LOCK & LOAD

LOCK & LOAD

ARMED FICTION

EDITED BY **Deirdra McAfee** AND **BettyJoyce Nash**

University of New Mexico Press   Albuquerque

© 2017 by Deirdra McAfee and BettyJoyce Nash
All rights reserved. Published 2017
Printed in the United States of America
22 21 20 19 18 17   1 2 3 4 5 6

Library of Congress Cataloging-in-Publication Data is on file at the Library of Congress

Cover illustration by Felicia Cedillos
Designed by Felicia Cedillos
Composed in Melior LT 10/14.25

With the hope that this book sparks discussion,
we dedicate it to readers across America

Contents

Introduction

Nothing says America louder than a gun. Without guns, our nation wouldn't exist. Musket fire at Lexington and Concord brought this country into being, the Winchester rifle and the Colt .45 expanded its boundaries, and the Spencer carbine won the Civil War. Though Americans view these events variously, firearms still pervade American life, looming as large in the national imagination as on the news. Gunfire even punctuates our language. Law-abiding citizens who have never owned or fired a weapon routinely refer to *the whole shooting match*; they don't want to *shoot from the hip* but they do want to *take their best shot*.

To write our own stories about firearms, we researched gun history and culture, paying close attention to how other writers used these powerful objects. Too often, a character simply chucked a shotgun into the pickup to manufacture drama or titillate readers, and too many scenes mimicked TV and movie gunplay. Wide reading revealed that the use, or non-use, of a firearm—that particularly American object— introduced fictional possibilities even more striking than those accompanying our nation's other preoccupations: sports and cars.

We sought stories that brought readers more than good guys against bad guys or shoot-'em-up clichés or lone-man-with-a-gun scenarios. We discovered fine examples of the kind of story we had in mind in world literature from Chekhov on, and in American literature beginning with Washington Irving. Our explorations revealed a number of established American writers who used firearms masterfully.

The few anthologies and single-author collections of gun stories available, however, dealt with war or hunting, not weapons. The writers were usually men, and usually dead. Nor did these books do justice to the force and meaning of guns in American life and thought today.

We resolved to remedy that. We sought out new work by both unknown and established writers, and we received a tremendous response. As writers ourselves, we looked not only for evocative language, engaging action, and complex meaning, but also for this hallmark of craft: a firearm used not simply as an object but as an essential object—something both real and metaphorical that not only advanced the story but deepened its resonance.

Throughout the months we planned and organized the project, thousands of hunters, marksmen, and hobbyists acquired and used firearms safely, as most Americans do. But shootings, large and small, also continued, including mass murders in Sandy Hook, Connecticut, and Orlando, Florida. Meanwhile, *Lock & Load: Armed Fiction* took shape, a group of varied, compelling stories that offered a bold, wide-ranging perspective on the real and symbolic power of firearms.

Authors in this anthology have long pondered the place of guns in American life. For example, Annie Proulx discussed American guns and their context eloquently in an interview with the *Missouri Review*:

America is a violent, gun-handling country. Americans feed on a steady diet of bloody movies, television programs, murder mysteries. Road rage, highway killings, beatings and murder of those who are different abound; school shootings—almost all of them in rural areas—make headline news over and over. . . . The point of writing in layers of bitter deaths and misadventures that befall characters is to illustrate American violence, which is real, deep and vast.

Some stories in *Lock & Load* do illustrate American violence, but the collection goes beyond that to illustrate American attitudes. During the past few years, while the severity and number of shootings increased and the political acrimony around firearms escalated, it became even clearer that contemporary American literature's treatment of guns held insights well worth considering.

Additionally, as women writers, we understood that women have more often been causes, or spoils, of armed conflict than actors in their own right—or actors with any rights. Our contributors themselves, however, challenge such assumptions. They show what women can do with guns, as writers and as characters, while firmly contradicting the idea that women have little interest in or knowledge of firearms.

We wanted, and found, thought-provoking, complicated stories that range from tender to violent, from chilling to hilarious. Love stories, war stories, coming-of-age stories, and revenge stories, they occur in landscapes familiar or ordinary, distant or dystopian, and they reflect Americans' particular obsession with—and paranoia about—guns.

Pinckney Benedict's "Mercy" simmers with the tension of colliding cultures and values in Appalachia, while Annie Proulx's "A Lonely Coast" explores the lives of contemporary women in the far West, where guns, trucks, and trouble ride together. Bonnie Jo Campbell's "Family Reunion" seeks rough justice for an unforgivable act, yet begins in a young girl's hunger to belong.

City life, too, can be armed and dangerous, as in Rick DeMarinis's "The Handgun," when a .22 revolver takes up residence in a fraying marriage, or when desperation drives an intelligent but aimless young African American man into a pointless, fatal confrontation, in John Edgar Wideman's "Tommy."

A gun's physical presence, even in memory, heightens tension and drives characters, as we see when the estranged wife in Sara Kay Rupnik's "An Act of Mercy" buys a pistol, fueling fantasies of her husband's return. The gun's existence is equally disquieting in Jim Tomlinson's "The Accomplished Son," which pairs the weight of loss with a veteran's pain, as a soldier back from Iraq recalls, and rediscovers, his dead father's hidden gun.

The young protagonist in Gale Walden's "Café Americana," an armed would-be robber, falls into a reverie, remembering the innocence of shooting for the first time on his father's farm. This almost arcadian, and deeply American, fantasy, recurs in a dreamy encounter between Vyla, the eldest of twelve children (living and dead) and a boy with a gun, in Nicole Louise Reid's "Pearl in a Pocket."

"Revealed," Mari Alschuler's horrifyingly amusing apocalyptic tale, takes gun fantasies a step further as Manhattanites tote mandatory pistols and mete out fatal consequences for subway rudeness. Joann Smith, meanwhile, in "Tuesday Night at the Shop and Shoot," offers an equally funny and disquieting tour of an imaginary attraction mixing consumerism, hatred, and target shooting.

Firearms are a massive presence, actually and historically, in American life and language. Americans' view of guns, shot through with ambivalence and strong feeling, remains a sore spot in the national psyche. Current events and clashing ideologies have scraped that sore spot raw.

Ambivalence and strong feeling, however, are where fiction starts. Like democracy, fiction invites us to participate and reflect. This is why *Lock & Load* takes no political stance: we believe that good fiction offers readers the freedom to ponder, not an agenda to march to.

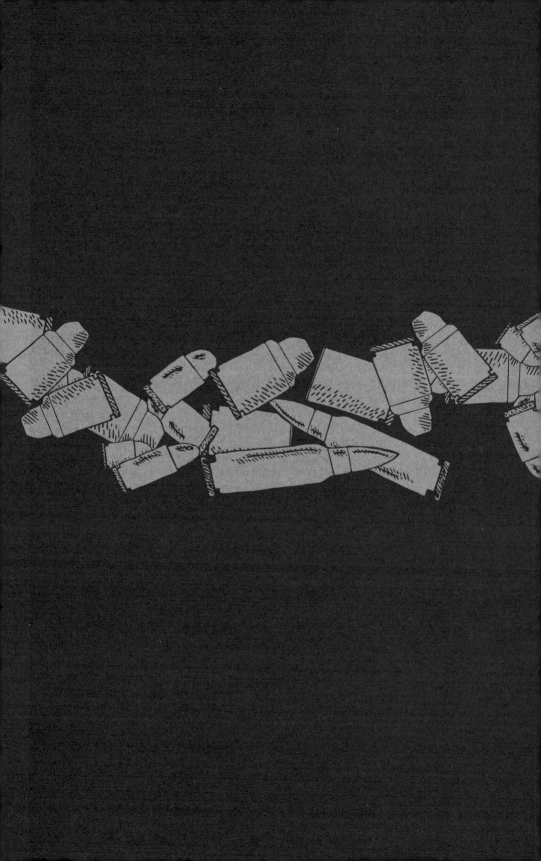

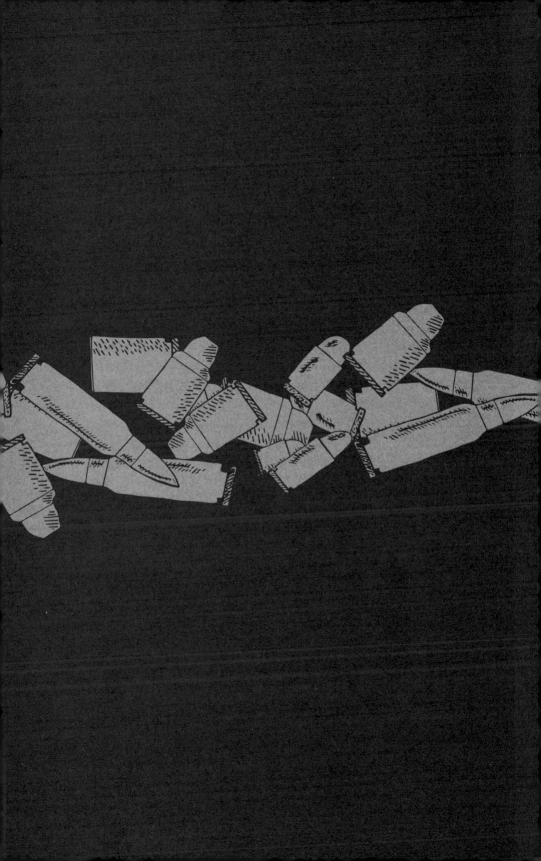

A Lonely Coast

Annie Proulx

YOU EVER SEE a house burning up in the night, way to hell and gone out there on the plains? Nothing but blackness and your headlights cutting a little wedge into it, could be the middle of the ocean for all you can see. And in that big dark a crown of flame the size of your thumbnail trembles. You'll drive for an hour seeing it until it burns out or you do, until you pull off the road to close your eyes or look up at the sky punched with bullet holes. And you might think about the people in the burning house, see them trying for the stairs, but mostly you don't give a damn. They are too far away, like everything else.

The year I lived in that junk trailer in the Crazy Woman Creek drainage I thought Josanna Skiles was like that, the house on fire in the night that you could only watch. The reason for it seemed to be the strung-out, buzzed country and the little running grass fires of the heart, the kind that usually die out on their own but in some people soar into uncontrollable conflagration.

I was having my own troubles then, a problem with Riley, my old boy, something that couldn't get fixed. There was a feeling of coming heat and whirlwind. I didn't have a grip on much.

The house trailer I rented was old. It was more of a camper you'd tow behind a car, so small you couldn't cuss the cat without getting fur in your mouth. When the wind blew I'd hear parts coming off it and banging along the ground. I rented it from Oakal Roy. He said

1

he'd been in the big time back in the 1950s, been a stunt man out in Hollywood. He was drinking himself down. A rack-sided dog hung around—I guess it was his—and once I drove in late at night and saw it crouched and gnawing at a long, bloody cow bone. He needed to shoot that dog.

I had a junior college certificate in craft supply merchandising— silk flowers, macramé, jewelry findings, beads, quills, fabric paints, that stuff. Like a magpie I was attracted to small bright objects. But I'd married Riley the day after graduation and never worked at the beads and buttons. Never would, because there weren't any craft shops in a radius of 300 miles and I wasn't going to leave Wyoming. You don't leave until you have to. So two nights a week I waitressed at the Wig-Wag Lodge, weekends tended bar at the Gold Buckle, and the other nights I sat in the trailer doing crossword puzzles and trying to sleep, waking always at the same hour the alarm went off at the ranch, the time when Riley would be rolling out and reaching for his shirt, and in the window the hard little dot of Venus rising and below it the thin morning.

Josanna Skiles cooked at the Wig-Wag. She'd had the job for seven or eight months. Most people quit after a few weeks. You had to learn how to make sushi and some kind of sticky rice. The owner was Jimmy Shimazo. Fifty years ago in World War II he was a kid in the internment camp at Heart Mountain, and he said that when his family went back to California with its cars and money and the bright coast, he missed Wyoming, its hardness imprinted on him. He came back years later with enough money to buy the Wig-Wag, maybe suffering some perverse need for animosity which he did find here. None of the others came back and who can blame them? All his guests were Japanese tourists who wandered through the lodge looking at the old saddles and cow skulls, in the gift shop buying little six-guns and plastic chaps for their kids, braided horsehair key rings made at the state pen. Jimmy was a tough one to work for, short-fused, but careful to pick women to yell at after the maintenance man, an ex–ranch hand from Spotted Horse, beat the piss out of him with a fence post and left him half dead next to the dumpster. Josanna never had a run-in with him until the end, but she was good at cooking that Jap food and out here everybody knows to leave the cook alone.

She had two women friends, Palma Gratt and Ruth Wolfe, both of them burning at a slower rate than Josanna, but in their own desperate ways also disintegrating into drifts of ash. Friday night was what they called girls' night out, margaritas and buffalo wings at the Gold Buckle while they read through the personal ads in the paper. Then they went to the Stockman for ribs. Sometimes Palma brought her kid along. The kid would sit in the corner and tear up paper napkins. After the praline cake and coffee they saw the movie at the Silver Wing, and they might come back to the Buckle or not. But Saturday night was their big night when they got into tight jeans and what Josanna called dead nigger shirts, met at the Rawhide or Bud's or Double Shot or Gold Buckle and acted wild.

They thought they were living then, drank, smoked, shouted to friends, and they didn't so much dance as straddle a man's thigh and lean in. Palma once stripped off her blouse to bare tits, Josanna swung at some drunk who'd said the wrong thing and she got slugged back, cussing pure blue through a split lip, kicking at the cowboy held tight by five or six of his delighted friends who urged her on. Nothing was too bold, nothing not worth the risk, they'd be sieving the men at the bar and cutting out the best three head, doing whatever drugs were going in the parking lot, maybe climb on some guy's lap in the cab of his truck. If Josanna was still around at two in the a.m. she looked like what she was, a woman coming into middle age, lipstick gnawed off, plain face, and thickening flesh, yawning, departing into the fresh night alone and sorry. When Elk came along she had somebody to go home with, and I thought that was the point.

Every month or so she went up to the Skiles ranch south of Sundance with a long-shot view of Black Buttes. She had a boy there, sixteen, seventeen years old, in and out of the detention home. Her folks had come through rocky times. She told me that their herd had carried the gene for dwarfism since her grandparents' day, back in the forties. They'd been trying to clean the snorters out for two generations, little by little. They should have sold every one of them for beef, started over, but somehow couldn't do it. The gene had showed up while her grandmother was running the ranch, the grandfather off to World War II with the Powder River Cavalry, the famous 115th. The government took their horses away and gave them trucks, sent those good horsemen to desks and motor pools. He came back home to stumpy-leg calves and did his best. In 1960 he drowned in the Belle Fourche River, not easy to do, but, Josanna said, her people had always taken the gritty way.

She brought me a jar of honey from their hives. Every ranch keeps bees. Me and Riley, we had twenty hives and I told her one time I missed the honey.

"Here," she said. "Not much but it's something. I go up there," she said. "That damn kind a life. Clayton wants a get out—he's talkin about goin down to Texas but I don't know. They need him. They'd take it wrong, I suppose, give me the blame if he went. Hell, he's pretty much growed up, let him do what he wants. He's headed for trouble anyway. Pain-in-the-ass kid."

Riley and me never had any kids, I don't know why. Neither one of us would go to a doctor and find out. We didn't talk about it. I thought it was probably something to do with the abortion I'd had before I knew him. They say it can mess you up. He didn't know about that and I suppose he had his own ideas.

Riley couldn't see blame in what he'd done. He said, "Look, I seen my chance and I taken it," reverting to Sweetwater home talk, where he comes from, and that was his last word on the subject.

Who knew better than me that he had a love spot on his body? She might have touched it. If she did he couldn't help it. Riley is just slat and bone, he has a thin, mean, face, one of those mouths like a paper cut and he doesn't say much. But you touch that love spot, you get him turned on, you lie down with him, his mouth would get real swollen, I'd just come apart with those thick, wet kisses and how big he got. Out of his clothes, horse and dog and oil and dirt, out of his clothes his true scent lay on his skin, something dry like the pith of a cottonwood twig when you break it at the joint disclosing the roan star at the center. Anyway, there's something wrong with everybody and it's up to you to know what you can handle.

In nine years married we had only one vacation, to Oregon where my brother lived. We went out on a rocky point and watched the rollers come in. It was foggy and cold, there wasn't anybody there but us watching the rollers. It was dusk and the watery curls held light as though it was inside them. Up the lonely coast a stuttering blink warned ships away. I said to Riley that was what we needed in Wyoming—lighthouses. He said no, what we needed was a wall around the state and turrets with machine guns in them.

Once Josanna gave me a ride in her brother's truck—he was down for a few days to pick up pump parts and some pipe—and it was sure enough a down-home truck, pair of chaps hanging over the seat back, chain, beat-up hat on the floor, a filthy Carhartt jacket, seven or eight torn-up gloves, dog hairs and dust, empty beer cans, .30-.06 in the rear window rack and on the seat between us in a snarl of wire, rope and old mail unopened, a .44 Ruger Blackhawk half out of the holster. Let me tell you that truck made me homesick. I said something about her brother had enough firepower, didn't he, and she laughed and said the Blackhawk was hers, she kept it in the glove compartment of her own truck but it was in the shop again that day with the ongoing compression problem they couldn't seem to fix; it was on the seat because she didn't want to forget it when her brother went back.

Long hair, frizzled and hanging down, was the fashion, and in the tangled cascades women's faces seemed narrow and vulnerable. Palma's hair was neon orange. Her brows were plucked and arched, the eyes set wide, the skin below dark and hurt-looking. Her daughter lived with her, a mournful kid ten or eleven years old with a sad mug and straight brown hair, the way Palma's would be if she didn't fix it up. The kid was always tearing at something.

The other one, Ruth, had the shadow of a mustache, and in summer heavy stubble showed under her arms. She paid forty-five dollars twice a month to have her legs waxed. She had a huge laugh, like a man's.

Josanna was muscular like most country women, tried to hide it under fuss-ruffle clothes with keyhole necklines. Her hair was straw-berry roan, coarse and thick and full of electricity. She had a some-what rank odor, a family odor because the brother had it too, musky and a little sour, and that truck of his smelled the same way. With Josanna it was faint and you might mistake it for strange Jap spices, but the aroma that came off the brother was strong enough to flatten a horse. He was an old bachelor. They called him Woody because, said Josanna, he'd come strutting out into the kitchen raw naked when he was four or five years old showing a baby hard-on and their old man had laughed until he choked and called him Woody and the name persisted forevermore and brought him local fame. You just couldn't help but look once you heard that, and he'd smile.

All three women had been married, rough marriages full of fighting and black eyes and sobbing imprecations, all of them knew the trou-ble that came with drinking men and hair-trigger tempers. Wyos are touchers, hot-blooded and quick, and physically yearning. Maybe it's because they spend so much time handling livestock, but people here are always handshaking, patting, smoothing, caressing, enfolding. This instinct extends to anger, the lightning backhand slap, the hip-shot to throw you off balance, the elbow, a jerk and wrench, the swat, and then the serious stuff that's meant to kill and sometimes does. The story about Josanna was that when she broke up with her ex-husband she shot at him, creased his shoulder before he jumped her and took the gun away. You couldn't push her around. It gave her a dangerous allure that attracted some men, the latest, Elk Nelson, whom she'd found in the newspaper. When they set up together he collected all the cartridges in the house and hid them at his mother's place in Wyo-dak, as if Josanna couldn't buy more. But that old bold Josanna got buried somewhere when Elk came around.

"Listen, if it's got four wheels or a dick you're goin a have trouble with it, guaranteed," said Palma at one of their Friday-night good times. They were reading the newspaper lonely hearts ads out loud. If you don't live here you can't think how lonesome it gets. We need those ads. That doesn't mean we can't laugh at them.

"How about this one: 'Six-three, two hundred pounds, thirty-seven, blue eyes, plays drums and loves Christian music.' Can't you just hear it, 'The Old Rugged Cross' on bongos?"

"Here's a better one: 'Cuddly cowboy, six-four, one hundred and eighty, N/S, not God's gift to women, likes holding hands, firefighting, practicing on my tuba.' I guess that could mean noisy, skinny, ugly, plays with matches. Must be cuddly as a pile a sticks."

"What a you think 'not God's gift to women' means?"

"Pecker the size of a peanut."

Josanna'd already put an inky circle around *Good-looking, athletic build Teddy Bear, brown-eyed, black mustache, likes dancing, good times, outdoors, walking under the stars. Lives life to its fullest.* It turned out to be Elk Nelson and he was one step this side of restless drifter, had worked oil rigs, construction, coal mines, loaded trucks. He was handsome, mouthy, flashed a quick smile. I thought he was a bad old boy from his scuffed boots to his greasy ponytail. The first thing he did was put his .30-.30 in the cab rack of Josanna's truck and she didn't say a word. He had pale brown eyes the color of graham crackers, one of those big mustaches like a pair of blackbird wings. Hard to say how old he was; older than Josanna, forty-five, forty-six maybe. His arms were all wildlife, blurry tattoos of spiders, snarling wolves, scorpions, rattlesnakes. To me he looked like he'd tried every dirty thing three times. Josanna was helpless crazy for him from the first time they got together and crazy jealous. And didn't he like that? It seemed to be the way he measured how she felt about him and he put it to the test. When you are bone tired of being alone, when you all want is someone to pull you close and say it's all right, all right now, and you get one like Elk Nelson you've got to see you've licked the bottom out of the dish.

I tended bar on the weekends at the Gold Buckle and watched the fire take hold of her. She would smile at what he said, listen and lean, light his damn cigarette, examine his hands for cuts—he had a couple of weeks' work fencing at the 5 Bar. She'd touch his face, smooth a wrinkle in his shirt and he'd say, quit off pawin me. They sat for hours at the Buckle seesawing over whether or not he'd made a pass at some woman, until he got fed up enough to walk out. He seemed to be goading her, seeing how far he could shove before she hit the wall. I wondered when she'd get the message that she wasn't worth shit to him.

August was hot and drouthy, a hell of grasshoppers and dried-up creeks. They said this part of the state was a disaster area. I heard that said before any grasshoppers came. The Saturday night was close, air as thick as in a closet with the winter coats. It was rodeo night and that brings them in. The bar filled up early, starting with ranch hands around three in the afternoon still in their sweaty shirts, red faces mottled with heat and dirt, crowding out most of the wrinkle-hour boys, the old-timers who started their drinking in the morning. Palma was there a little after five, alone, fresh and high-colored, wearing a cinnamon red satin blouse that shined with every move she made. Her arms were loaded with silver bracelets, one metal ring on another clinking and shifting. By five-thirty the bar was packed and hot, bodies touching, some fools trying to dance—country girls playing their only card, grinding against the boys—people squeezed eight to a booth meant for four, six deep at the bar, men hat to hat. There were three of us working, me and Zeeks and Justin, and as fast as we went we couldn't keep up. They were pouring the drinks down. Everybody was shouting. Outside the sky was green-black and trucks driving down the street had their headlights on, dimmed by constant lightning flashes. The electricity went off for about fifteen seconds, the bar black as a cave, the jukebox dying *worrr*, and a huge, amorous, drunken and delighted moan coming up from the crowd that changed to cussing when the light flickered back on.

Elk Nelson came in, black shirt and silver belly hat. He leaned over the bar, hooked his finger in the waistband of my jeans and yanked me to him.

"Josanna in yet?"

I pulled back, shook my head.

"Good. Let's get in the corner then and hump."

I got him a beer.

Ash Weeter stood next to Elk. Weeter was a local rancher who wouldn't let his wife set foot in a bar, I don't know why. The jokers said he was probably worried she'd get killed in a poolroom fight. He was talking about a horse sale coming up in Thermopolis. Well, he didn't own a ranch, he managed one for some rich people in Pennsylvania, and I heard it that half the cows he ran on their grass were his. What they didn't know didn't hurt them.

"Have another beer, Ash," Elk said in a good-buddy voice.

"Nah, I'm goin home, take a shit and go to bed." No expression on that big shiny face. He didn't like Elk.

Palma's voice cut through a lull, Elk looked up, saw her at the end of the bar, beckoning.

"See you," said Ash Weeter to no one, pulling his hat down and ducking out.

Elk held his cigarette high above his head as he got through the crowd. I cracked a fresh Coors, brought it down to him, heard him say something about Casper.

That was the thing, they'd start out at the Buckle then drive down to Casper, five or six of them, a hundred and thirty miles, sit in some other bar probably not much different than the Buckle, drink until they were wrecked, then hit a motel. Elk told it on Josanna that she got so warped out one time she pissed the motel bed and he'd had to drag her into the shower and turn it on cold, throw the sheets in on top of her. Living life to its fullest. He'd tell that like it was the best story in the world and every time he did it she'd put her head down, wait it out with a tight little smile. I thought of my last night back on the ranch with Riley, the silence oppressive and smothering, the clock ticking like blows of an axe, the maddening trickle of water into the stained bathtub from the leaky faucet. He wouldn't fix it, just wouldn't. Couldn't fix the other thing and made no effort in that direction. I suppose he thought I'd just hang and rattle.

Palma leaned against Elk, slid back and forth slowly as if she was scratching her back on his shirt buttons. "Don't know. Wait for Josanna and see what she wants a do."

"Josanna will want a go down to Casper. That's it, she will because that's what I want a do." He said something else I didn't hear.

Palma shrugged, shifted out into the dancers with him. He was a foot taller than she, his cigarette crackling in her hair when he pulled her close. She whipped her hair back, slammed her pelvis into him and he almost swallowed the butt.

There was a terrific blast of light and thunder and the lights went off again and there was the head-hollowing smell of ozone. A sheet of rain struck the street followed by the deafening roar of hailstones. The lights surged on but weak and yellow. It was impossible to hear anything over the battering hail.

A kind of joyous hysteria moved into the room, everything flying before the wind, vehicles outside getting dented to hell, the crowd sweaty and the smells of aftershave, manure, clothes dried on the line, your money's worth of perfume, smoke, booze; the music subdued by the shout and babble though the bass hammer could be felt through the soles of the feet, shooting up the channels of legs to the body fork, center of everything. It is that kind of Saturday night that torches your life for a few hours, makes it seem something is happening.

There were times when I thought the Buckle was the best place in the world, but it could shift on you and then the whole dump seemed a mess of twist-face losers, the women with eyebrows like crowbars, the men covered with bristly red hair, knuckles the size of new pota-toes, showing the gene pool was small and the rivulets that once fed it had dried up. I think sometimes it hit Josanna that way too because one night she sat quiet and slumped at the bar watching the door, watching for Elk, and he didn't come in. He'd been there, though, picked up some tourist girl in white shorts, couldn't have been more than twenty. It wouldn't do any good to tell her.

"This's a miserable place," she said. "My god it's miserable."

The door opened and four or five of the arena men came in, big mus-taches, slickers and hats running water, boots muddy, squeezing through the dancers, in for a few quick ones before the rodeo. The atmosphere was hot and wet. Everybody was dressed up. I could see Elk Nelson down the bar, leaning against Palma, one arm over her satin shoulder, big fingers grazing her right breast, fingernail scratch-ing the erect nipple.

They were still playing their game when the door jerked open again, the wind popping it against the wall, and Josanna came through, shaking her head, streaming wet, the artful hair plastered flat. Her peach-colored shirt clung to her, transparent in places, like burned skin where it bunched and the color doubled. Her eyes were red, her mouth thin and sneering.

"Give me a whiskey, celebrate a real goddamn lousy day."

Justin poured it high, slid the glass carefully to her.

"Got a wee bit wet," he said.

"Look at this." She held out her left hand, pulled up the sopping sleeve. Her arm and hand were dotted with red bruises. "Hail," she said. "I spun my truck in front a Cappy's and nicked a parking meter, busted the hood latch. Run two blocks here. But that's not hardly the problem. I got fired, Jimmy Shimazo fired me. Out a the clear blue sky. Don't anybody get in my way tonight."

"You bet," said Justin, pressing against me with his thigh. He seemed to want to get something going, but he was going to be disappointed. I don't know, maybe I'd think the score was even. But it wouldn't be.

"So, I'm goin a have a drink, soon's the rain stops I'm goin a get me some gone, try Casper is any better. Fuck em all, tell em all a kiss my sweet rosy." She knocked back the whiskey, slammed the glass down on the bar hard enough to break it.

"See what I mean?" she said. "Everything I touch falls apart." Elk Nelson came up behind her, slipped his big red hands under her arms, cupped her breasts and squeezed. I wondered if she'd seen him feeling up Palma. I thought she had. I thought he wanted her to see him handling her willing friend.

"Yeah," he said. "What a you want a do? Casper, right? Go get something a eat, I hope. I'm hungry enough I could eat a rancher's unwiped ass."

"You want some buffalo wings?" I said. "Practically the same thing." We called across the street to Cowboy Teddy for them and inside an hour somebody brought them over. Half the time they were raw. Elk shook his head. He was fondling Josanna, one hand inside her wet shirt, but looking at the crowd behind him in the bar mirror. Palma was still at the end of the bar, watching him. Ruth came up, slapped Josanna on the butt, said she'd heard what Shimazo did, the little prick. Josanna put her arm around Ruth's waist. Elk eased back, looked at Palma in the mirror, cracked that big yellow smile. There was a lot going on.

"Ruth, babe, I'm tired a this bullshit place. How about go down a Casper and just hang around for a while. I'm just goin a say fuck him, fuck Jimmy Shimazo. I said, hey, look, at least give me a reason. I put too much wasabi on the goddamn fish balls? Shit. He just fired me. I don't even know why."

Elk put in his dime's worth. "Hell, it's only a shittin job. Get another one." Like jobs were easy. There weren't any jobs.

"The latch on my truck hood is busted. I can't get it to stay shut. If we're goin a Casper it's got a be fixed." Josanna's truck had a crew cab, plenty of room for all of them. They always went in her truck and she paid for the gas, too.

"Reef it down with a little balin wire."

At the cash register Justin murmured to me what he'd heard at the back booths—Jimmy Shimazo had fired Josanna because he caught her in the meat cooler snorting a line. He was death on that. For now he was doing the cooking himself. He was talking about getting a real Jap cook in from California.

"That's all we need around here," said Justin. They say now the Japs own the whole southwest part of the state, refineries, big smoke-stacks.

Something happened then, and in the noise I didn't see them go, Josanna, Elk, Palma, Ruth and somebody she'd picked up—Barry, romping on his hands with whiskey. Maybe they left before the fireball. There is a big plate glass window at the Buckle onto the street, and outside a wooden ledge wide enough to set beer bottles on. Mr. Thompson, the bar owner, displayed his collection of spurs, coils of rope, worn boots, a couple of saddles, some old woolly chaps so full of moths they looked like a snowstorm in reverse in spring, other junk inside the window. The window was like a stage. Now a terrific, sputtering ball of fire bloomed on the ledge throwing glare on the dusty cowboy gear. It was still raining. You could hear the fireball roaring and a coat of soot in the shape of a cone and peck-speckled with rain was building up on the glass. Justin and a dozen people went out to see what it was. He tried knocking it off the ledge but it was stuck on with its own burning. He ran back in.

"Give me the water pitcher."

People at the front were all laughing, somebody called, piss on it, Justin. He poured three pitchers of water on the thing before it quit, a blackened lump of something, placed and set afire by persons unknown. There was a sound like a shot and the glass cracked from top to bottom. Justin said later it was a shot, not the heat. It was the heat. I know a shot when I hear one.

There's a feeling you get driving down to Casper at night from the north, and not only there, other places where you come through hours of darkness unrelieved by any lights except the crawling wink of some faraway ranch truck. You come down a grade and all at once the shining town lies below you, slung out like all western towns, and with the curved bulk of mountain behind it. The lights trail away to the east in a brief and stubby cluster of yellow that butts hard up against the dark. And if you've ever been to the lonely coast you've seen how the shore rock drops off into the black water and how the light on the point is final. Beyond are the old rollers coming on for millions of years. It is like that here at night but instead of the rollers it's wind. But the water was here once. You think about the sea that covered this place hundreds of millions of years ago, the slow evaporation, mud turned to stone. There's nothing calm in those thoughts. It isn't finished, it can still tear apart. Nothing is finished. You take your chances.

Maybe that's how they saw it, gliding down toward the lights, drinking beer and passing a joint, Elk methed out and driving and nobody saying much, just going to Casper. That's what Palma says. Ruth says different. Ruth says Josanna and Elk had a bad fight all the way down and Palma was in the middle of it. Barry says they were all screwed out of their skulls, he was only drunk.

We had a time with the calving, Riley and me, that spring. A neighbor rancher's big Saler bulls had got into our pastures and bred some of our heifers. We didn't know it until the calving started although Riley remarked once or twice that some of the heifers had ballooned up really big and we figured twins. We knew when the first one came. The heifer was a good one, too, long-bodied, meaty, trim and with a tremendous amount of muscle, but not double muscled, sleek and feminine, what we wanted in our mother cows, almost torn in half by the biggest calf either one of us had ever seen. It was a monster, a third of the size of its mother.

"That bastard Coldpepper. Look at that calf. It comes from them fuckin giant bulls, the size a tanks. They must a got in last April and you bet he knew it, never said a word. I guess we are goin a find out how many."

The weather was miserable too, spring storms, every kind of precip. We got through the first ten days sleepless, wet and cold, especially Petey Flurry who'd worked for us for nine years, out ahorseback in the freezing rain driving the heifers into the calving yard. Wouldn't you know, he got pneumonia when we needed him the most and they carted him off to the hospital. His wife sent the fifteen-year-old daughter over to help and she was a pretty good hand, ranch raised, around animals all her life, strong but narrow little hands that could work into a straining heifer and grasp the new hooves. We were all dead tired.

Around mid-afternoon I'd left them in the calving barn with a bad heifer, gone up to the house to grab an hour of sleep, but I was too tired, way beyond sleep, wired, and after ten minutes I got up and put the coffeepot on, got some cookie dough from the freezer and in a little while there was steaming coffee and hot almond sandies. I put three cups in a cardboard box, the cookies in an insulated sack, and went back out to the calving barn.

I came in with that box of coffee and cookies, pushed the door open gently. He'd just finished, had just pulled out of her, back up on his feet. She was still lying on a hay bale skinny kid's legs bent open. I looked at him, the girl sat up. The light wasn't good in there and he was trying to get it back in his pants in a hurry but I saw the blood on him. The heat of the coffee came through the cardboard box and I set it on the old bureau that held the calf pullers and rope and salve and suture material. I stood there while they pulled at their clothes. The girl was sniveling. Sure enough, she was on the road to becoming a sleazy little bitch, but she was only fifteen and it was the first time and her daddy worked for the man who'd done it to her.

He said to her, "Come on, I'm gettin you home," and she said, "No," and they went outside. Didn't say anything to me. He was gone until the next afternoon, came back and said his few words, I said mine and the next day I left. The goddamn heifer had died with a dead calf still inside her.

Most things you never know what happened or why. Even Palma and Ruth and Barry who were there couldn't say just how it came apart. From what they remembered and what the papers told it seems like they were on that street full of cars and trucks and Elk tried to get around a trailer loaded with calves. There wasn't a vehicle on the highway until they turned onto Poplar, and then there was the backed-up traffic from the light that's east of the exit ramp, traffic all around them and with it a world of trouble. While he was passing the trailer a blue pickup passed him, swerving into the oncoming traffic lane and forcing cars off the road. The blue pickup cut sharp in front of the trailer-load of calves. That trailer guy stepped on the brake and Elk hit the trailer pretty hard, hard enough, said Palma, to give her a nosebleed. Josanna was yelling about her truck and the baling wire on the hood latch loosened and the hood was lifting up and down a few inches, like an alligator with a taste in its mouth. But Elk was raging, he didn't stop, pulled around the calf trailer and went after the blue pickup which had turned onto 20-26 and belted off west. Josanna shouted at Elk who was so mad, Ruth said, blood was almost squirting out of his eyes. Right behind Elk came the calf trailer flicking his lights and leaning on the horn.

Elk caught the blue truck about eight miles out and ran him into the ditch, pulled in front and blocked him. Far back the lights of the calf hauler came on fast and steady. Elk jumped out and charged at the blue pickup. The driver was coked and smoked. His passenger, a thin girl in a pale dress, was out and yelling, throwing stones at

Josanna's truck. Elk and the driver fought, slipping on the highway, grunting, and Barry and Ruth and Palma stumbled around trying to get them apart. Then the calf hauler, Ornelas, screamed in from Mars.

Ornelas worked for Natrona Power Monday through Friday, had a second job nighttimes repairing saddles, and on his weekends tried to work the small ranch he'd inherited from his mother. When Elk clipped him he hadn't slept for two nights, had just finished his eighth beer and opened the ninth. It's legal to drink and drive in this state. You are supposed to use some judgment.

The cops said later that Ornelas was the catalyst because when he got out of his truck he was aiming a rifle in the general direction of Elk and the pickup driver, Fount Slinkard, and the first shot put a hole in Slinkard's rear window. Slinkard screamed at his passenger to get him the .22 in his rack but she was crouching by the front tire with her hands clasping her head. Barry shouted, watch out cowboy, ran across the highway. There was no traffic. Slinkard or Slinkard's passenger had the .22 but dropped it. Ornelas fired again and in the noise and fright of the moment no one grasped causes or effects. Someone picked up Slinkard's .22. Barry was drunk and in the ditch on the other side of the road and couldn't see a thing but said he counted at least seven shots. One of the women was screaming. Someone pounded on a horn. The calves were bellowing and surging at the sides of the trailer, one of them hit and the smell of blood in there.

By the time the cops came Ornelas was shot through the throat and though he did not die he wasn't much good for yodeling. Elk was already dead. Josanna was dead, the Blackhawk on the ground beneath her.

You know what I think? Like Riley might say, I think Josanna seen her chance and taken it. Friend, it's easier than you think to yield up to the dark impulse.

Não Faz Mal

E. G. Willy

THEY DIDN'T RECOGNIZE him. If they did, it wouldn't have mattered. He remembered them: Güero, José, and Ray, the López brothers, *norteño* affiliated. All members of the A Street crew, Hayward's oldest gang. Beside them on the curb, cousin Luís, who they called Speedy. They were the men who ruled this place, who noticed everything, every person that passes, every car that drives by, yet they failed to notice Paul twenty years later. Paul lay on the carpet, pondering this.

How can they miss you when you don't miss them? This place has changed, sure, but they should know you. Or were they pretending not to know you? Were they seeing through you like gangsters do, looking past you to a place that doesn't exist except to them? Were they positioned to do that? To not see you?

You're a man now, not a boy. Not even really a man, though, if your family were to consider it. You're not a man until you are thirty. But they gave you this man job, the fix-it job, the paint over and patch. It's your second time fixing this rental. You know the main rule: you stay in the house as you fix it or you come back to a home that's had every piece of metal stripped from it, every copper wire ripped from the walls, every fixture torn from its anchors. You get in and out, get the thing rented.

Paul was prepared. He had his golden beer and cheap cigarettes. Drunk just a little. The night was cool and hot all at once. Indian summer in Hayward. If someone asked Paul right at that moment, he

17

would say this is a good place, nice area to raise a family, prices didn't eat away at your paycheck. But this was the standard landlord lie. Like all the houses his family rented, it hadn't been a good place for some time now.

It had been Grandma Obrega's place before she died, then Paul's mom's, now Paul's responsibility. And it had declined with the years. He always kept a loaded gun and a knife hidden somewhere. Always loaded. Always ready. In his car, a golf club with the head removed, his whipping stick. That was the starting instrument. Next came the guns. Then knives. Bottles. Pipes. Nails. Rocks. Whatever it took.

The house was a dump. Right next to the railroad tracks. To friends he would say, "Close your eyes and think Bermuda grass, dog shit, old cars, pit bulls, fighting cocks, tough people, busted garbage cans. Fourth of July celebrated with weapon fire. Same as the New Year. Any birthday and full moon in between. Gunfire."

Paul rose. There was a noise outside like an insect buzzing. He was prepared. He had been waiting for this. He knew the sound but couldn't reproduce it. He could tell you it was the sound of raw emotion and that it came in many frequencies. Anyone who had heard this sound would know, too. Paul moved silently to the kitchen. He hadn't stored his *vergueiro* yet. It was leaning by the door. So he pumped a round into the chamber, threw the door open.

Choum. One slick dump of lead into the night. A hot round. A fat strike up to the hills, flying far, way up past Carlos Bee Boulevard, a good velocity, maybe a mile. After the shot, nothing. Not a sign. Just dark night and evening clouds. He looked across the street, saw the glow of a cigarette in the dark. Güero was out there smoking. Paul had seen him on the move in, recognized him. But Güero had only seen a man in a Chevy truck, not Paul, just the truck, something that didn't belong in the neighborhood, therefore something worth stealing.

Now Güero was playing lookout, sucking on his cigarette. The smoke was the sign in case someone showed up. Paul fired three more times into the air, *pop, pop, pop.* The old play. He knew plays. He knew this a million times a million. They didn't have to say a guy was hiding. He could smell the dude. The air was full of him. This was how it played. This was how Paul reacted.

Begin by getting respect. You react to whatever they present, then go tranquilo, tranquilo. *Set this up. Wait. Establish who you are. Give them a face to see. Respect begins by them knowing you. You know the game. Respect. Then trust. Then fill the rental with new people. Hope they stay as long as possible. Tudo bem. Tudo tranquilo.*

Paul went outside and checked his truck, saw bits of broken safety glass on the top of the passenger window where a metal instrument had stressed the beveled edge. A stupid amateur sloppy job. The *carnal* hadn't even used a slim-jim. Total crap. Paul held his gun with the barrel up so he could swing around in a tight spot.

You want him to see you and the vergueiro. *Show you are strong.*

He did a quick tour around the house, checked the gate and the back. He returned to the truck, said, "Dude, what the hell?" But he wasn't worried. He had released his fear, so there would be no problems now. They saw him. He saw them. He would take care of it the next day. Respect. Now trust. This was the play. It was how it should be. He went inside, lay on the carpet, wondered how the dude had gotten away. It took him an hour to realize what was wrong with the play.

Completely, stupidly not street-wise. You have no street. A guy comes up on you, you roll under the car. Everyone knows that. He was under your truck. You missed it. You must be tired. Or maybe you don't even really care. So not street. Or maybe you're getting old, like the A Street Boys. They figure you don't have hops because they don't have hops. You can't blame them for trying to jack you up. You would do the same if you were them. So let this go. If they don't remember you, it's okay. Can't change that. Don't care. Não faz mal. Tudo bem.

Paul went into his kitchen. It smelled of new paint, the rental home paint job to cover up the filth from the previous renters. He smoked a joint, felt the rhythms of the night, the words flying across his memory like liquid pieces of steel blue. He fell asleep.

It was morning now. Paul fried an egg Portuguese style in a big pan of olive oil, the egg snapping and cracking, then the bread right there in the pan. He didn't have to look outside to know the López brothers were hanging out in front of the garage, drinking beers, smoking *leños*, testing him. Paul finished his breakfast, got a six-pack out of the fridge, and went over to reintroduce himself.

They didn't want to speak to him. He understood that. They didn't remember him. That was a while ago, back when his grandma Avo Obrega was in the house. He would've been much younger, still not shaving. Skinny, too. Now he had the full form of a man. So they would see him differently. He waited until they were all holding cold beers, said, "Hey, some dude tried to break into my truck last night."

Güero was standing farther down the driveway, his shoulder turned toward Paul. He said, "I'm telling you, eh. You gots to watch out. People come walking through here, you don't know what's going to happen."

"I guess so," replied Paul.

"You guess right, holmes," said Güero.

They laughed. Paul felt the frown forming on his face, stopped himself.

They do this to show they're in charge. They know they live in a dump. This is their test. From their dump to your dump. Laughter doesn't matter. Those are the rules. Why harp on it?

Paul laughed, too.

Only Speedy was quiet. The *carnal* had a big frame and a baby face that hid the gauntness of years of shooting up. His sleeves were rolled down, hiding his condition. He was looking up the hill to the gravel yard.

Of course they send the junkie to rip off your truck. That's how it's done. Send the least important. The disposable one. The guy who takes the most risks.

"Well, I catch someone breaking into my truck again, I'm going to put a cap in his ass," said Paul slowly, letting them get every word. "I don't like to, but I don't appreciate someone coming up on me. I kind of react. I just do. Nothing personal."

José, the oldest brother, said, "Damn, dude, you're a badass."

Paul said, "Yeah well, I got my moments."

Silence. The homeboys thinking.

Güero asked, "You didn't see him, eh?"

"No. I saw one of you guys smoking, though. Saw the cigarette in the dark, you know, glowing."

An exchange of faces, guys blinking. Then, "Yeah, I saw you too, eh," said Güero. "You were walking around your house in your underwear."

"Yeah, I was," agreed Paul. He'd been waiting for this, the acknowledgment. If he were younger, he would've reacted differently, maybe thrown a fist, kicked Güero in the head, then the ribs, waited for his homeboys to pull him off. Instead he took a sip off his beer. No rush. It wasn't Paul's *bairro* any longer. Just a few Obrega left now. But the rules were the same.

José took it further, said, "Maybe you should've looked under your truck, eh. You might've seen what you were looking for."

A bunch more laughter.

Paul smiled, didn't show his teeth.

It's okay. Não faz mal. Let them get it out. You showed them you weren't to be messed with. You're almost done. Take it easy. Find the guy that might help with the painting. Get some money in his pockets. Bind him to you. He helps fix the house, the house becomes protected. The new renters are okay. Everything is tranquilo, tranquilo. *This is, after all, just business.*

Paul chuckled, said, "Yeah, I thought of that."

"Next time maybe you should put on some pants, eh," went on José.

"Maybe next time I start shooting. I start messing people up. I shoot one guy in the head. It goes *ping, ping, ping* in his head. Underwear don't matter if a dude has a gun. That is what it takes. Clothes do nothing."

The López brothers were laughing again.

Things are cool. They wouldn't be laughing otherwise. They get it. They feel my strength. They're starting to respect me. Tudo bem. Tudo controlado.

Güero put out his hand, said, "What the fuck, eh. We didn't know you was okay."

Paul said, "You don't remember me, do you?"

"What?" asked Güero, surprised.

"I'm Paul Obrega. That's my grandma's house over there."

"Shit, you're Paul Obrega?"

"Yeah."

"I didn't recognize you, eh."

"I'm older now."

"Well, shit, holmes."

"Well, shit."

"You were just a little fucking punk, eh. You know, tiny."

"I was. Now I'm grown up."

"Yeah, just a little bitch back then," added José.

"Ain't little now," replied Paul.

"Holmes, what you doing back here?" asked Ray, speaking for the first time.

"Working. Fixing up the house. Looking for renters."

Three heads nodding, thinking about this.

"You got work?" asked Speedy.

"I do," said Paul, then pointed with his jaw to his grandmother's house. "Fixing the place up, renting it out. Got lots of painting to do."

"You need any help, you just ask," offered Güero.

"Will do," agreed Paul. Then, "Hey, that reminds me. I got paint sitting out. Can't let it get dry. See you guys later."

They didn't reply. Watched him cross the street to his grandmother's house.

Let them think about this. I got work.

Paul painted until evening, returned after sunset with more beer. The door to the López garage was open. The crew was still hanging out, though this time they had moved from the street corner to the garage. Güero had the stereo pumped up, the speakers crackling and popping. He'd just come out of Santa Rita a few days before. He had the look of a guy that was all twisted up, pacing back and forth like a dog, jumpy.

Güero smelled like jail, the acid tang a convict gets on himself. The smell filled the garage. It would take a while to get it out of his clothes. Lots of washes. And the homeboy had a fresh tattoo that glistened in the light, a beautiful single-line prison tat of a crying woman whose back and feet were the body of a peacock.

You don't have to worry about him. Like all guys fresh out, he will stand at arm's length and never let you see his back. He is worried about himself. He could be the man for the job, though if you take him, he'll be yours forever, like the dog you get at the pound. Little jobs. Small repairs. And he'll watch the house. A Street Boys, they're good like that.

"Hey, thanks for the beer, man," said Ray. He was at the back of the garage, painting a *plaqueaso* of a girl he'd met a few days earlier in a dance hall. Even though he was already getting on in years, it was Ray's first *plaqueaso* that included himself in the story and he was painting proud. He was dipping his brush into the tiny bottles of paint kids used for plastic models, humming, acting like he was cool like that.

"You got it," said Paul. He registered Ray as the cool *vato*.

No trouble there. Just a dude getting by. Could help out with the painting. Make him your friend. Give him work. This is good. Things are working out. We are moving forward. We have options.

Speedy the junkie began to dance at the front of the garage, his face shiny from a load of Mexican Brown heroin.

With junkies there is no trust. No boundaries. He is nothing but the disposable shit. Do not engage him.

Güero put José Alfredo Jiménez on the stereo and they started tossing down *pistos* and singing. Paul too. Though he was a Portuguese homeboy, he knew the words. He'd had twenty years of learning them, Portuguese mixing with Spanish, working side by side with the homeboys from Michoacan. Many of them on his crew. His advantage, really. He would know Spanish. They wouldn't know Portuguese. The level of trust would be sixty-forty, just like with the Spaniards, because some things never changed.

Speedy messed up the lyrics as he danced around. He had a bag of candy in one hand, his junkie bag. And he was saying over and over, "I'm a man! I'm a man!" When he got close to the middle of the garage, they pushed him back. He wasn't ever going to get inside in the house. He had to be reminded who he was. So they had set the structure for him.

A young guy in a baggy flannel shirt came by. His eyes were

hollow from a load of heroin, and he was carrying a violin. Güero saw the kid coming and came out to greet him. As he was still in his prison senses, he was quick on picking up the vibe. There was a lot of talk about who knew who, checking the gang affiliations, *norteño* or *sureño*, making sure the kid was Mexican and therefore from the North. The kid talked slow, threw out names they all knew. Smart. No weapons, just the loot, traveling light. Knowing the names.

"Hey, any of you want to buy a violin?" the kid asked.

Ray looked up from his painting. "Naw, we don't play no violins down here."

Then everyone was talking about violins, how they didn't come down there, how only *jotos* played the violin. Paul listened, smiled so they could all see he was smiling, big and team. He wondered why the kid was playing it this way, trying to sell a violin he'd obviously stolen. If he stayed around, there would be a fight.

The kid finally picked up the vibe, crossed over to the tot lot and disappeared into a hole by the train tracks. The López brothers agreed the kid needed a good beating. A thief like that, you didn't need in the neighborhood. He stepped back here again, they were going to fuck him up permanent.

Once the kid was gone, Speedy took up his chant again, "I'm a man! I'm a man!"

Güero paced the garage, his face bloated from booze, wondering if the kid was *sureño*, if the names he'd given were lies, if he were connected somewhere else. "Where'd the *maricón* get the violin?" he asked.

Paul drank more, watched the crew, timed his own departure. It was midnight now, and he wondered why he was still there, the Portuguese kid hanging out with the *vatos*.

Ray painted in a fury. And the portrait of his blonde woman became uglier and uglier.

It was then that Paul saw Arturo's *placa*. Arturo, the second-oldest López brother. In the painting he had a *cuete* in his hand, was firing above a white mass that marked a paint-over. Next to the mass was written *pinche culero*. Paul turned to ask what had happened to Arturo, saw Güero was observing him, his face flushed from drinking.

Don't ask about this. You'll start something. You didn't remember Arturo. Just as they didn't remember you. You forgot a brother. So you are just as guilty of not remembering.

"No le echamos de menos," offered Güero.

"Arturo, your brother," said Paul.

"Se murió."

Paul lit a cigarette, stepped closer to the *placa*.

Güero is acting distant. I am supposed to guess what he means. No le echamos de menos. We don't miss him. Does he mean this about Arturo or the person in the paint-over? Am I supposed to decide who killed who?

Ignacio, the neighbor from around the corner, arrived at one. He was troubled. His hands were turned out, like a penitent to the cross. Ignacio was tall and round. A softy. Paul recognized him. They'd once watched trains, flattened pennies on the Southern Pacific tracks. Ignacio worked at the Napa Auto on West Tennyson. Paul bought parts for his truck from him a few times over the years. Ignacio wouldn't hang out with the López brothers. A homeboy when he was a kid, but it was over now. He would never be in the game. He was on his way out of the neighborhood, was taking classes at Laney College. A Street would soon be nothing to him.

"Hey, Nacho, what you doing here?" asked Ray. "We ain't seen you in a while."

"Yeah, I saw the light on," said Ignacio, shrugged.

"What up, holmes?" asked Güero. He held up his bottle of Thunderbird, the cheapest wine he could find at the corner market, now his favorite. "You want some wine?"

"No. I'm okay," said Ignacio, his voice smooth, not turned hard by booze, cigarettes, and marijuana. Not like Paul and the López brothers. No street.

They stood at the front of the garage, talking, asking Ignacio questions. He was slow in his answers, almost too flustered to reply.

"Hey, Nacho, what's bothering you, eh?" asked Güero. "You acting all clogged up. You don't come by no more, now you show up."

"Oh, I don't know," said Ignacio, his big shoulders rounded, his knees turned in, worried.

"Shit, don't give me the I-don't-know thing, eh," ordered Güero. "You speak your mind here."

"I guess."

"How long have I known you?"

"Long time."

"So?"

Ignacio nodded, said quietly, "Someone busted into my sister's room."

Ray looked up from his painting, said, "That ain't right."

"No."

Speedy said, "What they do to her? She okay?"

"She got pushed around a little," Ignacio replied quietly. "You know, made to do things."

"Goddamn, who was it?" asked Güero.

Ignacio glanced at Paul. He shook his head. "We all know him."

And then there were questions. No one asking details. Not talking about Mercedes and any shame. Just details about time. Which window? How many people? Ray and Güero pressing. Neither Paul nor Speedy asking anything. Ignacio uncomfortable, at last saying, "It was Rusty."

Paul felt his heart jump. Rusty's family was from Faial. Not mainlander Portuguese like Paul. A short, tough guy from the islands, Rusty because of his red skin, his *ruivo* hair. Part of the Machado clan. No one Paul cared about, but a dude he'd seen enough at the *festas*. He'd once gotten in a fight with Rusty during the *espiritu santo*. Two guys slapping each other, Rusty finally backing down when Paul's friends showed up. But still Portuguese like Paul. Still this division between Mexican and Portuguese, the López brothers looking at him, wondering if Paul was connected to Rusty. Paul sipped, waited for the next thing to happen.

"Ah, this *puto* has gone too far," said Shorty.

The brothers all agreed, but it was just Mario and Güero who strode off into the night, followed by Ignacio.

You're done here. This is not your argument. Let this one go. Rusty ain't worth this. Let him watch his own back. You don't play the affiliation game.

The garage door was drawn down.

Paul wandered across the street.

The night settled on the neighborhood.

Cool Hayward night, the fog creeping in slow.

Two Southern Pacific trains rattled by, just thirty feet away, shaking the house.

At four Paul heard shouts and screaming wheels. He opened his window, listened. Metal clanks, poles hitting solids, more shouts, a woman crying. Someone hurt.

Rusty won't be killed. Ignacio's there to remind them not to do this. He won't let them go all the way with the play. He's not an A Street member. Rusty will pay for what was done. Maybe wake up somewhere in bad shape, most likely down at the Hayward Airport, right along the water there, something broken. Not dead. Not your problem. Não faz mal. Tudo bem. Tudo controlado.

Paul turned over in bed, placed a round in his rifle. Fell back to sleep.

Dreams of dogs. In his garden. Six of them. Dogs in plastic bags. Paul wondered why they were in his dreams. He'd disposed of them the last time he came to fix the place up, reminders of the bikers that had lived in the house after his grandma died. Dogs buried right under the pigeon coop. Victims of men who fight pit bulls. Red dogs. White dogs. Small dogs mauled to death. And then a dark shape leaning over Paul, looking at him in his sleep. Paul could feel the shape's breath but couldn't open his eyes, no matter how much he willed it.

Paul woke late, ate the same breakfast as the day before. He smoked a joint, drank a cup of Angolan coffee. It was a warm morning, past ten.

Time to start painting the house, fixing things up. See if Ray is interested in work.

Paul stepped onto the stoop. No one was on the street except for Speedy. The sun high in the sky, acid yellow. Hayward perfect. A breeze coming in off the bay, like Lisboa, like Viano, like Coimbra. The reason the Portuguese came here in the first place.

Speedy was sitting on the curb, picking at an old Delco alternator with a knife. Cup in hand, Paul walked across the street. Even though he was mainlander Portuguese, he'd have to check on Rusty. It wasn't their *bairro* any longer but there was this cultural thing, this connection. Rusty was a tweaker now. Left behind in this shit neighborhood. His family never got out. But Paul would have to check anyway.

"What's up, Speedy? Where's everyone?"

"Holmes, it got ugly this morning, eh."

"Yeah, I heard the fight. Something go on?"

"Like I'm saying, things got ugly." And the way he said it showed he was involved. He was angry and distant all at once. "Something had to be taken care of, you know, what with Güero just coming out of jail. And that *maricón* with the violin, he came back with his old lady. Man, he was out of line." Speedy gave the alternator a jab.

Paul didn't want to push it much further. He sipped on his coffee, asked offhandedly, "Rusty make it out alive?"

"Shit, he needed showing."

"Hm."

Paul looked down the block. Five houses down was Rusty's. Painted aquamarine on the trim, just like his grandmother's. Aquamarine meaning you're Portuguese, the way all his people painted houses back then. The *norteños* and *sureños* had red and blue colors, the Portuguese had aquamarine. Back in the day the whole *bairro* was painted like this. Now they simply owned the houses, rented them out. No more folks from the Açores. It was Michoacan that came now, filled the old *bairro*. The *inquilinos*, the new renters Paul and his family looked for, the new people.

"He learned his lesson," offered Speedy, poking the alternator again with the knife.

Paul blinked, sipped his coffee, told himself to be calm, not to move, just to watch Speedy work. He let his gaze go from Speedy's shoulder to his hand, allowed his focus to rest there. It took a minute before he was sure. By then his heart was beating hard. He blinked, felt his eyes vibrate slightly in his sockets. A line of sweat dripped between his shoulder blades.

He's got my knife. That's my knife in his hands. That's the one my brother John gave me when I turned eight. An odd brand. US Army.

The same knife I used when I was twelve and tried to put it in that kid's leg over in Castro Valley. Tim Flores, family from Pico. The shithead had on blue jeans, and the blade bent right back onto my thumb. Not a good knife for fighting. Just a carver. And now Speedy has it. My goddamned knife, porra.

Speedy flicked the knife blade. It flashed in the sun, yellow and silver white. Paul saw the scratches on the blade he'd put there when he'd tried to sharpen it on a rock at Boy Scout camp in Kensington.

No, there's no mistaking. I know those scratches. I put them there.

"That's a pretty cool knife. Where'd you get it?" Paul asked casually, like it was no big deal, like he wasn't already starting to get a prickly feeling on his skin.

Speedy held up the knife and gave him a look. "Oh, yeah, my brother gave it to me, eh. It was like a gift when I turned eight."

Jacking me up after only one day. Goddamned fucking junkie. And then that dark shape leaning over me in my dreams. The breath. Shit, why didn't I see this? Junkie breath.

"Oh, really?" said Paul.

"It's got some scratches, eh," Speedy went on. "You know, like right here on the blade where I tried to sharpen it on a rock." He shook the knife.

How can he know this? Did I tell him about this knife all those years ago in the bairro? *Did he recognize me from the start? Am I like Arturo, how they didn't speak of him after he died? And how can Speedy have my knife just a day after my move in? I kept everything closed up. I was careful. I didn't let down my guard.*

Oh, but you did. The window. You opened it to hear what they were doing to Rusty. Then left it unattended. Stupid. Not street. Speedy didn't go off with his cousins. He stayed behind to take care of that moon-faced kid with the violin. And when he was done, he came into your house after you were asleep. You'd been drinking. They knew this. Because they'd remembered you all along. You wouldn't wake up when they came in. It's all part of the game.

"You sharpened it on a rock?" Paul checked.

"Oh, yeah," said Speedy. "I don't know if I knew how to sharpen knives back then. I was in Boy Scouts. But I tried."

Paul swallowed, said, "I see. And your brother gave it to you." A statement posing as a question.

"Yeah, like when I was eight," said Speedy. "Not good for anything but a tool. Not like a *filero*, eh."

Paul nodded. *No, not a* filero. *You couldn't stab a guy with that knife.*

"Good work knife, eh," said Speedy. "I can work with this."

"Yeah."

And now Speedy throwing it back in his face, almost too casual, like he didn't care in the least who he'd ripped off.

You let the truck incident go. You warned them with shots in the night. You shared beer with them, got them high, made a show that you got it. But now this. You don't play it like that.

Paul said, "Hey, I think I hear my phone ringing. I'll be back in a minute."

"Yeah, you go, dude."

Dude. Speedy saying dude like a gabacho. *Throwing it in your face.*

Paul didn't cross the road too fast or too slow. He went with deliberation. In the house he picked up his rifle. He sat in the kitchen, the rifle across his lap, picked up his phone and put it down. Talked to no one in particular, making up a conversation.

Point the gun at his stomach, demand the knife back. Get the knife, then kick him in the head. Show him who's boss. Junkie gets in your house, he figures it's a free pass. After that, he's coming and going, taking what he pleases. That's what junkies do. They work on your weaknesses.

There was a scrape, a sound of something in the backyard. Birds' wings flapping. A gate closing. Someone was in the yard. Paul stood. He went back to his bedroom. The curtains were billowing in the wind. Heavy Portuguese curtain boxes, the kind that hid the velvet curtains.

You left these windows open too. No one leaves windows open in this place. It's an invitation.

Paul turned to the closet. The door was opened.

Like that filho da puta *under your truck. Remember how you do this. You're cutting corners. You're losing it. Remember, their people rent from you. That's your plan. Once you rent, you have an obligation. They are your renters. You must be correct. Above all this. Check this. Make sure you have it right.*

He opened the box of his guy stuff, the souvenirs of his childhood and teen years. And there was his knife, sitting right there on top of all his memories. Paul swore, picked up the knife, opened the blade. The same scratches he'd seen a few minutes before. He checked the window.

Anyone with street knows you don't leave a window open. People come and go. And last night, things were getting ugly. You knew this. You didn't get it. Even after the warning. You passed out, lost your guard.

Paul sat down under the window, closed his eyes, took a breath.

He thinks he can come in and out without paying. First the truck. Now this. Taking your knife, then climbing through the window, putting it back while you're on the phone, messing with you. He's testing you, seeing what you got, showing he's faster. Why do you think he's called Speedy? The junkie's fast. Don't let A Street do this to you. They do this, they'll control this bairro. *They'll be your owner. This will no longer be your home to rent.*

Paul checked the chamber a second time, went to the door, went back to his closet again, took the knife out of the box. He walked out the door with the *vergueiro* leveled. Speedy was still on the corner. He had the alternator pushed into the curb, was poking it with a screwdriver. Paul took a breath, stepped toward the street.

Think. Think how this is playing. Are you doing what he wants? Is this part of the test? Is he getting under your skin just to get you going? Go soft. Tranquilo, tranquilo. *Don't fuck yourself. Be calm. This is business. You're going too fast. Fast is Speedy's territory.*

Two steps onto the driveway, he put the rifle on the hood of his truck. The rifle slid a few inches down the paint, stopped.

He won't have a firearm hidden. It will be a baseball bat or a steel pole placed in the yard. Ray will have the family gun on the inside of the garage door. Güero will have his rifle on the platform he's hung from the rafters in the garage. He sleeps up there with it. Speedy won't be holding. You've never seen a junkie strapped. So you go in straight.

Speedy looked up from his work. "You get that phone call?" he asked. He was smiling crookedly.

He's got some nerve, smiling like that, tossing it in your face that he's been in and out of your house twice already this morning, coming back like a dog to his own vomit.

"Yeah, it was a friend on the phone. We talked for a minute. And then I thought I'd pick something up and show it to you."

"Really? You got something for me?"

"Yeah, check this out." Paul pulled out his knife, opened the blade, thrust it in Speedy's face. "That's a knife," he said, shaking the blade. "My brother gave it to me when I was eight. I got the scratches on the blade from trying to sharpen it on a rock. Stabbed a kid with it when I was twelve. You know what I'm saying?"

"Oh, holmes, no way, eh."

"Yeah, way."

Now plunge the blade in Speedy's shoulder because he's still smiling stupidly, acting innocent. Punking you. Throwing it in your face. You do him now.

Paul waited for Speedy to make a move and give him an excuse.

Instead Speedy said, "Man, that's messed up."

"I know it is."

"So let me show you what I got for you."

Speedy reached in his front pocket. Paul stepped back. The sleeve to Speedy's flannel dropped down. Paul saw the black sores from the needle holes on his arm, was surprised at their infection. The boiled black blood. The blue-and-brown death.

He didn't recognize the knife for a second, the way Speedy had it cradled in his hand. Speedy was saying, "What are the chances of that, holmes? Two dudes with the same knife, scratching it up on the sidewalk. Same birthday too. They must've had a sale on at the sport shop. We both get the same thing."

Paul looked at his own knife in his hand. "Holy shit."

"Yeah, ain't that weird?" asked Speedy.

"The same knives," said Paul.

"What it is, homeboy. You can't make this shit up."

Paul glanced over at his truck. The rifle was pointing right at them. As if sensing his fear, the rifle slid a little farther down the hood, stopped, balanced, rocked in the breeze.

Speedy was speaking junkie slow about miracles and coincidences. Paul began grunting, shrugging, talking fast like a fool, wondering when Speedy was going to see the gun.

Lady Bird

Daniel Cox

 WALTER DEUTCHER HUNKERED in a copse of juniper
that grew halfway into the gravel turnaround.
The .30-06 lay across his thighs like a plank. At
3 a.m., he heard the big Ford grinding up the
switchback. He set the rifle's safety. He opened
the bolt to check the load.

The big pickup slewed into the turnaround. Lee Cole kicked open
the driver's door. A whip of smoke from the fat joint in his mouth
made him squint one-eyed like he was sighting a gun.

Lee jumped down. "Whew. I have to piss like a big dog." He
unzipped and let fly.

"Dog . . . dog," his brain-damaged brother Glenn blubbered from
inside the Ford.

"We didn't mean to hurt the dog, Glenn. It was an accident."

"No! No!" Glenn screeched. His feet slammed against the floorboard. He bucked his head against the back window. As he thrashed,
Glenn screamed, "Lady Bird . . . Lady Bird!"

Voices in Walter Deutcher's head screamed, too. Shrieks that
smothered him in cold blackness. That made him want to fling himself at the world with both fists. He stepped from the juniper. Eased
off the rifle's safety. A silhouette loomed beside the driver-side door.
Walter shot it and reloaded. A shadow slithered from the passenger
side, shouting, "Walter . . . Walter!" as if from a tomb. He fired again.
In Walter's cross-wired mind, the air itself exploded in a whirlwind

of fire and earth. The phantom blast's concussion rocked him, sucking the air from his lungs. He slumped to the ground.

Walter woke to a pale sun rising over the Sierra Diablo Pass. Shrikes darted in and out of the juniper scrub. They spooked a gang of vultures feasting on the drying eyes of the dead. He rummaged through the pickup's bed, shoving aside a gas can. He shook the can—half-full. A canvas tarp lay wedged under tools and shovels. Lengths of cotton rope secured the tarp.

He knifed the tarp in half, cocooned each corpse, and tied the ends. A narrow path behind the turnaround led to the tall grass where he'd hobbled his horse, Bob. He led the big gray gelding back to the truck and slung the first bundle over the saddle. Balancing the other over the horse's hindquarters, he tied off each parcel beneath Bob's bulging belly. He lashed a shovel and a spud bar to the saddle.

Walter doused the truck, inside and out, with gas. As the truck roared to flame behind them, Walter walked Bob into the winding canyon. The shrouded packages bounced in time with Bob's gait as the burdened horse picked his way among deadfall mesquite and piñon pine.

On April 12, 1969, two soldiers stepped out of the rain onto Beth Deutcher's front porch in Lobo, Texas. They had a telegram and their country's condolences to deliver. Beth's son, Walter, had been shot in Quang Tri.

Lady Bird, Walter's big yellow coonhound, saw them first. She shot from under the porch with bared teeth, growling low and hard. Beth glanced out. She shut her eyes and retreated to the parlor's shadows. With her fists at her mouth, she stared at the porch, praying that these men wouldn't turn the blue star in her front window—Walter's star—to gold. She sent eighteen-year-old Jessie out to talk to them.

"What kind of tree?" she asked Jessie when they'd gone.

"It's a place. They just say it like *tree*." She showed Beth the yellow telegram. "See? It ain't even spelled like a tree, Momma."

"Whatever it is don't sound like anyplace worth getting my boy shot over."

A week later, from someplace called Nha Trang, Walter sent them a letter. He included a photo of a flabby-faced officer fastening a medal to Walter's hospital pajamas. "That sure don't look a thing like Walter," Beth said, showing Jessie the photograph.

"Oh, that's Walter, all right, Momma. But he looks rough as a north-forty fence post." Jessie smoothed the folded letter. "Says here that medal's the Purple Heart. They give him that for getting shot."

"I know what they give it to him for. Your daddy came home from his war with a mess of iron in his back and shoulder and two of those things. He threw 'em in the top bureau draw and never looked at 'em again. They're up there still, buried beneath everything he could find to heap atop 'em."

Jessie's finger skimmed across the words. "Walter says he and some other boys took to calling it the Purple Shaft."

Beth Deutcher flushed. "My goodness! That don't sound a bit like Walter."

The first week in May, Beth and Jessie drove the spavined Chevy Apache to the El Paso airport to bring Walter home from the war. Jessie rode the worn clutch and ground through the gears. "This dang wore-out truck was old when Granddaddy was a boy," she complained.

"Be grateful we got this much to drive, child. Otherwise Walter would be taking the bus."

"Bet Walter would rather ride that bus than get bumped to death in this old rig." Beth Deutcher wanted to say that everything Jessie thought she knew about Walter had changed. That the man they'd fetch back would not be the boy they'd seen off two years ago. Beth knew.

Walter's daddy came home broken. Twisted. In such pain it broke her heart. The physical part was the least of it. Eventually he put most of the ugliness behind him. He'd made his peace, and made a life with Beth and the children. His day job was hauling pulpwood up and down this same highway. Five years ago, an accident at the pulpwood plant killed him, leaving Walter and Jessie to help Beth tend the ranch. Then Walter got drafted.

Now her boy was coming home. Thrilled and relieved, Beth was also afraid that darkness would dog Walter the way it did his daddy. "Go easy with Walter, Jessie."

"Easy? What you mean, easy?"

"He won't be like you remember."

"My brother Walter? As I remember he couldn't tie his own shoelaces without someone to tell him how."

"I reckon he's learned to tie his shoes. I'm just saying he'll be different, is all. He might not be as good-natured as you remember. Be patient. Don't push him."

"Shoot, Momma. I reckon I know my own brother."

When Walter finally stepped out of the plane, though, Jessie hardly recognized him. He was so scrawny he looked as if he might break. "Good Lord, Momma, he looks like a hungry wolf." Jessie plunged onto the landing strip. She threw herself into Walter's arms. He held her off, but she kept coming. He didn't feel scrawny, though. He felt like a hunk of steel before the burrs get buffed off. He held her at arm's length. The eyes that met hers were hard and cold as stone.

Beth followed Jessie. Just through the chain link gate, her knees buckled. She sank to the pavement sobbing. Two years of worry, seven hundred days and nights fearing the phone call or the knock at the door, had finally ended.

"Momma!" Walter said. He released Jessie and lifted his mother from the sweltering tarmac in one easy motion. Beth's gratitude almost sent her down again, a gratitude greater than she'd felt bringing Walter into the world twenty-one years before. She held to this scrawny, strong being. Her tears wet his neck and stained his shirt. Her firstborn had returned. Her long fret and wait while her son was among strangers and enemies was over.

Walter spent his first days home soaking in the tub and drinking cheap whiskey. What luxury! High piles of bubbles rode atop warm, soothing water, and washed away infected leech bites and scabby jungle rot. The last time he'd bathed in a tub was six months ago on R&R. "You number 10. You stink," the little Thai girl he'd bought for the week scolded.

She drew a hot bath and scrubbed him until the bathwater blackened. Draining that tubful, she drew another and scrubbed some more, all the time speaking to him in a beautiful, singsong dialect of which he understood not a word. After the third bath, she consented.

Walter took another slug, propped his feet on the tub, and peeled away saturated strips of dead skin. Months of arm's-length violence, bad water, bad food, and a worse climate had practically ruined him. Most of the truly awful stuff, though, he'd packed deep down inside. Whenever he slacked on the whiskey, painful sharp darkness leaked out. When he felt anxious or angry, he simply drank more rotgut. That quelled the anxiety, but the anger still smoldered.

At night, Walter's thrashing and screaming set Jessie off. She ran down the hall toward his bedroom. There, Lady Bird—named after President Johnson's wife the day Walter got his draft notice—stood guard. The hound had stationed herself outside Walter's bedroom door since his return, baring her fearsome teeth at everyone but him.

"Git, you old flea-bitten yellow turd!" Jessie kicked at Lady Bird, but the dog advanced. Jessie backed off, convinced of Lady Bird's resolve.

"Leave her be, Jessie." Her mother stood in the hall.

"Well, she's right in the dang way, and Walter's in there carrying on. He'll likely break something, and hurt himself while he's breaking it."

"Go on back to bed and leave Walter be. Ain't nothing to do, Jess. Your daddy acted the same when he came home. Just give Walter time. Be patient, like I said."

"How come you let that old dog up here? She don't do a thing but stink and growl, crouched there like a troll under a bridge."

"Lady Bird is Walter's favorite. She's his comfort. If she wants to lie outside his door, I'll allow it for a time. Now quit your sass or you'll sleep under the porch with the rest of the hounds."

"Well, ain't that a peach? You'd turn me out while this one lounges around and snarls?" Jessie harrumphed down the hall and slammed her bedroom door.

That darn Walter. Since he's been home, he's been a mystery. Don't want any company but a whiskey bottle and that old yellow dog. Well, dang it! Momma said to have patience. But 'twon't hurt none to push him a little in the right direction.

At sunup, Walter did the same thing all over again. Late that afternoon, Jessie could stand no more. She marched straight into that bathroom like there wasn't a naked man in the tub. Like she'd seen it all before. Lady Bird raised her head, growling a warning.

"Hush, dog!" The hound stared until Jessie crossed the room and seated herself on the hamper. "Walter. You can't soak in that there tub every day just drinking whiskey."

Walter hunkered into the soapsuds. "Why the hell not?" He handed her his half-empty bottle.

"'Cause there is work to be done around this place. In case you ain't noticed, me and Momma been hangin' on by our fingernails. We could use your help." Jessie took a long burning pull from the bottle, to show Walter she was a lady that knew how to handle her whiskey. "Besides, if you got dressed, it ain't too late to whip you at eight ball down at Tommy's." Walter sat bolt upright. Soapy foam dripped down his torso, revealing an angry rope of raised red skin on his shoulder.

"Is that where you was shot?"

"Yep. It went in here." He turned, exposing a puckered red-purple scar on his upper back. "Came out here."

"Dang!"

"Yeah, it sure is a mess. Want to touch it?"

"No!" Jessie jumped back. "I don't want to do no such thing."

"It's all healed up. It don't hurt none. When it happened, though, it burned like the devil. A hundred wasp stings all at once."

Walter popped the clutch and dogged the gas, fishtailing from the gravel drive onto paved road. "First thing tomorrow, we'll hit the parts store, get us a new clutch."

"We ain't got money for such. Plenty else needs fixin' before we waste money on this old thing." Jessie cranked her window to fend off agitated road dust.

"I got money," Walter said. "They give me all I had coming when

I mustered out. No fortune, but enough to fix what needs fixin'."
Walter pushed the Apache up to speed and shifted into high with a
thunk. "Rebuild this transmission, too."

"Big talk for somebody that lays up in the tub all day."

Before the curve that veered toward Lobo, Walter steadied the
wheel and straightened the truck. A battered Ford pickup in the
opposite lane overshot the curve, spinning toward Walter and Jessie.
Walter downshifted with one hand and leaned on the horn with the
other. He jerked the truck from the hard road to the sand shoulder,
and the rusted Ford shot past.

Walter wrestled the Apache back onto the blacktop. Jessie hung
halfway out the window, jabbing her arm at the sky, middle finger
extended. "That's that damn Lee Cole, and Glenn, his idiot brother!
Drunk as ten monkeys, no doubt." Walter grabbed her belt and jerked
her back inside.

Lee Cole palmed the steering wheel and gunned the Ford. He noted
the Apache in his rearview. Probably that old crone, Beth, and her
tasty little daughter headed to town for something or other. Two lone
women on that old broke-down ranch. Ought to go out there and
bend the young one over the porch rail. Maybe give Glenn the old
dried-up mother. Lee opened a fresh beer with his free hand and
handed it to Glenn. "Drink that slow," he told his brother. "You know
how you get when you drink too much too fast."

"Drink slow . . . drink slow." Repeating was Glenn's main form
of communication. Glenn possessed all the moving parts of a full-
grown man, and decent looks. Years ago he got brain-banged in a car
wreck, which left him duller than a stunted four-year-old with the
sensibilities of a puppy. The driver, Glenn's big brother, Lee, his
head full of whiskey and pills, zoomed the car from road to ditch to
tree. Afterward, a twisted mix of guilt and family feeling made Lee,
rough as forty hells and mean to the bone, poor Glenn's self-
appointed guardian.

In daylight, the Cole brothers hunted and fished the Sierra Diablo's
canyons. At dark, Lee pulled into one of the many dead-end turn-
arounds. There, in addition to drinking a great deal, Lee and Glenn

smoked weed until they passed out. The late afternoon of this particular day was no different.

Lee sucked in the belly that draped his lap like a feed sack. He
raked back his greasy shoulder-length hair. Wiping his mouth with
the knurled back of his hand, he said, "How about we go over to
Tommy's and see can we hustle some pool?" He spoke more to himself than to Glenn.

"Hustle pool . . . hustle pool!" Glenn pitched his empty from the
truck.

"Goddammit, Glenn. I told you not to drink that so fast."

Glenn squeezed his thighs tight. He clapped his hand over his
crotch to stopper the stream darkening his jeans.

"Shit." Lee stomped the brakes and swerved into a side road.
Glenn, pissing himself all the while, slid off the seat onto the floor.
Lee jerked Glenn from the cab and stood him up. The soggy patch in
Glenn's pants spread down each leg. "Goddamn, didn't I tell you?"

"Goddamn . . . goddamn," Glenn crowed, hopping from one leg to
the other. He began to blubber.

Lee grabbed him by the shoulders and shook. "Shut it! Quit your
crying. It ain't nothin' but pee. It'll clean up."

"Clean up . . . clean up," Glenn blubbered.

Lee pushed Glenn behind the truck. "Shuck those nasty britches,
and that underwear, too."

"Underwear . . . underwear?"

"You'll have to go without."

Lee jerked the tailgate down with a screeching crash. He scrounged
like a ragpicker through the junk in the truck bed. He unscrewed a
two-gallon water cooler and wet a filthy rag. "Here, swab off that
piss." Lee fished a pair of grease-stained overalls from behind the
driver's seat. "Put these on."

Clouds of cigarette smoke lingered over herds of empty beer bottles.
Tommy's patrons, the usual late-afternoon drunks, were too busy to
notice Jessie and Walter. They lined the bar, fussing at the early-
evening news on the color TV above them.

The same old thing the networks beamed every night, bad news from the battlefield. Oddly named villages that nobody could pronounce or find on a map. Walter glanced at the TV. He ducked his head and moved away fast, like if he stood still, the war would jump off the screen right on top of him.

The old drunks threw in their expert two cents, complaining about how the commies and draft dodgers, and especially the politicians, were ruining the country. The old jukebox crooned a cornball ballad about cheap bourbon and pearl-snap shirts.

"Three ball off the rail." Walter pointed with the tip of his cue. "Side pocket." With an easy motion, he drew back and struck the cue ball. The three ball clacked off the side rail, skedaddled the width of the table, and, as if possessed by some kind of magic, thunked into the exact pocket he'd called. The cue ball spun to a stop near the back rail.

"Blind luck," Jessie said. She stuck out her tongue. Her feeble shot scattered the table and blocked all but one corner pocket behind the cue ball. "Now what you gonna do?"

Walter chalked his cue. The eight ball sat at the opposite end, center table, a hair off the back rail. "Eight ball off the back rail, all the way down." Walter pointed to the open pocket behind the cue ball.

"No way in hell," Jessie taunted. "Way too much green, and that's a sure-enough scratch shot."

Walter planted his feet, hunched over the cue ball, and slid his stick back and forth between thumb and forefinger. He looked up midstroke. "You see, Jess, the trick is not to think. Once you figure your angle and English, put the shot out of your mind." Walter held her gaze as the white ball popped toward the table's other end.

The cue ball whacked the eight ball against the back rail, slamming it so hard into the far corner pocket that Walter jumped. The cue ball bounced off the side rail and spun to a stop in the middle of the table.

"Loser buys!" Walter crowed.

"You know I'm underage, dummy." Jessie fished a wad of bills from her jeans. She threw them on the table. "I'll pay, but you have to buy."

"Rack 'em up, little sister. I'll be right back."

"See if you can't find some decent music on that jukebox."

"I doubt they got any draft-dodger war-protester music in here."

Jessie shoved the remaining game balls into the pockets. Slotting a quarter into the coin slide, she jammed the slide home. A new rack clunked into the hopper.

"Rack 'em tight, there, darlin'." Lee Cole's grimy hand snaked out to squeak blue chalk over the tip of his cue. He leered at Jessie and swayed like a drunken tree. If trees wore unbelted jeans and dirty gray undershirts.

"We're on this table," Jessie said, wondering how she'd failed to notice the big, dumb troublemaker and his brain-damaged charge when she and Walter came in.

"We? Who's we? I don't see nobody else, sweet pea."

Lee's slow brother Glenn stood beside him in a sagging pair of overalls. Glenn fumbled with another chalk cube and cue, trying to imitate Lee but smearing his hands and face blue instead. Glenn dropped the chalk, picked it up, dropped it again.

"Don't call me sweet pea, you fat fuck."

"Well, would you listen to that mouth?" Lee poked Glenn with his chalked cue, provoking a giggle.

"Fat fuck . . . fat fuck," Glenn blurted.

Lee rounded the table, walking on the balls of his feet as if he'd caught his dungarees up his backside. "How 'bout we teach you some manners, Missy? Maybe show you what that pretty mouth is really for." Lee grabbed Jessie's wrists and pinned her to the pool table. Glenn squawked and giggled. He wiped his face with a slobbery smear of blue chalk dust.

"Let me go, Lee!" Jessie cried. Lee forced his beery face into hers. Day-old stubble burned her cheek.

With a crack that woke the barflies, Walter slammed two beers on the pool table's rail. Lee flinched at the noise, and Jessie broke away. Walter handed her a beer. He stared at Lee. "You two gents want to challenge, put your money on the table. You can play the next game's winner."

"Well, I'll be damned." Lee staggered backward into Glenn. "If it ain't little Walter."

"Walter . . . Walter," Glenn babbled. He slithered around Lee and caught Walter in a clumsy embrace. Walter wrapped Glenn in a soft headlock, roughed Glenn's hair, and kissed the top of his head. Glenn giggled and hummed.

"Leave him be, Glenn." Lee handed his brother the triangular rack. "Take this and stop acting like a dummy. Rack 'em up like I taught you."

"Dummy . . . dummy." Glenn plopped the rack onto the table's far end and scooped the balls from the hopper. Smiling like a toddler, he slopped most of them into the rack. He removed the wooden triangle, leaving a random, muddled mess. Lee glared down the table. Before Lee could make the usual mean, hurtful comment, Walter reached across and scattered Glenn's jumbled rack.

"Like this, Glenn," Walter said, placing the rack on green felt. "Start with a solid-colored ball at the top. Alternate with a stripe." Walter set them in sequence. "Here, Glenn, you can do it." Walter nudged the remaining balls toward Glenn, who filled the rack according to pattern. He cooed and hummed, a kindergartner solving a puzzle.

Walter handed Glenn the eight ball. "Now, this one goes right in the middle." Glenn shoehorned the ball in place. Walter positioned Glenn's hands on the rack. His hands atop Glenn's, Walter slid the rack in place. "Push your fingers between the wood and the bottom row of balls to tighten them. Press hard, now." Walter removed his hands and stepped back. "Okay, Glenn. Lift the rack." Slowly, Glenn removed it, leaving the balls in a perfect triangle. He looked at Walter and let loose joyous babbling.

Walter roughed Glenn's hair. "That's good, Glenn. Best rack I ever seen."

Glenn skipped the cue ball toward his brother. Walter intercepted it with a quick hand. "If you're challenging the table, it's my break."

"This table's open. Put that cue ball down, you hear?" Lee's cold stare bored into Walter.

Walter ran his hand along the table. The green felt turned gray. Color drained from the room, the place, the world. Time elongated like pulled taffy. Walter tracked the shadow of movement, Glenn sliding along the opposite rail toward Lee. The funk of decayed vegetation from the Asian plateau blew through Walter. Chaos pounded in his ears. That thing inside him, the not-so-distant voice of practiced survival, whispered its orders.

Glenn tugged Lee's arm. He pointed toward the perfect rack of pool balls. Lee nodded curt approval. He hefted his stick. "Put the cue ball on the table, Deutcher."

Walter looked at the ball in his hand. He stared up at Lee, whose face now wore the features of a cruel Asian enemy. Startled, Walter reached for his sidearm. It wasn't there.

"Hey, little man! You got shit in your ears or something? I told you to put the ball down."

Incomprehensible phantom singsong voices, coupled with a cataclysmic explosion, rang in Walter's ears. He threw the cue ball. Lee ducked. Glenn didn't. The ball flattened Glenn's nose. Glenn's face blossomed crimson. He yelped like a kicked dog. The bloodstained ball clattered to the concrete. Walter rushed around the table, sending beer bottles and ashtrays crashing. He lunged headfirst at Lee's chest, pinning Lee's arms in a bear hug so that Lee couldn't slash him with the cue.

"Hey! That's enough, you two!" Tommy's bellow quieted the ruined Glenn. Walter and Lee stopped thrashing but clung tight, waiting to finish each other off. Tommy reached into the scrum and forced them apart.

"Goddammit, Tommy, we was just trying to play a friendly game of eight ball and this peckerhead starts in. Look what he done to poor Glenn. You know I can't just let something like that slide." Lee made for Walter again but backed away when Tommy brandished the hard-bitten wooden club he used on troublemakers.

Tommy looked over Lee's shoulder. "Well, I'll be damned." He turned to Jessie. "Is that Walter?"

"Sure is."

"Dang, boy, I hardly recognized you. When did you get back?"

"Three, maybe four days ago."

Tommy looked Walter up and down. "Hell, looks like only half of you made it home. Don't that army feed you boys?"

"Some," Walter said.

Jessie grabbed Walter's arm. "Let's go on home," she said. "We got chores." Lee moved to follow. Tommy thumped him in the chest with the club. Hard.

"Where you off to, Lee?"

"This ain't over. I'm gonna take it outside."

"You ain't takin' nothin' nowhere till you clean up this mess and pay for what-all you broke."

"Me? What about them?" Lee stabbed a chalk-stained finger toward Walter and Jessie. "They started it. That shitbird up and smashed Glenn in the face with a pool ball for no damn reason. What kinda coward goes after a dummy?" As if on cue, Glenn covered his broken face. Sobs bubbled from beneath his bloody hands.

Tommy looked to Walter. "That true, Walter?"

"I don't know. I—" Walter looked from Glenn to Jessie. "I was seeing . . . hearing things." Walter shook his head to clear the gray fog from inside it.

"You don't look so good, boy. All right, you and Jessie clear out."

Lee cut past Tommy and went for Walter. "This ain't over. You hear?"

Tommy stepped in for a fistful of Lee's T-shirt. He laid the club upside Lee's head.

On the ride home, Walter checked and rechecked the rearviews, though he knew the thing following him couldn't be seen.

"Dang, Walter. What in hell was that all about?"

Walter shook his head.

"First, you bust up poor idiot Glenn's face, then, like a damn lunatic, you jump Lee. That dead-eyed hulk ain't got enough brains to get through the day, but he won't let that slide."

"I don't—I can't remember." Walter ground the gears.

"Can't remember? How can you not remember something like that?"

Walter shut his eyes. "It just comes out of nowhere. A smell or sound. Color drains away to black. Sometimes it's a warning. Sometimes it ain't. Sometimes it just happens."

Lee wet a rag. He daubed crusted blood from his brother's face, working in gentle swirls until he reached the blue-and-yellow mess of Glenn's flattened nose. "That goddamn Walter. That goddamn pissant."

"Walter . . . Walter," Glenn screeched. His nose whistled with each agitated breath.

Lee cleaned the ragged cut on the bridge of Glenn's nose. Glenn bucked and yelped. "Hold still, dummy." Tearing a strip from the cruddy roll of adhesive tape in the glove box, Lee smoothed it gently across Glenn's flattened nose. "Hurts, huh?" Glenn nodded.

Lee opened the driver's door. He reached behind the seat for his shotgun. He skinned off the case and slid five bird-shot shells into the magazine. He racked the pump and thumbed off the safety. "Remember what I taught you about shooting?"

Glenn nodded eagerly. "Shooting . . . shooting." His breath whistled through his nose.

Lee handed Glenn the weapon. "All right, it's loaded and dangerous. Keep it pointed at the sky."

The two brothers toked and drank. They killed flying beer cans until they ran out of empties. Building a fire against the night's cold, they sat side by side and drank some more. Glenn fell asleep.

Lee racked out the remaining bird shot. He exchanged it for a single double-aught shell and pumped the shell into the receiver. He straddled his sleeping brother. Glenn breathed in, then out, slow and relaxed. Lee dipped the barrel toward Glenn's head. Not enough sense left in there to care if the sun rose tomorrow or not. He eased off the safety. His finger moved inside the trigger guard. He considered how it would feel to be rid of this burden. His finger caressed the trigger's smooth, curved steel. Pull it. Just pull it. Glenn stirred in his sleep, burbling.

Lee jerked the shotgun skyward. He pressed the safety. Sweating, he shucked the double-aught from the magazine. He sheathed and stowed the shotgun. He fumbled in the truck bed, pushing aside a half-full gas can, wire cutters, two rusty toolboxes, a spud bar, and a spade. Caught in with them was a rolled canvas tarp, which he unfurled over his sleeping brother. Lee walked into the night, away from the fire's warmth. A cold moon rose behind the sawtoothed Sierra Diablo.

Two nights after the bang-up at Tommy's, Lee and Glenn swung off the hard road and up the Deutchers' gravel drive. Accompanied by shotgun blasts, the roaring pickup cut doughnuts in the front yard. A pack of coonhounds bolted from under the front porch, yowling like demons and snapping at the truck tires.

Walter scrambled downstairs in his drawers and a misbuttoned flannel shirt flapping at the cuffs. "Jessie, cut off the damn lights! Hit the floor and stay there!" He rummaged in the front closet for his granddaddy's old single-shot .30-06 and a handful of cartridges. He sprinted out the back door with Lady Bird on his heels.

The Cole brothers revved their big truck's engine and fired shot-guns at nothing in particular, spraying bird shot everywhere. A hound yelped, and Walter knew Lee managed to hit something. The pickup skidded to a stop. Walter hugged the corner of the house. He eased a glance toward the front yard.

Lee stood before his truck, silhouetted in the headlights' long yel-low cones. Walter slid a cartridge into the rifle's chamber. He locked the bolt forward. Something moved in the truck bed. Glenn Cole sat back there in a tattered old parlor chair with a white bandage on his nose and his shotgun trained on the front of the house.

Walter wondered if the dang thing was even loaded. Surely even Lee had more sense than to hand an idiot a loaded gun. Glenn's shot-gun discharged. Walter flinched and dropped into a crouch. Bird shot spattered the house like supercharged gravel.

Walter drew a bead on Glenn's bandage. He took a shallow breath. Just before he squeezed the trigger, he sighted farther right. A star-shaped chunk blew out of the windshield, cobwebbing the glass.

Minutes after her brother charged out the back door, Jessie heard Granddaddy's old deer rifle open up like a thunderclap. That old gun kicked like a mule, but what it didn't hit, it could sure enough scare to death. The noise must've made the Cole brothers think twice.

Jessie peered over the windowsill. The Coles' truck squealed into reverse and took the rutted driveway teeth-rattling fast toward the hard road. Walter continued firing steadily. A blown-out tire peeled from its rim, flaming and sparking like a Roman candle. The truck didn't slow.

Jessie waited till the Cole brothers got a ways down the road. She turned on the porch light. Long, thin shadows fell over the one shot dog. Walter bent over the other. The light was too dim to see for sure, but Walter's attitude told Jessie it was Lady Bird.

Jessie came up on them slow. She made sure to crunch the gravel good so Walter wouldn't spook. "Is she shot?" Walter shouldered the rifle. He ran his hands over Lady Bird until she let out a yelp and snapped at him.

"Back's broke. Must've got caught under the tires." Walter scooped Lady Bird into his arms. She whined and licked at his face, telling him she was sorry she'd snapped. "Jessie, bring a pickax and shovel from the barn."

Walter carried Lady Bird near the big weeping willow west of the house. He knelt beside her. She panted hard, whining with each breath. Her tongue lolled. A skim of blood-slobber covered her muzzle. Walter spoke to soothe her, but sobs and gasps choked his words. He gazed beyond her at the darkening horizon.

The purple mountains of the Sierra Diablo floated on a shimmering lake of moonlight. The dry, sage-scented breeze whispered from a great distance in a voice only Walter could hear. He stood. He cranked a cartridge into the chamber. The bolt slid home, cold and final. Lady Bird's ears cocked. Her brown eyes followed Walter's every move. "All right now, girl," Walter soothed.

Jessie closed her eyes. Walter pointed the barrel down at Lady Bird. The report rolled across the yard, hit the house, and rolled on. Its violence made Jessie jump and fussed the evening crows overhead. They rose, circled, and lit again in the willow's droopy arms.

Walter handed Jessie the rifle. "Go on up and fetch the quilt off my bed."

"Momma will have your hide." Walter burned her with a look that went through her. Jessie saw the darkness in her brother's eyes, hateful and cruel. She did as he asked and let him be.

Beth intercepted Jessie as she came downstairs.

"It's for Walter."

Beth extended her arm. "Give it to me."

"I'll take it back upstairs."

"No." Beth draped the quilt over her arm. "You stay on the porch."

"But Momma . . ."

Out at the willow tree, Walter bent to his labor. A grunt rent the night air with every swing of the pickax. Beth stopped between Lady

Bird and the edge of the deepening hole. She knelt and folded the quilt around the dead hound.

"This was my grandmother's mourning quilt. When your great-granddaddy passed, she sat in her room for six months and sewed away her pain. Into this." Beth brushed the worn patchwork. She fingered the stitching, loose now with age.

Walter paused, wiping his forehead with his shirtsleeve. His mouth trembled, and he sobbed.

Beth touched his shoulder. "Not one of us can fix all that's wrong with the world, Walter," she said.

Walter pulled away. He sat heavily on the edge of the blossoming hole with his head in his hands.

"Look at me, Walter."

He raised his head. His face sparkled with tears.

"No matter what manner of evil you think you've heaped upon the world, your mother loves you, will always love you." Beth stood. She shook the dirt from her nightgown. She held Walter's gaze for a long time before she turned and walked to the house. She took a seat on the porch beside Jessie. They listened to the pickax and shovel ring for hours, fighting hard clay and willow roots.

The narrow path dropped steeply into blackness. Walter slacked Bob's lead, letting the sure-footed horse find the way. Walter followed, listening for distress in the horse's breathing or a break in the rhythm of the horseshoes against the rock trail. The farther down they went, the more clearly Walter felt enemy eyes on him and heard whispering voices, still alive in that dark place where he'd sent all he'd seen and done.

Walter and the horse moved deeper and deeper into the folded canyon. The air grew frigid as they descended, the sun not high enough to warm the canyon walls. A line of scrub oak and knobby juniper woods marked the canyon floor's final descent to a level, ancient riverbed. Walter led Bob to a hidden draw, where a thin spring fed tufts of brittle grass. Walter unfastened the tools and hauled the shrouded bundles from Bob's back, releasing the horse to eat and drink.

He used the spud bar to bust the first six inches of hard-packed caliche. He shoveled out the loose clays. He busted six more inches and removed the overburden. Busting and shoveling, he tortured and pounded a rectangle into the earth, taking care to square its edges and sides as he went.

While he labored, he pondered what else needed doing: barn and stock pens reinforced; fence wire restrung; tractor and truck repaired. He straightened. He shook a bandanna from his back pocket and swabbed his forehead and neck. They'd need stock, too.

He levered out a rock the size of a man's head as if it would cause discomfort to the occupants. He tamped, leveled, and smoothed the rectangle's floor. If they ran stock, he'd have to get Jessie a proper cutting horse. Despite her sassy mouth, she was a good hand.

He split the canvases again with his hip knife and rolled Lee's body facedown into the hole. He lowered Glenn, however, as gently as he could, laying him faceup on his brother's corpse. Remorse pierced him, Glenn being no more harmful and not as smart as poor Lady Bird. It was a shame.

But Walter had many shames, this one not the worst. This one just another shame between the last one and the next. He jumped into the grave. Spitting on the kerchief, he rubbed the crusted blood from Glenn's mouth, the dirt from his forehead. He draped the bandanna across Glenn's face and folded Glenn's hands. Walter packed the caliche hard and flat. He swept the area with a juniper branch. The place ended as it began.

Café Americana

Gale Walden

IN THE MIDDLE of the Midwest, in a college town that could have been any college town, stood a coffee shop called Paradise Found. This shop had lots of windows, good coffee, and mediocre food. On every table, a flower, usually yellow, wilted in a blue glass vase that had previously held water from France.

At the very bottom of the vases lay marbles, which, though barely visible through the blue glass, still gave the effect of something bubbling up, about to surface. The vases made some people with laptops nervous. Those people moved the vases to other tables, so that by afternoon one table held most of the vases. The next morning, though, the flowers were always back on each table, the room's décor held hostage to style rather than practicality.

Up and down the cafeteria-style counter, behind curved glass filled with pies and quiches and sandwich wraps, young women and men stood ready to toast bagels, make smoothies, or foam organic milk for lattes or cappuccinos. Although the employees all wore long purple aprons, their hair was a study in quirky conformity. It was maroon, or orange, or platinum blond, cropped short or done up in dreadlocks or twists, or covered with bandannas or baseball caps.

There were pierced noses and tattoos and the occasional piece of metal darting from a tongue. Most of the employees were in their early twenties, in pause between one section of life and the next, but for a couple, the curved glass was the window into their dreams, and there they were, already behind it.

Customers came in and out through two glass doors. Cow-shaped aluminum wind chimes announced each person's entrance and exit. The girl at the cash register faced the doors, but she didn't usually notice people from a distance. She waited until customers were directly in front of her before she gave them her attention. An espresso machine separated her from her coworkers. She was the last person in the service line, and the only person every customer had to confront.

Her hair was usually the color of eggplant; she was roughly thirty pounds overweight, which didn't keep her from wearing tight sweaters that accentuated the large breasts resting on her ribcage. Silver glasses with a few rhinestones on them were her only jewelry. She was always spontaneously introducing herself. Her name was Eudora.

Eudora had decided somewhere along the way in her nineteen years of life that silence was a bad thing. She rarely had enough time to say everything that flitted through her brain, so she used her time at the cash register wisely. As soon as someone approached, she started to think about what topic might go with what person.

Eudora thought, for example, that her love of *Jesus Christ Superstar* was the type of information that the slightly frazzled woman with little tentacles of gray hair radiating about her head might appreciate.

The frazzled woman took this in without changing expression. She was Jewish. Her relationship with Jesus, while complicated, was nevertheless cordial—it was musicals she resisted, having played the lead in *Bye Bye Birdie* when she was seventeen, and having forgotten her lines at the precise moment she was supposed to be relating, over the prop phone, the news that Kim had gotten pinned.

Instead she blurted out the real news that Jenny had slept with Ken. Jenny never forgave her; Ken dropped Jenny, who hung her head the rest of senior year. In her yearbook, this customer had been labeled "Most Likely to Blurt Something Embarrassing."

This mistake resulted in a lifelong fear of saying the wrong thing, but also caused the frazzled customer to develop a fear of musicals. The customer even had an aversion to rain because it reminded her of Gene Kelly. Eudora couldn't have chosen a less appropriate topic.

"Did you prefer *Godspell*?" Eudora asked the customer.

At 10 a.m. on this particular day, October 11, in the Year of the Dog, ten tables were full and seven people waited to arrive at Eudora when the aluminum cows chimed and the boy with the gun walked in.

No one knew yet that the boy had a gun; it was the moment in time before people knew there would be an after, so people went on, oblivious to time and mortality in the face of a choice between a raspberry-almond and a blueberry-flax muffin.

The boy with the gun sat at a table near one of the floor-to-ceiling windows and looked outside, contemplating what he was about to do. Since he wasn't thinking about killing anyone, he didn't have to consider humanity at large, but if he had, he would have discovered quite a range of possibilities surrounding him.

In fact, Paradise Found was the kind of place that might figure in a commercial about America's diversity. At the largest round table, an elderly group chatted after the morning session of senior aerobics; at a table near a window, a woman lifted toddlers from a double stroller into wooden high chairs; at another table, a man dressed as a cowboy read from a King James Bible to two Korean students.

The boy with the gun, however, was not considering his surroundings' potential as the setting for a commercial; the boy was considering the gun. The boy was already a felon, having committed the felony of defrauding the government and having done time for it in a county facility for juvenile offenders. "Felonious" was practically a bubbly word to the boy, and he understood his offense as something that could be written off as mischief at a later point in time. The gun, however, nestled in the right pocket of the hunting jacket he wore, weighted everything like a promise he didn't want to make.

The first time he had ever used a gun was light and innocent—cans exploding and catapulting away on his father's farm, as if it were the Fourth of July. His father clasped his shoulder and said, "Birds of air, beasts of sea, which would ever be, shall be denied." Since his father never spoke in rhyme, the boy had listened and repeated the words to himself at night as both riddle and prayer.

The boy's father had died a sudden, ordinary death, a heart attack brought on by shoveling snow. The boy, who was thirteen at the time and not yet a felon, was the one who found his father in the driveway, spread out so much like a snow angel that at first the boy experienced a joy he hadn't known since before his mother left them when he was seven years old. For a moment, he thought his father was there on the ground to play. His father was there on the ground to leave the boy alone.

At the table behind the boy with the gun, a white, doughy man stuck somewhere in his twenties held court. This man, a coffee-shop regular, was promiscuous in his choice of conversational mates, which was one of the endearing things about him: he was an equal-opportunity talker.

He would even talk to the homeless: "Do you ever dilute the orange juice?" he asked the man he was sitting with, a man who, from the looks of him, was not all that familiar with water. He paused to let the man answer, and, when he didn't, offered full support for the silence. "You know what I'm talking about. I can see by the way you are looking at me."

Another pause ensued across the table. "I don't know what you are talking about," the more unkempt of the two confessed.

"With water. I often dilute the orange juice with water. That way there's more of it, and it's not as sweet." In this way, information was being exchanged up and down and across the United States.

But the boy with the gun was not taking in helpful tips. Nothing he was considering right then was in the coffee shop. After his father died, the boy lived briefly with Gus, his maternal grandfather. Gus's own wife had left him, just as his daughter had left his son-in-law, with the slight difference that Gus's wife had died.

Gus charged them both with abandonment and took comfort from his cigarettes and his basset hound, Sad. He hadn't had much previous contact with his grandson, though they lived in adjoining towns, and he hadn't been thrilled to be named the boy's guardian, but Gus was the only kin alive, with the exception of his no-good daughter.

The first night the boy was in his official custody, his grandfather took him back to his own frame bungalow, where it was immediately apparent that the boy was allergic to both smoke and Sad. He sneezed constantly, like an announcement. The boy's sneezes made Gus fear something dire would happen—they had enough force to be prophetic—and after a week, Gus got tired of smoking on the porch.

He told the boy he could go back and live on the farm that wasn't really a farm anymore but a house on some land the boy's father had inherited. Gus checked in weekly, leaving corn and tomatoes on the kitchen table along with his Social Security checks, which the boy cashed to pay for utilities and food.

At a table beside the boy, farther from the window, a bald-headed man was talking about passport problems, rather loudly, on a cell phone. A woman from another table got up to tell him he was talking rather loudly. "I'm talking loudly?" he asked, in a voice much louder than his original voice.

"Yes, you are talking loudly," the woman confirmed. "Other people are trying to converse." She was tall, with blond frizzy hair, which she'd tried to contain with a Guatemalan headband, an arc of worry dolls pasted atop bright fabric. She looked like she might have run a commune house-meeting and announced that whoever was in charge of sweeping the kitchen floor had missed the part under the refrigerator. The man she sat with actually tucked his head under his arm when she went to complain.

The cell-phone man expressed his umbrage in stages. The first stage was subtle and involved keeping his gaze on the woman who had expressed dismay while continuing his conversation. The second stage was to speak so loudly about the woman into the cell phone that she and others could hear. The third required taking the cell phone outside and waving his hands in front of the window, gesturing toward the woman.

That man was one of the lucky ones, the papers would say the next day, but even in this unrecognized moment, it looked from the inside as if somehow self-banishment had set him free. It was a crisp and lovely fall day; looking at the man outside, even those with little olfactory sensitivity noticed how muted the indoor air was in Paradise Found.

As the man glared through the glass, his gaze did not linger on the boy with the gun, although he would later correctly identify a cowlick and make an association with Dennis the Menace, also accurately alluding to freckles. In the moment, however, his gaze passed over the boy so quickly that he didn't notice he had noticed him. He was drawn past the boy toward the blonde with the headband, and also into his sudden hatred for her, from which he tried to move aside by considering a younger couple in which only one was animated.

If the glass and his own conversation hadn't interfered, the cellphone man would have heard the man with the ponytail give his girlfriend a pep talk about motherhood: "So you have to get up in the middle of the night when you're tired and change a diaper. It's a diaper. It's not like you have to solve a mathematical equation."

The boy with the gun overheard this and judged the young mother harshly. The burden of motherhood, he suspected, led to his own mother leaving. The first couple of years, she sent postcards from places with odd names: What Cheer, Iowa; Hope, Mississippi; Comfort, Texas; and finally Freedom, Wyoming. It seemed that the towns, rather than his mother, were sending messages. None of the messages said "I miss you."

The boy stood up to get in line in front of the curved glass and stood before the pan labeled "eggless egg salad" by a little card stuck into a wire. "Can I help you?" the boy in the bandanna in back of the muffins asked. His name was Brandon, and he and the felon had been in the detention place together. Brandon had told him that between 10:30 and 11:30, before the morning money was moved to the safe, the register usually held between $1,500 and $2,000. Brandon made eye contact with the felon but did not acknowledge familiarity.

"What is eggless egg salad?" the boy with the gun asked.

"It's really tofu salad."

"So why don't you call it that?" The boy was only seventeen, but he had already grown weary of advertising. The only thing that had been good about the juvenile detention center was that the warden did not allow television.

"Because people wouldn't buy it then."

Brandon owed the felon a favor and had already paid it in the form of information. He had instructed him where the key to the always-locked back door was, and explained that there were no security buttons or hidden cameras, and that the clientele was unlikely to be carrying concealed weapons. You couldn't say that about a coffee shop in Montana, which was where the felon was planning on going.

The last time Gus had visited the farm, he said he believed the boy's mother might be in Missoula. Gus gave the boy this information as if it might hold significance but he wouldn't bet on it. "That's where she was when she mailed me a birthday card two years ago," Gus said. "It doesn't mean she's still there; it just means she was there, and she said in the card that she had been there for a year. That's almost enough time to make a home, but it might be just enough time to get bored and move on."

By this point, Gus was carrying an oxygen tank, and his breath was so labored he had to pause between words. When the boy put them together into sentences, it was as if Gus had given him directions.

"I wouldn't have bought anything that looked like that, no matter what you named it. I'll just have a raspberry-almond muffin," the felon informed Brandon.

"You can pick it up at the cash register." Brandon tried to meet the boy's eye, but the boy wasn't looking back. Brandon was having second thoughts.

He knew the boy wouldn't rat—knew that it was a simple action and that he himself would then be free of the obligation he had incurred. A simple enough thing. Brandon had been involved in small robberies before. If you knew what you were doing, no one got hurt and everybody had a story to tell afterward, but still, Brandon was experiencing something like remorse.

It wasn't as if he liked this job or the people he worked with, especially the owner, but he had made the decision to keep working there rather than using the information for his own gain. Plus, they knew Brandon and, because this job was part of his rehabilitation program, they watched him.

He wished he could have been more removed from this particular situation: you aren't supposed to shit where you eat, and all thieves know that, but this wasn't really his shit and, in the end, he had decided it would look less suspicious if he was there with the others on the day this would go down.

He wasn't the only employee in the jobs rehabilitation program, and it couldn't be proven that he was the only one who had known the boy previously, but neither of the others was there this particular morning. From the coffee-break discussions (though most of the employees didn't drink coffee), Brandon concluded that what distinguished him from the others was not a moral code, but a willingness to take risks.

The boy with the gun made his way down to Eudora, who was speaking rapidly to the person in front of him. This speech went on longer than the boy with the gun thought the transaction should take. Brandon had not warned him of Eudora's proclivity for wanton confession.

The person in front of the boy on that fateful morning, Customer #73, had a talent for characterizing people by occupation or hairstyle. Whereas many preferred to think of Eudora as the cash-register girl because it distanced them from the exchange of money, Customer #73 preferred to think of most people by labels because that was more fairy-tale-like.

As she walked down the street and saw men carrying briefcases, she often thought "Lawyer Lad," or, if they wore certain kinds of glasses, "Computer Cad." Some of her fairy tales, especially the ones involving men, weren't exactly uplifting, but she couldn't get down the street without creating one, what with the sky-blue-and-yellow buses and deciduous trees. Customer #73, had she known the story of the boy behind her, would probably have called him "Orphan Boy."

With Gus's death, the boy had become temporarily invisible to various bureaucracies, and he didn't want to alert anyone to the fact that he was at the farmhouse alone—he knew the state would take him from the farm, and thus, away from the girl who had gray eyes.

The boy met her in tenth-grade Independent Living where they had received an egg for which to care. It was the girl who had broken the egg by cuddling it too close to her tiny breasts as if she were going to nurse it. The girl acted like this was a huge tragedy she was going to have to make up to the boy. The boy thought the whole purpose of the assignment was to get them to break the egg. What lesson would an intact egg serve? That they were capable of being parents?

The boy had to pretend he cared about the egg for the girl's sake. He had to pretend he would grow into the type of man who would be supportive should something tragic happen, which, of course, wasn't a broken egg. The girl's hair was stringy, but when he stroked it, the strings grew closer together and her hair got shinier. She smelled like baby powder.

She grieved over the egg so long that one day the boy sat her down and told her about things that were truly sad: parents leaving, parents dying, the way the sky gets at five o'clock Sunday afternoons and there's nothing you can do about it. Then he told her about things that should be sad but really aren't: three-legged dogs, Down syndrome children, coat-hanger TV antennas, broken eggs. They were things that offered hope or love or perseverance or a sense of relative unimportance.

Shortly after that speech, the girl started to look at the boy as the real egg she was not supposed to break. She spent as much time on the farm as she could get away with and the boy guessed that might have been one of the better times of his life. During that time, the girl, all long-limbed and shorts-wearing, had stroked his hair and made him iced tea and taken off her clothes for him and stood before him like a statue. All the boy remembered was that it was quiet everywhere around him.

The cell-phone abuser, who could see but not hear the boy with the gun walk up to the cash-register girl, had no idea there was a gun, nor could he see how the boy showed the gun, just the tip of it poking from under his jacket.

"Oh," Eudora said. "You have a gun." She didn't say it with alarm but in a matter-of-fact way that nobody heard, partly because the other workers had trained themselves to shut her out, and partly because the blender was in service making a mango-and-apricot smoothie.

"Don't say anything," said the felon. "Just put the cash in the bag with the muffin."

"My godfather has a gun like that," Eudora said.

"You aren't supposed to talk about it," said the felon. "Just charge me for the muffin and when you open the cash register put all the tens and twenties into the bag. I don't care about the ones."

After he got out of the juvenile detention center, which was really more of a concrete boarding school where they had them recreate Matisse paintings out of cloth, the boy was sixteen and could work, but the family they put him with was its own kind of prison. They had chore charts and color-coded systems for everything, including brushing teeth. His foster mother had cheeks like apples and eyebrows that scared him, and he wasn't allowed to see the girl, because the girl's parents had demanded a not-seeing after the girl had taken a bus out to the juvenile detention center, and so here they were, on the verge of running away.

He hadn't actually told the girl about this robbery part. Although she was devoted and ready to leave this town to be with him, she was ready for a road trip of youth and innocence, an escape into love. If she thought they were going to be fugitives from people other than her parents, the boy believed she would freeze into the expression that sometimes flitted across her face as she considered him. To call the expression doubt was not strong enough. It was resolve layered over doubt. For some reason the expression made the boy feel trapped.

The boy had pretended he had enough money to get them out of town and that it was important for her to wait for him in the Walmart parking lot close to the freeway so that no one would see them together in town. He had gotten an old truck running that his dad kept in the barn; the plates didn't have a current registration sticker but that seemed a minor point.

He stashed a bike at the back of Paradise Found and another in an alley on the way to the truck. The bike would go into the truck along with the girl's bike—they would ditch the truck somewhere in North Dakota or one of those states nobody cared about and ride their bikes to a train station. The plan was not to shoot anyone. The plan was to go to Montana.

The talkative girl opened the cash register and put all the bills except the ones into the paper bag with the raspberry-almond muffin and handed the bag over to the felon. Nobody was in the line behind him. Besides Eudora, the closest person was the fairy-tale girl, who was out of sight, directly behind the cash register at the table of sugar and nutmeg and honey and milk and soy milk.

The fairy-tale girl was so engrossed in her task that she didn't hear the felon. First she put in soy milk. One of the nice things about this coffee shop, she thought, was that they didn't pretend like soy milk was such an expense and a burden that they had to charge extra for it. She put in a brown packet of organic raw sugar, stirred it with one of the thin brown things that looked like Popsicle sticks on a diet, and topped the whole thing off with one sprinkle of cinnamon and one sprinkle of nutmeg.

She tried to fit the lid on tightly because there had been mayhem before when she hadn't, so she went carefully around the rim pushing down the cap. Yet somehow when she picked it up by the top, the cup mysteriously fell apart. The coffee splattered the floor. The fairy-tale girl screamed, not only because the spilt coffee was hot against her skin, but also because of the unfairness of preparing against an accident that happened anyway, and with more force than accidents she hadn't prepared for.

There were, at this point, as the newspapers would confirm the next day, thirty people in the coffee shop; seven were children, seven were senior citizens, and the rest were at various stages in the middle of their lives.

At one table, a mother and her very grown daughter were opening a present celebrating the mother's birthday. At the Bible table, the skinny, bearded man dressed as a cowboy revealed his true profession, explaining to the Korean women how people go either to heaven or hell. "Here in America," he said, "we believe in absolutes."

The preacher got shot first.

No one could have been more surprised than the felon. It was the first time he had ever fired this gun, and it went off a hell of a lot faster than he expected. He hadn't even aimed; there was an auto-matic release, but it wasn't that the gun had gone off accidentally. He had pulled the trigger.

The gun had been one of his father's. He didn't know much about this one—it was different from the rifle his father taught him to shoot with. It was the smallest one in the case his father had always kept semi-locked, with the key in the lock. The boy's father, a member of the NRA, had taught him that the person behind the gun was the problem, not the gun itself. "Guns don't just accidentally go off," he would say. "You have to pull the trigger."

The boy didn't completely understand that there was an internal trigger someplace, maybe in your soul, that allowed you to pull the other one. Now, it seemed like a decision he had always been going to make, maybe even before his mother left. Maybe she had left because in some mother way she knew that this was a decision her son had already made.

Outside, the cell-phone abuser, on yet another call, still peering inside, waiting for the blond woman to get up for a refill so that he could give her the finger behind her back, immediately went from being annoyed with the frizzy-haired, sensitive-to-noise woman to feeling a gratitude that bordered on love. Still, he wasn't able totally to deny a very small part of himself that was slightly pleased she had been punished. "Let me call you back," he said into the phone. "I have to call the police."

Back in the café, the preacher, writhing on the ground, thought for the first time about giving his life over to God. Until now, the status conferred on a preacher caused young girls to look up to him and, quite frankly, to let him get away with anything he wanted. He never actually slept with these young women, but he kept it in the back of his mind that he could, and he certainly kept it in the back of his wife's mind.

"What the hell?" said Brandon, "You had fucking bullets in the gun?" Immediately after he said it, he realized he had given himself away, but it wasn't information anyone in the moment picked up on.

"Not much use of a gun without bullets," a man in overalls remarked quietly.

"You're a fool to think such a thing right now," the woman sitting next to this man said. "You always think the wrong thing at the wrong time."

"I don't think I should be married to you anymore," the man said.

"See, that's exactly what I'm talking about."

But she was wrong. Those now forced to think about dying thought first about what they would do if they could just stay alive, even before they thought about how they were going to succeed in staying alive.

That is, the customers had this time of contemplation. The employees behind the case knew about the back door and the key, and all of them proceeded as if choreographed toward it.

"Don't anybody move," the felon said belatedly. Everyone behind the counter, with the exception of Eudora, and of Brandon, who was considering whether he could jump the boy with the gun, was gone. The fairy-tale girl might have remarked "in a poof," in a later telling.

The felon grabbed the fairy-tale girl, pointed the gun toward her head, and instructed Brandon to bolt the back door. For some reason Brandon, without understanding why, did just that and came back.

On the other side of the counter, everyone in the coffee shop remained perfectly silent, even the children. Only the frizzy-haired blond woman moved to bend down next to the preacher, her little worry dolls almost resting on his head. Blood spread on the checkered linoleum.

"Is there a doctor?" she asked, but everyone stayed quiet.

"Let me take the babies out." One of the men addressed the felon. "Let me just get the babies out there. They don't need to be seeing anything like this."

"Hide behind the babies. That's exactly like you," said the woman who had decided that if one of the last things her husband was going to think was that he didn't want to be married anymore, she would divorce him.

"Nobody is taking any babies out," the felon said. He motioned to Brandon and Eudora. "You two get in front of the counter where I can see you."

The fairy-tale girl had not come up with a way to figure out how she would match the story in her mind with what she had just seen.

She had not practiced for this, although she had practiced for several scenarios involving blood: automobile accidents, something crashing from above onto people—a piano, usually—but nothing like this.

The fairy-tale girl hated guns so much she didn't even incorporate them into her imagination. Also, she had always thought of a robber as being somebody with a bandanna over his mouth. Any thought of death had come accompanied by angels, or sometimes by a black-robed character with an empty face moving slowly through something like mud. None of her thoughts of death had involved soy milk.

"You don't need all of us to have a hostage situation," explained the man sitting at the table in what would be the last day of his two-year relationship with the cell-phone-complaining woman, a period of time in which he had reason to become intimate with his armpit. He chose this moment to become untucked. His whole head, followed by his neck, came up and stayed up in a stance that the frizzy-haired woman, looking over at him with surprise, recognized as stubbornness. "Let the women and children out first. That's what you are supposed to do."

"That's just sexist," the frizzy-haired woman tending to the preacher muttered. She had taken off her shirt and was putting pressure on the wound in his stomach. Everything around her was red. "We need to get this guy out to a hospital," she announced to the felon. She was determined not to let him bully her. She had faced worse during her sociology dissertation, all those white pompous men. She had forgotten how much she hated them.

Just then a three-year-old started to scream. It was unbearable. "All right," said the felon. "Only the children. The mothers can leave with their children."

"I told you we should have had children," a man reminded his partner.

The felon pointed at the frizzy-haired woman and the preacher. "And you should take him out. Take two other men to help you." All the men in the room stood up, but the felon pointed to two. "Him and him."

The man with the overalls and the doughy man accepted their task and picked the preacher up by shoulders and legs. The frizzy-haired woman kept her post at his center, still firmly pressing the preacher's wound. The girls he had read the Bible to stood up to say good-bye, and the felon waved his gun toward them.

The preacher, fading in and out of consciousness, tried to call to mind some scripture appropriate to the situation, but what he came up with made no sense to him, which in fact was often the case between himself and scripture, but, because of his job, he memorized passages anyway. What came to mind now—*and all creeping things that creep upon the earth, and all the men that are upon the face of the earth, shall shake at my presence, and the mountains shall be thrown down*—was not completely comforting.

The unwashed homeless man, who had not been chosen, stood up with his doughy table partner. He opened the door for the men and the women and just walked out behind them. He was used to people pretending not to notice him, and for once, that worked out. A woman from the senior-citizen table noticed him leaving and thought maybe she could do that also. She had been, as far as she could tell, completely invisible since the age of fifty-five.

The police station was a mile away, and sirens had begun to wail just as the mothers and babies were leaving. When the cars reached the building, they stopped, and all the sirens wound down like the tin toy engine the boy's mother had given him when he was very young.

In the parking lot, the cell-phone abuser had moved away from the window. The others who had come out were milling about giving accounts to people with pencils or sitting on the concrete with their heads in their hands. An ambulance was already there when the preacher was carried out, and he was immediately put on a stretcher. The sirens went on again.

Inside the café, the phone began ringing. "Pick it up," the felon finally commanded Eudora.

"Good morning," she said. She looked at the clock. "Good morning," she confirmed. "There is a gun pointed at me," she announced to whoever was on the other end. The police chief had a bullhorn but preferred to use the phone. He had called for help from nearby towns. "But it is pointed closer to someone else," Eudora said, looking at the fairy-tale girl.

Eudora put her hand over the receiver in an unnecessary gesture, and asked, "What's your name, hon?" but the fairy-tale girl couldn't think of a name that would fit this situation. Eudora removed her hand from the receiver. "Occasionally he waves it around," she informed the chief. "I'm a hostage," she said, trying it out. She had never said that before. It sounded strange so she repeated it.

"Ask him what he wants," the police chief instructed.

"What do you want?" Eudora asked. It was a good question. She was interested in the answer. She wondered why she had wasted so much time talking to people instead of taking full advantage of her position in life. She should have just questioned them.

Think of what wisdom she would have gained if all who stood in front of her had told her simply what they wanted. But, she reminded herself, they would just have repeated their order, except in the past tense. "I wanted a hot chocolate," they would say as if that desire was far in the past.

The boy was not as delighted with the question. It was a complicated one. He thought of the girl, in the truck waiting for him, or maybe already gone. Maybe her facial expression had loosened and she had gone back to a high school life. What did he want? Mostly what he wanted was for this not to be happening. He wanted his mother, who might or might not be alive. "I don't know," he said.

Eudora relayed the message, which wasn't one the police chief took comfort in. "It's a bad sign if they can't even come up with one demand," he said to his deputy. "It means he might have given up, and that is a very dangerous place to be."

By this time twenty police cars surrounded the building. Not all were from this town; three other towns lay within fifteen minutes' drive, each with its own sheriff and its own way of doing things, but the police chief kept control of the situation.

One by one people were let out, or two by two, until the only ones left were Eudora and Brandon and the fairy-tale girl. "You can leave, Brandon," the felon informed him. "You aren't doing me any good here. And when police shoot, they don't go, women and children first. I don't want anyone else to die."

"You may not have killed anyone," Brandon said. "That guy might still be alive." He was surprised that he wasn't walking out the door. It wasn't just the fairy-tale girl he was protecting. Suddenly, although Eudora had previously, well, just driven him crazy, she seemed dear. It didn't occur to him that she had fallen silent. The phone kept ringing, but the felon didn't want anyone to answer it anymore.

These small-town police hadn't much experience in this type of standoff. They thought back to TV shows they had seen and arranged their stances accordingly. It was now 11:30 a.m. The cow chimes rang four times. Another group broke through the back door.

Things happened. Things went wrong. The first shot was not fired by the boy, but the Force behind the chiming cows couldn't see that. "The right hand wasn't looking at the left," the police chief told the papers the next day in obfuscated explanation. Brandon had surprised himself by throwing his body over Eudora's; she had entered a silence so profound that every question she had never asked was answered.

The fairy-tale girl's tales did not turn immediately grim when the gunfire began. The flash reminded her of a summer night when she was a child and all the adults on the block were out front, grilling hamburgers and hot dogs. The children had been given sparklers and allowed to run up and down the block with them, and somebody had opened up the fire hydrant so that a fervent stream of water wet all those willing to get wet, in a night that kept turning a darker blue but never completely dark. The fairy-tale girl was glad to see that evening again, and to hear all the mothers call out their children's names like a song the whole city should hear.

The papers would say that the boy was called Levi. His mother had named him after her favorite pair of jeans. She had wanted to be a cowgirl. It was a name the fairy-tale girl would have made up for someone who was poetic, a little lost, a seeker into another world. Her name was Delia Conrad, the papers would say.

Tommy

John Edgar Wideman

HE CHECKS OUT the Velvet Slipper. Can't see shit for
a minute in the darkness. Just the jukebox and beer
smell and the stink from the men's room door
always hanging open. Carl ain't there yet. Must be
his methadone day. Carl with his bad feet like he's
in slow motion wants to lay them dogs down easy
as he can on the hot sidewalk. Little sissy walking on eggs steps
pussy-footing up to Frankstown to the clinic. Uncle Carl ain't treating
to no beer to start the day so he backs out into the brightness of the
Avenue, to the early afternoon street quiet after the blast of nigger
music and nigger talk.

Ain't nothing to it. Nothing. If he goes left under the trestle and up
the stone steps or ducks up the bare path worn through the weeds on
the hillside he can walk along the tracks to the park. Early for the
park. The sun everywhere now giving the grass a yellow sheen. If he
goes right it's down the Avenue to where the supermarkets and the
5&10 used to be. Man, they sure did fuck with this place. What he
thinks each time he stares at what was once the heart of Homewood.
Nothing. A parking lot and empty parking stalls with busted meters.
Only a fool leave his car next to one of the bent meter poles. Places
to park so you can shop in stores that ain't there no more. Remembers
his little Saturday morning wagon hustle when him and all the other
kids would lay outside the A&P to haul groceries. Still some white
ladies in those days come down from Thomas Boulevard to shop and

69

if you're lucky get one of them and get tipped a quarter. Some of them fat black bitches be in church every Sunday have you pulling ten tons of rice and beans all the way to West Hell and be smiling and yakking all the way and saying what a nice boy you are and I knowed your mama when she was little and please sonny just set them inside on the table and still be smiling at you with some warm glass of water and a dime after you done hauled their shit halfway round the world.

Hot in the street but nobody didn't like you just coming in and sitting in their air conditioning unless you gonna buy a drink and set it in front of you. The poolroom hot. And too early to be messing with those fools on the corner. Always somebody trying to hustle. Man, when you gonna give me my money, Man, I been waiting too long for my money, Man, lemme hold this quarter till tonight, Man. I'm getting over tonight, Man. And the buses climbing the hill and turning the corner by the state store and fools parked in the middle of the street and niggers getting hot honking to get by and niggers paying them no mind like they got important business and just gonna sit there blocking traffic as long as they please and the buses growling and farting those fumes when they struggle around the corner.

Look to the right and to the left but ain't nothing to it, nothing saying move one way or the other. Homewood Avenue a darker gray stripe between the gray sidewalks. Tar patches in the asphalt. Looks like somebody's bad head with the ringworm. Along the curb ground glass sparkles below the broken neck of a Tokay bottle. Just the long neck and shoulders of the bottle intact and a piece of label hanging. Somebody should make a deep ditch out of Homewood Avenue and just go on and push the row houses and boarded storefronts into the hole. Bury it all, like in a movie he had seen a dam burst and the flood waters ripping through the dry bed of a river till the roaring water overflowed the banks and swept away trees and houses, uprooting everything in its path like a cleansing wind.

He sees Homewood Avenue dipping and twisting at Hamilton. Where Homewood crests at Frankstown the heat is a shimmering curtain above the trolley tracks. No trolleys anymore. But the slippery tracks still embedded in the asphalt streets. Somebody forgot to tear out the tracks and pull down the cables. So when it rains or snows some fool always gets caught and the slick tracks flip a car into a telephone pole or upside a hydrant and the cars just lay there with crumpled fenders and windshields shattered, laying there for no reason just like the tracks and wires are there for no reason now that buses run where the 88 and 82 Lincoln trolleys used to go.

He remembers running down Lemington Hill because trolleys come only once an hour after midnight and he had heard the clatter of the 82 starting its long glide down Lincoln Avenue. The Dells still working out on *Why Do You Have to Go* and the tip of his dick wet and his balls aching and his finger sticky but he had forgotten all that and forgot the half hour in Sylvia's hallway because he was flying, all long strides and pumping arms and his fists opening and closing on the night air as he grappled for balance in a headlong rush down the steep hill. He had heard the trolley coming and wished he was a bird soaring through the black night, a bird with shiny chrome fenders and fishtails and a Continental kit. He tried to watch his feet, avoid the cracks and gulleys in the sidewalk. He heard the trolley's bell and crash of its steel wheels against the racks. He had been all in Sylvia's drawers and she was wet as a dishrag and moaning her hot breath into his ear and the record player inside the door hiccupping for the thousandth time caught in the groove of gray noise at the end of the disc.

He remembers that night and curses again the empty trolley screaming past him as he had pulled up short half a block from the corner. Honky driver half sleep in his yellow bubble. As the trolley careened away red sparks had popped above its gimpy antenna. Chick had his nose open and his dick hard but he should have cooled it and split, been out her drawers and down the hill on time. He had fooled around too long. He had missed the trolley and mize well walk. He had to walk and in the darkness over his head the cables had swayed and sung long after the trolley disappeared.

He had to walk cause that's all there was to it. And still no ride of his own so he's still walking. Nothing to it. Either right or left, either up Homewood or down Homewood, walking his hip walk, making something out of the way he is walking since there is nothing else to do, no place to go so he makes something of the going, lets them see him moving in his own down way, his stylized walk which nobody could walk better even if they had some place to go.

Thinking of a chump shot on the nine ball which he blew and cost him a quarter for the game and his last dollar on a side bet. Of pulling on his checkered bells that morning and the black tank top. How the creases were dead and cherry pop or something on the front and a million wrinkles behind the knees and where his thighs came together. Junkie, wino-looking pants he would rather have died than wear just a few years before when he was one of the cleanest cats in Westinghouse High School. Sharp and leading the Commodores. Doo Wah Diddy, Wah Diddy Bop. Thirty-five-dollar pants when most the cats in the House couldn't spend that much for a suit. It was a bitch in the world. Stone bitch. Feeling like Mister Tooth Decay crawling all sweaty out of the gray sheets. Mom could wash them every day, they still be gray. Like his underclothes. Like every motherfucking thing they had and would ever have. Doo Wah Diddy. The rake jerked three or four times through his bush. Left there as decoration and weapon. You could fuck up a cat with those steel teeth. You could get the points sharp as needles. And draw it swift as Billy the Kid.

Thinking it be a bitch out here. Niggers write all over everything don't even know how to spell. Drawing power fists that look like a loaf of bread.

Thinking this whole Avenue is like somebody's mouth they let some jive dentist fuck with. All these old houses nothing but rotten teeth and these raggedy pits is where some been dug out or knocked out and ain't nothing left but stumps and snaggleteeth just waiting to go. Thinking, that's right. That's just what it is. Why it stinks around here and why ain't nothing but filth and germs and rot. And what that make me? What it make all these niggers? Thinking yes, yes, that's all it is.

Mr. Strayhorn where he always is down from the corner of Hamilton and Homewood sitting on a folding chair beside his iceball cart. A sweating canvas draped over the front of the cart to keep off the sun. Somebody said the old man a hundred years old, somebody said he was a bad dude in his day. A gambler like his own Granddaddy John French had been. They say Strayhorn whipped three cats half to death try to cheat him in the alley behind Dumferline.

Took a knife off one and whipped all three with his bare hands. Just sits there all summer selling iceballs. Old and can hardly see. But nobody don't bother him even though he got his pockets full of change every evening.

Shit. One of the young boys will off him one night. Those kids was stone crazy. Kill you for a dime and think nothing of it. Shit. Rep don't mean a thing. They come at you in packs, like wild dogs. Couldn't tell those young boys nothing. He thought he had come up mean. Thought his running buddies be some terrible dudes. Shit. These kids coming up been into more stuff before they twelve than most grown men do they whole lives.

Hard out here. He stares into the dead storefronts. Sometimes they get in one of them. Take it over till they get run out or set it on fire or it gets so filled with shit and nigger piss don't nobody want to use it no more except for winos and junkies come in at night and could be sleeping on a bed of nails wouldn't make no nevermind to those cats. He peeks without stopping between the wooden slats where the glass used to be. Like he is reading the posters, like there might be something he needed to know on these rain-soaked, sun-faded pieces of cardboard talking about stuff that happened a long time ago.

Self-defense demonstration . . . Ahmad Jamal. Rummage Sale. Omega Boat Ride. The Dells. Madame Walker's Beauty Products.

A dead bird crushed dry and paper-thin in the alley between Albion and Tioga. Like somebody had smeared it with tar and mashed it between the pages of a giant book. If you hadn't seen it in the first place, still plump and bird colored, you'd never recognize it now. Looked now like the lost sole of somebody's shoe. He had watched it happen. Four or five days was all it took. On the third day he thought a cat had dragged it off. But when he passed the corner next afternoon he found the dark shape in the grass at the edge of the cobblestones. The head was gone and the yellow smear of beak but he recognized the rest. By then already looking like the raggedy sole somebody had walked off their shoe.

He was afraid of anything dead. He could look at something dead but no way was he going to touch it. Didn't matter, big or small, he wasn't about to put his hands near nothing dead. His daddy had whipped him when his mother said he sassed her and wouldn't take the dead rat out of the trap. He could whip him again but no way he was gon touch that thing. The dudes come back from Nam talking about puddles of guts and scraping parts of people into plastic bags. They talk about carrying their own bags so they could get stuffed in if they got wasted. Have to court-martial his ass. No way he be carrying no body bag. Felt funny now carrying out the big green bags you put your garbage in. Any kind of plastic sack and he's thinking of machine guns and dudes screaming and grabbing their bellies and rolling around like they do when they're hit on Iwo Jima and Tarawa or the Dirty Dozen or the Magnificent Seven or the High Plains Drifter, but the screaming is not in the darkness on a screen it is bright, green afternoon and Willie Thompson and them are on patrol. It is a street like Homewood. Quiet like Homewood this time of day and bombed out like Homewood is. Just pieces of buildings standing here and there and fire scars and places ripped and kicked down and cars stripped and dead at the curb. They are moving along in single file and their uniforms are hip and their walks are hip and they are kind of smiling and rubbing their weapons and cats passing a joint fat as a cigar down the line. You can almost hear music from where Porgy's Record Shop used to be, like the music so fine it's still there clinging to the boards, the broken glass on the floor, the shelves covered with roach shit and rat shit, a ghost of the music rifting sweet and mellow like the smell of home cooking as the patrol slips on past where Porgy's used to be. Then . . .

Rat Tat Tat . . . Rat Tat Tat . . . Ra Ta Ta Ta Ta Ta Ta . . .

Sudden but almost on the beat. Close enough to the beat so it seems the point man can't take it any longer, can't play this soldier game no longer and he gets happy and the smoke is gone clear to his head so he jumps out almost on the beat, wiggling his hips and throwing up his arms so he can get it all, go on and get down. Like he is exploding to the music. To the beat which pushes him out there all alone, doing it, and it is Rat Tat Tat and we all want to fingerpop behind his twitching hips and his arms flung out but he is screaming and down in the dirty street and the street is exploding all round him in little volcanoes of dust. And some of the others in the front of the patrol go down with him. No semblance of rhythm now, just stumbling, or airborne like their feet jerked out from under them. The whole hip procession buckling, shattered as lines of deadly force stitch up and down the Avenue.

Hey man, what's to it? Ain't nothing to it man you got it baby hey now where's it at you got it you got it ain't nothing to it something to it I wouldn't be out here in all this sun you looking good you into something go on man you got it all you know you the Man hey now that was a stone fox you know what I'm talking about you don't be creeping past me yeah nice going you got it all save some for me Mister Clean you seen Ruchell and them yeah you know how that shit is the cat walked right on by like he ain't seen nobody but you know how he is get a little something don't know nobody shit like I tried to tell the cat get straight nigger be yourself before you be by yourself you got a hard head man hard as stone but he ain't gon listen to me shit no can't nobody do nothing for the cat less he's ready to do for hisself. Ruchell yeah man Ruchell and them come by here little while ago yeah baby you got it yeah lemme hold this little something I know you got it you the Man you got to have it lemme hold a little something till this evening I'll put you straight tonight man you know your man do you right I unnerstand yeah that's all that's to it nothing to it I'ma see you straight man yeah you fall on by the crib yeah we be into something tonight you fall on by.

Back to the left now. Up Hamilton, past the old man who seems to sleep beside his cart until you get close and then his yellow eyes under the straw hat brim follow you. Cut through the alley past the old grade school. Halfway up the hill the game has already started. You have been hearing the basketball patted against the concrete, the hollow thump of the ball glancing off the metal backboards. The ball players half naked out there under that hot sun, working harder than niggers ever did picking cotton. They shine. They glide and leap and fly at each other like their dark bodies are at the ends of invisible strings. This time of day the court is hot as fire. Burn through your shoes. Maybe that's why the niggers play like they do, running and jumping so much cause the ground's too hot to stand on. His brother used to play here all day. Up and down all day in the hot sun with the rest of the crazy ball players. Old dudes and young dudes and when people on the side waiting for winners they'd get to arguing and you could hear them bad-mouthing all the way up the hill and cross the tracks in the park. Wolfing like they ready to kill each other.

His oldest brother John came back here to play when he brought his family through in the summer. Here and Mellon and the courts beside the Projects in East Liberty. His brother one of the old dudes now. Still crazy about the game. He sees a dude lose his man and fire a jumper from the side. A double pump, a lean, and the ball arched so it kisses the board and drops through the iron. He could have played the game. Tall and loose. Hands bigger than his brother's. Could palm a ball when he was eleven. Looks at his long fingers. His long feet in raggedy ass sneakers that show the crusty knuckle of his little toe. The sidewalk sloped and split. Little plots of gravel and weeds where whole paving blocks torn away. Past the dry swimming pool. Just a big concrete hole now where people piss and throw bottles like you got two points for shooting them in. Dropping like a rusty spiderweb from tall metal poles, what's left of a backstop, and beyond the flaking mesh of the screen the dusty field and beyond that a jungle of sooty trees below the railroad tracks. They called it the Bums' Forest when they were kids and bombed the winos sleeping down there in the shade of the trees. If they walked alongside the track all the way to the park they'd have to cross the bridge over Homewood Avenue. Hardly room for trains on the bridge so they always ran and some fool always yelling, *Train's coming* and everybody else yelling and then it's your chest all full and your heart pumping to keep up with the rest. Because the train couldn't kill everybody. It might get the last one, the slow one but it wouldn't run down all the crazy niggers screaming and hauling ass over Homewood Avenue. From the tracks you could look down on the winos curled up under a tree or sitting in a circle sipping from bottles wrapped in paper bags. At night they would have fires, hot as it was some summer nights you'd still see their fires from the bleachers while you watched the Legion baseball team kick butt.

From high up on the tracks you could bomb the forest. Stones hissed through the thick leaves. Once in a while a lucky shot shattered a bottle. Some gray, sorry-assed wino motherfucker waking up and shaking his fist and cussing at you and some fool shouts *He's coming, he's coming*. And not taking the low path for a week because you think he was looking dead in your eyes, spitting blood and pointing at you and you will never go alone the low way along the path because he is behind every bush, gray and bloodymouthed. The raggedy, gray clothes flapping like a bird and a bird's feathery, smothering funk covering you as he drags you into the bushes.

He had heard stories about the old days when the men used to hang out in the woods below the tracks. Gambling and drinking wine and telling lies and singing those old time, down home songs. Hang out there in the summer and when it got cold they'd loaf in the Bucket of Blood on the corner of Frankstown and Tioga. His grandaddy was in the stories. Old John French one of the baddest dudes ever walked these Homewood streets. Old, big-hat John French. They said his grandaddy could sing up a storm and now his jitterbug father up in the choir of Homewood A.M.E. Zion next to Mrs. Washington who hits those high notes. He was his father's son, people said. Singing all the time and running the streets like his daddy did till his daddy got too old and got saved. Tenor lead of the Commodores. Everybody saying the Commodores was the baddest group. If that cat hadn't fucked us over with the record we might have made the big time. Achmet backing us on the conga. Tito on the bongos. Tear up the park. Stone tear it up. Little kids and old folks all gone home and ain't nobody in the park but who supposed to be and you got your old lady on the side listening or maybe you singing pretty to pull some new fly bitch catch your eye in the crowd. It all comes down, comes together mellow and fine sometimes. The drums, the smoke, the sun going down and you out there flying and the Commodores steady taking care of business behind your lead.

"You got to go to church. I'm not asking I'm telling. Now you get those shoes shined and I don't want to hear another word out of you, young man." She is ironing his Sunday shirt hot and stiff. She hums along with the gospel songs on the radio. "Don't make me send you to your father." Who is in the bathroom for the half hour he takes doing whatever to get hisself together. Making everybody else late. Singing in there while he shaves. You don't want to be the next one after him. "You got five minutes, boy. Five minutes and your teeth better be clean and your hands and face shining." Gagging in the funky bathroom, not wanting to take a breath. How you supposed to brush your teeth, the cat just shit in there? "You're going to church this week and every week. This is my time and don't you try to spoil it, boy. Don't you get no attitude and try to spoil church for me." He is in the park now, sweating in the heat, a man now, but he can hear his mother's voice plain as day, filling up all the empty space around him just as it did in the house on Finance Street. She'd talk them all to church every Sunday. Use her voice like a club to beat everybody out the house.

His last time in church was a Thursday. They had up the scaffolding to clean the ceiling and Deacon Barclay's truck was parked outside. Barclay's Hauling, Cleaning and General Repairing. Young People's Gospel Chorus had practice on Thursday and he knew Adelaide would be there. That chick looked good even in them baggy choir robes. He had seen her on Sunday because his Mom cried and asked him to go to church. Because she knew he stole the money out her purse but he had lied and said he didn't and she knew he was lying and feeling guilty and knew he'd go to church to make up to her. Adelaide up there with the Young People's Gospel Chorus rocking church. Rocking church and he'd go right on up there, the lead of the Commodores, and sing gospel with them if he could get next to that fine Adelaide. So Thursday he left the poolroom, *Where you tipping off to, Man? None of your motherfucking business, motherfucker*, about seven when she had choir practice and look here, Adelaide, I been digging you for a long time. Longer and deeper than you'll ever know. Let me tell you something. I know what you're thinking, but don't say it, don't break my heart by saying you heard I was a jive cat and nothing to me and stay away from him he ain't no good and stuff like that I know I got a rep that way but you grown enough now to know how people talk and how you got to find things out for yourself. Don't be putting me down till you let me have a little chance to speak for myself. I ain't gon lie now. I been out here in the world and into some jive tips. Yeah, I did my time diddy bopping and

trying my wheels out here in the street. I was a devil. Got into everything I was big and bad enough to try. Look here. I could write the
book. Pimptime and partytime and jive to stay alive, but I been
through all that and that ain't what I want. I want something special,
something solid. A woman, not no fingerpopping young girl got her
nose open and her behind wagging all the time. That's right. That's
right. I ain't talking nasty, I'm talking what I know. I'm talking truth
tonight and listen here I been digging you all these years and waiting
for you because all that Doo Wah Diddy ain't nothing, you hear, nothing to it. You grown now and I need just what you got. . . .

Thursday rapping in the vestibule with Adelaide was the last time
in Homewood A.M.E. Zion Church. Had to be swift and clean. Swoop
down like a hawk and get to her mind. Tuesday she still crying and
gripping the elastic of her drawers and saying *No.* Next Thursday the
only singing she doing is behind some bushes in the park. *Oh, Baby.*
Oh, Baby, it's so good. Tore that pussy up.

Don't make no difference. No big thing. She's giving it to somebody else now. All that good stuff still shaking under her robe every
second Sunday when the Young People's Gospel Chorus in the loft
beside the pulpit. Old man Barclay like he guarding the church door
asking me did I come around to help clean. "Mr. Barclay, I wish I
could help but I'm working nights. Matter of fact, I'm a little late now.
I'm gon be here on my night off, though."

He knew I was lying. Old bald head dude standing there in his
coveralls and holding a bucket of Lysol and a scrub brush. Worked
all his life and got a piece of truck and a piece of house and still running around yes sirring and no mamming the white folks and cleaning their toilets. And he's doing better than most of these chumps.
Knew I was lying but smiled his little smile cause he knows my
mama and knows she's a good woman and knows Adelaide's grandmother and knows if I ain't here to clean he better guard the door
with his soap and rags till I go on about my business.

Ruchell and them over on a bench. Niggers high already. They
ain't hardly out there in the sun barbecuing their brains less they
been into something already. Niggers be hugging the shade till evening less they been into something.

"Hey now."

"What's to it, Tom?"

"You cats been into something."

"You ain't just talking."

"Ruchell man, we got that business to take care of."

"Stone business, Bruh. I'm ready to T.C.B., my man."

"You ain't ready for nothing, nigger."

"Hey man, we're gon get it together. I'm ready, man. Ain't never been so ready. We gon score big, Brother Man . . ."

They have been walking an hour. The night is cooling. A strong wind has risen and a few pale stars are visible above the yellow pall of the city's lights. Ruchell is talking:

"The reason it's gon work is the white boy is greedy. He's so greedy he can't stand for the nigger to have something. Did you see Indovina's eyes when we told him we had copped a truckload of color tee vees. Shit man. I could hear his mind working. Calculating like. These niggers is dumb. I can rob these niggers. Click. Click. Clickedy. Rob the shit out of these dumb spooks. They been robbing us so long they think that's the way things supposed to be. They so greedy their hands get sweaty they see a nigger with something worth stealing."

"So he said he'd meet us at the car lot?"

"That's the deal. I told him we had two vans full."

"And Ricky said he'd let you use his van?"

"I already got the keys, man. I told you we were straight with Ricky. He ain't even in town till the weekend."

"I drive up then and you hide in the back?"

"Yeah, dude. Just like we done said a hundred times. You go in the office to make the deal and you know how Indovina is. He gon send out his nigger Chubby to check the goods."

"And you jump Chubby?"

"Be on him like white on rice. Freeze that nigger till you get the money from Indovina."

"You sure Indovina ain't gon try and follow us?"

"Shit, man. He be happy to see us split . . ."

"With his money?"

"Indovina do whatever you say. Just wave your piece in his face a couple times. That fat ofay motherfucker ain't got no heart. Chubby his heart and Ruchell stone take care of Chubby."

"I still think Indovina might go to the cops."

"And say what? Say he trying to buy some hot tee vees and got ripped off? He ain't hardly saying that. He might just say he got robbed and try to collect insurance. He's slick like that. But if he goes to the cops you can believe he won't be describing us. Naw. The pigs know that greasy dago is a crook. Everybody knows it and won't be no problems. Just score and blow. Leave this motherfucking sorry ass town. Score and blow."

"When you ain't got nothing you get desperate. You don't care. I mean what you got to be worried about? Your life ain't shit. All you got is a high. Getting high and spending all your time hustling some money so you can get high again. You do anything. Nothing don't matter. You just take, take, take whatever you can get your hands on. Pretty soon nothing don't matter, John. You just got to get that high. And everybody around you the same way. Don't make no difference. You steal a little something. If you get away with it, you try it again. Then something bigger. You get holt to a piece. Other dudes carry a piece. Lots of dudes out there holding something. So you get it and start to carrying it. What's it matter? You ain't nowhere anyway. Ain't got nothing. Nothing to look forward to but a high. A man needs something. A little money in his pocket. I mean you see people around you and on TV and shit. Man, they got everything. Cars and clothes. They can do something for a woman. They got something. And you look at yourself in the mirror you're going nowhere. Not a penny in your pocket. Your own people disgusted with you. Begging around your family like a little kid or something. And jail and stealing money from your own mama. You get desperate. You do what you have to do."

The wind is up again that night. At the stoplight Tommy stares at the big sign on the Boulevard. A smiling Duquesne Pilsner Duke with his glass of beer. The time and temperature flash beneath the nobleman's uniformed chest. Ricky had installed a tape deck into the dash. A tangle of wires drooped from its guts, but the sound was good. One speaker for the cab, another for the back where Ruchell was sitting on the rolls of carpet Ricky had stacked there. Al Green singing *Call Me*. Ricky could do things. Made his own tapes; customizing the delivery van. Next summer Ricky driving to California. Fixing up the van so he could live in it. The dude was good with his hands. A mechanic in the war. Government paid for the wasted knee. Ricky said, Got me a new knee now. Got a four-wheeled knee that's gonna ride me away from all this mess. The disability money paid for the van and the customizing and the stereo tape deck. Ricky always have that limp but the cat getting hisself together.

Flags were strung across the entrance to the used car lot. The wind made them pop and dance. Rows and rows of cars looking clean and new under the lights. Tommy parked on the street, in the deep shadow at the far end of Indovina's glowing corner. He sees them through the office window. Indovina and his nigger.

"Hey, Chubby."

"What's happening now?" Chubby's shoulders wide as the door. Indovina's nigger all the way. Had his head laid back so far on his neck it's like he's looking at you through his noseholes instead of his eyes.

"You got the merchandise?" Indovina's fingers drum the desk.

"You got the money?"

"Ain't your money yet. I thought you said two vans full."

"Can't drive but one at a time. My partner's at a phone booth right now. Got the number here. You show me the bread and he'll bring the rest."

"I want to see them all before I give you a penny."

"Look, Mr. Indovina. This ain't no bullshit tip. We got the stuff, alright. Good stuff like I said. Sony portables. All the same . . . still in the boxes."

"Let's go look."

"I want to see some bread first."

"Give Chubby your keys. Chubby, check it out. Count em. Make sure the cartons ain't broke open."

"I want to see some bread."

"Bread. Bread. My cousin DeLuca runs a bakery. I don't deal with *bread*. I got money. See. That's money in my hand. Got plenty money buy your television sets buy your van buy you."

"Just trying to do square business, Mr. Indovina."

"Don't forget to check the cartons. Make sure they're sealed."

Somebody must be down. Ruchell or Chubby down. Tommy had heard two shots. He sees himself in the plate glass window. In a fishbowl and patches of light gliding past. Except where the floodlights are trained, the darkness outside is impenetrable. He cannot see past his image in the glass, past the rushes of light slicing through his body.

"Turn out the goddamn light."

"You kill me you be sorry . . . kill me you be real sorry . . . if one of them dead out there it's just one nigger kill another nigger . . . you kill me you be sorry . . . you killing a white man . . ."

Tommy's knee skids on the desk and he slams the gun across the man's fat, sweating face with all the force of his lunge. He is scrambling over the desk, scattering paper and junk, looking down on Indovina's white shirt, his hairy arms folded over his head. He is thinking of the shots. Thinking that everything is wrong. The shots, the white man cringing on the floor behind the steel desk. Him atop the desk, his back exposed to anybody coming through the glass door.

Then he is running. Flying into the darkness. He is crouching so low he loses his balance and trips onto all fours. The gun leaps from his hand and skitters toward a wall of tires. He hears the pennants crackling. Hears a motor starting and Ruchell calling his name.

"What you mean you didn't get the money? I done wasted Chubby and you ain't got the money? Aw shit. Shit. Shit."

He had nearly tripped again over the man's body. Without knowing how he knew, he knew Chubby was dead. Dead as the sole of his shoe. He should stop; he should try to help. But the body was lifeless. He couldn't touch . . .

Ruchell is shuddering and crying. Tears glazing his eyes and he wonders if Ruchell can see where he's going, if Ruchell knows he is driving like a wild man on both sides of the street and weaving in and out the lines of traffic. Horns blare after them. Then it's Al Green up again. He didn't know how, when or who pushed the button but it was Al Green blasting in the cab. *Help me Help me Help me . . .*

Jesus is waiting . . . He snatches at the tape deck with both hands to turn it down or off or rip the goddamn cassette from the machine.

"Slow down, man. Slow down. You gonna get us stopped." Rolling down his window. The night air sharp in his face. The whir of tape dying then a hum of silence. The traffic sounds and city sounds pressing again into the cab.

"Nothing. Not a goddamn penny. Wasted the dude and we still ain't got nothing."

"They traced the car to Ricky. Ricky said he was out of town. Told them his van stolen when he was out of town. Claimed he didn't even know it gone till they came to his house. Ricky's cool. I know the cat's mad, but he's cool. Indovina trying to hang us. He saying it was a stickup. Saying Chubby tried to run for help and Ruchell shot him down. His story don't make no sense when you get down to it, but ain't nobody gon to listen to us."

"Then you're going to keep running?"

"Ain't no other way. Try to get to the coast. Ruchell knows a guy there can get us IDs. We was going there anyway. With our stake. We was gon get jobs and try to get it together. Make a real try. We just needed a little bread to get us started. I don't know why it had to happen the way it did. Ruchell said Chubby tried to go for bad. Said Chubby had a piece down in his pants and Ruchell told him to cool it told the cat don't be no hero and had his gun on him and every-thing but Chubby had to be a hard head, had to be John Wayne or some goddamned body. Just called Ruchell a punk and said no punk had the heart to pull the trigger on him. And Ruchell, Ruchell don't play, brother John. Ruchell blew him away when Chubby reached for his piece."

"You don't think you can prove your story?"

"I don't know, man. What Indovina is saying don't make no sense, but I heard the cops ain't found Chubby's gun. If they could just find that gun. But Indovina, he a slick old honky. That gun's at the bottom of the Allegheny River if he found it. They found mine. With my prints all over it. Naw. Can't take the chance. It's Murder One even though I didn't shoot nobody. That's long, hard time if they believe Indovina. I can't take the chance . . ."

"Be careful, Tommy. You're a fugitive. Cops out here think they're Wyatt Earp and Marshal Dillon. They shoot first and maybe ask questions later. They still play wild, wild West out here."

"I hear you. But I'd rather take my chance that way. Rather they carry me back in a box than go back to prison. It's hard out there, Brother. Real hard. I'm happy you got out. One of us got out anyway."

"Think about it. Take your time. You can stay here as long as you need to. There's plenty of room."

"We gotta go. See Ruchell's cousin in Denver. Get us a little stake then make our run."

"I'll give you what I can if that's what you have to do. But sleep on it. Let's talk again in the morning."

"It's good to see you, man. And the kids and your old lady. At least we had this one evening. Being on the run can drive you crazy."

"Everybody was happy to see you. I knew you'd come. You've been heavy on my mind since yesterday. I wrote a kind of letter to you then. I knew you'd come. But get some sleep now . . . we'll talk in the morning."

"Listen, man. I'm sorry, man. I'm really sorry I had to come here like this. You sure Judy ain't mad?"

"I'm telling you it's OK. She's as glad to see you as I am . . . And you can stay . . . both of us want you to stay."

"Running can drive you crazy. From the time I wake in the morning till I go to bed at night, all I can think about is getting away. My head ain't been right since it happened."

"When's the last time you talked to anybody at home?

"It's been a couple weeks. They probably watching people back there. Might even be watching you. That's why I can't stay. Got to keep moving till we get to the coast. I'm sorry, man. I mean nobody was supposed to die. It was easy. We thought we had a perfect plan. Thieves robbing thieves. Just score and blow like Ruchell said. It was our chance and we dead now if it was me Chubby pulled on. I couldna just looked in his face and blown him away. But Ruchell don't play. And everybody at home. I know how they must feel. It was all over TV and the papers. Had our names and where we lived and everything. Goddamn mug shots in the Post Gazette. Looking like two gorillas. I know it's hurting people. In a way I wish it had been me. Maybe it would have been better. I don't really care what happens to me now. Just wish there be some way to get the burden off Mama and everybody. Be easier if I was dead."

"Nobody wants you dead . . . That's what Mom's most afraid of. Afraid of you coming home in a box."

"I ain't going back to prison. They have to kill me before I go back in prison. Hey, man. Ain't nothing to my crazy talk. You don't want to hear this jive. I'm tired, man. I ain't never been so tired . . . I'ma sleep . . . talk in the morning, Big Brother."

He feels his brother squeeze then relax the grip on his shoulder. He has seen his brother cry once before. Doesn't want to see it again. Too many faces in his brother's face. Starting with their mother and going back and going sideways and all of Homewood there if he looked long enough. Not just faces but streets and stories and rooms and songs.

Tommy listens to the steps. He can hear faintly the squeak of a bed upstairs. Then nothing. Ruchell asleep in another part of the house. Ruchell spent the evening with the kids, playing with their toys. The cat won't ever grow up. Still into the Durango Kid, and Whip Wilson and Audie Murphy wasting Japs and shit. Still Saturday afternoon at the Bellmawr Show and he is lining up the plastic cowboys against the plastic Indians and boom-booming them down with the kids on the playroom floor. And dressing up the Lone Ranger doll with the mask and guns and cinching the saddle on Silver. Toys like they didn't make when we were coming up. And Christmas morning and so much stuff piled up they'd be crying with exhaustion and bad nerves before half the stuff unwrapped. Christmas morning and they never really went to sleep. Looking out the black windows all night for reindeer and shit. Cheating. Worried that all the gifts will turn to ashes if they get caught cheating, but needing to know, to see if reindeer really can fly.

Action Adventure

John P. Loonam

KIM WAS IN no mood for last-minute customers. "Ki–im!" Jamal moaned. Bigelow, the fat manager, instead of locking the door and letting them prep for closing, giggled in the corner with Jamal. Kim ignored the knot that tightened in her stomach every time Jamal used her name, the same knot she'd ignored since they hooked up in Amanda Richardson's bedroom eleven nights ago.

At least Jamal had the sense to move toward the door. Bigelow followed like R2D2, spinning the keys on his fingers. The last customer—a scruffy man in a Mets cap and a three-day beard—handed her *Pulp Fiction* and *The Red Shoes Diaries*. His thumbnail was blue and cracked. He smiled and said, "Good evening." Kim thought he was flirting. The front door's electronic gong distracted her from this thought. In with the cool March breeze came the real last customer, a skinny guy in a floppy green hat, sunglasses, and a corduroy jacket.

Kim was swearing off boys forever when this guy grabbed *Finding Nemo*. He stepped to the register in one swift movement, filling the space Red Shoes had barely vacated.

Kim blinked. A gloved hand at the end of Finding Nemo's corduroy arm held a pistol—large and squarish, like something from a movie. "Empty the register." With his free hand, he reached across the counter for one of the store's blue plastic bags and shoved it at her chest. "Use this."

Red Shoes, on his way out, turned. He stepped back inside and shouted, "Hey, you can't do that—"

Finding Nemo shifted his right shoulder, extending the corduroy arm across his own chest. He did not turn his head or look away from Kim but squinted so hard his face folded into itself. The gun went off, cracking the air in half.

The scruffy man's face exploded, blowing off his Mets cap. A red haze hung in the air. The rest of the man jumped backward through the front window. Shards blew back and bounced off the counters, musical in the sudden silence. They glittered on the gray carpet.

The man with the gun turned toward the destruction. He fired through the broken window into the night. The second gunshot reanimated Video World. Bigelow screamed. He tried to dive behind Action Adventure. Instead, he crashed into a rack of *Spiderman 2*. The cases hit the floor, and silver plastic circles rolled across the gray. The shooter looked up. Jamal, protecting himself from falling glass and second shots, crouched the way Lee Harvey Oswald did in Kim's American studies book. A dark stain spread across Jamal's crotch.

"Get busy!" Finding Nemo yelled, his voice rough, his hands shaking. He wasn't squinting. He was looking straight at her, his eyes wide and shining. She could smell his sweat. Kim looked down at her own hands methodically stuffing cash into the plastic bag. It was Thursday night, the night no one went out, as Mr. Neagle reminded them at every team meeting, the night people watched a movie instead. Tonight it felt like everyone in Bay Ridge had come in.

The register was overflowing, and the lockbox at Kim's feet held at least $5,000, cash that Bigelow was supposed to have deposited in the office safe at the 8 p.m. shift change, according to the Shift Activities Checklist taped to the counter beneath the blue bag Kim was loading.

Finding Nemo, as if reading the list himself, leaned over the counter and shouted, "Get me that fucking box, too." He yanked a black knapsack from under his jacket and jammed the box and the plastic bag into it. He streaked through the IN door, setting off the alarm because he took *Finding Nemo* with him. Kim saw him put the gun in the back of his pants like Jack Bauer on *24*. He tossed the floppy hat and sunglasses in the trash can and walked quickly out of the window frame. That was when Kim screamed.

The phone rang while I pondered the suitcase in my living room. I'd come in from a double shift in the ER at Victory, happily expecting a dark, empty house. The kids were at Grandma Betty's, Frankie never came around anymore, and I'd left a half bottle of rosé chilling in the fridge.

I stumbled over the suitcase on my way to the wine. I walked more carefully back to the couch, turned on a lamp, and contemplated my blue Samsonite bag and the box beside it. My husband's possessions. Packed and ready to go, but not gone.

The box held his Springsteen CDs, along with his fishing tackle, his tool belt, and, on the plastic lanyard Meghan made at day camp, his union card. The CDs said he was leaving for good, since the Boss goes where he goes, but my suitcase suggested he was coming back, if only to return it. Frankie, the kind of husband who'd cheat openly and leave suddenly, would not steal my suitcase.

The phone rang while I pondered all this. A Detective Cooperman called to tell me that Frank Walsh had been shot to death at Video World. He was polite in that informative way the doctors at Victory use with the relatives. His sorrow at my loss was another piece of information on top of the information he'd called with.

Which was how I took it. I filed away my wondering about the suitcase with other wonders: why would a man stop for a video in the middle of abandoning his family; why would anyone have a second child with such a man; why had marrying him seemed better than single motherhood in the first place.

Last Thursday a gunshot wound came in, all torn flesh and ruined organs. Everyone but his wife knew he was past help. I realized I hadn't asked the detective where Frankie got shot. I shivered and stopped myself from wondering that.

I poured more wine and propped my feet on the suitcase. Margaret arrived. She gently removed my feet. She pulled the bag upstairs, its wheels hitting each step like a dull clock striking. Frankie's dresser drawers opened and closed. The empty suitcase skidded back under the bed. A wave of the guilt that broke whenever Margaret had to take care of me swept me off the couch.

I put the CDs back into the entertainment center, filling the hole they'd left. I dragged the cardboard box across the kitchen floor and into the garage. I poured Margaret some wine and set it on the counter. When she came down, she took away my glass and hugged me. "Oh, Brianna," she said into my hair.

There, breathing into my sister's neck, I saw life without Frankie stretching out ahead of me almost as it would have if he'd finished leaving me for Claudia, but without all the awkward conversations. Meghan and Little Frank hovered over this vision, and I realized, surprised at my own selfishness, that it would be easier to tell them that their father was dead than that he had moved in with his girlfriend.

"How long do you think we have before people show up?"

"I'm surprised no one's here yet," Margaret said. "Vito was working the precinct house desk when the call came in. I won't be the only one he tells."

I broke away from her hug. While she wiped her streaking mascara with the heel of her hand, I bent over the counter and started a shopping list. "Well, let's hope Tommy gets here first. I can send him to Pathmark."

"A brother's duty. If he's sober enough to shop." Typical Margaret. I took a deep breath.

The witness had two piercings in each ear and a small chain tattooed around her wrist. Nothing extreme for a girl her age—Cooperman figured Kim Soong to be sixteen—but he was old-fashioned. The tattoo and piercings, plus the cigarette, and the way she squatted expressionless against the counter where the shooter stuck the gun in her face, gave Cooperman the feeling she'd be hostile in some way.

"Could we get her a chair?" he asked Kessler, the responding officer. Kessler had called the detectives in.

"There's only one back there—with chunks of dead guy on it," she answered.

Cooperman scanned Kessler's notes. "She said the hat was gray green?"

"Her exact words."

"What color would you say that hat is?" Cooperman gestured to the hat recovered from the trash, now in a Ziploc on a shelf labeled "New Release: Comedy."

"Gray green."

"So these other details: corduroy jacket, hair color, boots—they're probably going to check out?"

"She's pretty confident."

Cooperman crouched in front of the girl, his face level with hers, leaving a couple of feet between them. "Mind if we talk?"

"Am I in charge now?" The polite way she blew the cigarette smoke left and down, away from his face, blunted her sarcasm. Cooperman noticed she had a nose piercing, too—a tiny fleck of silver above her right nostril, something gentle enough to soften the other markings' impact.

"I'll make this quick. Your parents will be here soon."

"My grandparents."

"Where are your parents?"

The girl gave Cooperman a look. "Wonjul. Korea."

"OK, your grandparents. Let's get started so you can go home with them. Your description of the guy is incredible. We hardly ever get that kind of detail—the hair color, the accent, the clothing . . ." Cooperman paused.

The girl said nothing. Waiting for the questions.

"In my experience when a description is that detailed—well, I have to wonder if there were mistakes. Witnesses have a hard time remembering everything, and it usually takes lots of questions to get any detail at all.

"But sometimes in the rush to tell us everything they know, to be cooperative, witnesses will tell us more than they actually do know. Enhance the details. So the shirt's stripe is blue rather than green, or maybe was on some other customer, earlier in the day."

Kim closed her eyes. "His shirt was off-white, with stripes—" She splayed her fingers and drew lines down her own chest. "The stripes were dark, but I couldn't tell black or blue or green. That's what I told that woman cop." Her hand flicked toward Officer Kessler. She opened her eyes and looked directly into Cooperman's.

Cooperman bounced slightly forward onto his toes. "Or the witness might leave out something. Despite all the details, sometimes a witness holds back the most important one. Like maybe she'd seen the guy before. Somewhere. Maybe knew the guy. Sometimes witnesses are afraid to admit that they knew the suspect. Anything you might be afraid to tell us?"

"Why would I be afraid?" Sarcastic again. She took a long drag. Her hand shook.

Cooperman smiled reluctantly. "Sometimes if a witness admits to knowing the guy with the gun, they think they'll become suspects or we'll consider them accomplices."

Still staring at him, the girl leaned in close. She locked into his gaze. Her eyes filled with tears. She said, more intensely but no louder, "You think I knew this guy?" Her voice cracked. Cooperman itched to reach out and comfort this little girl whose tough act just broke down.

A commotion started outside. An elderly Asian couple pushed to get in. The woman's gray hair hung to her shoulders. She stretched her arm past the officer on the door. She leaned around him as if she could reach all the way to Kim Soong, crying on the floor near the blood-soaked circle of carpet.

On the pavement outside Video World's broken window, meanwhile, wailing commenced. A well-dressed man, whose tightly pulled electric-blue tie matched his yarmulke, shouted hoarsely and repeatedly, "My store, my life, I'm so sorry! My—" He stopped abruptly, his voice dropping to a whisper. He stepped through the frame, avoiding the window's jagged remains, and skirted the bloodied carpet.

He reached Kim just as her grandparents eluded the officer and scuttled to her side.

Kim got to her feet. The three adults surrounded her, close but not embracing her. They reached out tentatively, touching her shoulder. They offered half words, quiet sounds, as if aware of how meager their comfort was.

Cooperman stood, too, feeling his knees crack. The room filled now with family grief. Relatives of the dead customer and the bruised coworker poured through the door and the window. They cried and hugged, pointing to the cash register, the counter, the carpet. Cooperman picked up the Ziploc beside *Zoolander* and headed to the clutch of officers standing in Drama.

I took the steps two at a time but paused before Meghan's door, where the Britney Spears poster stared back at me. I still had all the papers in the funeral home envelope. I turned to toss it through my open bedroom door. It hit the bed, but a Mass card fluttered to the floor. I took a deep breath, knocked, and barged right in.

Meghan was reading. Little Frank, who I guess was now just Frank, played a computer game involving soldiers, shooting, and bizarre balls of light and smoke. Both kids jumped up to hug me, Meghan quick and full of spiky energy, Frank slower and rounder, his head down, his step already long and lumbering like his father's.

Meghan's arms circled my waist, her face pressed against my ribs. Frank wormed one shoulder and his cheek between his sister and me, keeping an arm around Meghan's back, his other hand tapping nervously against my thigh. We stood like this. A moment later, I shuffled us all over to Meghan's bed, where we sat in a tangle. Meghan cried, sniffing loudly. I touched her hair, in which blond had already lost against my ratty brown genes. At the touch, she jerked up and stared.

"Are you all right, Mom?"

"I will be." I tucked her head back under my arm, felt her wipe her nose on the ridges of my ribcage. "I didn't think you guys would already know. Who told you?" I looked around her room, a clash of personalities. Pink cashmere and black denim, stuffed animals and soccer trophies, the world of a girl who'd quit trying to figure out how to be a girl and started trying to figure out how to be a woman.

"Meghan told me," Frank said into my shoulder. I could feel his embrace slowly stiffening, him growing bored with all this affection.

Meghan looked up, her guilt quick and contagious. "I heard Grandma Betty."

I pulled her into me again and put my hand back on her hair. We sat in our three-person heap. Someone knocked. Grandma Betty,

Frankie's mom, cracked it open, whispered too loudly, "Father Clement is here."

"Oh, fuck," I said, rubbing my face. I unwrapped myself from the kids and stood up.

When Kimmy took a cigarette from the red-and-white pack and stretched backward, leaning away from the dining table to work the lighter from her jeans pocket, Kalie knew that all the rules had been suspended. "Halmoni!" Kalie whispered, pointing at the kitchen, but Kimmy waved her sister off.

She leaned forward to light the cigarette and blew smoke in Kalie's face. Missing school was not allowed even more than smoking was not allowed, but not only did Kimmy get the day off for seeing a man get shot in the Video World at midnight, Kalie had to stay home to comfort her.

That turned out to mean playing Monopoly since breakfast. Kalie watched Kimmy smoke, flicking the ashes onto the deed for Ventnor Avenue, held flat in her palm. Kimmy already had the B&O and the Short Line. Her silver shoe was four spaces from Reading Railroad. If she hit that, she would buy it for $200. If she got the fourth one, she'd win.

Kimmy's school friends, who normally weren't allowed to call until Kimmy's homework was done, interrupted the game all day. Kimmy's cell hadn't quit. She asked them a million questions. "Yolanda, are you in Holsbach's class? Is Mercedes there? Did Jamal come to school?"

Kalie thought that everyone would want to know what it was like to see a man get shot at the Video World at midnight. Except Halmoni and Grandpa, who refused to ask, and the kids at school, who just gossiped and giggled. Maybe if Kim rolled a four, Kalie could ask again, very politely.

"Tell Mercedes I'll be back tomorrow. She better stay away from Derrick or I will kill her." Even though she rolled a three and got Community Chest, Kim laughed. Community Chest sucked. Who was Derrick anyway? Kim was seeing Jamal.

Kalie waited last night until they were both in bed—very late, later than Kalie had ever been up before. "What was it like?" she asked. "Did you really see it?"

Kimmy didn't move or speak for so long that Kalie thought she was asleep. Kalie was trying to get up the courage to shake her awake and ask again when Kimmy said, "Nothing." She turned her face to the wall. "It was like nothing."

As Kalie drifted to sleep, she heard Kim crying. She got up and sat beside her. Too afraid even to touch Kim's shoulder, Kalie just sat on the edge of the bed and watched her sister cry.

"You gotta remember, he was trying to help that girl," Margaret's husband Vito said, for the fourth time since walking into the viewing room. Praising Frank's bravery seemed to be Vito's duty as a brother-in-law.

"Did you know her?" asked Paul, Frankie's construction buddy. Because Vito's a cop, Paul assumed Vito knew everyone in Brooklyn. "Chinese girl?"

"Korean," Vito said, in his cop voice. "She was Korean."

"Heard she was from up to Eighth Avenue?" Paul said. "Thought that was Chinese?"

"Mixed," Vito said.

Margaret turned to me. "You knew her, though, Bree. She used to play on Meghan's soccer team."

"Pretty girl," I said. I kept my back to Frankie's coffin. Somebody'd stood our wedding picture on top, and I didn't want to see.

"That figures," Paul laughed. "Frankie always did have a nose for a damsel in distress." Vito backhanded him in the chest to shut him up. I would not miss Paul. I flashed them my best tight smile and moved away so they could whisper and giggle about Frankie's nose for damsels.

A disturbance at the door, quickly hushed, caught the crowd's attention. Claudia, in a dress too short for those damn legs, slunk to the far end of the room. Margaret cut across to intercept her, steering her to a couch. I turned back to Vito and Paul. They stood silent, staring stiffly at the carpet.

The talk dropped to whispers, a wave of breathy voices rolling across the room. Everyone here, from Grandma Betty to Bill Sears to the McConnell girls in their Bishop Kearney uniforms, knew who Claudia was and why she was crying. Those with half a brain knew why I was not.

"Excuse me," I said, slipping through to the ladies' room. That was packed, too, full of women answering a sudden urge, the moment Claudia walked in, to freshen their makeup or use the toilet. Now, as I stood in the doorway, interrupting their gossip circle, they forgot those urges, colliding with each other to avoid touching me as they left.

I closed the door and leaned against it. I sucked air down my throat to stop the sob in my stomach from working its way up. Breathing and crying reached a standoff in the middle of my chest. Someone pushed against the door, interrupting the struggle: Margaret to the rescue.

I pivoted, wedging my hip against the ladies' room door until I could lock her out. I fumbled with the handle, an ornate brass monstrosity, looking for the latch. Margaret, meanwhile, forced open the door and squeezed her fingers through, knowing I wouldn't push back and slam it on them. She reached around and touched my hand.

"There's no lock on this door!" I wheezed.

"People lock the stalls, Bree." Margaret shoved, hard. I let go. She stumbled in. The door banged off the wall so hard it slammed itself closed. "Why would someone lock the whole room?" Margaret asked.

"Maybe someone wants to be alone. Maybe someone is distraught. It *is* a goddamn funeral parlor. People *do* get distraught." I turned on the hot water. We stared at each other in the mirror. "People do get distraught."

"I know. Give me a minute to get rid of her. The stupid bitch should know better, but I need a minute to do it quiet." Margaret looked into my reflected eyes as steam rose from the sink. The mirror clouded. My face floated above the fog.

"You never thought she was stupid before," I sighed.

"I barely know her."

"You liked her. After Isabella's bachelorette party, you told me about her. You said she was smart and funny and—well, smart."

"That was before. I didn't know she was going to . . ."

"No, of course not." I waved her off. "Only Frankie knew." I sighed again. "Only Frankie ever knew."

"She's not even that pretty."

"But Frankie was charming and funny. And flirtatious." My face got lost in the mist. "I loved it when he flirted. I'll tell you, if he hadn't gotten himself killed, he'd have given that Korean girl quite a thrill. Driven her home. Smiled that smile that made you forget."

Margaret returned to the door. She opened it just wide enough to ease out. "I'll get rid of her," she said. I turned off the water and wiped the mirror.

As he slid through the barely open door, Jamal tried to kiss Kim. She held her face at such a stiff, sharp angle that his lips puckered against her chin. He blushed and whispered her name short and quick. The sister took off for the kitchen.

Jamal and Kim sat in the straight wooden dining room chairs. Jamal talked in ragged bursts, telling a story about gym class, asking when she'd return to school, offering to do her Spanish homework. Kim smoked, but when he pulled out his Marlboros, she waved her hand.

He slipped them back into his gray hoodie, but he plucked Kim's cigarette from the teacup where she'd balanced it and took a drag. Kim grabbed it, snubbing it on the saucer. Jamal felt a wave of loneliness mix with his need for nicotine. He knew Grandma was in the kitchen, as usual, listening, as usual, but he couldn't imagine what she understood.

"More tea? Cup of tea?" the old lady called.

Kim yelled "No!" and whined something in Korean. Jamal looked down at the Monopoly board. He licked his sleeve and tried to rub a dark stain off Ventnor Avenue. He shifted in the chair. He scuffed the rug with the heel of his sneaker. "You were very . . . brave."

Kim said nothing.

"I peed myself . . . literally." He laughed as if self-mockery might hide the memory of the dark stain, the tang of urine mixed with the odor of blood.

The dining room window had no view, but the sun lit the curtains, a square of glowing yellow. The leaves of a tree moved in shadow.

Kim stared at the shapes. "I had trouble moving," she said. "All I could do was just . . . see things."

"They used your description to catch the guy."

"I wanted to move, or scream, or anything."

"He'd have shot you."

Kim closed her eyes. Jamal watched her still face, caught the hint of movement as her eyes shifted behind her lids He felt a surge of relief that he had not seen what she had, then he felt guilty.

"Neagle closed it again today," he said. "They haven't fixed the window, but he patched the carpet. He tried to clean that chair, the one behind customer service, with Resolve, but he had to throw away the chair. Bigelow told me. Resolve."

Kim opened her eyes. They shone with tears. Jamal reached for her hand. He tried to bring it to his lips, but she held it so stiffly that he had to twist it to his mouth. Feeling the strain on her wrist, Jamal got scared and let go. Kim folded both hands in her lap. She looked past him at the yellow window.

"While your sister's gone, you should steal her Get Out of Jail Free card."

Kim smirked. "She's listening."

"More tea," Halmoni called. "Who wants tea?"

Grandma Betty took the kids Monday night. She planned to fill them with her cooking and her opinions, both of which she preferred to mine. Their absence made Margaret talk up the idea that I shouldn't be alone. "We don't even have to speak," Margaret said, running a hand through her fading blondish perm. She shook out her curls and resumed wiping down my kitchen counter.

I focused on the brown roots along her part. "Marge, you need to go."

"I'll just help you get set up."

"It's my house." I needed to pee. I needed Margaret gone even more. One leg shook nervously. "It's already set up."

"I'm worried about you alone."

"You saw the suitcase. I'd be even more alone if Frankie were alive."

"I'm just afraid it hasn't hit you yet." She was right. It hadn't. I was still adjusting to Frankie living over on Fourth Avenue with Claudia, still worried I'd run into him in CVS or at the bank.

It was as if a song I expected to hear had started, but the music changed after I'd already begun dancing. I had just this one night alone. Tomorrow Meghan and Frank and I would be back to living together, our new life same as the old life. Almost.

Kim waited across Eighty-First Street, leaning against the print shop window full of faded wedding invitations. She gave Mr. Neagle time to turn on the lights and get all the way back to his office before crossing to Video World. She flattened her palms against the plywood, feeling its cold roughness. She pushed through the door. The gong announced her.

Neagle said, "We open in an hour," then froze. They looked at each other down the long New Releases aisle. She knew he wouldn't get up, so she stopped at the register to slap at the new chair and watch it spin. She inspected the carpet, the seam between old and new. Resolve hadn't worked on those bloodstains, either.

Kim shook that thought, walking quickly between Comedy and Classics to the office door. Neagle was dismissive of the kids who worked for him, just short of unfriendly. Now, though, he half-stood and waved Kim toward the only other seat. Plastic DVD cases packed the space, and boxes full of rolled-up posters that stuck up at odd angles. Old soda bottles and register tapes littered the desk.

"I hope—" Neagle began. He cut himself off. His long soft fingers caressed the gray in his neatly trimmed beard. They skittered down to tighten the knot in his tie, and up to fiddle with the bobby pins in his matching yarmulke. "I was going to come by, but I didn't want to disturb—" He cut himself off again. "You know you don't have to work today. Take time. As much time as you need. Your job will be waiting." He looked into her eyes as he said this, and Kim thought he would cry.

"I won't be back," she said. Her voice sounded mechanical. She couldn't hold it steady unless she spoke in a monotone.

He seemed relieved, but his voice was frightened. "Why not? I hope you're not afraid?"

"No," Kim said. "I'm not afraid. I just don't want to . . ." She stopped. Silence filled the office.

Neagle sputtered. "I've ordered a new security system. Cameras and sensors—" There was another silence as Neagle's protest faded.

"I can't . . . imagine it," Kim said. "It might be the same as before, help kids find Disney movies, ignore men who rent porn. It might not be different." Kim looked at the carpet. She rubbed her shoe along the nap. "But I can't imagine it. Not at all." She stopped. Neagle shifted uncomfortably.

"That guy," Kim said. "He had a nice smile. And he reached out. . . ." She shifted her hand from one knee to the other. She stiffened, remembering the shock. "I don't want to be that girl. The one who saw." Her hand moved back to its original knee.

"I never meant for anything like this to happen. I bought this store . . . I thought I would not have to be here very often. It would run itself." He swiveled his chair to face the aisles of films, the brightly lit posters. "I think I will be here a lot now. All the time, maybe."

"I won't," Kim said, and heard finality, energy, enter her voice.

Neagle smiled. "You live with your grandparents?"

Kim nodded. She stood, eager to move. She shifted from foot to foot.

"I would like to stop by sometime, pay my respects."

Kim wondered who he'd pay them to. No one in her house was dead. Yet it seemed the kind of thing Grandpa and Halmoni would appreciate. Kim wondered if Neagle was secretly Korean. She shrugged and said, "If you want. My halmoni—grandmother—doesn't speak much English. But Grandpa's a big talker. They'd probably like that."

Neagle snapped out of his reverie and turned back to the desk.

"I owe you some money. I think three shifts?"

"Just two." Kim said. "You were closed Saturday."

Neagle winced. "Let's call it three."

Margaret's final gesture had been to cook a chicken for my next dinner. First thing Tuesday, I threw that chicken into the trash. I fired up Frankie's pickup and went to buy my own damn groceries. The weather, cold and clear, matched my mood. I'd get the kids from Grandma Betty in the afternoon. Their last day out of school. Maybe we'd catch a movie.

I passed the girl on the way. If I'd been thinking, I'd have gone around the block to avoid Video World. I wasn't thinking, and there she was, a pretty Korean girl in front of the plywood barrier where the window Frankie fell through used to be.

Plenty of pretty Asian girls in the neighborhood these days, but I knew who it was. She wore all black—black denim jacket, black knee-length skirt and high black socks. Her little bit of face, framed by straight black hair, seemed to disappear into the pale wood. I kept her in the rearview and nearly hit a stray dog crossing Third Avenue.

I bought beer and frozen burritos, laundry detergent, and a box cake for the kids. On the way back I stopped for a latte at Starbucks. I had to double-park, so the whole time on line I watched the truck nervously. As soon as the guy put down my cup, I grabbed it and ran.

I practically knocked the girl over as she came in. I caught her arm just below the elbow to steady her. She regained her balance. We faced each other. We held each other's gaze. Her eyes widened.

She seemed to look at me in a kind of panic. Her eyes darted past me into the store. Then she looked into my face, calmer now, then back over my shoulder. A nervous calm, though, that mirrored my own feeling—a rushed, anxious encounter whose only benefit was that it would soon be over.

The girl was small. Pretty as I remembered. The light sparkled off the tiny jewel in her nose and made her prettier. I understood why Frankie had the urge to protect her. I had the same urge now—to pull her close as though she were a child, as though she might cry on my shoulder. She stiffened, though, and pulled back her arm, which told me to hold my pity and allow her her toughness.

"I'm . . . sorry," she said, pausing long enough between the words to make me think she meant to introduce herself.

"I know," I said. "Me, too." I meant it, which surprised me.

I studied her face and she studied mine, looking for fear or grief or strength or hope. Each of us found all that. Her eyes were wet but clear; the wind whipping into the coffee shop suppressed any inclination toward tears.

She smiled briefly and looked beyond me into the crowded coffee shop. I released her arm. We continued past each other. On the sidewalk, I stopped and took a deep breath. Then I ran for the truck, just ahead of the meter maid.

Six Cents

Mary D. Edwards

THE GUN CLOSET is built into the wall on the steps that lead into Mama and Father's room. It is 1953. Andy is eight and I am fourteen. Father puts his brass key into the lock and opens it. Inside, the shotguns stand on their stocks. Father reaches behind them.

"Look, Sarah," he says, unwrapping a rumpled chamois. "It's a Smith & Wesson." The barrel and cylinder are black. The grip's wooden panels have cross-hatched grooves. The smell of oil rises from the metal. "Twenty-two caliber. I got it at Anderson's last Saturday." Father stuffs a red box into his trouser pocket. "Let's go."

Andy and I follow him down the back stairs, through the screened porch, and across the backyard. The April air is warm and clear. The three of us enter the patch of scrub oaks, passing the steel petroleum drum where we burn trash. We squeeze through the V-shaped kissing gate, wide enough for us to enter but too narrow for the horses, and step into the pasture. Ahead is the elm tree where Cousin Beebe peed when he was in second grade and I was in sixth. Beyond is the asparagus patch.

"Where are we going?" I ask.

"Halfway down the hill," Father says. "The embankment." His blue-and-red suspenders, buttoned to the back of his trousers, move ahead of me. His white shirt luffs in the breeze like the sail of our boat. "We must shoot into that."

102

"Why?" Andy asks.

"So no one'll get hurt."

We loop around the sandstone ledge where I made a campfire last summer to the mound beside it. We face the mound. The bluestem grass surrounding us is damp and matted. Back in the woods, a bob-white calls. I found a bird's skeleton there.

Father takes the box from his pocket. He pulls up the lid. He counts out cartridges. "Here, Andy." He hands the box to my brother. "You hold this." Dropping the chamois onto the grass, Father flips open the cylinder and loads the pistol. "This box cost over three dollars," Father says, snapping the cylinder shut. "Six cents a cartridge."

He turns toward the mound and takes aim. "You hold a revolver straight out in front. Like so. To protect yourself." He tenses his jaw. A tiny cut from his razor stands out. The sun glances off the pistol's barrel and I remember how he told me to hold scissors the same way, with the points forward. So you don't get stabbed if you trip.

"Then you aim." He sucks in his breath and pulls the trigger six times. The cracking sound fills the woods clear to the barn, the creek, and Grandma's house. Maybe even downtown to Oklahoma City, where Father's office is.

"Sarah, you try now." He opens the cylinder. The empty brass casings fall onto the horse trail with a clinking sound. He inserts fresh rounds into the holes.

The grip's wooden panels press into my palm. "Farther out," Father says, grasping my hand and pulling it away from my body. "And hold it level. Not like a ping-pong paddle, the way those Hollywood cowboys hold their sidearms."

I straighten my arm so that it is like his.

"Now squeeze the trigger."

Bam! The kick lifts my hand a couple of inches into the air.

"Both hands. Use both hands."

I wrap my left around my right. I pull the trigger five more times, watching the embankment, where the bullets kick the red dirt. The acrid smoke stings my nostrils. I look down at the pistol, then up at Father. I am elated. I just put six bullets into a mound! I hold the barrel with my free hand and rock the pistol back and forth as if it were mine. "Can I shoot again?"

Father frowns. "It's six cents a bullet."

Andy has set the box on the horse trail. I never thought about bullets as money.

"Let me!" Andy squeals.

"Just one load." Father takes the pistol from me and empties the cylinder. He plugs in new cartridges. "Six cents a bullet. Thirty-six cents a load." He stands behind Andy, nestling him between his legs and handing him the pistol.

"It's heavy," Andy says.

"Let me help." Father folds his hands around my brother's and lifts the gun. Andy jerks at the trigger. Bam!

"It's so loud," says Andy. He laughs and squirms in his yellow T-shirt. Slowly, carefully, he shoots the rest of the bullets into the mound. All of them enter it in exactly the same place because Father holds the pistol steady.

"Can I shoot again?" Andy asks.

"Well, all right. One more load for each of us," Father says. "But only one. This costs a lot." He reloads and takes his turn. Then I take mine. This time I don't enjoy it, not even when I shoot. Each time the gun fires, I think of six cents and feel guilty.

Andy takes his turn. "That's it," Father says. "Let's go up for dinner."

"One more?" Andy asks. "Please?" Father shakes his head.

I shrink back, upset that it is over so soon. Andy puts his hands on his hips and looks angrily down at the weeds. Father picks up the red box and shoves it into his pocket. He rewraps the pistol in the chamois and starts up the hill.

Andy and I linger, staring at the mound, then we follow the path far behind Father. At the gate, Father turns. "You children did a good job. Not like those Hollywood cowboys."

I place my hand on Andy's shoulder and shrug, resentful of the compliment. Looking down at Andy, I say, "I wanted another turn."

"Me too," Andy says.

When Andy and I reach the back lawn, Father has already gone inside. Through the junipers, we see the station wagon and know that Mama has come home. We walk to the car. The door is wide open, and Mama is reading the mail.

"We shot the pistol," Andy says.

Mama looks at us. "How was it?"

"Well, Father kept talking about money," I say.

"Six cents a bullet!" complains Andy. "He ruined it for us."

Mama nods solemnly but says nothing.

The next afternoon, I climb the three steps beside the gun closet and enter Mama and Father's room. Father is lying on the spread of their bed, alone, wearing flannel trousers and an undershirt. Around his neck he has a red bandanna, the one he ties across his eyes when he naps so he can fall asleep. "Sarah? Is that you?"

"Uh-huh."

He rolls onto his side and props himself up with one arm. "Come here, won't you?"

I walk over to his side of the bed, close enough to see the pock-marks on his nose. "When I came back from college, I worked in Dad's office." He means the Terminal Building downtown. "That was in 1928."

I look out the window behind him. The sky is a clear blue, but the tips of the blackjack oaks sway as if nervous. "The crash came the next year." His voice is hushed and his green eyes seem to tremble. "We lost money every day." He leans toward me. "Each morning when I went to work, I was afraid Dad would jump out the office window." He looks down and purses his lips. "Like the brokers in New York City."

I saw Grandpa three times when I was little. Twice in 1945, sitting up heroic in his sickbed, a cigar in his hand, a smile on his face. Once in 1946, in his coffin. I can't imagine him scared and about to jump.

"Then came the Depression," Father says. "Poor people with no food stood in long lines for soup outside the office. Business got so bad we had to lay off all three men." He squeezes the edge of the bedspread into a ball. "I took a salary cut. I was slated to be dropped next." He relaxes his fist. The bedspread falls into place. He looks into my face again. He shakes his head slowly and winces. "That's why I can't help but remind you that each bullet costs six cents."

He stares at me a long time. Finally he covers his face with his bandanna and rolls over. He could have been fired. I never knew that. Beneath his undershirt, his shoulder juts like a wing. Or a bone. I move a step closer. I extend my hand, then let it drop. I begin to understand.

The Handgun

Rick DeMarinis

EVERY MORNING AT 3 a.m., a dog would sit in front of our house and bark. It was a big dog, a wolfhound of some kind—Irish or Russian—and its bark broke into our sleep like a shout from God. More than loud, it was eerie. The barks came up from the street with an urgency meant to induce panic. The Huns were at the gate, the tidal wave was almost here, the volcano was about to blow. Every night, I fell out of bed in a running crouch, my heart looking for a way out of its cage.

Then I'd get back into bed and pull the pillow over my head. But Raquel, stiff with rage, wouldn't let me have this easy escape. She would sit up in bed, turn on the weak lamp, and light a cigarette. "I am losing my mind," she said. "How can you expect me to go to work every morning without sleep?"

Finally, after the tenth night of the punctual dog, Raquel said, "I want you to buy a gun."

Her face was a spooky, hovering oval in the lamp's yellow glow. Her eyes were fixed on a resolute vision. I'd seen her pass through some alarming changes since I had lost my job and she had become chief breadwinner, but this tightly focused rage made me believe significant trouble was on the way.

"We can't afford a gun," I said. Which was true. We were barely making our house payments on her secretarial wages. "Not a good gun anyway. A good rifle with a scope runs four or five hundred."

"My hunter," she said, a sneer curling her lips. "I am not talking about a rifle. I want you to get a pistol. Just a .22 target pistol. They sell them even in drugstores."

I knew it would grate on her but I tried a patronizing chuckle anyway, hoping to deflect her anger to me and thereby leave this gun business far behind. "You can't go out on the street and shoot animals. This is a neighborhood. People will get upset."

She turned to me—mechanically, I thought. Her smile would have done credit to the Borgia family. The warmth of the bed was dissipating noticeably. "I thought of that," she said. "But it's almost the Fourth of July. The neighbors will think it's only boys who could not wait to blow up their firecrackers. No one will get out of bed to investigate."

"You've been thinking about this for some time," I observed, mostly to myself.

"Yes, I have. And we won't go into the street. We will shoot from the window, behind the curtains. We will put Kleenex over the barrel so that the flash will not be seen."

"You'd be murdering someone's companion, a pet . . ."

She gave me a lingering, abstracted look, the look she might give a complete stranger who had offered a demented opinion. "You," she said, "suffocate me."

The distance between us enlarged. Madness does that. It seemed like a trend. Her response to straightforward remarks might come from left field or from outside the park. I thought she might be in the early stages of a breakdown. The thought depressed me. I got up and went into the bathroom, where I took an Elavil.

I didn't want a gun in the house. I'd recently read a sobering statistic: Of all handgun deaths in private homes, only a tiny percentage involved intruders. The majority of victims were members of the gun owner's immediate family. The usual motive was suicide. And sometimes, but not rarely, murder *and* suicide. I thought: *Baloney.* Then I saw that it made perfect sense. I couldn't count the number of times I'd raised my finger to my head and said "Bang" after reading, say, a turn-off notice from the power company, or a credit-threatening letter from Penney's or Sears. A finger to the temple and the sadly muttered

"Bang" is a clown's gesture, wistful at best, but signifying the ever-present wish to put out one's lights.

"Go to Mel's Pawnshop tomorrow," Raquel, or the person Raquel was in the process of becoming, said when I came back to the bedroom. "They sell fine guns there for under one hundred dollars."

She'd turned out the lamp and was sitting naked next to the window, looking down on the dog. It had quit barking and was just staring, like a rejected lover, at the cold beauty of Raquel's unforgiving silhouette.

"It's against the *law* to shoot fine guns in the city," I said, mocking her lambent Hispanic fire and lilt. "It's a felony."

"I am not interested in your *putrefacto* laws," she said.

"What do you know about Mel's Pawnshop, anyway?" I said. I stepped behind her and put my hands on her moon-dusty shoulders. The moon was nearly full and she was incandescent with a chalky light. Given the state of our lives, 3 a.m. sex was unlikely, but this crazy moonlit woman in the window broke the spell hard times put on flesh. I slipped my hands down to her breasts like a repossessor.

She hunched away from me. "I want to put a bullet in that dog's throat," she said.

I went back to bed as the dog resumed its pointless assault on our lives. "I am not going to Mel's," I said.

"Fine, St. Francis," she said. "I'll go."

But she didn't go. She was afraid to. The pawnshop area of town was full of aimless psychotics. Now and then one of them would be picked up for a crime committed in another part of the state or country. In fact, a serial murderer had been arrested in Mel's a year ago as he was trying to trade a necklace made of human kneecaps for a machete.

The next night a weather front moved in and the air was stifling. The changed atmospherics improved the acoustics of the neighborhood. The dog, it seemed, was in bed with us.

"I can't stand it!" Raquel screamed. "You have to do something!" She pulled the pillow off my head and threw it across the bedroom.

I got up and opened the window. "Shut up, dog!" I yelled, but I might as well have been arguing with a magpie. We were not on the same wavelength. The odd timbre of the dog's bark gave it an almost human quality. I could nearly make myself believe I was hearing a kind of garbled English. "What what *what?*" or "Hot, hot, what?" But there was also a forlorn tone that was not translatable. A canine refusal to accept some wrenching loss. I went back to bed.

"I've got this feeling, hon," I said. "Like that dog is in mourning for its lost mate." We'd called the Animal Control cop days ago and his white van toured the neighborhood, picking up strays. Maybe the big dog lost his ladylove in that sweep.

Raquel turned on the bed lamp and studied my face for signs of mockery or perhaps derangement. "Are you *crazy?*" she asked. "Dogs don't mate for life like *swans.* They screw any bitch in heat. Don't try to turn that monster into a brokenhearted family man."

Then she said the thing that forced the issue. "Look, *hon,*" she mocked. "Either you get that gun or I am going to find somewhere else to sleep at night."

My joblessness, and now my refusal to take action in an emergency, had turned her against me. "All right," I said. "I'll get the gun."

The next day, after I had made breakfast and Raquel had gone to work, I walked through the neighborhood looking for the dog. I'd already done this several times, but now I knocked on doors and asked questions. No one would admit to owning such a dog, not on our street or on the several adjacent streets. But even more curious than this, no one admitted to having heard the dog bark. Evidently its tirades were sharply directional, like the beam from a radar antenna, hitting only the thing it aimed at.

"Did you get it?" Raquel asked me when she got home from work.

I stalled. "Bindle-stiff chicken tonight, darling," I said. "Plus asparagus à la Milwaukee vinaigrette." These were recipes I had invented. I was proud of them. They were Raquel's favorites.

"You didn't get it," she said.

"All Mel had were big-caliber revolvers—.357s and .44s. Nothing we could use comfortably. We'd wreck the neighborhood with those cannons."

"You didn't go," she said.

I stuttered, a dead giveaway, then faced a wall of spiting silence the rest of the evening. She didn't touch my wonderful dinner.

The following morning at nine-thirty I saw Dr. Selbiades, my shrink. I told him all about the dog, the gun, and Raquel's threat. I had not called him up about this crisis, and I could tell that it miffed him a bit.

"So," he said, in that loftily humble, arrogant, self-effacing way of his. "Your wife wants you to get a . . . *gun.*"

Selbiades is not a Freudian, so this was only a joke—meant, no doubt, to get even with me for keeping secrets.

"I've decided to get one this afternoon."

"Just like that?" he said, rocking back in his five-hundred-dollar leather-covered swivel chair.

"Yes. A .22 automatic."

"It would be a mistake, my friend," he said.

"Probably. But I don't see that I have a choice."

He stood up and flexed his hairy arms over his head and yawned. His yawn was as healthy and as uninhibited as a lion's. He scratched his ribs vigorously, then sat down again. He was wearing a T-shirt and Levi's and running shoes. He never wore anything else, at least in his office. "Christ, man," he said at last, his thick neck corded, it seemed, with redundant veins and arteries. "Of course you have a choice! Unless . . ."

I bit. "Unless?"

"Unless you hate her."

"*Hate* her? I love her! What do you mean, *hate*?"

"It just sounds like some classic passive-aggressive bullshit, my friend. You're giving her enough rope to hang herself with."

"I am terrified of losing her," I said, my voice ragged.

Selbiades swiveled his chair around abruptly, so that he now faced the window behind his desk. "There is, of course, a level on which what you say is true," he said, his tone suggesting a far too intimate knowledge of mankind. His window gave out on a view of fields, freshly scraped down to naked earth in preparation for a town-house development called Vista Buena Bonanza. He clasped his hairy hands behind his head and contemplated this field. He owned it and was a partner in the new development. I envied him: he was the happiest man I knew.

"What about bullets?" Raquel asked that evening. I gave her the small paper bag that had four boxes of .22 ammo in it. She snatched the bag from me and inspected each box.

"No blanks," I said, thinking that blanks would have been fine. I was sure all she wanted to do was scare the dog off, not actually wound it.

She looked haggard sitting at the kitchen table, holding the pistol in one hand and sorting through bullets with the other. Then she put the gun and bullets in one messy pile and shoved them to the center of the table. She stood up and hugged me. "I am so proud of you at this moment," she said.

But it was a soldierly embrace. French or Russian, it would have involved tight-lipped kisses on both cheeks. A distinct warpage had entered our lives.

While I did a stir-fry, she paced around the kitchen smoking cigarettes, lost in strategy. She had been putting on weight and her heavy stride made the wok shimmy. I guessed that she'd put on twenty or thirty pounds since she'd taken the job at the courthouse. I hated to see that. In spite of our quick lip service to the contrary, physical attraction is the first thing that draws men to women, and vice versa. Time and mileage do their damage, but Raquel was too young to lose her figure. She had the long-muscled legs of a Zulu princess, along with the high-rising arch of spirited buttocks. Her torso was wide and ribby, the breasts not large but dominant and forthright. But now that rare geometry had been put in danger by the endless goodies office workers have to contend with every day. The county office in which she processed words seemed more like a giant deli than an arm of government. Often she would bring me pastries oozing lemon curd or brandied compote, or giant sandwiches on kaiser buns thick with ham or beef, and on special occasions, such as office parties, entire boxes of sour cream chocolate cookies, brownies, or bismarcks. She wouldn't step on the scale. When I suggested it, she snapped, "I know, I know, I've put on a couple of pounds. I don't need to have it shoved in my face."

But it was more than her waistline that was changing. She began to embrace opinions that seemed alien to her nature. She'd sit on the sofa in front of the evening news with watchdog attentiveness. ("See how Rather works in the knee-jerk liberal point of view?" "Look at the expression on Brokaw's face when he mentions the Contras. Looks like he wants to spit.") In the past she had no coherent politics. She was resolutely apolitical, in fact. But now she was listing sharply to the no-nonsense Right.

"The people are going to take law and order into their own hands if the courts keep turning loose the rapists and killers," she once said.

"That's how a society destroys itself," I suggested, fatuously, I admit.

Raquel scoffed. It was the first time in our eight-year marriage that she had shown outright contempt for me. It stung. The scar is still warm. "That is how a society *saves* itself," she said.

And, on another occasion, she said that the bureaucrats didn't care a bit about the common man. "All they care about is raising taxes so they can keep their soft jobs." She had good evidence for this, having spent the last six months working for the Department of Streets.

That first night of the gun was electric with adrenaline. We couldn't sleep at all. We watched TV until 2 a.m., then went up to the bedroom. We got undressed—no pajamas or nightgown, as it was another hot, humid night—and got in bed. Raquel was giddy with high excitement. I was tense, and not looking forward to the dog's appointed hour. I wished now that my passive-aggressive bullshit had not expressed itself so classically.

The bed got swampy with body steam. Raquel threw off the sheet and thin blanket and sat up. She took the gun off the night table and couched it on her belly. Goosebumps, triggered by the cold steel, radiated upward to her breasts, stiffening the nipples, and downward to her thighs, making them twitch. The moon was on the wane but still bright. A thin film of sweat made her body glow metallic. *Oh rarest of metals!* I thought, choking back a desperate love. The gun muzzle slipped down into the dark delta at the vertex of her thighs. Perversions of wild variety and orientation presented themselves to me.

"Forget it," Raquel said, sensing my state of mind. "He might start any minute now."

"It's not three yet. It's only two-thirty."

I was pleading. I hated myself, a beggar in my own bed.

"Afterwards," she said, her voice oddly abstract in the abstract light of the moon. "It will be *better* afterwards."

I couldn't see her eyes, just the black skull-holes that held them. She was smiling.

I snapped on the bed lamp, but didn't look at her. I wanted to avoid her, to organize my thoughts; I wanted to hold back the clock. I picked up a *Newsweek* from the magazine rack under the night table and flipped it open. I read about a woman in Pennsylvania who boiled her baby and sent the parts of the cooked body to a newspaper editor who had denounced abortion. Another article suggested that eighty percent of all children under the age of twelve will one day be the victims of a violent crime. I switched to the opinion columns, but those genteel, sharp-witted souls seemed to be writing about a world in which sanity was a possibility.

Then it was three o'clock. "How do you shoot this thing?" Raquel asked, looking at the gun as if for the first time.

"You aim and pull the trigger. It's easy," I said. I heard my passive-aggressive bullshit sprocketing these words out of my lungs.

"Isn't there something here called the safety?" she asked. It made me happy that the enormity of the coming violence had made her a bit timid.

"That little lever, up on the handle, I think." Actually my knowledge of guns was not much better than hers.

"*Where?*"

"Push it up, or maybe down. I don't know."

The gun, wobbling around in her hand, gradually aimed itself at her throat as she fiddled with its levers and knobs.

"Jesus Christ!" I said, grabbing the gun away from her. It went off. It shot a Currier and Ives print off the wall. It was an original, given to me by my grandmother. *Fast Trotters in Harlem Lane, N.Y.* Men in silk hats driving fine teams of horses down the dirt roads of nineteenth-century Harlem.

Raquel burst into tears. It shocked me. Not the tears but the realization that I could not remember the last time she had cried. I put my arms around her, half expecting her to shove me away. She didn't.

Then something else happened. Or failed to happen. It was three-fifteen and there was no dog in the street calling to us. "Listen, honey," I said.

But her sobs had been on hold too long to be put off. She cried for another five minutes. Then I said it again, as gently as I could. "Listen, Raquel. No *dog*."

We both went to the window. The street was empty. Whatever the big dog had wanted to get off its chest was gone. He had exorcised himself, or at least that's what I hoped. There was the possibility that he'd taken a night off and would come back. But I didn't have to think about that now. Thinking about that, and what I would have to do about it, could wait.

I went downstairs and made a pot of hot chocolate. I brought two big mugs of it back to the bedroom. But Raquel was already asleep. I was too rattled to sleep. I went back down and drank hot chocolate until 5 a.m. The dog never showed up.

When I went back upstairs, the sun was flooding the bedroom with its good-hearted light. It was the same good-hearted light that fell on the heads of baby boilers and saints alike, unconditionally.

The last thing I saw before dropping off to sleep that morning was the gun, shining on the night table like a blue wish. I had one of those half-waking dreams that give you the feeling that you've understood something. I understood that the barking dog had been a sponsor for the gun. The gun had sought us out, and found us, with the assistance of the dog. *Go to sleep, you fool*, Raquel said. But that was the dream, too, and I realized that the gun had summoned, again with the aid of the dog, real changes in Raquel.

Morning dreams always wake me up, insisting that I register their fake significance. I got out of bed and went to the bathroom. I took a long look at my face. It had more mileage on it than my life justified. I rummaged through the stock of pills in the medicine cabinet, then went back to bed armed with Seconal against smart-ass dreams. The gun caught my eye again. It had a tight, self-satisfied sheen, like a deceptively well-groomed relative from a disgraced branch of the family who'd come to claim a permanent place in our home.

EVERYONE IN NEW York carried revealed. By law. All taxpaying citizens of the five boroughs were required to carry a 9-mm Beretta pistol in a standard cop-blue fanny pack. These City-issued accessories came with the owner's ID laminated to the front. A zippered inside pouch held alcohol wipes, a tourniquet, and compression bandages. In addition, the City provided one daily bullet per person. Which didn't mean people couldn't hoard them for massacres or family celebrations, or melt them down.

Each adult over eighteen received a morning bullet from the super upon showing the pistol's empty magazine. The trick was to use the bullet wisely. Endless choices presented themselves: graffiti artists, litterers, aggressive panhandlers, kids who looked at passersby funny, or reminded those passersby of the playground bully who punched them at recess.

It soon became obvious that the policy worked. Graffiti dropped by eighty-seven percent. The streets looked as they had in an earlier era. No litter clogged the drains, no spent newspapers wrapped them-selves around people's heels to trip them up. The boroughs cut back sanitation crews.

During the policy's first six months, cemeteries filled to capacity, which meant that crematoria did big business. So did charter boats: for fifty dollars, loved ones could scatter the ashes of their dead at sea

like old sailors. A brisk black market in non-sanctioned weapons—
Colts, Lugers, semiautomatics—grew up, too.

Sydney Simich woke into a blustery October Wednesday during the
policy's second year. Rain was expected. Winds whipped the gingko
trees outside her window. On this particular morning, she shook off
a dream of her estranged cousins, Max, Avon, and Ruthie, and her
Aunt Julie, their mother. Her Uncle Glen, in real life a convicted,
imprisoned pedophile, had won back his family.

In the dream, they lived in the same ranch house they'd always
shared, in the Indianapolis suburbs. The children were as young as
the last time they'd all played together in real life—Max was eight,
Avon just five, and little Ruthie, three. But in the dream they were
tiny: Syd saw them as if they were miniaturized dolls in a dollhouse.

She woke queasy and sweaty. Glen was still in prison, but the
thought of what he'd done made her reach reflexively under her pillow for the Beretta. She sat up, rubbed her clammy arms, and sighed.

She was not bitchy with PMS for a change. The hormones pervad-
ing the food supply made PMS universal; women got two extra sick
days each month. Men complained so bitterly against this discrimi-
nation that some companies gave male employees two sick days a
month for the Beasties, caused by overimbibing, nonfatal bullet
wounds, divorce or breakup, or the death of a friend.

Matt thought Beastie Days Off were ridiculous. "Syd, a BDO means
you can't hold your liquor or you're a whiny baby! Besides, if I take
a single day off—for anything—they'll think I'm a pushover." Matt
was angling to make partner; he couldn't afford to show weakness.

And even if he wanted a day off, where would he escape? They
shared his one-bedroom on the Bowery, but even combining Syd's
income as a City welfare worker with Matt's as an investment company attorney, they could barely afford it. The tub was in the kitchen,
the toilet was in a hall closet they shared with their neighbors, the
Saxons. The room with the toilet had no sink.

At first, Sydney had been appalled. How did you go to the bathroom without a sink? She was glad she'd left Long Island's fancy
North Shore for Lower Manhattan, and for Matt Gleeson, Esquire, but

she missed the spacious, modern bathroom attached to her ample, airy bedroom. She missed the bookshelves and doodads that had lined the marble mantel above her fireplace. She missed Mirta, the family maid, so good at cleaning and cooking, the linens that washed and folded themselves behind Sydney's back, the lint and dust that disappeared like magic—all the being-done-for.

She loved Matt. Sometimes she wasn't sure why. He was so . . . average. He had thinning reddish hair. A nearly hairless barrel chest with tiny pink nipples. He was not well endowed. "Make do with what you have," she told herself as she tried to feel him inside her.

The policy had made it terribly hard to meet new people. Most people had to use the Internet, which wasn't very safe. Sydney had met Matt the old-fashioned way, though, just before the policy came in: her parents knew his.

Her mother introduced them at a cocktail party when Sydney and Matt were home from college for winter break. The two of them took off for her upstairs bedroom, donned latex, and made love. A typical first date: no talking, just sex. Two days later, Syd called Matt for a date. They talked over dinner but not during sex.

Soon they saw each other regularly, at her parents' house, where she still lived after graduating from college, or at Matt's. They spent nearly every evening and most weekends together until Syd moved in. His place offered an escape from her parents' rules and quirks. She was tired, too, of riding the Long Island Rail Road.

Meanwhile, the new policy took effect. At first, the whole idea disturbed them both. Over late-night dinners and microbrews, they spent hours arguing with each other and friends. In the end, though, no one refused: to remain a City resident, a person had to carry a gun. Period. Licenses, Berettas, and fanny packs came by mail, automatically, like voter registration cards or jury duty notices.

As New Yorkers do, Matt and Sydney adapted. After a disgruntled client, a stockbroker, gunned down Nate, Matt's law school classmate, on the courthouse steps, they accepted reality. Nate had been one of the few in their circle who favored the new policy. "Think of all the lying, cheating scumbags we won't have to protect anymore, Matt," he'd said.

Sydney's college friend, Francesca, also supported the law. Repeatedly sexually harassed by a workmate, she quietly confessed to Syd and Matt one night that she'd taken matters into her own hands. Francesca's attitude, even her posture, had changed: no more sloped shoulders, downcast eyes, shaking hands. Francesca seemed almost radiant. Free.

The new policy had virtually dismantled the justice system. Like those old state mental hospitals emptied decades before, prisons stood vacant. Courts dealt only with contracts and regulations. Corporate lawyers like Matt just droned on, stupefying the few spectators who still bothered to attend. Divorce, custody, and personal-injury cases almost always settled out of court, usually with gunplay. Dockets cleared quickly. Lawyers and judges had more time than even they wanted for golf and racquetball.

Matt was happy that Syd could protect herself; work gave him enough to worry about. On beautiful weekends, he and Sydney wandered the High Line. They took target practice at the shooting range there, and then, over lunch, enjoyed the view of the Hudson. Sydney was surprised at how good it felt to squeeze the trigger. She couldn't figure out why she was so hesitant to use her pistol on people instead of pigeons or paper targets. No one had enraged her enough, she supposed. Not even Gus, her boss. Not yet.

Matt hadn't said whether he'd killed anyone yet. She was glad when he came home intact, with clean clothes. Walking to work, though Wall Street was two miles from the Bowery, made that easier. Neither of them could help getting blood on their clothes sometimes. The bottle of OxiClean under the sink saved dry-cleaning fees.

"I see you're up," Matt said. "Gotta dash. The board's trying to decide whether to prosecute or execute that guy I told you about. How about drinks and dinner at that place near the Exchange?"

Syd nodded. The door slammed behind him. He hadn't bothered locking it again. "Why should I?" he always said. "You're armed and dangerous. Everybody is now."

Sydney ran tepid water into the kitchen tub, feeling queasy after the dream. A sheen of sweat covered her. Shivering, she perched on the tub's edge for a quick sponge bath. She tossed talcum powder every-where. She dressed for their date in a pale blue skirt and pink silk blouse.

She checked her Beretta, zipped it into the fanny pack, and snapped it around her waist. She chugged eight ounces of enriched soy milk with an Abilify and Cymbalta chaser, plus a horse-sized multivitamin. "Breakfast of Champions," she said aloud, smiling crookedly.

She donned her tweed overcoat and tossed a mini-umbrella into the outer pocket. Freddy, the building superintendent, was at his post two flights down, counting out bullets to Nikki and Josh Saxon.

Before the new policy, Freddy had never bothered about the ten-ants. He barely responded to dire requests to fix a backed-up toilet or dripping sink. Now he was Mr. Punctuality, dispensing each morn-ing's bullets with a solicitous grin.

Nikki waved good-bye as she and Josh left for work. "Hey, Freddy," Sydney said in a monotone. She hated his smug face. She racked the Beretta's barrel and kicked out its magazine. Freddy made a big pro-duction of handing her a dun-colored bullet. "Have a nice day," he said insincerely.

She gave him a leftover fragment of her lopsided grin. "Yeah, you too."

The early drizzle became a downpour. Sydney opened her umbrella and marched the four blocks to the Spring Street station. 8:43. Damn, she'd never get a seat. The crush of people pressed the gun into her ribs, which nudged her into each commuter's morning ritual, considering whom to shoot today and why.

The conductor, if he closed the doors before she got on. That smartly dressed businessman, if he beat her to a seat. Gus, right between the eyes, if he so much as raised an eyebrow when Syd came in a few minutes late, or tried one more appalling double entendre. Her secre-tary, Blanche the Avalanche, if she guessed again what Syd was think-ing before Syd knew it herself. The sandwich man, if he slathered on too much mayo or forgot the thin-sliced tomatoes yet again. Sneering Freddy. No, leering Gus. No, her fucking pedophile Uncle Glen!

Revenge fantasies flooded her. She pushed through the turnstile. Today as always, vibrant images filled Sydney's commute: gray-black gunshot residue on a firing hand; bystanders' blood-spattered, overly bleached dress shirts; hiked-up skirts showing the holey underpants of women who'd never listened to their mothers; redness ebbing from noses, ears, corners of mouths. Sydney was inured to violence; everyone was. It was just another day in the City.

Inside the Fourteenth Street station, Syd hit the stairs for the northbound N and R. Of course a Q came instead, followed by an L on the opposite track. Syd grew more and more impatient. Three S shuttles came and went. She got mad at herself for not going over to the S platform. But she stayed where she was, waiting more and more impatiently for the 7. She paced and pursued her fantasies, murdering a potential mugger, a muttering old lady, a kid who stared at her two beats too long, and anyone else whose gaze was too direct.

An R train finally screeched out of the darkness. People crammed themselves through the opening doors. Syd knew she'd never get a seat on the shorter trip to Times Square. She clutched the closest metal pole for balance. Her umbrella puddled on the floor, rain mixing with old blood. People jostled for a handhold on the center poles. The train swung along a curved embankment, and everyone swayed together like a choir.

One bullet. Just one. Some days she saved it for her walk home, especially in the early dark, on a windswept day like this. Other days, she shot a pigeon, or the occasional sparrow or wren, or a screaming cat being screwed in an alley. She hadn't shot another human. She'd come close. Some days she didn't use her bullet at all. Saving for a rainy day. Maybe this was that day. Syd looked at the dripping people and umbrellas crowding onto the car and hummed the old song to herself.

Finally, just before Twenty-Eighth Street, her second-to-last stop, Sydney wedged herself into a seat, grateful for the respite. No one who'd pissed her off enough to invite a shot remained in the car. She avoided others' eyes, though. No way to tell when someone might get annoyed because she was staring. Syd chewed her lip and kept her head down. Yesterday replayed in her head.

Three went down. An elderly woman shot a young man in low-riding jeans who sat too wide. "Gimme one of them seats, boy," she'd demanded. He ignored her and spread his legs wider, owning his double space. Everyone else inspected the swaying subway floor but kept talking or chewing gum.

The old woman unzipped her pack. She hauled herself to her feet. She stood before the arrogant punk, gripping her pistol two-handed. Its muzzle nudged his torso. The Beretta's report cracked across the noisy, crowded car. A few passengers jumped, but most continued studying the floor.

The teenager gasped. A crimson zero appeared below his left clavicle. His mouth gaped. A trickle of blood seeped from one corner. His legs twitched closed, releasing the seat. He slid to the floor, clutching himself, and curled up. Shoving him disdainfully aside with a booted foot, his executioner took her seat. She beckoned to a stooped middle-aged man with a cane. He took the now-vacant place beside her.

A businessman in a sleek Prada suit pressed himself too closely behind an attractive young woman. At first she seemed to allow for it; bodies jam-packed the car. She must have felt him stiffen. She unzipped the blue pouch with one hand and clung to the pole they shared with the other. She drew her black Beretta stealthily, made a tight pirouette, and fired, winging him in the shoulder.

He threw up his hands instinctively, which made him lose his balance and fall to the floor. She kicked him several times. At the train's next stop, he staggered to his feet, stumbling off with a blood-soaked arm. The woman pulled a wipe from her fanny pack and dabbed the blood spray off her jacket.

The third one dropped on Sydney's way home, a few stops before Spring Street. A teenager in a slick red poncho glided a slim hand inside an older man's tan raincoat. As the hand closed around his wallet, the man cursed. He reached into the back of his pants for his Vietnam-era Colt .45. He stepped back, crouched into shooting stance, and plugged the kid in the shin.

The boy dropped, screaming, his leg shattered. His own unsheathed Beretta clattered along the aisle. A middle-aged woman helped the boy, still screaming, drag himself toward the next car. She pulled him onto his good leg. He leaned on her and wrenched open the heavy inner door.

He fell through. The door slammed shut. A tide of his blood seeped underneath. The corrugated steel floor between the cars was slippery with it. The older man fled at the next stop, afraid he'd be questioned. The policy imposed a heavy penalty for unauthorized weapons.

Finally: Times Square at Broadway. On the platform, stretcher bearers awaited other cars' dead and maimed. Ambulance drivers were as rich these days as plumbers and City officials. Upstairs, Syd got on line at the coffee truck for her usual, a large cappuccino and a low-fat blueberry muffin. The nearby fruit vendor had mangoes on special, three for five bucks. Their green had matured to matte ruby. She hadn't realized how hungry she was. She bought three.

Provisions in both hands, she caught the elevator to work, pushing 11 with her elbow. On her floor, she glared into the retinal scanner. The doors whooshed open. Sydney stepped out facing her agency's logo, a giant fist holding a nautilus shell. Light rays pierced both skin and shell. Sydney remained puzzled about who might have designed it, or for what purpose. She couldn't see what the fist, the shell, or the rays had to do with the City's welfare system. Well, maybe the fist.

The few clients still eligible for welfare were the Verys: very ill; very old; very disturbed. They shuffled in each week for their paltry allowance and one of the pantry boxes lining the welfare office's shelves, pre-packed with dried pasta, canned tuna and beans, Spam, the rare apple or head of lettuce.

In exchange, they donated a pint of blood or plasma, or a day of labor. The need for these, especially labor, was great. The Verys carried subway stretchers, filled in for the suddenly dead as temporary workers, or stoked the fires of the competing crematorium conglomerates.

Most of the needy had been picked off during the first few months of the new policy, dispatched by the trigger-happy as leeches or ingrates, worthless vermin, or lazy good-for-nothings. The survivors, however, became essential; their work was critical to keeping the City's streets, subways, and buildings clear of the dead and clean of the mess. They rarely had time to pick up their boxes, though their paperwork still flooded in for Sydney to fill out and file.

Wednesday remained uneventful. The most memorable thing Syd did was to strip the first ripe mango. She leaned over the staff lounge sink, tearing off great gobs of drippy flesh with her teeth. Gus came in, slamming the door as usual. He pulled a yogurt container from the fridge and peeled off the foil. Catching Sydney's eye, he licked the foil slowly. She dropped her gaze. If Gus broke the silence with one more rude pun or sexist joke, she'd let him have it right where it counted.

He winked elaborately and left. She ate the second mango quickly. It nauseated her, but she peeled and ate the third, ripping the skin from its flanks with her teeth, exposing and devouring the yellow meat. She no longer tasted the subtle, musky flavor.

Her secretary, Blanche the Avalanche, plopped down on a molded plastic chair that barely held her. She watched Syd clear the mango mess and wash off the dripping yellow juice. "He bother you?" As usual, guessing Syd's thoughts before Syd knew what they were. Which annoyed Syd no end.

"Of course not. I pay him no mind." Syd ticked a mental checkbox: shoot Avalanche soon. Between the eyes but up a bit, blinding her third eye.

Sydney returned to her office. Stacks of forms and reports buried her City-issued metal desk. The files seemed to replicate. Each case she closed added two others. Fewer Verys were benefit-eligible, but meanwhile, a tidal wave of death certificates, changes in custody arrangements when one or more parents were killed, job assignments, and performance reviews rolled across the agency.

Five thirty came and went. Shit, she was late. Again. She slid pale-pink gloss across her lips, preparing to meet Matt. She envied the fact that he walked to work most days, despite the distance. Pedestrians were far safer than those cramped into metal boxes on bus lines and subways. Matt probably had to take the First Avenue 15 bus today, though, because of the rain. It would be jammed. Good. Gave him a taste of what she dealt with daily.

She checked herself once more in the bathroom mirror and

shrugged on her tweed coat. Its pocket was still damp from her umbrella, which she slung over her wrist. The wind was still strong, but the rain had turned to fine mist. Stowing her umbrella in the other pocket, Syd bought a one-dollar spritz of Chanel No. 19 at a perfume wagon. These had cropped up all over town, entrepreneurs' savvy but unsuccessful effort to mask the smell of death and soiled underwear profitably.

Three blocks to the Crosstown 7. On the platform, she reached under her coat to adjust her fanny pack. Her hand brushed the gun through the nylon. Though her last imaginary score-settling took place eight hours ago, fantasies and memories spooled out again in lurid color like an uninterrupted movie.

She got to Grand Central and waited for a southbound local 6. That would get her to Chambers, where she'd change for Wall Street and meet Matt. *Cli-ick, cli-ick.* Though she'd heard this dull, distinct sound so often, the hairs bristled on her neck. Sydney held her breath; she didn't dare glance back. Anything could happen. Sometimes people got shot just for looking. Or looking at the wrong person the wrong way.

The sound of the gun cocking made Sydney aware that she was tired, bone tired. The southbound 6 to the financial district was even later than that morning's R. She had to keep still.

Station benches were long gone, replaced by low, narrow perches that commuters could lean against but homeless people couldn't sit or sleep on. Sydney leaned until the train came.

Maybe it wasn't physical weariness. Maybe she'd just had enough of her job, her colleagues, the gory commute, the endless slog up subway stairs. She was sick of the sludge of caked blood, the refrain of gunfire and screaming.

She might even be tired of Matt. Her father had been eager to get her out of his house. "Start making babies," he said. Nobody had grandchildren anymore, and he wanted one. Even though she and Matt stopped using condoms, she still got her period. Despite their mothers' hectoring, they still hadn't set a wedding date.

The train hurtled from the dark tunnel, brakes screaming. Syd jumped from her perch and pushed into the waiting car. A large man shoved her from behind, like a Japanese pusher during Tokyo rush hour. The rankness of sweat, congealed blood, and evacuated bodies filled the car. As Syd hustled for a seat, she snatched bleach swabs from the overhead dispenser and held them under her nose. The bleach, meant for disinfecting flesh wounds, did little to overcome the stench.

No seats. Sydney grabbed a metal pole, wedging her hand between two others. Something slimy seeped beneath her hand. Blood. She tightened her grip as the train lurched forward. She and the others swayed with the train, bending their knees in unison. All kinds of people, just riding home at day's end. Furled umbrellas dripped onto the floor, liquefying the day's dried blood.

She scanned the lucky sitting ones. A well-dressed woman juggling shopping bags from Henri Bendel and Saks to keep them from touching that floor began the transit pantomime signaling imminent departure. She slung the bags from her shoulder and reached beneath her Burberry to adjust her fanny pack. Sydney, too, prepared to move, shifting the pistol under her drab tweed coat.

Releasing the sticky pole, Sydney pushed up the aisle and stood before the woman, waiting. She grasped a ceiling pole to steady herself. The woman stayed put. The next stop came and went. Syd's feet throbbed. Oh, how she wanted to sit down. She glowered at the elegant, obstinate woman.

At the next stop, the woman abruptly hoisted her bags and exited with the hordes. "Mother—" Syd muttered. She aimed for the vacancy, landing hard against the knee of a neighboring woman.

"Ow! Goddamn it, bitch, get off me!"

Syd pressed her thighs together, shrinking into her just-claimed seat. "I'm so sorry," she said.

The woman raged unappeased, ignoring Syd's apology. "Watch yourself, asshole!"

Syd froze. She faced forward, molding herself into her narrow space. Still cursing, the other woman dug around in her clothes. She unzipped her fanny pack. Sydney couldn't look, of course, but fumbled for her own pistol. The woman whipped hers out first. In a single fluid movement, she cocked and aimed. As she squeezed the trigger, though, the train jolted. The round hit Syd's left bicep instead of her chest.

Shock stunned Sydney for a few seconds. Pain, sharp and terrible, came next. Sydney smothered a scream. She shook herself and looked at her ripped and bloody coat, grimacing in pain and disgust. Though the thick tweed caught most of the bullet's force, blood soaked through her blouse and coat. Sydney raised her arm and held it up. Only a flesh wound, no broken bones. The boy with his shin blown away came to mind. Sydney closed her eyes, grateful that the train, and the tight quarters, spoiled the woman's aim.

The shooter calmly replaced her pistol. She sighed, avenged, and closed her eyes. Her angry face settled into a glum mask. She dozed.

Fury replaced shock. Sydney hadn't meant to knock into that bitch! She fumbled for her Beretta. She straightened and swung around. Remembering how the older woman took care of the wide-sitting teenager, Sydney pressed the muzzle to her sleeping neighbor's forehead. She pulled the trigger.

The woman's eyes bugged out in surprise, even though she died instantly. The back of her head split open. Brains and blood spattered surprisingly far, stippling Syd and those nearby, as well as the car's wall and window. Everyone looked elsewhere or pretended to sleep. The woman crumpled forward, falling heavily onto the floor. As the train advanced south, her body, like an oversized bowling ball, rolled away and back.

Unlike the S yesterday morning, this car's interior was silent except for the train's racket and the rails' squealing. Sydney shrugged off her coat. She folded it into her lap, noticing that the right sleeve was already stiff with the woman's blood and brain glop.

Blood flecked Sydney's pink blouse and soaked the sleeve. Wincing, she raised her arm again, rotating it to see if the bullet went through. She smiled at the bloody, jagged exit wound. With her good arm, Syd pulled another bleach pad from the dispenser and swabbed the wound, flinching at the pain.

The train pulled into Canal Street. She rummaged in her fanny pack for a pressure bandage. Another passenger helped her apply it. She thanked him, but their eyes didn't meet. Keeping her wounded arm above her head to make the blood clot, she settled back until the next train change.

At Chambers, she waited for a 4 or 5. Two more stops. She groped one-handed in her fanny pack for a pre-wash and dabbed awkwardly at her bloodstained blouse. Feeling rocky but more in control, Syd caught the next 4. Two short stops later, she tugged on her overcoat carefully and climbed to Wall Street, over an hour late.

Sunset faded behind the old stone buildings, tinting their granite steps gold and rose. Time had worn away the lions' faces, but they still stood regal and calm, flanking the esplanade.

Sydney strode up the steps and into the restaurant's dim foyer.

She paused in the doorway. Matt sat unruffled at the tall mahogany bar, relaxing. He stirred his martini idly and signaled for another. Perched there, stooped over his drink, silent and distant, he looked like all the other men. He didn't see Sydney. He didn't see her leave.

WHAT IT COMES down to, Doc, is—bang!—I lost my mind! Presto! Reducto! Had it. Lost it. Gone! Alles kaputt. Whoever that asshole was who said a mind is a terrible thing to lose, Doc, he had it all wrong. I mean look at me, little ol' Andrew, for cryin' out loud. Three squares a day. Baskets of apples all over the place, art therapy classes! I mean, I've never seen such a confabulation of crap.

Not to mention the hour a day I get to spend with a hottie like you. Can you believe it, Doc? No, sir, a mind is most definitely not a terrible thing to lose. I should know. For sixteen years, I had one. Then bang! Oh, excuse me, Doc. Poor choice of words. Under the circumstances. No pun intended, unless Freud was right and there really are no accidents. In which case, "bang" certainly was intended, but only by my subconscious.

That Billingsley, what a dumb shit. It was freaky, Doc. Ambulances, firetrucks everywhere. And cops. Christ, I never saw so many cops. Big fat cop bellies hanging over their belts like blubber awnings. All standing around. I never saw such a concentration of cluelessness. Not to digress, Doc, but after watching those cops that day, I honestly don't think they've got much in the way of minds, know what I mean? I mean, would they even know if they lost theirs?

As far as my own mind, though, I say, *Quod cito acquiritur cito perit*: easy come, easy go. People lose things all the time. Doc.

Direction. Virginity. Even their looks. Think about that one, Doc. Kind of scary, isn't it? I mean, "Love goes toward love as schoolboys from their books," as the Bard says, but how is a hottie like you gonna hold their interest once old tempus fugits? Botox can't redux. Kaputt!

Know what I think is more interesting to lose? Your temper. Think about it, Doc. I mean, you have a temper. I have a temper. My brother has a temper, like when I used to hide his little sock monkey. My point is that all God's chillun got tempers. But how do we know we got them? By losing them, that's how.

Your temper's there, but nobody can see it, or touch it, or hear it. It's just there. Like a nano-nuclear reactor perking away. Then—bang! You lose it. And suddenly everybody knows you've got one. Only you *don't*. Why? Because you've lost it. Isn't that weird? I love meta-physical shit like this, don't you, Doc? It's so freaky.

Take my dad. He's temperless. Most of the time he has absolutely no temper. He can't. It would be impossible: he loses his constantly. He's a real Temperless Joe, my dad. I mean he loses his temper all over the place. The one person who could always find it was my mom. She could find my dad's temper like that. Especially before they split. Now, not so much.

He loses his temper other places, too. One time even in Mr. Tilley's office. You know Old Tilley, don't you, Doc? The headmaster at Pelham Academy. It was something to see. Dad screamed so loud I thought he'd bust a gut.

The occasion was my Personal Bizarro Day, in freshman year. When I threw the desk out the window. Shit, throwing a desk seemed perfectly reasonable at the time. I thought I'd get the freshman Latin prize, you know? But that dickhead Gorman got it. I mean, I lost out because that asshole Mr. Turner didn't like me. So I threw the desk. It seemed like a reasonable alternative to punching Asshole Turner's fat face in. Of course, I should have been more careful. How was I supposed to know that Mrs. Tilley had picked that very moment to show the gardener where to plant her flowers?

Mr. Tilley told him I was suspended. That's when my dad really lost his temper. He started yelling that with all the money he and Uncle Deke give Pelham, Tilley was dumber than a box of rocks to do such a thing. Tilley could go fuck himself if he thought my dad was still going to be chairman of the Fall Bullroast.

And then, even though he'd lost it in Tilley's office, I guess my dad found his temper somewhere on our way home. See, Doc, when they split, my mom started working. Tilley couldn't reach her, so he got my dad instead.

At first my dad's driving all stonyfaced, but by the time we got to the house, I guess he found his temper. My mom was home from work, digging in her garden. She saw my dad and got all worried: what was I doing home when I should have been at lacrosse?

"What's happened? What's happened?" she kept saying.

My dad starts screaming, "Tell her. Tell her about the stupid ass- hole thing you did, Andrew." So I told her I threw the desk. I thought my dad was going to smack me, because, see, he's a lawyer and he knows all that shit about the whole truth. He yells at me, "You tell her everything, damn you, Andrew!"

So I told her how the desk almost fell on Mrs. Tilley.

And my dad goes, "And—? And—? Tell her the rest, Andrew, or I swear I'll break your arm."

So I say, "And I'm suspended." And my mom's holding this heavy flowerpot and standing there like she doesn't know what to do with it. She just sort of hugs it and wipes her face, because she's crying a little, which makes her face all muddy. I felt real bad about that.

Then my dad says, "It's not that bad." He tells her he got sus- pended once, and so did Uncle Deke. He doesn't want her to feel too bad, because she feels so bad already, because of the split and all. She's got custody, but our dad, he's a good guy, Doc. He really is. Peter and me, we can't complain. Some dads, when there's a split, they're such dicks. But our dad, he's okay. He gets us almost every weekend. I can tell his girlfriend doesn't like it, but he still gets us and does stuff with us.

Even with her working, usually it's our mom who picks us up at school. But the afternoon of Grand Bizarro Day, it was my dad. That's how I knew something had happened. I don't know how I knew, but I did. And I knew my mom had to be with Peter.

They wanted to herd us into the field house—after Columbine, they knew they had to keep us together—but it was being renovated. So they put us on the bleachers at the football field. And it started raining. Not heavy, but steady. The drops were big. You know, Doc, this is going to sound crazy, but it made me think of nuclear rain. Everything was so gray.

Man, it was weird. Parents were running up and down the rows of bleachers looking for their kids. Kids were crying. And I don't just mean little kids, either.

The faculty? Man, they were freaky, too. They looked sort of dazed. Usually they strut around like the Lords of Pelham, but I tell you, Doc, on Grand Bizarro Day, they looked just plain scared. I heard some of them saying Mr. Turner got hit. They said Billingsley went into the faculty lounge and just opened up. A lot were dead. Nobody said "shot."

Everybody was surprised it was that asshole Billingsley. He was real quiet, you know. Not freaky, just real quiet. He never really hung out with anyone. He *was* freaky in one way, though: his mother drove him to school every day. Here he was a senior, and his mother drove him to school. I mean, how weird was that?

People said it was because he didn't get accepted anywhere. That would sure do it to you. Twelve years at Pelham and getting in nowhere. That would do it. I mean, that's what Pelham's all about, isn't it? Getting in somewhere good.

With the rain and all, I was glad I had on my lacrosse uniform, so at least my mom wouldn't freak about me getting my good pants wet, because, you know, she's working and she doesn't have a lot of time now. I kept standing up, concentrating on trying to find Peter where they had the lower-school kids. I thought he'd spot me easier in my uniform.

Peter, he is such a little kid. Even before Grand Bizarro Day, he did weird stuff. He made these nests on the floor with his blankets and slept there. I used to call him birdbrain. He was so little and dumb he didn't even know I was making fun of him. It was pathetic.

Like once, two years ago, we couldn't find him. It was night, we'd just started Christmas break, and my mom and dad were still together. My dad was putting up the tree. We had this tradition, you know: we always started the tree with the star. Most people do the star last, but we did it first. Every year, my dad picked up Peter so he could put it on top. And every year my dad made a big deal out of how heavy Peter was getting and how he could barely lift him. So that year, it's time, we're ready for the star, but there's no Peter.

I mean, we can't find him anywhere. Not in the house. Not even the garage. And my mom's getting all hysterical, 'cause Peter was only six then. So my dad and me go looking for him. It was dark and cold. Really cold.

My dad goes one way. I go the other, toward this big old Episcopal church at the end of St. Bart's Way. Every year they put up a big Christmas scene. It's huge, with cows and sheep and the Wise Men and all. I swear to God, that's where I found Peter. Right in there with all the animals and angels. He had his old blanket. He was wrapping it around Baby Jesus.

Know what he said? "I just wanted to cover Him up. He was cold. He needed a blanket." That's what he said, Dr. Joyner. I swear to God. I told you, Peter did some weird stuff.

On Grand Bizarro Day, Peter could have been anywhere. So I wasn't too worried. But still, I wanted to see him. I kept getting down to look, but they kept making me go back to the bleachers. I didn't want to get suspended again, you know, Doc. I mean some colleges will overlook one suspension. But not two. So I went back. And then, Mrs. Tilley—she came and sat with me. She just came and sat with me and put a blanket over me. After what I almost did to her, I felt sort of bad about that, but I let her do it. And she held an umbrella over me.

It was getting dark. Every time I saw headlights swinging into the drive, I thought to myself, "That's Mom." Because, see, even then I still thought it would be Mom who came for us. Mrs. Tilley's arm must've gotten tired, though. The way she started holding the umbrella, I couldn't see the headlights any more. I kind of pulled the blanket around me and just waited for whatever. But I still wanted to find Peter.

When I looked out again, the bleachers were almost empty. A few middle schoolers huddled in a corner. Out of the whole upper school, though, I was the only one left. Then I knew why Mrs. Tilley was being so nice. My dad was coming down the path. He had Uncle Deke with him. I could barely make them out in the dark. I stood up so they could see me. I didn't lose it or anything. I didn't get all blubbery like those other assholes. I just stood there and waited, you know?

My dad took the bleachers two at a time. He could do that because his legs are real long, Doc, you know? I'll probably be real tall, too. Did I tell you he was third in his class? And my uncle Deke, he was somewhere the hell up there, too. They both got into Yale.

And now that I'm in this place, I'm wondering if I'll even be able to get into Hip-Hop Community College. All because of Billingsley. Christ. Nowhere. Can you imagine that? Nowhere? No wonder he shot himself.

But sometimes I think it isn't worth trying to get in somewhere. Sometimes I just want to be real small. Like when I was under Mrs. Tilley's blanket, and I kept having this crazy thought that if I didn't move or anything, I could become real little. Yeah, that's what I wanted to be, Dr. Joyner. Little, but dense. Really, really dense, so that I wouldn't lose hardly a single particle of light. So that if people stepped on me, they'd feel me and say, "What the hell was that?"

And I'd think to myself, "You dumb shit, you're so dumb you can't even see what's right under your foot. And even if you did, you'd just think I'm a piece of dust or something, but I'm right here." You know, Doc? Like I could be perfectly still, too, and all my organs and all my cells would gravitate toward the center of my body. Like it was a black hole.

I just felt I could do that if I could stay in my closet. Everything was going fine, super-duper—lacrosse, my grades, all super-duper. And then—bang! I just woke up one day and felt like being in my closet. So I sat there all scrunched up, with the door open so I could see what was going on and still get out if I wanted to, wishing I was a nano-me. Small, but really, really dense. And I just wanted to sit there, getting denser and denser, and holding all the light, watching every move they made.

The Weight

Elaine LaMattina

DON'T THINK YOU can change my mind, Martin. No. Not even if you beg. I won't listen this time. The weight of the children, of what they meant and needed, always tipped the scale in your direction, but tonight will be different. You'll see. That's what you always say: *You'll see.*

Three weeks I've watched you. Three long weeks since you smacked around a twelve-year-old girl who's braver than her mother. You're such a creature of habit! You leave the HR office at precisely 5:05, sick of politeness and tired of all the company's whiners, your tie already loosened and hanging off your neck. You haven't noticed me. Not once in all these weeks. Ha!

But I'm not really surprised. Your mind is already in another place—smoky, dark, crowded. You already have the taste of tequila on your lips. Another Friday night, like so many others. You, predictable as ever, will crunch across the gravel to that shiny new F-150—another possession, like me and the girls.

You'll open the door, fumble in your pocket for keys, and start to whistle the hook of an old song: *Go down, Miss Moses, ain't nothin' you can say.* You'll slide into the driver's seat, yank off the tie, rev the engine, and take off.

No need to follow. I know where you go. Down Columbus, right on McClain. TOMMY'S BAR & GRILL—AIR CONDITIONED—2 FOR 1 HAPPY HOUR—FRI NITES. Jose Cuervo. Tommy knows that's yours.

You'll toss back six shots, exchanging lewd remarks with the other guys each time a woman walks in. Oh, if you could just see yourself.

No! I want you to see me instead. Me. Sitting there at the other end of the bar with a man you don't know. I want you to watch the way he takes my hand, presses his lips to my wrist. It might be worth the risk just to see the look on your face. Me, running my fingers through his hair as he gazes into my eyes. A man who sees me, Martin. Who knows I'd never cheat on him.

You can't believe that, can you? All your harsh accusations for all these years. You made holding a job impossible for me, going after the men I worked with, threatening to call their wives. This man would never do that. He would never raise a hand.

I want you to see him hook his thumb into the back pocket of my jeans, watch him open the door as we leave. Later, much, much later, I want you to notice that I'm whistling when I come home, that tune you whistled earlier. And I want you to wonder why.

Ah, I can anticipate your every gesture. The way you'll push yourself up from the recliner in the darkened living room, take hold of my arm, raise your fist, and slam it again and again into my ribs. Never my face, no, never. You'll hear me cry and beg, but you won't stop. You never do. That's not your habit. Still, it might be worth all that to give you, just once, a reason. To make the puzzle mean something I can almost understand.

You won't see me at Tommy's, though. You could never imagine me there. You're so sure I'm home, warming dinner, waiting for your plate to hit the wall, for you to yell, "You expect me to eat this shit?" But you won't give me a thought until you get up to go. Take your change off the bar, pat your pocket for your keys. *So long, Tommy. Catch ya next week.*

You'll stumble to the truck, rev the engine twice, and roar away. Up McClain slowly, left on Spruce, five blocks, now right on Hotchkiss. Just three more blocks. No sign of the police. You're going to make it. Pull into the driveway.

But tonight the house is dark. Where the hell am I, anyway? Kill the engine. Open the door. That's right, open it all the way. Get out, still wondering. Where could I be? In bed? At my mother's with the kids? Now slam out of the truck, hard enough to wake me if I'm asleep. Stagger to the porch, unlock the front door.

Oh, but something's wrong, isn't it? Your house key's missing. You really should take better care of things. You'll have to break the glass. Careful. Don't cut yourself. There. That's better. That should wake me up. Now reach through the broken pane and let yourself in. That's right. Slam that door, too, just in case. Now yell. Go ahead. Scream my name. No one but me will hear you, Martin. Why don't I answer? Where do you suppose I am? Silence. Is it possible you're all alone?

Switch on the hall light and climb the stairs. Head down the hall. Open the bedroom door. Grope for the switch. Darkness. Go ahead, try again. Still darkness. What the hell? Is it possible you've lost control? Curse now, yes. Wait. Curse again. Scream my name.

Do you feel it? The weight's shifted. Now it's in my hands. You're a dark shape in the doorway, Martin. Oh, what was that? An almost-remembered scent. Oil. Gun oil. Yes, that's it. A hard, metallic click.

The Glock in your nightstand. You'd never lock it away. You liked to ram in the magazine, rack the slide, aim it straight at me. Our intimate ritual. To tell me how important it is to hold it steady. Use both hands. Keep both eyes open. Aim and squeeze. *Go ahead and try it*, you said. *Try leaving. You'll see. I'll kill you before I let you leave.*

Go down, Miss Moses. Darkness. A dark target. Your curse, my name. Can you see me, Martin? A blinding flash. Yes, it's me. My face. *You'll see.* And I'll see you dead. My face burned forever into your darkening eyes.

The Accomplished Son

Jim Tomlinson

ONE SUMMER AFTERNOON when Toby Polk was
eleven years old, he found a rag-wrapped pistol
hidden in a slot up under his father's workshop
bench. At first he thought some stranger must
have put it there, a burglar, maybe, or a vagrant
passing through. His father, after all, was a quiet
man who spent his days alone in the workshop building chairs. To
the boy, Earl Polk seemed no more likely to own a pistol than a
howitzer. Still the gun was undeniable, solid in his hands. He
considered every possibility, and when he finally decided that it
must be his father's, a frizz of energy ran through him. Toby imagined
their lives changing again, things somehow returning to the way
they'd been before—before Arnel Embry, before his father's wounding,
before the hard times came.

He put the handgun back, then slid it out again. How perfectly it
fit, as if the slot were built just for this gun. Six months before, his
father, still clumsy in his wheelchair, had hired a carpenter. Together
they remodeled the workshop behind the family's Lily Road home.
They widened doorways and lopped lengths off the angle iron legs of
the radial arm saw and wood lathe. They built ramps in the shop, in
the house, and in between. It was then, the boy decided, that his
father must have chiseled the pistol slot.

Toby turned the thing over in his hands. The bright and oily heft
of the pistol surprised him. In years to come, he would know it as a

.38 Special, nickel plated, a dreamer's weapon, perfect for his father. But on that hot Sunday afternoon, as the boy crouched in crisp shavings of pine and cherry wood, he knew only that this was a powerful thing, and that the sensation he felt holding it was a pleasurable one. He wrapped the pistol again and put it back where he'd found it.

Toby didn't tell his mother, and he didn't tell Mike, the younger brother from whom he'd been hiding that afternoon. He kept the knowledge to himself, a private nugget, a secret charm of sorts.

In the next few weeks Toby would sometimes dream that his father, .38 in hand, rose up from his wheelchair. Balanced precariously, strangely invisible on his flimsy legs, he'd kill Arnel Embry, the man who had launched a thin metal dart from a pistol crossbow and paralyzed him, had sentenced him to life in that chair. Some nights Toby dreamed that his father tucked the muzzle under his own chin, and, draping a plastic shower curtain over his head to contain the mess, pulled the trigger. And some nights he dreamed that his father, joystick wheelchair revved up and power geared, pursued Toby's mother through the house and into the yard, bullets flying wildly, his aim spoiled by bumpy ramp joints.

Army Specialist Tobias Polk, just back from Iraq, remembers all this as he drives across Kentucky. It happened twelve years ago. The sun, low ahead and rising, burns red through June fog. Beside him, his wife, Inez, is buckled in. She adjusts the visor and loosens the Camry's shoulder belt around the ripe bulge of her belly. She says it's safer this way, safer for the baby she carries inside, leaving the belt slack across her.

Polk's six-month tour in Iraq, his third, has been shortened by a month. He'll be here in the world for the birth. His unit is in Kuwait now, decompressing, recharging before going back—Fallujah this time, if rumors prove true. He doesn't talk about any of this, not with Inez.

Polk's tooth, a molar, starts aching again. He takes out a small vial of clove oil, gets a drop on his finger, and rubs the gum. They'll be back in Arizona next week. He'll see a dentist then, have the damn thing pulled, once this family business is wrapped up.

As he drives, Polk stays alert—alert to other cars, to a small white pickup truck and a cadre of motorcycles, to a black plastic trash bag beside the roadway. He accelerates past a derelict Olds Cutlass abandoned in the breakdown lane. Freshly patched pavement disappears beneath the Camry's wheels. He squeezes the steering wheel. Polk has survived by being aware of such things. All his wife knows to worry about is seat-belt safety for their child.

"Do you miss it?" she asks. "Kentucky?"

Polk glances over. She has a cherub's profile, all upturn and roundness. An Arizona girl, her skin keeps its tan even in winter. Her hair is spiky and short, bleached platinum this week. He enjoys looking at her, feels calmer when he does. He reaches across and touches her belly. He wants to love this child she carries. On the first ultrasound, Inez thought she saw the nub of a penis. Later ones haven't shown it, though. He mulls this endlessly on nights when he can't sleep, trying to imagine it—Toby Polk, father of a daughter. It seems unreal.

"Do you?" Inez asks again. "Miss it?"

"Kentucky? Sometimes." He draws his hand back. "When my parents divorced, that part sucked."

"You don't talk about it."

"Shit happens," he says. He rummages in the console, clatters plastic cases, searching for music to play.

"You were happier," Inez asks, "once she left, once she took you to Phoenix?"

"What do you think? New state, new school, her scrambling for work, me all of fifteen? That sound like a picnic to you?" He remembers school fights, battles at home. "Can we talk about something else?"

"I'm just asking, Toby." She wears her hurt expression now. "Married people do that, have conversations, talk about things."

"And I've told you before." Polk lets the console lid slam shut. "Life was shit for Mike and me. And when we moved in with Ma's jerk boyfriend . . . ," he says. "What the fuck. You met Barry. You know."

Not half of it, really, does she know.

Or need to know.

The roadway dips. Fog drifts across in wispy patches. On an

overpass ahead, two boys straddle bicycles. Their hands are stuffed in the pockets of camouflage jackets. Polk's mouth goes dry, the pain inside a dull ache. His hands tighten on the steering wheel. He waits, waits, waits, and then he swerves the car into the breakdown lane.

Inez lurches sideways, grabs the door handle as they speed beneath the boys. "Jesus, Toby! What was that?"

"Couple of punks," he says, "loitering on the overpass."

She's quiet for a minute. Then Inez reaches a hand across the console, and she squeezes his shoulder. It's a gesture of love, he thinks, or maybe sympathy. He can't tell for sure anymore.

"Sorry, babe," he says.

Her hand slides to the back of his neck. Her fingers work on the tension there. "It's okay, Toby," she says. "Honest. It's okay."

Toby steers the car up the gravel driveway and parks behind his brother's rust-rotted pickup truck. Mike Polk pushes a sputtering lawnmower across the splotchy yard of the house on Lily Road. An oily exhaust hangs overhead in a flat blue cloud.

"This is it?" Inez asks, lowering the car window and shading her eyes.

"This is it," Toby says. He shifts into park and sets the brake.

"I imagined it bigger."

"It was," he says, "when I lived here." He gets out and goes around the car to help his wife. She's already out, stretching, hands braced low on her back when he gets there.

Mike stops the mower long enough to wipe his brow with a sleeve. He shouts over, asks if they've gone by the cemetery.

"Not yet. This here's Inez," Toby shouts back.

Mike waves and tells them he'll be done mowing in two shakes, that he wants the place looking good for them. "Go right in. Make yourselves homely," Mike tells them, and a stupid grin cracks his face. "Help yourselves to whatever you need."

Toby reaches into the car and lifts out his wife's shoulder bag. Mike yanks the starter cord and the mower clatter-roars again. The sudden racket startles Toby, sends an electric buzz down his back and legs. Across the yard, the machine kicks up dust whorls.

Inez grabs his arm. "Some welcome," she says in his ear.

He takes her hand, squeezes it lightly. "Don't," he says. "Okay?"

Her gaze goes to the gravel between their feet. She draws a breath like a diver getting ready, then lets it out in a slow, hissing leak. It's her way of relenting.

Toby shoulders the bag strap, and he leads Inez past his brother's truck, up three leaf-stained concrete steps to the side door. He pauses there, the doorknob familiar in his hand, and he looks back. The long ramp is gone. What remains of it is piled out back, the weathered lumber a haphazard stack. Bent nails point every which way.

"Arnel Embry came to the funeral," Mike says in the kitchen. He opens the refrigerator, stoops to look in. His long hair, still wet and comb-streaked after his shower, slips like a curtain across his cheek. "You drink beer?" he calls to Inez. They left her in the front room with a photo album.

"Gave it up." Her voice has a drifty sound, as if she's distracted. "Pregnant, you know."

Mike grabs two bottles from the refrigerator, hands one to Toby. "I shoved the old man's stuff to the back," he says. "Maybe I should throw it out." He looks at Toby as if it's a question.

"Embry showed up?" Toby says, twisting the cap off. "Some nerve."

"Nine people came to his goddamn funeral." Mike holds up fingers. "Nine, and that includes me, and it includes the preacher, and it includes the fucking mortician."

"But Arnel Embry?" Toby says.

Mike huffs out a sickly laugh. "At least he came."

Toby takes a drink and looks around the kitchen. "He died here?"

Mike points his bottle at the chrome-rimmed table. "Over there." He starts toward the front room. In the doorway he says, "Embry asked about you, why you weren't there."

"What balls," Toby says.

In the front room, Mike drops into their father's chair. "I told him you were busy snipering some Taliban."

Toby Polk winces. "Wrong country," he tells Mike. "Different bad guys." The air in the room is viscous now, hard to breathe. He goes to a window, opens it, and leans on the sill looking out. His pulse throbs in his tooth, his jaw, everywhere in his head.

Inez has his wrist, then his hand, and she tugs him back to the couch to sit beside her. She takes up the photo album again and opens it across their legs. "You were one darling boy," she says. He feels the sting of her pity. It's the last thing he wants from a wife.

Long past midnight, Toby Polk lies on a cot in his childhood bedroom. Inez sleeps in a twin bed nearby. Nighttime sounds filter through the window screen, a dog barking at the night, crickets chirping back and forth, a rooster mistaking moonlight for an early dawn. In the ceiling cracks and textures, Polk finds familiar faces, ones he'd found there as a boy—gnarled witches, midgets and gnomes.

Despite the beers, he hasn't slept, can't sleep, like so many other nights. In Iraq they've got combat pills to keep you awake three days straight—longer if you need. And they've got pills for sleeping afterward. Trouble is, lately those don't work. And now the damn tooth makes sleep impossible.

In his mind, Polk replays that evening's visit to his father's grave, the sad look of the place, how a kind of rage rose up in him just seeing it, a nothing place, hardly there at all. It shouldn't bother him so. He knows that. He worries that his life is coming loose again, imagines himself careening, crashing. Each time his mind drifts toward sleep, a jolt of dread yanks him back, even more alert. Panic lurks behind his eyes waiting for any brief unguarding. It could happen soon, he knows, very soon, any moment now.

The throb is deep in his jaw now, its taste like tin under his tongue. He remembers the time he fractured a front tooth in a fight with Lonnie McCray. He must have been seven then. Maybe eight. His mother wrapped two cloves in a fresh mullein leaf. She told him to hold it against the tooth, said the pain would go away. Instead it got worse. So his father took him back to the workshop, and he brought out a cloth pouch. Inside he kept dried jimsonweed.

"Our secret," Earl Polk said, and he waited for his boy to nod that it was. Then he packed a pipe and lit it for Toby to puff. The smoke tasted harsh. At first Toby coughed. The world got weird then, and he thought he was floating, his pain drifting miles away. He slept, and next morning his mother shook him awake and drove him to the dentist in town.

A dog barks outside. Inez rolls onto her side and mumbles into her pillow. Polk swings his legs off the cot, and he sits in the dark room. For a minute he watches the slow in and out of his wife's steady breathing. Then he gets up. He quietly gropes for his pants, shirt, and shoes. Carrying them, he feels his way down the dark hallway to the kitchen.

He rinses his mouth with Jack Daniels, a bottle he's found deep in the refrigerator. He spits the mess into the sink. It's no help for the pain. So he pours more, three fingers, and gulps it from the glass. It burns his throat going down. Then he pours more and sips as he dresses.

The key is still hidden low along the doorframe. Polk takes it from its nail. In the dark, he jiggles the key into the padlock and twists. The lock pops open, the sound solid as a stone in his hand. He unhooks the padlock, slips the hasp off the staple, and opens the workshop door.

Inside, he flips the wall switch. It takes a moment before the fluorescent lights blink on. In that last dark moment, he remembers how it was, the benches tall, shelves high, the lathe still long-legged, back before things went bad, before the ramps. Then the lights buzz, flicker, come on fully bright. Chairs without seats huddle together like leggy children. Chisels are scattered across the bench. A chair back is clamped in the bench vise. Rubber straps bind the uprights to carved rungs, the glue set long ago.

He steps around a pile of swept shavings and sawdust. He opens drawers, searches shelves, and he finds the old pipe in a low nail bin. There's no cloth pouch anywhere, though. Polk draws in the empty pipe, then flings it away and turns to leave.

At the door he stops. He goes back to the workbench and kneels there. One hand grasps the edge for balance. He ducks down and reaches up. His free hand finds the slot and the rag-wrapped pistol.

Old sawdust drifts down as he slides the thing out. A stale smell is in his nose, a dry taste in his mouth.

He folds back the rag. Under fluorescent lights, the .38 Special shines silver bright. The cylinder, heavy with cartridges, spins easily under his thumb. It feels reassuring in his hand, a calming thing. Polk's breathing settles now.

The June night sky is clear, the stars bright away from streetlights. Polk wears the denim jacket he found hanging in the shop, its cuffs hiked up on his wrists, sleeves worn ratty by wheelchair rails. The pistol is tucked behind him, beneath his belt, snug against his spine. With each step, he feels a solid kneading.

Polk reaches Arnel Embry's place with no memory of walking there, no sense of intent. Still, it feels inevitable. The pain in his mouth has become a wet throbbing again. The tooth must be abscessed now, poison leaking into his blood.

The house is split-level, white clapboard, a wide garage extending to one side. The lawn and blacktop driveway slope up to the house. A privet hedge tall as a man runs along the roadway and up either side of the yard. The house is dark except for an upstairs window where a pink night-light glows.

Polk walks past, crosses the road, and settles onto the dark slope of a weedy hill. Dew soaks his blue jeans. A shiver races up his back and across his chest. He remembers the heat of Baghdad, how he'd crave a chill like this as he lay waiting, helmeted, body armor zipped and snapped. He'd baste there in his own sweat drippings, eyes stinging, his M-24 sniper rifle braced and waiting for another kill. Polk is an expert marksman, one of the best. And waiting is something he's always done well.

Lights inside the house come on at five fifteen, first one room, then another. A dingy Plymouth chugs by, slowing slightly. The driver lobs a rolled newspaper toward the driveway. Polk raises an arm, starts to turn away, to duck, imagining the thing exploding. Instead, it lands with a dull thud on the asphalt, just a newspaper after all. A queasy feeling washes over him, so damned jumpy, so chicken-shit back here in the world, all these miles from war. Relax, he tells himself. Block everything else and stay focused. You can do this.

The sun is up, hanging somewhere below the trees, when Arnel Embry comes hurrying down the driveway. A tall, ruddy-faced man, Embry is narrow across the chest and shoulders, thick around the waist. He's dressed for work, a lawyer—tan slacks, blue shirt, striped necktie, red and blue.

Polk crosses the road quickly and skirts the hedge. He's only a few feet away when the man, stooped to pick up his newspaper, sees him. Embry straightens slowly, momentary confusion showing on his face. "Morning," Embry says, and he turns and starts back up the drive.

"Arnel Embry," Polk says, stopping him.

Embry turns, peering at him, the rolled newspaper held like a club. Then his face brightens. "Toby Polk," he says, stabbing two fingers at him. "Am I right? Your brother said you were coming to town. Listen, I'm really sorry about your father. Earl was a good man. Like I told Mike, it's senseless, him dying young."

"Senseless," Polk says.

"You missed the funeral."

"I was overseas," Polk says. "The army didn't get word to me in time." He hates that he's explaining.

Embry gives out a grunt. "That's rough."

"How come you showed up?"

The expression on the lawyer's face tightens, and his gaze steadies on Polk. "It's a funeral, son," he says. "You let bygones be."

"You know damned well that's not what he'd have wanted."

"What do you want from me, Toby? Why are you here?"

"Yesterday, I went to the cemetery," Polk says, beside him in the driveway now. "Everybody near him, every grave in the section, they've got upright tombstones. My old man, he'd bought himself a lay-down-flat one, the kind they just mow over. They don't even have to trim. Grass clippings already cover the thing."

"You want a different gravestone—"

"No. What I'm saying is that's how he was. He couldn't let things go, but he didn't do anything about them either." Polk moves closer now, inches from the man's face. "I'm someone else. You walk into my father's funeral like it doesn't matter, like you never did a thing, like it wasn't you started all the damage."

"It was an accident," Embry says, "a fucking accident."

"You show me," Polk says. His body feels its adrenaline now. The pain in his mouth hardly matters. "Show me exactly how it happened. Make me understand."

Embry steps back and glances at the house, the front door. For a moment Polk thinks he might bolt. But then Embry's hands come together. His thumb works deep in the palm of the other, rubbing the soft middle. "It was this pistol crossbow," he says, "a Belgian design, eighteenth-century replica."

"Show me." Polk grabs the man's elbow, gives him a shove up the driveway.

Embry stumbles. "I busted it up, Toby," he says, regaining his balance. His hands lay open to the sky now. "I didn't want the damn thing around."

"So get another. Show me with that," Polk says. "All those trophies you've won, all those ribbons shooting crossbow, don't tell me you don't have others."

In the garage, hunting bows with sculpted shapes, strings slack, hang from pegs along a side wall. Beneath them, the fletched ends of arrows protrude from green plastic tubes. Several crossbows are mounted along the back wall, shoulder-fired models with wood and plastic stocks, and off to the side, three smaller ones with pistol grips. Embry touches a metal-handled model. "Something like this, except the Belgian had a carved oak stock. More like a dueling pistol."

Polk lifts the weapon from its wall hooks, slides his hand along the body, studies the aluminum dart rail, the woven wire string, the black-anodized cocking lever. "This the safety?" he asks, diddling a switch he knows must be.

"The Belgian didn't have one," Embry says. "A safety."

Polk picks up a metal dart. It's long like a pencil but slender, plastic-fletched in canary yellow. The tip end is surprisingly heavy. He probes the point with a fingertip.

"Careful," Embry says. "They're sharp."

Polk holds the tip to the light, squinting. Then he trails it across the back of his hand. Behind the point, the scratch brightens and a string of small blood drops appears. It's bright red, not nearly black as he'd expected.

"Like I said . . ."

Polk mounts the dart on the rail and hands the uncocked weapon to Embry. "Show me, Arnel." His voice starts to tremble. "You show me how this thing happened."

For a moment Embry looks at the pistol crossbow as if it's something he's never seen. Then his gaze comes up, and his head tilts slightly. Polk returns the look, waiting. Something like a smile assembles itself on the lawyer's face. "You have a right to know," he says. He grabs a candle stub from the bench and walks to the door. "Come out back."

The yard is wide, the air outside noisy with morning birds. Saplings in mulched circles are staked and wired upright. The lawn fades into dark woods at the back, where a dozen straw bales are stacked. A paper target shaped like a man is draped across the center bales. It is peppered with holes.

Embry sights the weapon. "You been back long?" he asks.

It takes Polk a moment to understand he means Iraq. "Few days," he says.

"Takes time," Embry says. He rubs the candle along the crossbow's dart rail. "I was in Vietnam—Da Nang. Twenty-Seventh Marines."

Toby Polk tries to imagine this man young and lean, tries to imagine him without the gut, imagine him in uniform, in camouflage and heat. "Different war," he says.

"You guys are heroes," Embry says. "That's what I say."

When Polk doesn't answer, Embry adds, "It's not everyone can fight a war." He sights down the dart. "Not everyone's got the constitution."

"That's it," Polk says. "The constitution." He turns Embry's word over in his mind, trying to make it fit. It doesn't, not exactly. Polk knows inside who he is, what he is, knows it better than words can say.

The lawyer slides the dart along the track. "You kill anyone?"

Polk shrugs in a practiced way. "Who knows?" he says. He does know, though. He remembers every one, remembers them clearly. Each time his eyes close, he sees them, the crouched silhouettes of rooftop fighters. They drift into his realm, his night-vision world, a place all scintillating and green. They come believing in the hiding power of Iraqi nights and dance briefly with his silent crosshairs. Then the slow trigger-squeeze, and they fling dark emerald splatters across bright cinder-block walls. This knowledge Polk won't give up, not to Embry. He hasn't even told Inez, not yet. Maybe he never will.

"Vietnam was jungles," Embry says. He straightens and draws air into his chest. "Over there we shot all the time, single rounds, bursts, not really aiming. It was jungles everywhere, and Charlie was clever. He never left bodies behind. So we never knew."

Polk's voice is a taut whisper. "Maybe my father was your first kill?"

"Jesus, Polk! It was an accident! Your father said so. Sheriff Tate, too." His grip tightens on the weapon's handle, tendons moving beneath skin. "Besides, he didn't die."

"Not fast, maybe. Not that day or year."

"I'm sorry. You've got to know," Embry says his expression crumbling now. "It was just this horrible, freaky thing."

"He died slow," Polk says, the words tight in his throat. "He took twelve years doing it—"

"You can't blame—"

"—twelve years turning rancid in that wheelchair, watching his wife walk away with his sons, watching her leave for some sack-of-shit boyfriend still tooled to satisfy. That, and he'd beat on us when she thought we needed it."

Embry straightens again, making himself tall. "You'd better leave."

"My father's dead now. His grave is marked by a fucking apology of a tombstone. Who gives a shit anymore? And here you come, parading yourself at his funeral like a friend, as if none of us matter, as if his life didn't really end years ago."

"You're trespassing, son," Embry says. He turns and faces Polk, the metal dart in the track pointed his way. "Leave now."

"This how it happened?" Polk asks.

"I'm done talking." Embry's hand steadies.

"You forgot to cock it."

Embry works the crossbow's cocking lever and threads the wire string in the slot. "That seem right to you?" the lawyer asks, showing it. "Now go!"

Polk reaches over and releases the safety catch. "There," he says. He steps back and opens his jacket.

The crossbow wavers in Embry's hand, the aim loose. "Louise!" he calls hoarsely. "Louise! Call Sheriff Tate."

Polk turns and reaches a hand back under the denim jacket and brings out the .38. "This thing doesn't have a safety," he says. With his thumb, he cocks the hammer. He feels solid now, more alive than he has in weeks.

"Jesus, kid!"

"Like it? My old man got it after you shot him." Polk holds the pistol sideways to show him. "Every week I'd go check in his shop where he hid it. I kept telling myself he was biding time, that any day he'd collect his payback."

The lawyer stares at the pistol. "He wasn't like that," he says. Then he calls again, "Louise!" her name a bark this time. "Call Tate."

"Sometimes a fantasy helps a man keep going," Polk says. He sidles around until he can see Embry and the back door, too. "A handgun hidden away, or a bottle, or maybe a woman he sees on the side."

"You got children?" Embry asks. "They change things, how things look."

Polk starts to tell him to shut up about that, intends to say that he isn't here to talk about kids. Before he can, the back door bangs open. He turns to look. A round-faced woman in a pink housecoat comes onto the porch. She's aiming a shotgun his way. "Louise, no!" Embry yells. "Get back inside."

As Polk's pistol comes up, a pain stabs deep in his right side. He grabs at the place, and his hand feels an inch of fletching and the shaft end. The sound of a shotgun blast shatters the air, shakes him bone deep. He ducks belatedly and rolls onto his side, the stab deeper now, rolls once to a kneeling stance. He raises the .38, all adrenaline now, as the shotgun clatters over the railing and pinwheels down to the ground. The woman lets loose a horrified scream and crumples to her knees.

Embry moves toward his wife. "Hold it!" Polk yells. Embry slows, his hands wide out to his sides and empty. Polk feels the blood on him now, a warm trickle inside his shirt from the crossbow dart. The shotgun blast, he's pretty sure, missed him entirely.

At the porch steps now, Embry takes a slow step up. "I said hold it," Polk says. He raises the .38, aims and fires. The slug splinters the railing ahead of the man's hand. The lawyer stumbles back against the bright house. A burnt cordite smell etches the air. It stings and dries Polk's eyes.

"My wife," Embry says. "Please. She's no part of this."

With his free hand, Polk opens his shirt. His fingers find the dart's notched end and grip it. He pulls, feels it budge, slide out an inch. His blood flows more freely now, pulsing deep red around the yellow-fletched shaft. He presses a hand over the wound to slow the flow. A taste like new pennies fills his mouth.

"Think this through—," Embry says.

"Over there." Polk waves the pistol, indicating the corner of the house. His wound burns now, as if probed by a blacksmith's cherry-hot poker. A dizzy confusion fills his brain. This isn't how he wanted things to go, isn't how he planned. It's all messy now, noisy with the woman's wailing, pulsing with pain. Morning sunlight reflects from the white siding, unbearably bright, harsh behind his squinting eyes.

Embry moves back along the house, his hands out to shield his face. "Please," he says. "Oh God! Please."

Ten feet from the man, Polk raises the pistol. He brings his left hand, sticky with blood, up to the butt and steadies his aim. He draws a deep breath and holds it, squinting against the glare. "No," the man says, and then he repeats the word, keeps repeating it like an incantation. Polk tells himself he's done this before, for God's sake, killed total strangers in that place of silent, shimmering green. He can kill this man now, this Arnel Embry, this man who first poisoned their lives.

Seconds pass, ten, twenty. A rumble like a freight train fills his body. His breath comes out ragged and wet. Toby Polk, fevered and trembling now, tries but still he can't bring himself to squeeze, can't make himself do this one simple thing.

The Shield of the Norns

Deirdra McAfee

THE BERSERKER SWUNG us so hard and high against the cloud-roof that Wayne and I could count the people with regular jobs snailing home on I-95. The roller coasters and the water park spread below us like a kingdom, while the ever-glowing sun drowned below the world's edge and dimmed the lovely roof.

Down we skidded. The interstate vanished, the blacktop came at us. Wayne's girlfriend stood at the gate, a bright ant under our shadow. A grown woman who looked like a child. Weak fall sunlight caught her straw hair and fake gold nails, and she shouted his name. "We'll deal with it later, Trisha," he said, exactly loud enough for her to hear.

"Not if I see you first!" she screeched. We lurched up. She flounced off. She was younger and prettier, but she'd never see thirty again either. Skinny enough to wear those sprayed-on pink-and-yellow leggings, loud hot colors that sallowed her even more.

She reminded me of girls I knew in prison over in Goochland years ago. Hairdresser, said those talons and her bleached-out shag. Waitress, maybe even bartender. Dog groomer. Jobs I've worked, too. The kind that didn't check references too close. The kind where she mostly saw people she knew, so she could look however she pleased.

We didn't talk about her. We were screaming ballast strapped to a monstrous motorized pendulum. We were Vikings burning our way through the wind-weaver in a swift black dragon-headed ship.

It was my fourth or fifth time that day but Wayne's first ever. I'd had my eye on him. Trisha made things easier by picking a fight at the gate and refusing to ride. When the attendant sprang the safety harness and seated Wayne beside me, I was glad. I knew he'd seen action. The way he looked and carried himself, even standing in line, even fighting with Trisha, told me.

I didn't look like her. I'm short and dark—"Bernadette, you're built for comfort, not speed," Gary Grice, my first boyfriend, used to say. Pretty enough once, now I was creased and graying like a picture left out in the weather. I carried some weight from the job, telemarketing at Storm King Weatherproofing. Grice was long gone, of course, lived by the sword and died by the shank. Never made it to Valhalla to drink with the valiant dead. Grice wasn't brave, he was impulsive. Me, I was a brooder.

Back and forth I sailed with Wayne, up and up, the air tight with speed, our throats thick with curses and prayers. After Grice, I almost forgot fear; practically the only time I felt it now was on the Berserker. That's why I bought a season pass: to remember.

The Berserker hit apogee and kicked all the way over. Screams flew from us like crows. For thirty-six seconds, the sky went all wrong, the dragon head gazed at the ground, and gravity gnawed us like Fenris, the world-devouring wolf.

On his ninth day noosed to the World Tree, one-eyed Odin grasped the runes, the mystic letters that contain all knowledge, mystery, and wisdom. The burden of understanding was unbearable—it killed him—but understanding was unconquerable, it brought him back to life. Like Odin, the Hanged Man, Wayne and I waited between worlds, upside down and outside time. Unlike him, we were mortal, purified by the sacred fear that scours the rust off existence, yet unopen to truth.

The Berserker pulled itself through the hole in the up-world and became a pendulum again. While it kept its strict trajectory toward the rushing ground, I savored the high-altitude chill of winter on the way and looked into Wayne. Sweat bloomed through his blue bandanna. Wind whipped his face into a mask above the beard. He licked chapped lips and roared, fought for breath and roared some more. Compared to him, I was almost not afraid.

At the end, Wayne stumbled from the gate, dazed and grateful to be alive. I slipped my arm around him and carried him off to a kiosk, where I braced him up with a beer. I paid, but he didn't notice. We fell onto a red metal bench near a sun-bleached fountain. The fountain's hot mist blew across us as we slugged our drafts.

"Want to go again?" I asked, teasing him as if we knew each other. As if more than our hips had connected. As if my fingers had touched his bare arm instead of his frayed Redskins windbreaker.

"No, thanks," he said, staring into his go-cup. "I used to jump out of airplanes. This was the same deal exactly."

"Were you afraid?"

"Damn right," he said, grinning, suddenly boyish despite the gray in his beard, the out-of-fashion hippie hair his bandanna couldn't tame, the look in his eyes of having seen too much. "Scared shitless," he said, leaning back on the uncomfortable bench. "Like any sane person would be," he said, squinting up at the park's fake Eiffel Tower as if gauging the drop.

"How did you do it?"

"Shut my eyes and stepped out behind the next guy. Made sure I never led off. Left that to the glory hogs.

"Hell, most of us were the same. Joined this special unit to quit being cowards. Didn't work, though," he said, and grinned again. He scanned the crowd, looking for Trisha, maybe, or looking to leave. It was too late to ride again even if he'd wanted to; after Labor Day the park stops at sundown.

At Ashland's best barbecue joint, we let our talk glance off important things enough to see each other's depths. I followed him to Mechanicsville. His rented house needed paint, but it was solid, with a tidy yard. No furniture to speak of, a beat-up sofa and love seat in the living room, no tables or chairs. The bed was a king-sized mattress on a bolted-together gray frame, a frame we banged into the wall doing some of the things we did next. I meant to snare him, to create an obligation. I wanted him to teach me of spear-din and the weather of weapons.

The real berserkers were crazy. I read about them twenty years ago when I was supposed to be shelving. The correct term is *berserks*, from *bear-sarks*, the bearskin shirts they wore instead of chain mail. Berserks worshiped war-loving Odin, the Spear Shaker.

In the weather of weapons, which is battle, they foamed at the mouth, bit their leather shields in bloodlust, and howled havoc at their foes. Odin brought out the beast in them, and he protected them. While he favored them, fire and steel touched them not.

Books never attracted me until I learned the truth about people, that they were perverse, hungry, and wild. Beasts more vicious than the kind I'd met in myself. Then I couldn't read enough. In books, rules and plots kept the story orderly. You knew what would happen before it happened, instead of sitting in a car somewhere hoping everything went right and knowing it didn't, or sitting in a cell somewhere else hoping you wouldn't get hurt. The words stayed in lines, the pages happened in order, the stories came out as they should.

The library had a strange assortment, as if Corrections rummaged through secondhand bookstores and dead professors' houses. There was no system; shelving meant just that. Musty old sets of Scott and Stevenson brooded beside Pythagoras and pocket Shakespeares. Buried in a box of engineering texts was the treasure: *Hero-Tales of Northern Lands*.

That's how I entered Odin's holy realm, a place that made sense, the threefold world where honor was revered and blood debt repaid. There dwelt the Valkyries, the Choosers of the Slain. "Some sources call them hell-hags or ravens, battlefield scavengers who ride wolves," the book said, "but they are more commonly thought of as beautiful flying goddesses on horseback."

Odin summoned them from the mist, and they flew into battle with swords drawn, goading the chosen into spear-din, slaughter-dew, and sword-sleep, and leaving the cowards for crow-food. The bravest dead they escorted above, to Valhalla, Odin's palace. There he restored the heroes' health with magic learned from Freya, the goddess of love, fertility, and lust.

In return, she took half the men home to sleep with her. The rest fought fiercely each morning; their radiant sword-dance electrified the air and drenched them in death-dew. At noon the dead rose, the wounded healed, and everyone trooped to Valhalla to feast all night.

They quaffed the sacred mead and savored the succulent meat of Sæhrímnir the boar, made whole again after their banquet, to be roasted again in the morning.

At Storm King the next day, my night with Wayne inspired me to high performance. *Most calls completed* and *Most appointments set* said the tote board beside my name. Marcella, my supervisor, stalked past, glaring and muttering. She'd hated me from the start, though I couldn't tell why. She was just as bad to some of the black girls, so it wasn't that. To keep my numbers down, she made me work mornings. This left afternoons free for the Berserker, and then Wayne, but was further evidence that Marcella considered me prey.

Day calls were easier. The housewives, retirees, and shut-ins who answered were lonely. And lonely people were nice to strangers. Five years ago, just out of stir, trying to do better after what I'd done with Grice, telesellers were the only human voices I heard. But day calls had no money. Even the cheap-ass roofing and siding I tried to sell them were more protection from the Fates than they could afford.

Which was why setting records on the day shift was impossible. When I set some, it just pissed Marcella more. And Marcella killed for sport. "Silence Is Golden," warned yellow signs throughout the soundproof gray-carpeted boiler room, a restriction Marcella routinely ignored. She cut into calls to chew me out. She broke the connection before I could close. She got in my face and glared, she came up beside me and cursed, she wrote insults on her clipboard and shoved it under my nose to rattle me. The rest of them watched, and Marcella enjoyed that, too.

I kept my headset on and my mouth shut. Answering back or objecting would have let her twist my words and plant them in my file. She'd made others into raven-food; she waded through blood wherever she went.

The season pass said the Berserker closed October first. August faded into September and brought me Wayne. September now fell into the dark and frosts of the finished year, but Wayne and I continued. And I continued punctual and thorough at Storm King, setting records every week. The better I did, the harsher Marcella became. Despite September's upturn, she aimed to slay me.

I blame Odin. He wasn't bloodthirsty, but he stirred strife. Because of Ragnarok, the Twilight of the Gods, Odin needed new recruits. Not only the god of magic and wisdom and war, when he hung from the tree, he also foresaw apocalypse. The wise crone Wyrd, one of the Fates, or Norns, confirmed it.

The Norns were sisters—sparse, wrinkled Wyrd was the Past, dew-fresh Verdandi, the Present, and silk-shrouded, gray-veiled Skuld, the Future. They decided destiny, recording it in runes on a burnished shield. "The gray wolf watches the halls of the gods," Wyrd warned, pointing her bony finger at the shield.

There, Odin read that he, too, would die during this final struggle, swallowed whole by Fenris, whose jaws reached from the ground to the sky. Though they would perish honorably, Odin and his army of gods and heroes would lose to the frost-giants, dwarfs, and cowards.

Wayne had guns, as I expected. His daddy's over-and-under and his own deer rifle waited, racked and peaceful, in Wayne's only beautiful thing, a shining glass-and-walnut cabinet. In the ammo drawer beneath, cleaned and oiled in a soft leather holster, slept Wayne's old Vietnam .45.

We'd become close, closer than I meant. Love was never Odin's plan, nor mine; Odin is jealous of Freya, whom he desires and can never have. When Wayne and I were apart, I argued against him, but when we were together, I fell into him. Wayne thought I was only a woman, something I'd never been before.

He charmed and delighted me despite myself; the boyishness always ready in the man lit me up. He was direct, guileless, uneducated, skilled (a carpenter), and true. We sampled stock car races, truck pulls, and slo-pitch, what Wayne called the redneck pleasures of this part of Virginia, and he made them pleasures all.

We spent each night in Freya's precincts, where sometimes I read to him: "Valhalla's roof is built of shining shields, its walls of gleaming spears. Eight hundred warriors can march abreast through each of its five hundred grand gates of jewel-encrusted gold. Inside, the

Valkyries pour mead, the sacred fermented honey that Odin stole from the giant's daughter for gods and men."

"Is mead like ale?" Wayne asked. I put down the book. He smiled and looked at me, the deep clear gaze of an innocent man.

"Not at all," I said. "Listen."

"I am," he said, and settled me against him. He ran his rough palm along my thigh, turning me to tinder. I cleared my throat.

"The warriors' goblets are the skulls of the vanquished, whose bodies were left to rot ignobly on the field and seep down to the goddess Hel's dark hall. There, gray wraiths—the dishonorable dead—stumble through rivers of blood while venom drips down on them from the bony ribs of the serpent-spine roof.

"Mead brings on the mystic drunkenness of poetry, which names and celebrates the gorgeous temporary world." Wayne kissed my forehead, and I read on. "Poetry calls battle *sword-storm* and *spear-din*, calls the sea *whale-road* and *swan-path*, and calls the earth *beast-sea* and *storm-hall floor*. All realms belong to Odin's troops. They go where they wish, even to the underworld."

The underworld was where Grice and I went, too. Unlike Valhalla's heroes, we never returned.

Wayne and I shot skeet. This was my idea, and I thought disturbing thoughts as Wayne surrounded me, helping me manage the shotgun and lead the brittle bird. I loved Wayne, as much as I could love. I wanted to make him happy, but it was too late. I wanted to wake to him forever as I'd been doing, bedding down so beautiful and free at night and staying on. But I knew I couldn't.

I felt him, tight and wiry and steady, and I smelled him, the rich scent of tobacco and Old Spice. Then came the cracking report and the sharp dangerous reek of gunpowder. Then the smithereens of clay. Wayne congratulated me on my aim. He didn't know he'd given me the highest gift, the means to make things right after all these years. For that, I loved him even more. Still, my fealty to Odin outweighed Freya's to me: honor is higher than love.

Eventually I got Wayne to show me how to load and shoot the .45. On mild gold evenings, we took target practice across the fallow field

next door. I knew the hole a piece like that could leave. I'd learned
with Grice.

The gas-station owner went down and never got up again, but he
splashed all over the point-blank shooter. The police pictures showed
a face without a face.

"Drive, Bernadette," spattered Grice said hoarsely, taking a running jump into the car, and I did—I drove him to big time in state
prison and myself to the Women's Facility. When you drive the
shooter, you're a shooter, too, the judge informed me: felony murder.
Twenty years.

The .45 kicked hard, but Wayne helped me hold it.

"Not bad for an old broad," I said, and he laughed and unloaded.

"Exactly how old a broad?" he asked, leaning back against his
side-yard fence and lighting a cigarette, his eyes on me warm.

"Thirty-eight," I said, "the last twenty rough, even with time off
for good behavior." Wayne disbelieved me, of course.

"Just a baby," he said. He took the cigarette from his mouth and
wedged it between two fence boards to keep me from catching fire
while he kissed me, but it didn't work.

A call complained. Mrs. Cox, rude and rich in her fancy zip code,
annoyed to be caught in the tub. She spat me out and asked to chew
on my manager. Although I'd followed procedures—apologize and
try to close—Mrs. Cox had a piece of her tiny mind to share. Because
we remained invisible, and because they knew we had rules at our
throats, some of them were beasts.

"You say you went by the book. Mrs. Cox says you talked back,"
crowed Marcella.

"Well, it's my word against hers, isn't it?"

"Word?" Marcella laughed. "You don't have a word. You're fired.
Pack up." Verdandi steadied the shield while Skuld and Wyrd bore
down on the burin to engrave Marcella's name. I left my dead folks'
pictures, two pens, and a vase. Things I'd have to come back for. So
said the runes.

Thus the spirit of strife that Odin stoked in Marcella entered me
and made me his handmaiden. I could have evaded the task,

dedicating myself to Wayne and serving Freya. Choosing Wayne's light and warmth would have been so easy, and so wrong. I answered the iron summons instead, entering the fiery ruckus of battle.

I'd taken the easy way once, falling in with Grice and doing what I was told. For love, I thought. But really for death. This time I was stronger, strong enough to take the hard way. The way that looked like death but stood for honor. The way that abandoned Wayne, a loss to us both, but made partial payment for not abandoning Grice. The way that took me into Odin's domain, because Valhalla was my final hope. To bathe the ignoble in slaughter-dew, thereby discharging the blood debt. But bravely.

Twenty years back, the light and air were like this, burnished, the bright trees stripping themselves barer with every breeze. In those days, on the unbuilt western flank of Richmond—on the way, in fact, to the cage of girls in Goochland where I spent the rest of my youth— stood an old drive-in movie. It still struggled along on weekends but looked abandoned.

"Here," Grice said, jerking the wheel to make me turn. We bumped along a gravel path that wound behind the screen. Weedy bushes climbed the structure's rusted legs, cans and bottles splashed beneath like tidal debris. The path ended in a thicket of scrub beside a swamp.

"Hurry up," he said, pulling the bank pouch full of bloody cash off the floor. He cradled the gun against his black-leather chest like a father keeping a loved child from harm. The trigger was touchy, and he'd been too busy to set the safety. Grice often acted before he thought.

Sweat greased his face and stained his bright hair; senseless slaughter is heavy work. He jumped out running and I followed. He stashed the pouch in a rotten stump, then jogged past the scrub to the swamp where bleached corpses of drowned trees poked the sky. He splashed into the murk, cocking the muscled arm that pitched a string of no-hitters before we dropped out. But he threw wild.

The gun banged a branch and fired before it sank, a thunderclap Grice seemed not to hear. He slopped out and pulled me to him, hardmouthed and hungry. I could taste the dead man's blood.

I could feel the death, the nothing, the hole in Grice's heart that made him not sorry. I was afraid—for the last time in my life, as it turned out. After that, only the Berserker made me feel fear. Only its height and speed and doom could shock me back to the clean and easy life before that day.

"Come on, Gary," I whispered, wooden in his grasp. "Let's go." It was already too late. A bird watcher in the white-boned trees heard the gun. Heard me sweet-talking Grice to ride for the Blue Ridge and disappear. Grice always believed what he wanted, and right then he believed we were free and clear and could go on home.

I coaxed Grice west by suggesting we celebrate. The witness's sharp binoculars spotted tag numbers as well as birds. State troopers found us at a seedy motel near Zion Crossroads, entertaining ourselves but unprepared for guests.

"Tell me more of those stories," Wayne said the night I got fired. I never talked about work.

"Odin's name means fury or madness, but he is also a seer and sorcerer," I read. "He wandered the nine worlds as a slouch-hatted blue-cloaked vagrant. Before he read the runes and studied the secrets of the dead, he plucked out one eye to pay for a swig from the well of wisdom.

"But Odin is fickle," I continued. "Sooner or later he deserts his warlike worshippers. That is why he is also the god of death by violence." Wisdom and death, they make war in you. They tell you the same stories but don't tell you how to believe.

"I like these weird myths," Wayne said. "They're like fairy tales. But they're all wrong about battle and bravery. What I know about death, I wish I didn't. War is ugly and scary. And death makes a scar. Bravery's what you do when you're too scared to think. These stories don't mention all that. Like they damn sure didn't mention it in the service.

"We jumped in the mountains behind enemy lines, and came down on them like wolves. But wolves with weapons. Including fixed bayonets. Against little fellas in pajamas.

"They didn't run like we expected. They stood and fought with antique guns, with knives and sticks. They made us slaughter every last one of them. That was their curse on us, to make us wade through blood, like Odin in your stories.

"Mine, a skinny snaggle-toothed guy with an old Red Chinese rifle and a machete in his belt, crashed into me out of nowhere, too close to shoot.

"He was old. He kept his long gray hair back with a piece of green silk," Wayne said, touching his own bandanna. "Hair that flew out behind him like silver every time he lunged. And that's what he did—jumped into me, sort of shoved me, then jumped back, like he was dancing. While he whispered to himself.

"He came in too tight for me to get my gun up. And he moved too quick to sight. His eyes were black and wild. His skin wasn't yellow, it was just like mine. He looked like he was smiling, but that was fear." Like Wayne looked when the Berserker dived for earth.

"We'd seen each other's faces," he said. "That made us enemies, not just a couple guys out walking in the woods. Two hunters trained to hunt each other.

"When you see their faces, it's almost impossible to hurt them. Or kill them. In basic training, they told us that would be tough. They drilled us against sawdust dummies. We ran up and stabbed them as hard as we could and shouted the bayonet cry."

"The bayonet cry?"

Wayne got up. He stood sideways at the foot of the bed, charged the wall, and shouted, "The spirit of the bayonet is to *kill*!" He bounced off the wall and came back to bed. I laughed.

"Not funny," he said. He sat up beside me, frowning. Staring else-where. "The spirit of the bayonet kept running through my head. That little gook could see right through to how scared I was. I wasn't scared of *him*, even. I was scared to be a soldier. I was scared to be a coward, too. But I was both. Hand to hand with an old man.

"The spirit of the bayonet is to kill. I pointed my gun down and looked away, then dropped my shoulders and cowered. He slowed his dance, tricked into making his move, and went for his knife, not his gun. Turned out his gun was empty. Before he could pull the machete, I'd skewered him. Just like in training. Only he wasn't sawdust.

"It was sickening. He watched me the whole time, still whispering. His innards drenched us both. He reeked. Then his eyes went out and his smile sagged, and the end of my weapon hoisted a red-soaked heavy thing. So heavy I could hardly let it down. So heavy I could hardly keep from dropping into the dirt beside it.

"He was dead but he kept bleeding. I remember getting him off the bayonet and trying to keep from stepping in it. Just killed a guy, and all I could think about was keeping his guts off my boots. Then I started puking. I thought I'd never stop. And I wanted to keep my feet out of that, too.

"My buddy Arnie busted through the trees. He pulled off the guy's headband for a souvenir, but I couldn't open my hands to take it. They stayed curled up like claws, still helping me shove that bayonet home.

"I killed other guys, he was just the first. But bullets, you know, they keep your distance. You don't have to see. I never forgot him. And he'll never die now. He can't. Instead he has to die in my head whenever I remember him. Right now he's dying again. I wish I hadn't killed him. But I didn't have the choice. I wanted to be brave like those guys in your stories. But isn't it cowardly to kill someone who has no chance against you?

"Your stories don't tell the truth, Bernadette. Freya is more important than Odin. Death is just death, we get that whether we go to war or not. But love is different."

I changed the subject then, and did something about love so he wouldn't talk about it anymore. Wayne was right. Love is different. Although Odin longs for Freya, although he watches her covetously and yearns to possess her, he can never be at home in her halls, nor she in his. He loves her but hates her. As death hates life.

The next day at Storm King, after I cleared my desk, iron-shower felled Marcella; serpent-sting of bullet-bite brought her sword-sleep. On her, ravens banqueted. I wasn't sorry, but I didn't enjoy it.

Well, I did enjoy watching her crawl and cry beforehand, a coward as expected. I worried all along that when she did so, she might sway me. While she carried on, though, I remembered the others she'd wrecked and knew that teaching her to treat people right wouldn't work. She had no aptitude.

When she stank out loud because I hit her in the gut, and when she dragged herself across the boiler-room floor in a bloody smear, I did regret that. I was aiming for her head, quick and clean, but my hand shook. Grice killed a man without thinking and died in captivity, where I died, too. Marcella murdered many face-to-face, and nothing happened until she opened fire on me. Then Odin finally went against her. She should have known that was a risk.

I fired again, to finish her pain, and soundproof gray swallowed that shot, too. "Silence is golden," I said into silence, dropping the gun beside her carcass. Soft carpet soaked up the blood. Let her sink to the halls of Hel, I thought, where the cowardly dead are always thirsty and the cupbearers serve forth goat piss. The sounds she made before she died were disgusting. But I felt no worse than if I'd crushed a cockroach or snapped a rat's filthy neck in a trap. I felt ready for the mead and well able to drink it from her bare skull. For a while.

The Valkyries kept the goblet-skulls overflowing, and Valhalla's roofs and walls rang with battle songs and poetry. Under the spell of the mead, shining with daily victory and perfect health, the heroes were comely and their words the same. They sang of sky, the wind-weaver, the up-world, the lovely roof, the dripping hall; and of sun, the ever-glowing, the fire of air, the all-seer; and of night, the obscure, the shadow-mask, the star-meadow.

The sun was slipping, but the season pass was still good. I craved another ride. Nobody stopped me. At Storm King, they ran. Beside the Berserker, they evaporated. Silence is golden. Grice was never sorry, and I didn't want to be. But when I boarded the Berserker, I still saw Marcella draining away. Did I break her bone-house to feed the ravens, or did I just dream I did? Did she read the runes and return?

Alongside the pleasant spectacle of Marcella groveling for her life, I saw the less pleasant sight Grice saw so long ago, saw how fragile and tender flesh really is, how easily it tatters and explodes and takes the inconvenient occupant elsewhere. The gas-station owner fell down and stayed. Marcella crawled and bled. Wayne warned me, but Odin made me deaf.

Clots of color covered the ground, human shapes with upturned faces. Splashes of sound drifted up, sharp shards of bullhorn. The loudspeakers tried to call me but didn't know my name. All distant empty noise, and not just because I was so much nearer the sky. They think I'm dangerous. They're sure I'll shoot. But I'm not, and I won't.

The dragon-headed prow pierced creeping shadow-mask, swung straight into high blue cloud-sea. Until it failed. The whale-road rider shuddered and jerked. It halted: park security had hit the switch.

The harness came half-open. Defeating the latch wasn't hard, but my hands fumbled, same as with the gun. They didn't want to help; they'd helped already. Finally, just in time, my fingers cooperated. With the crisp click of release, the second release in my life, the cage moved up and off me

Though Odin blurred the rest, I remembered what Wayne said the night we met: everyone's afraid. I saw Wayne in an airplane, the belly of it dark because the open door was full of light. I saw him young and beautiful, self-sufficient, self-contained, wearing his complicated necessary equipment. Another man blocked the light, then fell, and another. Then Wayne. His eyes were shut, and he stepped off into air, into cold brightness, heart-stopping speed, cloud-power.

My eyes were open and I was next. I was not afraid or exultant. All of that had fallen away, left behind on the roped-off blacktop and in the staring faces. I couldn't see Wayne, but I could feel him near in the waiting darkness, surrounding and steadying me. While the gun and Marcella exploded and exploded inside.

There I hung, between two worlds, until Wayne called my name. I gazed down at the floor of the storm-hall, that sea of beasts where Wayne was. I stared up at the world-tent, past the dark margins of star-meadow and into the fire of air, and pushed aside the harness. I whispered Wayne farewell so I'd fly free.

Then I saw the women, plunging through the lovely roof on their airy horses. Riding to meet me. The dying fire of heaven dazzled nine shields and breastplates. Its brightness, red-gold as Freya's tears, harshly hit the helms that hid their faces. They reined their restless, champing steeds to a cloudy standstill, so close I felt the horses' breath and smelled straw-sweat.

The first dismounted and drew near. She raised her visor, revealing her terrible face: the face of Marcella in agony. She exhaled flesh-stench. The second did the same, displaying the bloody emptiness Grice had killed, faceless where Grice shot him. She breathed carrion wind. The last showed Marcella again, gray, ruined, rotten. She exuded miasma. They showed Marcella twice to punish my deep-planned and dishonorable transgression. I meant to make her raven-food, but, unarmed, she became my Ragnarok—dispatching the weaponless wasn't brave.

Behind those three, the shadowy troops rattled their swords, hissed in scorn, and doffed their helmets. They were beautiful at first, ripe young women in their prime. Then that whirling scythe, the rising moon, overtook sun's embers, changing their faces to skulls, their horses to wolves.

Shrieking like ravens, they wheeled; spurring their hideousness homeward, they vanished. Disdaining me dead or alive. Leaving a revelation unendurable, an understanding unbearable: the way that looked like death but stood for honor was really only death. But understanding is unconquerable; even Odin became its vassal and could not die.

When the long last of the all-shining faded to bright cold moon-way, sorrow climbed me down to what was now only earth—where Wayne, only a man, waited. Where we had something different, and where Odin had no dominion. Where I was only a woman with hard time ahead.

An Act of Mercy

Sara Kay Rupnik

I BOUGHT THE gun in August, right after Sam left. "I'm frightened," I told the guy at the sporting-goods store. "I have trouble sleeping. I hear noises."

He made sympathetic sounds. "You want security. Maybe something for your bedside table?" He pulled small silver pistols from under the glass countertop. They looked like the cap guns my brother and I had growing up.

I almost said, "No, I want a real gun," but he spoke about them seriously, as if I were an ordinary customer. I had to put my fist against my mouth to keep from smiling. His speech ended and I looked up. He was waiting for me to respond to whatever he had just said.

"I lost my husband." Probably not the answer he wanted.

"I'm sorry." His tone downshifted. "We get a lot of widows in."

"He left," I said. "He didn't die."

"I see. So basically you live alone, and you want something for protection?"

"I want something easy. Not too big, heavy, complicated, or expensive."

He picked up the daintiest of the toy weapons. "Any .22 could fit in your pocket or purse, but you'll need a permit unless you carry it in plain sight. You probably don't want to wear a holster." He smiled and presented it in his palm. "Try it," he said.

I wasn't ready. I figured it would come in a box with instructions. I hadn't counted on such personal attention.

"It's not loaded."

"I realize that." I lifted the gun quickly from his hand, curving my fingers around its coldness. I liked its surprising solidity, the sleek feel.

"We'll need to wait a couple days for the state police check," he said. "You can get a gun permit at the courthouse."

"I'll keep it at home," I said. "You don't check on that, do you?"

He laughed as if maybe I could be sane after all. I started to give him a credit card and hesitated, considering the anonymity of cash. In the back of my mind, I heard my friend Alice say *once a plan is put into action, Lila, there's no sense trying to alter its course.* I handed him the Mastercard.

He needed my full name for the state police check, and I wrote it out in block letters: LILA MARY JACOBS HERLIHY.

"Sam's wife?" I nodded, suddenly regretting that I'd come to downtown Prattsville, where every red-blooded man of a certain age would remember Sam from high school. I should have taken my chances at Walmart's less-personal gun counter.

"I'm sorry about Sam," the gun guy repeated. I gave him a closer look. His eyes were clear and honest. His face was tanned and pleasant. Before Sam, and even when things were good with Sam, I would have found this guy attractive. I might have even flirted with him a little. Now I decided I was way too wild for him. I looked into his open face and knew I would only shock him.

I didn't go back for the gun right away. Great disorder had accumulated in the weeks since Sam walked out, saying he had to find himself or understand himself or find someone else more understanding, I was not clear which. Just as I was certain he was gone, I was also certain he would return. I wanted to be ready. I dusted furniture and polished woodwork and shined windows and imagined that moment.

I am in the kitchen. He comes in the back door. He gives me that look that means he is too emotional to speak. He stares straight at me and brushes back his sandy hair with those long fingers. I don't talk, don't make it too easy for him to slide back into my life.

Finally, he gazes at the floor and gives the hoarse laugh that only I know comes from embarrassment. He says softly, "So, can I come home?"

"Yes." I smile. "Always."

He moves toward me with his arms wide. I open the pot-holder drawer. I hold the gun straight before me with both hands. I aim somewhere toward his right side. "C'mon, baby," he says. "You wouldn't shoot me." His breath quickens, fast and deep as when he wants me. His eyes flare like the flick of a lighter. "Put that damn thing down, Lila, you hear me?" Then he catches on. The spark fades. "I messed up, didn't I?" He sees what he's lost. Not for long, though. The trigger answers my touch.

I spent a lot of time considering what part of Sam's body would make the best target. Upper shoulder would be good, I think, but he is a tall man and I don't want to damage his face or nick his jugular. His leg would be easier to hit, but I love to watch him move, his long limbs fluid and easy. That is one part of him I do not want to change. The part of him I want to change is his mind. Shooting any part of him probably would not accomplish that.

Still, I wondered what kind of mark the bullet would leave, whether it would produce a geyser of blood or a small black burn. Whether he would slump over or jerk backward, cry aloud or pass right out.

When the guy from the sporting-goods store called, I was tempted to ask him. I said instead that I would be in soon. At the store, he was friendly but intent on instructing me about the safety catch and ammunition. I tried to look attentive, but he said nothing within my grasp.

I grew to love the gun. I took it with me everywhere. I liked its hard bounce against my hip when I carried it in the bottom of my purse. I liked its cold comfort when I slid my hand under Sam's vacated pillow. Mostly, I liked its reassurance that I could go anywhere unthreatened, that no one else could come along and take what was mine.

Autumn deepened without word from Sam. I woke unwillingly,

earlier and earlier each day. While I waited for the dark to pale to another gray dawn, my mind picked through my list of grievances against him. I altered and justified that list until it was perfect. He loved me. He married me. He left me. Despite how hard I loved him back. Then I replayed the kitchen scenario: Sam in the doorway, the hand through his hair, the hoarse laugh, the quiet plea, the gun in my hand, the calm purposeful squeeze, and Sam's face, asking my forgiveness.

Alice called weekly with secondhand news bulletins. Where Sam was seen, what he'd been doing, who he'd been with. None of it sounded much different from what I knew of Sam when he was here. She also begged me to help her out with the truck stop's early shift. "Just until that new girl gets over her foot surgery," she promised. I said I'd think about it, but I had no intention of leaving the house for any length of time. I had to be here when Sam came back.

I began wearing an old flannel-lined jacket that Sam had overlooked in his rush from our life. One morning, in that purple hour when night turns to day, I slid the gun into the jacket's cavernous pocket and started walking. Fog hung like a web, muting my footsteps and the neighborhood dogs and the trucks on the interstate. Fallen leaves clumped to my damp soles. I kept to side streets and passed only three cars. Their headlights picked out the movement of the swirling mist but missed me, striding toward the edge of town.

By the time I reached the Methodist cemetery at the intersection of Grove and Church Roads, the sky was silver. The sun burned through in one great dazzle. It touched my shoulder and twisted me toward the crest of the hill, where a school bus moved through an arc of scarlet and golden trees. That solitary bus on a dirt road lined with light struck me as terribly lonesome, and I turned back, stilling the gun's movement against my thigh with my hand.

I took Alice up on her offer the next day. I knew I needed to be with people again. And, I told myself, I would work only the hours Sam would be at his job. I was surprised to find my old uniform in back of my closet. My first job out of high school had been at the Prattsville Diner in town. Sam stopped in every morning for breakfast because his first wife liked to sleep late, out there in posh new Cherry Creek.

When Sam married me, I figured I'd never live in Prattsville or wait-ress again. I thought I might even leave Washington County.

"Still fits," I said, twirling before Alice.

She shook her head and smiled. "Black polyester skirts and scratchy white shirts never go out of style," she said. "But you are awful thin, Lila." She reached toward me. "I'm sure glad you're here. Let me take your jacket." I remembered the gun.

"Just show me where to put it, Alice. I need to learn my way around." I hung the jacket from a hook in the little pantry just off the kitchen. While I was arranging it so the heaviness in the pocket was not noticeable, May came to welcome me. May and her second hus-band started Ernie's Truck Stop twenty years ago as I-99 came through. After Ernie died, May expanded the place.

"Most of 'em are fine," May said. Alice and I waited. "Had a fella in here last week, though," she continued, "who thought he needed my undivided attention. It was slow, so I sat to talk a spell. Next I knew, his hand came crawling up my leg. Now I want you girls to know I smiled real nice. Politely told him it was time to leave. No, sir, he stayed put. So did that hand. I leaned over and burned the top of it with a cigarette."

"I didn't know you smoked, May," Alice said.

"It was his cigarette."

Alice and I laughed, exchanging surprised looks. "Good one," Alice said, high-fiving May. "Remind me to keep a cigarette handy." She swept back into the dining room.

"Here's my point." May fixed me with a stern look. "I don't expect anyone to have to put up with that nonsense." I nodded, counting the steps it would take me to get from the dining room to the jacket pocket in the pantry. Security. After a few weeks, I relaxed and started hanging Sam's jacket inside the kitchen door.

The place usually cleared out for a time around 10:30, and May and Alice and I took a coffee break in the back booth. May talked about the many men in her life, Alice talked about her husband and kids. I listened.

"I am one tired girl." May kicked off her shoes. "I went to the Grange square dance last night."

"This a new man, May?"

"More old than new." She grinned. "Real lively fella for his age, though."

"Jim and I haven't been to a dance in years. We chaperoned the prom last year. We didn't do any dancing."

"How about you, Lila? You a dancer?"

"Not even close."

"You know—" Alice sat up straight against the red vinyl. "I should fix you up with my cousin. His wife left him last year. Gives him a hard time about seeing his son. It's a sad thing."

She caught my look. "Lila, it's been how many months now?"

"Three." Three months was nothing. A single season. Barely time to grow a garden.

"I'll just get us a refill." May walked to the kitchen in her stocking feet.

"He'll be back," I told Alice. "He always returns eventually. If he thinks I'm seeing someone, it might slow him down."

"I've heard he's seeing someone."

"Who?"

"Karen somebody, a little blonde thing."

"The Kmart cashier?"

"Could be."

"I heard he was seeing her before he left."

"What's with this sense of loyalty? You shouldn't be alone too long. Being alone will warp you."

"Don't worry. I've been warped quite a while now."

Esther Steele called me at Ernie's just as I was shrugging into my jacket. "I don't know whatever made me think you would be an easy person to find."

"How are you, Esther? How's the baby?"

"He walks, he talks, he climbs out of his crib."

We laughed and then her voice changed. "Listen, Lila, I'm afraid this is a business call."

My mind went blank until I remembered: Esther had gone to work as a paralegal after the baby was born. "What's wrong?"

"You know Sam's been in to see us?"

"Oh?"

"The papers are ready."

"Papers?"

"To initiate the divorce. Can you stop by and sign them some day after work?"

My mind halted. My thoughts evaporated.

"Lila, you have talked to Sam?"

"No, I haven't. I haven't seen him. I haven't had a chance to—" I almost said "shoot him," but my words quit forming.

"I understand. Would it be better if we just sent the papers to your attorney?"

"I really don't think I'm prepared."

"You do have an attorney, Lila?"

"I have nothing," I told her. "I'll be right over, okay?"

"We'll be here."

I grabbed my keys and went out the door, grateful that May and Alice were deep in conversation across the dining room. I could not face the Broad Street Mall traffic, so I took the back way—Green Glen Road. It follows the creek, cuts over Thompson Hill, and comes out on the north side, near Memorial Hospital.

I couldn't concentrate. My mind clung to my kitchen scene and replayed it: Sam in the doorway with his soft look and hoarse laugh, my hands around the gun and his expression of regret, of apology.

I passed a slow-moving Jeep headed up Thompson Hill. At the crest, where boulders jutted from the hillside, the road narrowed. I started down. My mind struggled, seeing Sam's face, hearing his laugh, his words. Feeling the weight of the gun.

At the foot of the hill, just where the road curves into the one-lane bridge over Limestone Run, stood a pickup. The driver's door hung open, blocking passage. I jammed on the brakes, skidding close to the truck. The cab was empty. Someone moved into the woods.

I closed my eyes and dropped my head to the steering wheel, feeling too much. Anger rose over everything else and pushed me from the car. The truck was still running. I'd lost sight of the driver. I waded into the roadside brush toward a dense clump of leafless trees. "Hey, what's going on?" I shouted. "I almost plowed into you."

The shot was close. The echo bounced off the truck behind me. I froze in a patch of spent milkweed, ducking into the split, empty seedpods. They were dry and brittle, worthless as dust. Not a single seed left to fly away in her feather-white skirt. The woods crackled. My hand closed on the gun.

Twigs broke, leaves crunched. A man wearing a camouflage jacket and carrying a rifle emerged from behind a solitary blue spruce. I stood my ground, the gun warming in my hand. I was suddenly weary. Weary of waiting, weary of all my life's delays. The man approached. Blood streaked his chest. My head swam.

The man looked over his shoulder to the creek. "A dog came up from the stream." His mouth set in a line. "I hit her."

"You shot her?" I caught on now. "You shot someone's dog?"

"I picked her up. She was in bad shape," he said defensively. "Suffering. There was nothing else to do." He turned toward me. His tone changed. "Hey, lady, are you okay?" He put his bloody hand on my elbow.

"Fine." I pulled away, trying to focus on my car.

"You look washed out. I'm real sorry if I scared you." He dropped his hand. "Look, she was suffering. Leaving her in pain is far worse than ending it. You know that, right?" He insisted on walking me to my car and shutting my door for me. He made a big production of following me into town.

I'd told him I was on the way to the hospital to visit my husband. I couldn't think of a better explanation for my sudden weak spell, and in a way, it seemed like the truth. I turned right at the hospital parking lot and waved. He waved and kept going. I drove through the lot and came out at the top of Broad Street.

Esther took one look at me and rushed over. "Lila, I'm sorry. I didn't know this would be such a shock. I thought you and Sam had talked this out."

"It's okay."

"It's never easy." Her tone gave me no comfort. She glided to her desk and picked up a folder. "Do you want to sign them now?"

I held out my hand. "I'll take them with me." The folder felt too light to contain anything as substantial as a marriage. I gave her a steady look, forcing myself to make polite small talk. "How is he?"

"I hear he got the electrical bid for that new middle school over toward Burton."

"He's happy?"

"Seems to be doing all right."

I fanned my face with the folder. "So what's the hurry?"

Her eyes took in the floor, the door behind me. She finally focused on my chin. "I don't want to be disloyal to either of you," she whispered. Pity, not confidentiality, lowered her voice. "Don't say you heard it from me, but Karen is pregnant."

I slid Sam's jacket off and resumed fanning myself, blinking now against the shimmering room, the glaring lights. I noticed a smear of blood on the jacket sleeve. Bloody fingerprints.

Esther followed my gaze. Maybe she thought it was my blood. "I have just the thing for that." She pulled a white plastic bottle from her desk drawer.

Maybe I thought it was, too. I stood so fast the gun shifted off my lap and banged my shin hard. "Please, I'm fine. Don't bother."

"No bother, Lila. I'm happy to help you."

I gathered Sam's jacket in my arms. "I'm just not ready for help today, okay?"

"Sure." Her voice was soft. "Take the bottle along. You can bring it back with the papers."

I clutched the whole mess—papers, spot remover, jacket—to my chest and walked out. Alone in the elevator, I thought about the man in the woods. How quickly I mistook his actions for cruelty instead of kindness. How doggedly I believed that every wound could heal, that suffering somehow offered its own splendid reward.

Out on the bright street, my thoughts went back to that man leaping from his truck, bending over the dying dog. He'd scooped the creature from the road and carried her gently into the trees. He'd done the only thing that could relieve her pain. Now, set loose in this torn November day, I wished life would offer me such tenderness.

Pearl in a Pocket

Nicole Louise Reid

VYLA WANTED TO run when Momma was like this. She wanted to swim a little, maybe even flirt with losing her breath beneath the putrid green waters of the Pearl that rimmed their yard.

Today Momma sat swollen on the porch, rocking on Daddy's round-bottomed stool, humming a little. He scrubbed his scaler over the flesh of a shrinky bass. Prill watched Daddy with the mess all over his hands. Loewy combed out the snags of Hepsey's hair.

All day Momma had been barking at Vyla because she was the oldest. The whole day showing her what-all she did wrong. "Don't just tip and tail those beans, girl—show the babies."

Hepsey and Loewy dragged themselves over, Loewy's two fingers still gripping hanks of her sister's hair. They weren't babies anymore, Hepsey four and Loewy seven, but Vyla didn't say anything, just held up one of the mammoth, brown-rubbed string beans Momma'd left growing too long, methodically demonstrating the process. Loewy looked back at her hands that were moving again. Hepsey winced twice, and Vyla snapped the stem and pulled the string down the fraying spine of every bean.

But Momma was watching the yard, Prill and Daddy making puce handprints of God knows what along his slab, a low table made of nothing but four mason bricks stacked on four more to be a square covered in red blood and yellow-and-green guts. So the girls went on braiding and Vyla made quick work of the beans she knew would chew like sodden cardboard. All this in Momma's quiet.

Tonight Vyla would slip away. There was a boy she knew. They'd been meeting some nights, when she could. Down by the river.

What Vyla knew by heart was the water stretching on and on, the way it felt to sit hours on the pebble shore waiting. The Pearl was long and thin here, turning like an elbow, for years pushing through with just enough speed to lose your flat sheet to the current before you'd finished wringing the fitted; these days it hardly moved at all.

Stinking of paper mills and streaky fish heads Daddy used for bait. So cloudy in its stillness that she quit sticking her toes in while she sat thinking about the boy. Or about the girls: there were babies in this river. Her sisterbabies born broken or cold. All of them sisterbabies, and so many gone in that way. So she knew where to go to talk to them and she knew which nights to sleep heavy.

For years she'd woken in the pillows when the prick of something—needle, knife, shard of glass, pointed handle of a rat-toothed comb? she didn't know—scraped at her forearm, the instep of her foot, then stole back into the hallway and the dark. Because it had happened in the night, another early stillborn, and Momma wanted Vyla with her to tie the rock because Daddy was ruined for one more time.

One night Vyla slipped the knot around her own finger and when Momma shoved the little wrecked thing into the river water, Vyla jumped in after it and let the rock find its ground before even thinking of coming up for air. She just wasn't sure. And so she kneeled in the rotten slurry of silt and stones and older death on the bottom of the Pearl, with that baby in her lap, its empty head trying to rise up through the water, light as an apron. Vyla opened her own fist but would not shake free her end of the rope. She felt the way her hair tugged up toward the surface, how each section moved independently like so many snakes. The tight pursing of her lips and shut eyelids made stars in her darkness. Even when the vacuum of her lungs came to feel like all the trees along all the rivers, standing on her chest, still she would not come back.

Momma waded in after a bit but she seemed to want to wait until Vyla was sure either way. Then she trudged deeper into the river, to the center where Vyla's last bubbles had broken. She splashed around in the black water, slapping the surface and kicking. Her toes grazed Vyla's temple. A hand moved across Vyla's face, brushed open her lips, and Vyla couldn't help but fill herself with the Pearl. She let go then. Of the baby and her rope.

Momma had Vyla by the nightgown and the slime-shiny hair. She dragged her to the edge of the river and, still knee-deep in water, Momma leaned herself out upon the bank—bosoms and all the drapings of deflated baby-stomachs like rings of a tree made of fat, hoisted up.

It was her breathing Vyla still remembered, how her momma panted like a dry-mouthed dog, lying bent across the hard-packed dirt becoming mud beneath the triangular spread of her housecoat. Vyla began to drift from the shallows. Momma had let her go, she would always let her go.

She was never sure if Momma had thought her gone, if Vyla sleeping curled and coughing in the raggedy marigolds aside the front stoop in the morning was a surprise or not. Still damp, Momma peeled off Vyla's nightgown, her pants, and replaced the latter with a fresh pair, the former with a short, dirty dress of Prill's—much too small for Vyla. There were three years and as many other sisterbabies between Vyla and Prill. But Momma laid her back down so nice and sweet to sleep more in the patch of garden fenced in with bent-up metal hangers so rusted now they were beyond real identification.

Vyla had been there that day bending the things, folding and pulling as well as she could, watching how her mother gripped the metal, seemed to jab the straightened neck at herself and then at the girls. Baby Glenys was just to walking then, pedaling around the yard with one of the hangers, Momma watching to see would she fall.

Yet Vyla was whole. Whole as a girl can be when some of her sisterbabies are gone and some are not, and she was big enough to be certain of her own permanence. Almost certain. Fourteen now and taller than Momma, though Daddy still towered above her. But Daddy wasn't any danger. He was quiet and still and hardly breathed for fear of disturbing the air of the universe. He baited his trotlines and picked off dead catfish he'd left too long, said little prayers over having wasted them. Other times he'd bring home a heap load and dress them in the yard on his slab.

And now, now Momma was pregnant again and so it had been smooth for a while, but soon back to the river in moonglow. Each baby, each of the twelve that came after Vyla—she wasn't sure how many might have come before her—each one was either living broken or sleeping in the current.

Simon, the boy she knew, was younger by a year, just thirteen, and she'd known him all her life, but in a way of not knowing him one bit. He was just always there. But last summer she'd found him at the water, watching it, thinking to do something permanent.

"Simon Cale, you'd better watch what you do, those feet stay on land."

He spun his head around, tucking his knees to his chest, almost a lame dog looking down the barrel.

Vyla sucked in her lips worrying over having sounded a thing like Momma. She squatted in the sand and wispy grasses, tore out grips of the stalks. "What're you doing?" she asked him, more easy this time.

"Why you love this river so much?" He kept his eyes on the water. "You're always here."

Vyla inched closer but seeing how the ground beneath his feet was dusty, loose earth that crumbled away from the roots of the trash trees growing sideways out of the bank, she stepped back, kept some distance. Instead, she sat in ivy and weed that brushed the backs of her legs and stuck in the drops of sweat behind her knees.

"You wouldn't understand," she told him.

He didn't answer; didn't turn in on himself regretting the question, or push her to give it up. The two sat until the sun lost itself behind tiny puffs of nothing-clouds right low on the horizon. Not much to tell: he wasn't beaten at home, no bullies chased him from the corner drug, no brother slipped into death sheets.

One day he said, "Shut your eyes."

She did and then she didn't but he took her hand and fed it inside his jacket pocket anyway. She let her fingers open against the inside fabric between her palm and his skin, but there was something else.

"It's a gun," he said.

"I know." But did she? She wasn't certain. "Why?"

He pulled her hand out. "You don't understand."

Every day they met, he wore his jacket no matter the heat. When Vyla left, some nights she dreamed his hand putting hers in the pocket again but when her fingers opened, she could feel him breathing against the denim fabric separating them. She woke flat on her back, the sheet thrown off of her, one leg hanging over the side of the mattress, and Prill next to her, breathing steam into one of her ears.

The next evening, she put her own hand back inside his pocket and pulled the gun from within. She did not know why. She held it loosely in both hands, appraising it like one appraises the runt of a litter one has chosen to love. There were no bullets, it had no hammer. She slid a finger along the trigger and there wasn't even resistance.

"It's mean, you know? I like the feel of that, of something so mean."

Vyla laughed, holding the gun out in front of her. What little a boy could understand of longing or meanness. The worst he had it was a mama who wanted so much more for him she wouldn't let Simon get by without quadratic equations and logarithms.

Vyla realized he was silent. She looked at him.

What he wanted was all the tracings his finger made in the sand, the arrangements of grasses collaged into the buttonbush. And for some reason these made him sad, in a way she knew, and so they leaned against each other some, leaned and let their arms press close, and wondered things about skin and touching skin and the way it is to feel a pulse that's not your own creeping up your veins.

Simon and Vyla met on the bank as much as they could, which meant whenever Momma was sleeping or fierceangryblind to her, and when he could get away from working the imaginary numbers. She liked to hold the gun whenever he brought it and she kept her finger on the trigger and took careful note of the way such a thing made her hand that much heavier. Even so, it seemed a toy for it nearly fit in her palm and had nothing to make fire and wasn't in any way a weapon.

He hadn't kissed her yet. She thought about this when the first light of a day crept through her window and two of her sisterbabies were quiet enough to work a thought through her head start to finish. Then she could breathe. No more black taking up Momma's insides, no more dark to feel under the water. So she thought about Simon and his mouth which was freckled and pink and small like a girl's. She sometimes dreamed him shutting his eyes and she'd wake sucking her fist to her lips.

"Pass them beans, girl." No telling how long Daddy had been waiting on her.

"Mmm-mm," Momma said, shoveling another bite into Glenys's mouth and then her own.

Vyla worked fast at her plate, chewing up those beans, dry and tough as they were. She scooped up the turnip greens and sopped the juice with a lardy biscuit. "Daddy, may I be excused?" She'd hardly swallowed.

But Momma cut in: "Child, what you up to these nights? Don't you get no ideas."

"She's got a boy she sees." Prill tucked her greens beneath a third biscuit she'd only nibbled from.

Daddy just looked at her, at Vyla. Looked at her eyes and her mouth and seemed to see what she was, as if just this morning he'd been toting her, rice-sack style, over his shoulder. Her hair was grown out of its bob now, and she liked to swing it around to her back in one long sweep. Her skin was like early sun, all pink and golden. She'd always had those eyes that change color and now, right this instant, because of how much she wanted whatever it was, they were green. He didn't dare look lower than her shoulders, she could see him stop his eyes from even finding out. "Go on then," he said and she was gone out that house faster than the blood pushing through her, the sound of Momma's jaws grinding through those beans entirely lost on Vyla.

He wasn't there, Simon Cale. Their bank was bare, just two

half-moons worn in the disintegrating earth near water's edge. She didn't sit now, but instead went along the water touching all the trees, the water oaks and the tag alders. She saw how the low-hanging whips of willow were snapped and crushed from careless fishermen pulling at the world they walked through. She studied the bends and shredded leaves.

Today the Pearl moved so slow it was almost still, and she could feel every hair up her arms and down her legs, knew where each pore was because of the heat that gloved her. She wondered what it would be like to swim. She thought about Momma and all the sisterbabies, and wished, as sometimes she did, that she had just stayed under. Then she fought back and wished she could drown Momma instead. Either way, it was no use.

She dreamed a rock where someone lay curled. Up, out of the water running thick and white around it. Someone whose arms were trying to hold to that bit of earth because anything else meant being gone for sure. Vyla, in her sleep along the bank, flew over that water and to that rock. And as she neared, she could tell it was her own thin, streaky hair covering the shoulders and arms of the girl. It was her own long foot and small toes angling out from beneath the body.

She reached an arm to the girl, feeling in some ways frightened of touching herself, and the face turned up and it wasn't Vyla, it was years-ago Momma. From pictures of her and Daddy before the new Ford truck, his arm around her waist, her fat cheeks smiling. And with that girl, her head lifted up to see Vyla flying over, there, wrapped up tight in that girl's arms, covered like ducks by a downy wing, were all the others.

Then there was a hand on her. Something real or imagined, she wasn't sure. But somewhere, someone was pressing her. The murky sleep and visions gave way to late-evening sun in her eyes, and there was Simon. His hand touching her side in a place somewhere between shoulder blade and breast, a place left exposed by an arm falling forward into the grass while she slept. She sat up blinking for the light. She said his name and was sure his hand was still pressing that little bit of tender skin, but she could see he had both arms propping him up now in the shifting sand.

"There's people I don't know in there," she told him. "Sometimes I think through their names just to be sure I've saved each one whole. Other times I sit here scared to try because I'm sure I've lost the sister-baby came just after me."

What she couldn't tell him was that she believed there had been a moment when Momma wanted to love every single one of the sister-babies right—gentle and sweetly kind, tenderhearted and sort of broken—and that Vyla should have seen this and saved that bit of time like a pearl in a pocket. That she should have tried.

She wished she could remember everything of the dream, more than just the rock and the dead ones piled beneath her, more than just the black hair that is her hair, the face that is her face. She wished there were more for her to see than that.

All she said was, "Do you think you'll kiss me soon?"

His face went strange. His girl lips folded in on themselves, rearranging themselves. He leaned forward and she leaned forward and what it was, was like Daddy saying good night. Just softness pressing. Just a little time, heads so close together.

"Good," she said, and walked straightaway home.

Prill was sitting in Vyla's bed waiting on her, fussing with the one inch of hem left on the edge of the blue curtain. Vyla pulled her T-shirt over her head.

"You're getting boobies, Vyla," said Prill, still messing around with the curtain.

"*Getting?* Where've you been, dumbass?" She pulled down her shorts and tossed them back into her dresser drawer. Wash was her job, and sisterbabies and Momma made enough work for anyone without her adding to it. "Quit it," she said and swatted Prill's hands out of the stitches they were pulling.

So now Prill's fingers found the frayed selvage rim of Vyla's bed sheet. "Will there ever be a boy?" Prill asked.

Vyla stopped moving about the room tidying up after all the rest had been in there the whole day, pulling out and then leaving anything they wanted to touch. "There'll be somebody, Prill. I know you." She stood looking out at Momma's tree and the half-moon lighting the water and bark. "He kissed me tonight."

"He did?" Prill sat up on her knees. "Tell me, tell me everything."

"Well." Vyla blushed. "It was just once and nothing extreme, but it was nice. And I'll go back. And he'll go back. And he'll want to do it more and more." She was walking around the room making dramatic folds in each piece of clothing she picked up. Feeling tall.

"Will you marry him, Vyla?" Prill was so obviously only eleven.

She sat down on the bed next to Prill. "No, I don't think I will." She said this as though she carried the weight of the world, as though nothing could save her, as though she were goddamn Joan of Arc.

Prill's face asked for her: Why? it said.

"I'm not sure, Prilly." She put her arm around this sisterbaby and leaned her head to Prill's shoulder. "I just don't know if I want that. Not everyone makes promises. We can go on. We can be in love."

"Oh." To look marriage and escape in the face and turn away, that was unspeakable bravery, and Prill sat silently absorbing her sister's courage. Until finally she spoke again, "I meant Momma. Before, when I asked if it might be a boy."

"No," Vyla said. "I don't think so."

In the kitchen Daddy was fixing coffee and Vyla breathed it in deep. She heard Glenys paddling around in the hallway: taking a few steps and falling to her hands, then crawling the rest of the way. Daddy's slippers scuffed into the front room where he offered Momma a cup of coffee or a sweet from the pantry (hidden at the back of the top shelf against all of them, Vyla knew) or maybe a dance. First Momma was quiet, humming that thing she sometimes got fixed in her head and couldn't lose. The two of them spoke smoothly and Vyla wanted to sneak into the hall to know what it was making Momma so soft right now.

Glenys made her way into the bedroom where Vyla and Prill were sitting on the bed staring into the opposite wall. When Prill saw Glenys, she leapt from the bed and swooped her up to dance her around the room. "We'll find beautiful, rich, rich men, won't we, baby?"

"Mind you don't spin those beans right out of her," Vyla said and left them dreaming.

Daddy was on the porch now and Vyla sat with him in the swing.

Quiet for a long while, just watching the moon spread over the water. His breathing was slow and steady and she worked to match his rhythms with her own even though doing so meant breathing in the stench of the water.

"So you got a boy now?" he asked her, running his palm down his neck against the sprouting stubble there.

Vyla's rhythms lost time. "I don't know," she said.

"Well . . ."

Vyla kept quiet a good wait in case he changed his mind but he didn't. "There's something wrong with Glenys," she said, "isn't there?"

He put his hand over hers, in thanks or fear, she could not know.

"She's started losing her steps, Daddy. Just a few months back she was walking all through the yard. No trouble. Now she falls to her knees and crawls the whole way."

"No," he said.

"She's fine every other way."

They sat in each other's quiet and the small, bright glow of porch bulb.

A fresh shift at the mills was pulping. Vyla could feel the sulfur stream cross the Pearl and come to live inside her in ways she was sure she would never be rid of. Especially now if she'd go roll around in it in bed.

Daddy's hands were splayed on his thighs like a man set to rise. In the dimmer edges of light, the tips of his fingers, stained like his gutting slab, looked dark with blood. Vyla knew better, though, that this was just the nighttime playing tricks on her. Still, she looked away from him now, his hands.

"A boy," Daddy said. "A boy would be nice."

Vyla turned back to him now, to his face. The bulb lit up his forehead, his nose, and cheeks. But what she wanted to see, his eyes, were now sunk into the night. "Will she keep it?" she whispered.

"It's got to be whole."

"What about Glenys?"

"A losing proposition—"

"But Glenys."

"—trying to make her love something she thinks don't want her. She's a woman got to get something back from people she chooses."

Vyla thought about Simon and felt something ugly push through her. She knew she was just as ugly, that she wanted something from him, too.

"I see it in Prill sometimes," he said. "That girl hungers." He rubbed one eye until Vyla thought he'd pop it right out his head.

"I've seen it, Daddy."

"A woman like that's got accounts in her head. And what's a baby got to give her?"

"No," said Vyla, thinking of one night soon when Momma would lug another rock onto Vyla's bed. She stood up out of the bulb's cast, her own face now as dark as the river. "Just tell her the baby's loving her. Tell her you're loving her and it. Tell her every time she feels it shifting in there, that's it telling her she's the one. Tell her and she'll know it, Daddy. Doesn't she love you? Doesn't she love any of us enough?"

When Vyla next went to the river, Simon was there waiting and she almost knew the something different between them. Almost. His fingers were still, not etching the bank with some vision of space and movement. She didn't trust in it, though, this change she could smell as acrid as weeklong breath or isopropyl spilled onto the floorboards to evaporate. She breathed down deep this new air, this new way he was sitting all folded up on himself, chin to knees.

"Can I ask you something?" he said.

The way he turned from her, wouldn't dare look, how could she think anything but his hand finding her face again, his eyelashes skimming her cheek, his girl's lips so fine?

"Sure." She reached in his pocket, felt the gun warm and left it there.

"Would you mind . . ." He troubled over a fleck of scab covering the bony rim of one knee. It was old scab, thick. Fresh skin as pink as pearls peeking from beneath. He bent a bit of it back, pushed it to and fro as if on a hinge.

"Tell me." She couldn't stand this anymore, wondering if he'd give up before getting through however it was he aimed to tell her she was his one.

"I just mean," he started up again and now tore off the entire heel of old scab at once.

"Simon—" The bare slick of pink prickled with his blood. She wanted nothing more than to touch it. And for him to speak. "Say whatever it is." She put a hand on his arm.

He turned to look at her. Hazel eyes. That sweet mouth. "Don't come down here tonight."

She didn't speak.

"Please." He grabbed hold of her fingers, suspended her arm in the air between them, that creeping bit of widening world, then pressed her hand to his face, his kiss. "I don't mean anything by it."

"I won't come," she said and left him on the riverbank.

She took the quick way home straight through the stand of white pines even though it meant ruining her good shoes and wearing mud-socks until she was through the wash one more cycle. The trunks of the trees were like the faces of traveling circus elephants, their eyes so wet and tearing with sticky white sap. The needles a matted bed of sorrow turned to sugar.

She stopped a minute and looked back up the bit of path she could see. Just swamp privet, just some young fringetree swaying. She kept on. It wasn't hard to imagine what he had in mind. Even so, she fooled herself wondering if it might be a surprise for her, a test to see if she could keep away and if so, then she must not truly love him.

He'd have a blanket draped over their by-now bare seats in the grass. He'd have a ribbon to tie around her wrist or her neck. She would kiss him again. Touch his face memorizing where the bones turned out and in, where they gave up and seemed stunted.

He'd said a name once, asked Vyla what she thought of Fay Molene, a girl they knew from school. Half Choctaw, though her house was three miles up the river and far enough off the one reservation that sitting with a boy might seem a little romantic, a little dangerous.

Vyla wouldn't go to the river. Not tonight. Not any night. She would let Daddy teach her the two-step again and again because she wasn't any good feeling the music. She would let Prill ask her anything she wanted, anything at all, and she'd answer every last question. She'd squeeze a nice lemon fizz for Momma and give it to Loewy to take to her.

Vyla was still fixing this list of all she'd do tonight and every night when she walked right up on the real reason she wasn't supposed to go this way. Not anywhere near the Delpy house, which wasn't the Delpys' anymore. Grown men used it as one big duck blind in season and nearly grown men used it like that all of the other months. She could turn around. She could always turn around, but the path folded back on itself all the way back to where Simon sat. She was not crying now but, well, she kept on past the Delpy house.

The closer she came, the faster her heart. Three windows faced her path. Two of them, the glass was knocked out, a red and white gingham towel hung instead in one. She moved her eyes from each of the three windows as she walked on by, but as she rounded the corner of the house, she was struck by its porch and a small potted plant sitting in a pie tin at the front door, as if someone had left it as a welcome gift. She didn't know why the Delpys left. It was just the couple, just the woman and man—they'd had no children.

Vyla was standing still in front of the steps up to the Delpys' front door. She climbed the steps to pick up the plant. It was long dead but, by the look of it, had been a geranium. She was back to her own yard, the tree, Daddy's slab, the marigold flowers, and Vyla still held the pie tin and the geranium. She had not intended to steal it, and she had certainly not intended to be holding proof of walking the route she'd walked when first seeing Momma. She set the pie tin on the ground, leaned a hand to their own front steps, peeled the ruined sock from her foot, and stepped back into the gritty footbed of her shoe, letting the slimy sock drop to the hangers surrounding the flowers. She repeated the process, her bare toes feeling nearly like they were digging their way deep in the mucky sand.

From inside the house, something slammed. Vyla picked up the geranium and ran to the river. She kneeled there and held the root ball under until it took on enough weight the thing sank down without a trace. Except the pie tin. She began to hold it down, too, but then ran back up to the house—careful, with it behind her back just in case. She threw it under the porch steps, without a single reason why.

As soon as Vyla walked through the front door, there was Momma panting in her cotton slip on the front room floor. Daddy and the sisterbabies sweating and red-faced looking at Vyla come in, with all sorts of hopes she might take over this production.

"She's doing it, Vyla!" Hepsey cried out.

"It's coming," sang Loewy.

Vyla pushed off her shoes again. The floorboards were grit gluing to the bottoms of her feet but she could hardly complain this time.

"I've been hoping on you," Daddy told her.

Glenys teetered up to start over to her, then collapsed into a fish-tailed crawl.

"Everything going good, Momma?" Vyla touched her face and studied her eyes for any sign of things turning.

"I won't stand for this much more. 'Bout to break my back, this one."

"Just a bit more, Momma. She's come this far. Just a bit," said Vyla touching Momma's foot and then taking back her hand real quick when Momma took a deep breath in and was ready to scream through that next rush of tearing free inside.

She didn't scream. Just took in as much air as she could and then held it in her fat cheeks, her puffed-out face holding it until she went blue and purple. This was how she'd done the last two, but each time Vyla expected the terrifying shrillness of her sound.

"When did it start, Daddy?" Vyla asked.

"Second you swung the door leaving."

She redoubled her efforts: touching Momma's foot or counting how long she was holding a breath.

"Help me up," said Momma.

"No, right here's best, love. Right here," Daddy said, looking scared as all. Daddy even pinned down her right hand and gripped her knee.

Momma put an arm to the wall behind her and started mustering the strength to hoist herself up despite all their force to keep her down.

"Please, Momma," said Vyla. "Please don't. This one's going fine."

"I can feel it. It's all wrong. I can feel that, you know."

"She can feel it, Vyla," said Prill, holding her arms tight around herself.

Then she was standing and they all knew there wasn't a thing they could do about where she was headed. Out the door she went, lugging her eight-month belly. Fifty yards upriver and she pushed out in the boughs of the old snap-limbed swamp hickory grown right up out of the river wall, leaning across to almost center of the slow water. Just like a mama cat nesting in barn hay, hissing and spitting at anyone come near. Moving slow as all, checking each branch for what it would take of her. Taking each foothold and grip worlds serious.

Every other time, Momma had lain in the crotch of several limbs hitting the trunk and when she pushed, Daddy and Vyla and whoever else hadn't already gone to the river watched breathless from a window in the house, hoping to God she'd catch the thing when it came out. And she always did. But she'd stay up in that tree for days afterward holding on to the dead thing or gripping the breathing one, waiting to see how long she'd get to have it.

This time, the whole troop of them waited on the bank looking like stargazers come too soon. Even Glenys padded along on all fours then to stretch her neck up at this first new chance since she came to be. No one spoke except Daddy. And he didn't really speak but whispered a sort of terror Vyla'd never heard in him before. He called up to her, "This one's different, Layla. Make it different."

She went on as though she'd not even heard.

"You can do that. You just come down and kiss me and let's let it be."

The day eased into dusk and Glenys slept on her back, Hepsey and Loewy sitting in the grass tugging up bits of it and tracing single blades along their calves. Prill held Vyla's hand. And Daddy touched the thin, scaly trunk of Mama's tree. Then Hepsey was up and Loewy with her, tugging at Glenys to come inside. Loewy slung the baby over her shoulder and carried her home. Vyla watched the lights come on in the front room, in their bedroom, and then in her and Prill's room. Prill saw it too, and Vyla could feel the worry in her hand that they were getting into things they had no business with.

Vyla had little in there to protect, but Prill had secrets any eleven-year-old thinks she's the first to ever hold.

"Go on," Vyla told her and Prill's eyes went teary just for wanting to be as good as Vyla. As grown. Still, she went into the house.

So it was just Daddy and Vyla now. And she didn't know a thing to say or do. Momma was still heaving and grabbing hold of so much air Vyla sometimes struggled to get any at all for herself.

"It's different this time," he called up again. "I just feel it. I know it."

Vyla could hardly stand this. The way he'd wrapped himself about the trunk of the tree. That she wouldn't offer him any scrap of hope or love.

"Promise me you'll let it be whatever it wants to be," he said.

"It's dead. I know it is," she hollered and the leaves shook.

"It's been kicking. It loves you. It wants to be with you."

"It's the cord, then. Something. It's got to be something."

"Please." He was crying.

Vyla pressed herself to his back, squeezed herself to him. It was all she could do. She didn't have any power here. And neither did he.

When the last push came, Momma's breathing eased some and Vyla could see her cleaning it on her belly, wiping at it with the white of her slip. Touching it. Daddy's head was glued to the red bark of the hickory. "It's breathing?" he asked real low.

"For now," she called down.

Vyla stepped to the edge of earth and water and then stepped in. Slowly, deliberately. Feeling her toes in the gravel and the silt clouding around her feet. Not even minding the stench of the mills and water-treatment runoff. No one said a word to her. Not one shred of worry for her finding another rock to hold to her lap. Not one ounce of thinking people ought not do whatever it is they want with their own selves.

She aimed to wait at the sandbar, beneath Momma and whatever it was up there with her. And she did wait. Long enough to hear Momma begin cooing and Daddy start to come out of his death grip around her tree. Then Vyla lay on her back because she thought the water wasn't even moving. And she was tired and the moon was wide tonight.

She didn't feel the drifting. Didn't know the little bit of current was pushing her far enough to where Simon Cale and Fay Molene were sitting right in Simon and Vyla's same spot. And she wouldn't have known at all because she was back in her dream floating over the girl on the rocks with one more baby crawling out from under her white cotton slip, except for Simon crying out, "Vyla!" and then splashing in after her.

She folded in half from the fright, and lost her breathing underwater. He grabbed her sleeve and tugged her up, treading water there with her in the middle of the river, not twenty feet from a brown-haired Indian girl sitting there watching.

"What're you doing?" he asked her in a sort of holler. He hadn't let go of her sleeve and his grip was serving the current to pull her to him.

"She had it, the baby. All day long. Until finally, and Daddy couldn't bear it and all I wanted was to catch the thing if she didn't want it. But then she was loving it. Or starting to. And so I thought I'd float there beneath her and it and whatever was coming next."

His mouth was wet from swimming to her, spitting out his breaths in trails of even bubbles. And now he just bobbed before her, fanning his one free arm and swishing his feet to keep him up. He just looked at her in that way of knowing something.

"Simon?" It was the girl. Standing now. Being separate from all this commotion. Wearing a cardigan sweater hung around her shoulders for God's sake.

He didn't answer. And still had hold of Vyla's sleeve. Then he kissed her. A swift-enough pulling to her that dragged them both under some. So they breathed what each other had and then pulled back up.

"Simon!" She sounded just like a girl left on a riverbank.

He didn't even look.

"I'm leaving then." And she did.

He kissed at Vyla's face again. Looked right in her green eyes. Vyla could feel them being green with all there was she wanted in this world. But it wasn't real. She started paddling for shore. "You don't mean this," she said.

He followed. "It was all wrong tonight," he said between strokes. "She's all strange to me."

Vyla felt things moving in her but this time knew better. She got up on her feet when the water was too shallow for swimming. She sat, dripping, taking care not to sit where Fay had been. He sat down beside her, facing her, wrapping his arm around her back and swarming every bit of her as if trying to make her body his.

"She isn't—I want you."

"It's a losing proposition."

"What?"

"This doesn't change a thing, Simon. Of who you love or don't. Don't fool yourself into thinking it does." She didn't touch his face or sigh, like someone in the movies might. But she did run her finger through her name already traced there on the bank beside her. She didn't consider letting him be a grand gesture of selflessness. All she knew was it was done. To be sure, she reached for his pocket and felt the cool metal there. That wasn't mean or even the way it felt to miss someone. It was wet and broken and now very, very uninteresting.

"It's just the moon's trick," she told him. "Think of me in the river in midday. Think of me floating through because I meant to grab up this bit of her and me—it having nothing to do with you—and you'll see what a wider slip of silver can change, if you can see better. I'm just a girl you know."

"But that's it: I know you!" He tried to kiss her again, his chin awkwardly coming at her but she pushed him back down. "It's the same midday. I don't care how much sunlight's shining. I don't care if it's blinding bright. If you're in the Pearl, I'm coming in after you."

Vyla watched the water seeming not to move—everything around here was a trickster. She thought of Momma and Daddy and whether she'd come out of the tree or he'd gone up. She didn't even know if this might be a brotherbaby. It didn't matter really, because she'd chosen. Momma had held this one. Loved it. Slipped the pearl into her pocket. There wasn't any undoing that. Momma's first and only choice.

Simon was wrong, of course. There was always—no matter who— just one choice ever: a yes or a no. A first and only. That's all. She'd thought he'd said yes at first. He thought so, too. "I'm just a girl you know," said Vyla, kissing his cheek, fingering the little bits of plant and sand in her own pocket. "And you're just a boy."

Family Reunion

Bonnie Jo Campbell

"NO MORE HUNTING," Marylou's daddy rumbles. Mr. Strong is a small man, hardly bigger than Marylou herself, but he's got a big voice, and some people call him just *Strong*, without the *Mister*. "We got more than enough meat. You understand what I'm saying, child?" He stands up from the stump where he's been sitting, sharpening the butcher knife, and glances around, looking for her, and Marylou fears he will also spot the yellow paper stapled to the beech tree. Marylou has just noticed the paper herself, and she is sneaking around the side of the house, intending to jump up and yank it down before he sees it, but she is not quick enough. He puts down the butcher knife and whetstone and moves to the tree.

Strong is freshly shaven for work—the new job makes him go in on Saturdays—and Marylou can see his jaw muscles grinding as he reads. Under his green wool cap, his forehead veins are probably starting to bulge. She didn't notice anybody putting up the invitation, but maybe one of her cousins snuck over here after dark last night. Uncle Cal couldn't have posted it himself, because of his tether and the restraining order, in place on account of the trouble at last year's Thanksgiving reunion party. Ever since Grandpa Murray died, though, Cal has been the head of the Murray family (not to mention president of Murray Metal Fabricators, the only shop in town paying a decent wage), and so in Strong's eyes, the photocopied invitation has come straight from Cal.

Marylou and Strong have just finished stringing up a six-point buck, Marylou's third kill of the season and two more than the legal limit. When Strong found her dragging the body toward the house an hour ago, he reminded her that being only fourteen didn't make her exempt from the law. Some day she would like to try hunting with the new Marlin rifle she won in the 4-H competition, but they live below Michigan's shotgun line, and, anyway, she knows a .22 bullet can travel a mile and a half, far enough that you might hit somebody you never even saw. Not that Marylou has ever missed what she was aiming for. She took this third buck in the woods at dawn, and the single shotgun blast echoed along the river and awakened Strong. He used to get out of bed early, but nowadays he usually stays up late and sleeps until there's barely enough time to shave and get to work.

But Strong seems to have forgotten about getting to work now. He shakes his head and says, "Son of a bitch." All he needs to see are the words *Thanksgiving Pig Roast*, and he knows the rest, that it's the famous yearly family gathering of the Murrays, when uncles and aunts and truckloads of cousins come in from out of town, and even outside of Michigan, to play horseshoes and drink beer and eat pork. Worst of all, the paper is stapled too high for Strong to reach up and tear it down.

He storms off and returns a few minutes later with his chainsaw and yanks the starter until the motor roars. He jabs the tip of the saw into the beech, knee-high. Sawdust flies, and with one clean, angry slice, the adolescent tree is free of its roots.

As the beech falls, Marylou notices the few marks where she and Strong carved dates and lines for her height in the smooth bark. The tree is taller than she has realized, and the top hangs up on a big swamp oak before breaking free by taking down one oak arm with it. When the beech lands between Strong's truck and the venison-processing table, it smashes a honeysuckle bush. Strong puts his foot on the downed trunk and cuts some stove-length pieces. When he reaches the invitation, he shreds it with the chain.

"Nerve of that bastard." His white breath mingles with the oily blue smoke.

When he notices Marylou staring at his face he says, "You got something to say, child, say it."

Marylou looks away from him, across the river, toward the Murray farm, toward the white house and the two red barns. The big wooden barn would be full of hay this time of year, and she knows how the cold morning sun streams through the cracks inside, the shafts of sunlight full of hay dust. Behind that barn is the hill where she used to shoot targets with Uncle Cal and her cousins, before all the trouble.

She decided to stop talking last year because she discovered that she could focus more clearly without words, and by concentrating hard with her breathing, she has gradually learned to slow time by lengthening seconds, one after another. In target or skeet shooting, she sometimes used to fire without thinking, but on opening day this year, she took her first careful, deliberate aim at a living thing. As she set her sights on that buck, she found she had all the time in the world to aim—up from the hooves and legs or else down from the head and neck, smack in the chest, touch the trigger, and *bang*.

On the way to his truck, Strong is shaking his head in exasperation, and once he's inside, he slams the door hard. When he pulls away, the truck's back wheels dig into the ice crust of the two-track. Marylou hears him throw up gravel on the road, and she hears the truck's noisy exhaust as it crosses the bridge downstream. No, she doesn't have anything to say, yet. And it was not just out of loyalty to the Murrays that she wouldn't open her mouth for a trial last year— her daddy is wrong there. At the time she didn't have things figured out, and even now she is still puzzling through what really happened.

This morning she puzzles about the invitation on the tree. It certainly wasn't meant for her mother, Cal's sister—she ran off to Florida with a truck driver and only calls home a few times a year. And it definitely wasn't meant for Strong—although he worked for the Murrays for years, they've never liked him. *The man broods*, Uncle Cal has always complained. Even Anna Murray used to say, *Loulou, don't brood like your father.* Marylou tried to defend him, but the Murrays could not understand that a person sometimes needed quiet in order to think about things.

The invitation on the tree has to mean that, despite all the trouble, the Murrays want to keep Marylou in the family, and Marylou feels glad to be wanted by them, by Anna who taught her to cook, and by Cal who taught her to shoot. And having boy cousins has been as good as having brothers.

Marylou kicks at the lengths of wood Strong has cut. The beech is too green to burn or even split this year. She retrieves the sharpened knife from the stump and returns to her strung-up buck. She wants to hurry and get the first long cut behind her. She will be fine after that, once the guts slosh into the galvanized trough, but she hates that first slice that turns the deer from a creature into meat. Strong would do it if she asked, but Grandpa Murray always told her, from the time she was little, how important it was to do a thing herself. She reaches up and inserts the knife about a half inch, just below the sternum. Pulling down hard and steady on the back of the blade with her free hand, she unzips the buck from chest to balls, tears through skin and flesh, and then closes her eyes for a moment to recover.

A gunshot yips from the Murray farm across the river, and Marylou drops her knife into the tub of steaming entrails. A second shot follows. Uncle Cal's black Lab begins to bark. Marylou has known this day would come, that Strong would one day kill her uncle with the pistol he carries behind the seat of his truck. And now Strong will go to jail, and she will have to move to Florida to live with her mother. Two more shots echo over the water.

Marylou considers the hole she has dug for the deer guts, and she knows she has to act fast to cover up her daddy's crime. She will bury Cal. Except she'll have to get the tether off somehow, so the police won't locate his body. She grabs the shovel and the bone saw from her venison table, carries them to her rowboat, tosses them in, and rows a hundred fifty feet across the current to the other side. She ties up to a fallen willow near Uncle Cal's hunting shed, where the trouble occurred. This is the first time she's been on the Murray property in almost a year. She climbs the bank, ignoring a sick feeling as she passes the shed, and makes her way across toward the Murray farmhouse. There she sees how Cal's new white Chevy Suburban is sunk down on flattened tires. Cal stands alongside the vehicle, yelling at the banged-up back end of Strong's departing Ford.

"Strong, you son of a bitch! Those were brand new tires!"

Cal's wife stands beside him, wearing a dress with pockets, holding an apple in one raw-looking hand and a peeler in the other. Marylou feels bad she didn't consider Anna when she was thinking about burying Cal. Marylou wonders if Anna is making pies for the party.

Tuesday, two days before Thanksgiving, Strong comes home from work to find Marylou dragging the warm, soft body of an eight-point buck by the antlers across frozen leaves, toward the venison table. She has to stop and rest every few feet.

"Marylou, what the hell are we supposed to do with all this meat? We've got no room in the freezer." He shakes his head. "Even if you aren't going to talk, child, you've got to listen."

Strong would be even madder if he knew she shot the deer across the river, because he doesn't want her to set foot on that bank for any reason. But Marylou was on her side of the river, watching the shed, puzzling through a few things, when the buck came high-stepping down the trail to the river's edge. Marylou aimed the shotgun and calmly fired. She wasn't sure she could hit at that distance, but the buck collapsed to his knees on the sand, then to his chest. She carried the knife across with her, dreading the prospect of finishing him off, but by the time she got there, he was dead. Dragging the buck into the wooden rowboat was difficult, and she was lucky nobody saw her. He was bigger than she realized, and the weight across the prow made it hard to fight the river current.

"Listen," Strong says. "The Murrays could make one phone call, and if those DNR sons of bitches open our freezer, we're in big trouble."

Marylou isn't worried. The Murrays always avoid the law, always figure they can take care of their own problems—apparently they haven't reported Strong for shooting out Cal's tires the other day.

Strong helps her string up the buck and then stands back. "You are one hell of a hunter, though. You always hit what you're shooting at, child of mine."

Marylou squeezes her daddy around his middle, and he puts his arms around her as he hasn't done in a while. Over his shoulder, across the river, she notices Billy, who is her age, dragging out the pig-roasting barrel from the barn. At last year's party, Marylou ran around with Billy and a whole flock of cousins, and some of the boys spit into the men's foamy draft beers while the men were tossing horseshoes. Billy has gotten tall this year, maybe tall enough to staple an invitation way up a tree, but when he or any of the other cousins see Marylou in school, they always turn away.

Aunt Anna appears by the water's edge, wearing insulated boots and a coat almost as long as her dress. She messes with an orange extension cord to light up the waterproof tube lights before she even starts stringing them around the dock. Last year Marylou helped Anna attach hooks for those lights.

Strong pulls away from Marylou's embrace and turns to look at what's caught her attention.

"I know you miss your aunt Anna," he says, shaking his head. "But don't you even think of going to that party."

Before Marylou can look away, Anna drops her string of lights into the river, and Marylou sees the end waggle and sparkle a few yards downstream. Anna is probably laughing as she fishes the lights from the cold current. Anna has always pulled Marylou out of being serious by saying, *Quit brooding and sing with me, Loulou!* or by letting Marylou bake something sweet in her kitchen, a place with all kinds of sweet smells, like vanilla and nutmeg.

"You don't seem to understand what's been done to you by those people," Strong says. "If you would have spoken against Cal at the trial, he would not have been able to plea bargain down to a damned ankle bracelet."

When her father goes inside, Marylou lets herself puzzle again about what they did to her, what Cal did. She still doesn't know why she followed Cal into his shed—Strong had told her a hundred times to stay away from Cal when he was drinking. Even before Uncle Cal shut the door, she knew something was wrong by the anxious way he was breathing, but she never grabbed the door handle to leave the way she thought about doing.

What the men did to each other afterward was more violent than what got done to her, wasn't it? Just after she crawled into a corner to gather herself together, Strong busted into the shed. Marylou heard bones crunch, and two red and white nuggets—Uncle Cal's front teeth—bounced on the plank floor. The men growled like bears. With all the noise and fury, Marylou forgot how Cal had insisted he had to teach her that afternoon how to dress out a deer—he said if she wanted to hunt, nobody was going to do her gutting for her. When they entered the shed, she was surprised to see it was a doe hanging there.

Anna Murray showed up a minute after Strong clobbered Uncle Cal. First she knelt beside Marylou and said, "What's the matter, honey? What happened?" But when Anna saw Cal's bloody mouth, she moved away to help him. Then Cal sputtered those words Marylou has just remembered. "The little slut lured me in here," Cal said. "And don't let her tell you any different." After that, Anna didn't look at Marylou anymore.

Cal had busted open Strong's cheek, and later at the hospital they shaved off his beard for the stitches. Marylou hardly recognized him as her father—going home with him afterward was like going home with a stranger. He hasn't grown his beard back because of his new job, which pays only about half what he made at Murray Metal Fabricators. The nakedness of his face still sometimes startles Marylou.

On Thanksgiving morning, Strong says, "I can't have you killing any more deer, child. I'm taking the shotgun with me. I'll be home from work at six." He slides the twelve-gauge into its case and hangs it in the truck's window rack. His old job with Murray Metal gave him holidays off, and Marylou can't help thinking that everything was better the way it used to be. Used to be when Strong was at work, she could spend time across the river being the girl that Anna and Cal said they always wanted, maybe still wanted. Grandpa Murray used to say that your family was all you had, and that a strong family like the Murrays could protect a person. He said it even when he was sick and dying, said he didn't care what her last name was, she was a Murray.

Instead of stalking another buck, Marylou sits on the bank all morning and watches vehicles pull in at the farm across the river, and she studies each Murray through the scope of her Marlin rifle. After a few hours, Marylou is sick with yearning to be on the other side of the river, to hear the old-fashioned country music from the outdoor speakers, to smell the meat roasting, and to see heaps of Murray cousins wrestling in their winter jackets. She pulls the rifle strap over her shoulder and rows her boat across. She ties up at the willow near Cal's shed. She slowly narrows the distance between herself and the shed as she kicks out rabbit holes in the yellow grass to keep warm. She is listening to the clinks and shouts from the horseshoe pit, wondering what the Murrays would do if she walked over and took a can of pop off the table. But then Strong's truck pulls into the driveway at home, hours before he is supposed to return.

She knows he will see her rowboat tied up, so she runs down the path to the river and waves her arms until Strong sees her, to let him know she is not at the party. As he pulls out of the driveway, Marylou notices her shotgun in the truck's window rack. Luckily Cal is nowhere around. But then, as if conjured up by her thoughts, Cal stumbles out the shed door, looking drunk and sleepy. Marylou silently hoists herself onto the lowest branch of the snake-bark sycamore. Uncle Cal doesn't even glance up as she climbs higher into its leafless branches. She straddles a smooth branch and looks through the window into the shed, looks for another girl like herself who might have gone in there with Cal, but she sees only a skinned carcass hanging.

Cal closes the shed door and steps around to the river side of the building. He puts a red-and-white beer can on the windowsill, and he leans against the unpainted shed wall. Marylou hears Strong's noisy exhaust on the road bridge, but Cal lights a cigarette and doesn't pay any special attention to the sound. Marylou is fifteen feet off the ground, high enough to see her daddy's Ford when it pulls up outside the rail fence a hundred yards away. Cal fumbles with his zipper, and when Marylou realizes he is going to pee right there on the path, she looks away. Then she looks back. Cal doesn't seem to hear the truck door creak open or slam shut. He continues to draw on his cigarette and stare down at his pecker in his hand, waiting for something to come out.

Marylou concentrates with her breathing to slow everything down so she can think better. Strong might kill her uncle, and Marylou knows he would not survive being locked in jail. She also knows he won't shoot a man on the ground, so maybe Marylou should take Cal down herself before Strong gets there, injure Cal rather than kill him. Marylou grips the branch with her legs, pulls the rifle off her shoulder and takes aim at one of Cal's work boots. At this short distance, she could shatter the white radio box tethered to his ankle.

Marylou sights Cal's kneecap. Strong won't kill a man who has fallen forward as though he is praying or begging forgiveness.

She aims at his thigh. For a split second Cal wouldn't know what hit him. A stray horseshoe? A biting snake? Then he would clutch his leg in confused agony. The bullet would continue through the side of the shed, bury itself in a floorboard.

Years ago Marylou's cousins held her down and put a night crawler in her mouth, and Billy once put a dead skunk in her rowboat to set her off. But she always got revenge—she chased Billy down that time and rubbed his face in cow manure until he bawled. Her cousins always enjoyed teasing her, enjoyed her shrieks, and afterward she evened the score, and they all got along again.

Uncle Cal wasn't teasing her, though—he wasn't even listening to her begging him to stop. Over the last year, she has been going back and forth, not knowing for sure if she had begged out loud, but looking at him now, she knows she said, "Please no, Cal," over and over.

"I know you want this, Loulou," he said, as though having him on her was a nice thing, like a hunting trip, like sitting down to a piece of pie. That afternoon, she saw past Cal's shoulder, through the dirty window glass, three little Murray kids peeking in. They looked terrified, and when she looked back at them, they ran off. Whatever they saw scared them enough to go get her daddy from the party.

Marylou looks past the beer can on the windowsill, past the table with the knives and saws, past the newly skinned carcass, to the place on the floor where Cal pushed her down. She has been puzzling about whether he really did push her down, but when she looks at Cal from up high in this tree, things get clearer. A year ago Marylou didn't know about slowing down time to study a situation, to make sure her aim was perfect or to avoid a terrible mistake. Those little kids were two girls and a boy, and Marylou thinks she knows what they saw, what scared them: they saw Cal had opened up Marylou and was gutting her there like a deer on the plank floor.

As Strong reaches the place where the path widens, Marylou realizes he doesn't have the shotgun or even his pistol. Seeing him unarmed now is as shocking as first seeing him without his beard at the hospital. Under his Carhartt jacket he still wears his blue work smock. He hasn't left work for the day, but has just come home to check on her.

Marylou looks through the scope at Cal's eyes, where she sees the same expression of concentration as when he was holding her down, so far from the door handle she could never have reached it. She looks at a patch of Cal's chest—it is amazing Strong was able to hurt such a big man at all. She moves her sights down farther to where a button is missing from his flannel shirt—why hasn't Anna sewn that button back on for him? Marylou moves the tip of her rifle down to Cal's hand, loosely clutching his pecker, from which a poky stream dribbles. She has to do this thing for herself; nobody is going to do it for her. She aims just past his thumb. She knows she is good enough to take off the tip of his pecker without hitting any other part of him.

The shout of her rifle is followed by a silent splash of blood on the shed wall and one last horseshoe clink from the pit. Cal's mouth is open in a scream, but it must be a pitch discernible only by hunting dogs. Marylou grasps the branch above with her free hand to keep herself from falling. The weight of the .22 in the other keeps her from floating up. She closes her eyes to lengthen that perfect and terrible moment and hold off the next, when the air will fill with voices.

Laser Vision

BettyJoyce Nash

VAYDA MANEUVERS THE ancient Mercedes into the bus depot. A tall guy with no hair turns and stares, but he can't be Josh. He's wearing her brother's jeans and busted-up bomber jacket, though. She's so busy gawking at him she thunks into the guard post.

Her seat belt yanks her back. She jams into reverse, clashing the gears. She cuts the engine and breathes deep: time to assess the damage. The tall guy gallops up and jerks her door wide open. He stands there grinning. "Way to go, Sis," he whoops. "How'd you convince the state of West Virginia you could drive?"

"Josh!"

He pulls her into the cold air and squeezes her breathless. "Merry Christmas." He inspects the bumper. "Barely crimped. This thing's a tank."

"My first solo." She makes a face. "I can hear the lecture now. Let's get out of here."

"OK, baby driver." Josh laughs. He pitches in his duffel and sits beside her. "What's new? Bruce still around?"

"He lost his job at the machine shop, so Mom's pulling extra shifts." Vayda, numb with cold, hauls her door shut on the third try. She frowns at Josh. "You look like a zombie." Like he just escaped from the pen. Like Dad near the end.

He reaches over and tugs a spike of her hair. "Uncle Sam paid for mine. Who swiped yours?"

She glares. "Locks of Love." She jerks her bangs so hard her eyes tear. "I don't recognize myself in the mirror. Made Wayman cut it; he bitched the whole time." She'd dyed what was left copper. Josh eyes her. Before leaving the house, she'd smushed gel into the copper. Black tights and black suede boots with ice-pick heels, and a black skirt hiked thigh high, completed the look.

"But your hair was you." It's true. Ash-blond waves had flowed past her shoulder blades.

"So was yours." A year ago, Josh turned eighteen and enlisted. Deserted her. Left her alone with their dead father, their mother, and their mother's obnoxiously undead boyfriend, Bruce. To celebrate a crappy Christmas. Until now: Josh is home.

He leans back, shoving sunglasses over his eyes. "Won't need hair where I'm going. Some R&R and then the Big Dune for me. Time to be a hero. I'm finally good at something besides meatball specials at the Hurricane Deli." He lights a Camel and exhales.

Vayda coughs at the smoke. She puts her hands at ten and two. She looks both ways and pulls out smoothly. She gets the Benz up to forty on the state road before speaking. "So you ship out. Where does that leave me? How do I survive the two long years until I turn eighteen?"

He takes another drag. "We've been over this. I couldn't stay. Period. Mom loves Bruce. I don't. What's going on with you?"

"Still at QwikPik. And Wayman's passing chemistry, thanks to me." After Josh left, she'd chased and caught Josh's best friend, Wayman. He smells like her old life. Same as Josh, same as Dad. Old Spice. Her chem teacher says the sense of smell wakes up a person's earliest memories. Vayda's memories never sleep.

"Wayman's already given me my present. Metallica tickets. Why? I hate Metallica. At least I get to blow town for one night. Maybe Bruce will lend us this heap." The concert's in Huntington, an hour away.

"Speaking of the Way Man, me and him are getting high tonight. Drive around, drink some beer." He cracks open his window to toss the cigarette.

The state road runs past their old farm, owned now by the bank.

Mom couldn't hang on after Dad died. The valves chatter as they top the snow-dusted hill. Vayda jerks the car into the shoulder's brittle grass. A freezing wind jangles the FOR SALE sign chained across the driveway. Sun bronzes the farmhouse's empty upstairs windows. They jump the chain. Vayda's heels catch and sink; she'd saved for the boots this whole wet fall.

"Wait," Josh says. He hops over the chain and sprints to the car. He rummages through his duffel. This time, he steps over the chain with care. He reaches into his bomber jacket. "Merry Christmas. She's a thirty-eight."

"She! She! A girl gun." Vayda grabs it by the barrel. Its weight surprises her. She drops it into the weeds.

"Hey! Careful." He retrieves the gun. The wind stirs. He prowls around a catalpa, its seed pods rattling. He squeezes the pistol's grip; a thin, red beam lights a hawk perched near the top. "Laser sight— lights your target."

She shivers. Josh, sideways, grips the gun two-handed and fires. Vayda's ears ring. She works her jaw.

"Sorry you don't like my present."

"Worse than Metallica tickets."

"I get him?" The hawk drifts from its branch unharmed, so close they see its mottled wings.

"He's coming for you," she says through clenched teeth. Fierce eyes glare above the curved beak. Clamping an unlucky mouse, the hawk blends back into the tree. Josh now smells nothing like her father or Wayman. He smells like a spent firecracker.

"Your turn to feel the magic," he says.

She shakes her head.

"You have to. So you'll understand." He nudges a half-buried beer can from the ditch with his boot and props it on the fencepost. He empties the cylinder and points to a button inside the grip. "Activates the laser. Go ahead. Dry-fire a few times."

"I understand plenty." She hesitates but tugs off her mittens and stuffs them into the pocket of her parka. She rubs her numb hands together until feeling returns. She takes hold of the gun and aims. Josh plants his boots beside hers and bends until their heads touch. He reeks of smoke.

She sucks in her breath, holds it, and places her left hand over her right knuckles. Her heart beats hard. She shrugs and pins the tiny red spot on the can's faded blue ribbon.

"Line your trigger finger along the barrel till you're ready to fire. Number-one safety rule."

She nods. Slides her finger onto the trigger, pulls back the hammer and fires. Again. Again.

"Let's load her up for real. You do it."

She shifts the gun to her left hand. She unsnaps her parka. "Hand me those things." She nods at the cartridge box. Her fingers, now warm and limber, chamber six rounds. She clinks the cylinder home.

"The smaller the target, the more time you take," Josh says. He engulfs her hands with his as they sight the ribbon. Then he releases her hands and steps aside.

Under the rubbing catalpa pods, she pulverizes the ribbon. She breathes in slowly to keep her teeth from chattering, then whips around. Whoom! She blasts the FOR SALE sign four times. It thuds to the ground. She takes three steps, stands over it, and shoots it dead.

"This place is ruined." She kicks the sign.

He gives her a thumbs-up and takes the gun, turns, and salutes the farmhouse. Her right hand burning, she jerks the door handle, swings the door wide, and gets in. Josh stashes the gun in his duffel. "Shooting opens you. You feel it? I know you did."

She says nothing. Sweat trickles from her armpits, the smell of her own fear.

Back at the rental house, neighbors have already piled torn boxes that only hours ago held fire engines or doctor kits. Vayda and Josh walk the strip of sidewalk between rectangles of brown grass. Behind the storm door, Flaps, Bruce's three-legged dog, barks, filming the storm door's glass with his hot bad breath. The brittle tree's lights blink a mechanical welcome.

Inside, Josh heads for the kitchen. Vayda pauses to inspect her hair in the hall mirror. "I look like shit," she says to no one. Josh's duffel thumps on the kitchen floor. He gives Mom a loud smacking kiss.

"Merry Christmas," he says. "I hear you're working extra shifts at the call center since the man of the house got laid off."

Behind Vayda, on his way up the basement stairs, Bruce calls, "Ho, ho, ho." His man funk arrives ahead of him. Bruce smells nothing like her dad. Or like Josh used to. Bruce appears beside her. Vayda squints into the mirror and holds her nose. He's wearing his Metallica "Ride the Lightning" T-shirt, and a sweatband girds his shaggy hair.

"Worked out," he says, sucking in his gut.

"I can tell." She elbows past.

"Hey! I let you drive my valuable antique vehicle, and this is how you thank me?" He follows her into the kitchen. "Lighten up. It's Christmas Day." Flaps guards Josh's duffel.

"For what exactly do I thank you?" Vayda says over her shoulder. "And quit telling me to lighten up." Bruce's presence spoils Vayda's private pretense that her father isn't buried-dead, only make-believe dead.

Their mother interrupts. "Thanks for coming up to greet Josh, Bruce." She's wearing the color-blind Bruce's Christmas gifts, a screaming orange turtleneck and matching slippers. When Vayda unwrapped her own lime-green version, she stuck her finger down her throat. Who looks good in lime besides a zombie?

"Yeah, coming out of his man cave so he can butt into everything," Vayda says. "Like he's one of us." Her best friend, Sheila, insists Bruce is permanent, but Vayda refuses to ask. Mom's got more than her crappy job and unpaid bills worrying her: a combat-ready son.

"Let's toast Josh," Mom says. She lines four goblets on the counter and fills each with clouded-over cider. "Not our worst Christmas, especially now that Josh is home." Josh and Vayda clink glasses, avoiding eye contact; instead, they inspect the cider. Josh and Bruce hook elbows and chug theirs. Mom sips.

"Nope. That was the one when Dad died," Vayda says flatly, and drains her glass. She turns to the sink, sponges the goblet clean, and rinses with hot water. "Or did everyone forget?" She rubs the rim until it moans in the silent kitchen.

No one speaks. Finally, Bruce pops Josh on the bicep, quick-hugs him and pushes off. He says, "Got ripped in basic. And without all that hair, you look almost grown."

Vayda's sigh scrapes the air. She upends her glass in the dish rack.

"Bruce bought dinner fixings," Mom says. Mom's eyes loom like burned-out bulbs above the orange sweater. "Vayda, will you brown the taco beef?"

"Make Josh. And whatever happened to turkey and dressing and cranberry sauce? Josh's last Christmas—" Her mother looks up sharply. "Last Christmas home for a while," Vayda finishes.

"Turkeys go half price tomorrow. Then we'll really celebrate," Bruce says. "In the meantime, Vayda, jack up that mood. Josh is home." He rips open a box of taco shells and lines a roasting pan with them. "I got some listening techniques to help you get in touch with your feelings, Vayda."

"Fuck you. I'd feel fantastic if it weren't for—"

"What?" Bruce says. "Nice mouth. Cut up an onion, would you?"

"No," Vayda says.

"We don't want Josh working his first day back, do we, Flaps?" Bruce rubs the dog's ears. Vayda drags Flaps to the floor with her.

"Army's not a bad gig, huh, Josh? Works good because of order." Bruce tosses the onion from one palm to the other.

"Bruce's been like this ever since you enlisted," Vayda says, her cheek against Flaps's fur. "Acting like he's the one headed for the desert."

"All right, Josh," Mom says, cutting her eyes at Vayda, who ignores the stare. She hands him the ground beef. "Have at it."

"Want help?" Bruce asks, peeling the onion's first layer.

"No," Josh says, too agreeably. "I got it." He pulls out the skillet. He switches on the radio, and sopranos belt out, "A thrill of hope, the weary world rejoices . . ."

"Do you know," Vayda says, from the floor, "how sick I am of Christmas music?" The high-pitched voices hurt her ears, still ringing with the revolver's reports.

"Alice," Bruce says, "turn it off. Princess PMS is sick of Christmas music. Vitamin B, Vayda, a mood miracle. I saw an infomercial about it."

At the stove, Josh whispers to their mother. "Why did you let her donate her hair? She looks ridiculous."

"Don't talk about me in the third person," Vayda shouts. "Besides, Mom likes it; she's donating hers, too, right?" Her mother nods.

"We could've shared our memories about Dad at the farm," Vayda says. "But no, instead he pulled out a gun and shot at a hawk."

"Yeah, and your baby girl here murdered the sign."

"What sign?" Mom asks Vayda. "What gun? What's going on?"

"I don't want to talk about it." Vayda's heart lurches crazily when she remembers the sign, the shooting. Josh's thumbs-up. To Josh, she says, "Why'd you mention that?"

"Excuse me, Sis, who brought it up?" He dumps the beef into the skillet and disappears with his duffel. He reappears with the gun.

"Sweet, huh, Broofus?" The barrel overshoots his palm. "Vayda's Christmas gift. We tried it out."

"Wish you'd quit calling me Broofus," Bruce says. He inspects the revolver.

"Sorry, man."

Mom's face darkens when Josh produces the gun. "Where'd that come from?" Her voice is harsh. She yanks her hair up and pulls a rubber band off her wrist to make a ponytail.

Josh turns. "Bought it off a buddy. Need to get a permit."

"We'll go to the range," Bruce says. "Family outing." He hefts it. "Nice weight—probably low recoil."

"Don't bet on that," Vayda says under her breath.

"This laser sight lights your target." Josh bounces the beam at his boots, then across the vinyl floor. "Cost extra."

"Bet it did," Bruce says. "A hunting buddy of mine's got one on his rifle."

Vayda sticks her tongue out at Josh. He shoots her a look. The beef sizzles and smokes. She jumps up and dials down the flame.

"I discovered my talent," Josh says. Flaps circles the men, waiting for attention.

"Yeah?" Bruce kneels to rub the dog's neck. "Army'll man you up if you learn to take orders. Not your thing, as I recall."

"We don't take 'em from you," Vayda interrupts. She flops into a chair and lays her head on the kitchen table.

"What'd you do in the army, Bruce?" Josh takes Vayda's place at the stove. He stirs the beef.

"Motor transport. Skills for life. How do you think I brought that old Benz back? How about you?"

"Machine gunner. Well, assistant."

"Set the table, hon," Mom says. She leans down and caresses Vayda's spastic hair, massages her scalp. At her mother's touch, Vayda stiffens then softens her spine.

"Might get the top job," Josh says. He lays the revolver on the table and takes a shooting stance. "Couldn't do much at first, but then instinct kicked in when we got these M4s." He pounds his fist into his chest. He thuds onto his knees and aims his imaginary weapon at the door.

"Eh-eh-eh-eh-eh," he chatters, a little kid's machine-gun fire. "You squeeze off round after round, and the whole time, the music's blasting, not just inside your head. For real, inside the Stryker. Even old Metallica's in there riding the lightning."

Mom's hand stops moving through Vayda's hair.

"You're right down to it: Live or die. Lose or win." He rises, slinging his invisible weapon over his shoulder. "Punish the deserving!"

The neglected meat spits. Smoke swells above the skillet. Vayda gasps and flings open the back door. Mom cuts off the stove and says, "Dinnertime. Let's eat in the living room beside the tree."

"Not me," Vayda says, coughing. "Gotta get to work."

She ditches the skirt and boots for jeans and sneakers. While everyone's eating tacos in the living room, she stops in the kitchen and jams the gun into one parka pocket and a handful of cartridges into the other. She jogs the three blocks to Alonzo's QwikPik.

"You'll be okay alone. It's Christmas—no beer sales. Probably all we'll sell is eggnog," Mr. Alonzo says. "Lock the money in the drawer."

QwikPik used to be an insurance office. Six short aisles cram the inside. The cold case up front holds milk, eggs, cheese, and Crazy Eight malt liquor. The meat case in back is cold but dark. No one's replaced the lights. "Or the meat," Josh said last summer, squinting into the glass before he left.

She sets the gun beside the register. She sniffs its handle, scented slightly with Josh's aftershave. She swings out the cylinder and slides the brass cartridges in and out. Her fingers memorize their shape and weight, and her ears, their metal-on-metal sound. She rubs the barrel; she steadies her hands and clutches the grip. She sets the laser on the Crazy Eights and then lets it follow the second hand on the clock above the door.

She lays the gun on the counter and presses her sweaty palms together until they stop trembling. Wiping her hands on her jeans, she organizes the ancient register's paper receipts: cash, charges, checks. At nine, a disheveled couple in Santa hats enters. Vayda stashes the gun under the counter. They get a carton of eggnog and ask for two Pick 3s. "Wish you luck," Vayda says.

"I already have luck. You, Junius," the woman says. She gives him the tickets. "Merry Christmas." His grin opens his face.

Vayda smiles. They leave and she reaches for the gun. She stashes it again when Josh and Wayman push through the door. Josh jumps and jangles the overhead bell a couple more times. Wayman's watch cap makes him look twelve. She giggles. He grins, and she remembers how much she enjoys their tutoring sessions. Now Wayman understands chemistry. So does she.

"Thought maybe you'd stay in and hang with Mom and Broofus," Vayda says. She rings out the drawer, lifts the tray, and slips the receipts underneath.

"Later," Josh says. He holds up his thumb and forefinger and sucks an imaginary joint. "This time, I got money." He heads to the cooler. His last night home, he and Wayman stopped by QwikPik and lifted two sixes of Crazy Eights. She paid their tab before Mr. Alonzo found out.

"You got a new identity also? One that allows you to purchase alcohol?" she asks.

Josh and Wayman guffaw.

"You and Mr. Wayman here just trash yourselves to hell, but buy somewhere else. I can't sell alcohol at all, much less to you. I could lose my job. Then what? I'm too young to enlist." She glances through the front door's burglar bars. Across the street, Mr. Alonzo's house twinkles a red-and-green rhythm in sync with her hammering heart.

"Who'd know?" Josh asks. "No cameras."

"Don't." She fires her evilest eye at them.

"Cool," Josh says. He and Wayman cruise the aisles. They hop onto the counter with Hostess cupcakes, Slim Jims, and a jumbo bag of Cheez Doodles. They cram Cheez Doodles into their mouths. Day-Glo orange crumbs fall everywhere.

"Ten dollars and twenty-seven cents. With tax. Fork over. Then clean that up," she barks. Josh tosses the bag and catches it. He pops it between his palms. Day-Glo dust falls like snow.

"Goddammit. Get the broom. Brush those crumbs back in the bag." She reaches under the counter for the gun and makes the red dot skip along the fluorescent ceiling fixtures. She lowers the gun, lighting first Wayman, then Josh.

Josh freezes, suddenly pale. "We're a little high is all; we're not messing with you." He wipes the checkout counter with his sleeve while Wayman sweeps. "Don't aim that thing at people. Keep your finger off the trigger like I showed you!"

"Yes, sir, GI Josh!" she says, mockingly, stung at his rebuke. "Who's feeling the power now?" She jitters the dot from the cooler to the Slim Jim jar to the clock. "Outside," she orders, still in her angry voice. She waves the weapon one last time. Before locking up, she drops a cartridge into each chamber. She stuffs the gun into her pocket.

Josh drives. Wayman lets Vayda ride shotgun. Her eyes light on a six of Crazy Eights. God. Josh and Wayman chug two each. Josh slows as a cop car passes in the opposite direction. Vayda nurses her beer. "What if a cop stops us?" she hisses. "We're drinking and I've got a gun." The phrase shocks her. Josh glances at her like he understands.

At the farm they cut the lights and park at the chain. The yard jumps with full-moon shadows. Josh kicks his door open. Vayda follows Josh, and Wayman lags behind with her. Josh waits on the porch. He wrestles open the living room window and climbs through. "Need to see the old place again, case I get greased."

"Don't talk like that," Vayda says. Her breath ghosts the air. Wayman gives her a leg up. Once he's inside, the window falls shut. They face the hearth and smell the smoke of old fires. Vayda stamps her numb feet. The floorboards shudder and a branch rasps a window. Somewhere, a coyote complains and more join in a yipping chorus: *I've got my gun, I've got my gun.*

The boys troop through the house, their boots resounding like a platoon on parade.

"Wait!" she shrieks. Wayman reappears and escorts her upstairs. Josh stumbles along the hallway, a palm against each wall.

"He's in a spiritual daze," Wayman whispers. He pulls her to him. She buries her face in his jacket and inhales the hollow of his throat: weed, beer, Old Spice.

"More like a Crazy-Eight-and-weed daze," she says.

Josh enters their parents' bedroom and walks to where the bed once stood. He sits in a pool of moonlight. "The wasting. But you," he points at her. "You shouldn't have butchered your hair. He wouldn't have wanted that, never mind your good reasons."

She shrugs. She floats to the window and tugs off her mittens. In the bright yard below, the catalpa pods' shadows make splayed fingers. She reaches into her pocket. She pulls the gun from her coat and turns around. Less target. More time.

"I'll shoot you. Just your toe. Then you can't go back."

Wayman hoots. "Ha! You're joking, right?"

Josh gets up. "So shoot. I saw today you might not miss. But don't forget the blood. Somebody's gotta clean up the blood. That's what people forget. Dad did, too. Otherwise he'd never have made that mess. Then again, he wouldn't have pulled the trigger if I'd heard him." He pauses.

She holds her breath.

"Remember how even sitting up exhausted him? He'd opened the nightstand drawer, probably looking for pain pills. I could've gotten them. But I didn't check on him—too scared. Mom's the one found him." Josh gazes around the room. "Look how clean it is. We scrubbed like hell."

"Clean! Blood's covered everything since he died," Vayda shouts, waving the gun. "I'm not stupid. I knew there was more."

He paces. "Mom drew second shift that weekend. You slept over at Sheila's, remember how her dumb mother pitied us? I was supposed to be at Wayman's." Josh grabs Wayman's lapels. They stand nose to nose in the middle of the room. "We were going to trick the girls, right? Rub branches against the screens and hide."

Josh's voice is one Vayda's never heard, businesslike but urgent, like he's selling something. She bites her lip. She squeezes the grip. The red beam hits Josh's boot. "But you had strep," he reminds Wayman through gritted teeth. "So I stayed home." He releases Wayman's jacket and sits down, hard, on the floor. "Goddammit, I stayed home so I wouldn't catch it."

"Later, I got up to pee. That's when I heard it." He bangs the floor with his fist. "Like the house cracking open. Louder." He looks at the ceiling. He whispers, "I went back to bed. Heard Mom come in a few minutes later, though. At midnight." He laughs harshly.

"I tried their door. It was locked. I knew she was in there. I knocked. 'Go back to sleep, Josh,' she said. I said, 'Did you hear that?' But she answered, 'Go back to sleep.' And I said OK. Then she opened the door." The moonlight silvers his stubble. He looks like an old man.

Vayda shivers and so does the dot on his boot. Wayman slips into the shadows by the door. "She had to," Josh says, walking toward Vayda. "He'd sprayed himself all over the room." She stares into the yard. Josh joins her at the window.

"Still doesn't explain why you enlisted."

He shrugs. "Mom moved on. So did I." He stares at her, then at the gun. "I'll make things right. Kill fear, so I'll be ready for anything."

She blinks rapidly. "You don't deserve any more punishment. Tell me how shooting strangers fixes things."

"I'm a sharpshooter. Death is indiscriminate. I won't be."

"I know death. And I know worse—deception." She stares into his moonlit face. "Now I really want to shoot you."

"I know."

The gun in her hand feels alive. She can hurt him. The moonlight slicing through the room makes it so easy. The army will let him go. He'll move home. The three of them—minus Bruce—will be each other's again.

"Don't forget the blood. And don't think shooting me will put things back the way they were."

"Not that much blood, not this time. It would be worth it."

"Do it, then."

She nods. But he's too close. "I need to take off this parka," she says. He extends his palm. She lays the gun on it, steps back, and shucks her coat.

"Thanks." She grips the gun and licks her lips. The coyotes must be asleep. Everything's quiet except for Wayman's loud breathing. Good old Wayman. She presses her lips together and raises her eyes to Josh's, but he's shut his. She squeezes the gun's grip and makes the red dot dance.

She grabs his hand with her free one. Her trigger finger pulses as she slides it into position. She steadies the gun, turns, and fires. Josh jumps and Wayman howls. Her first round punches a hole in the window. She fires again and again.

Her next five blow the window into the yard.

Freezing air floods the room. Behind her, Josh holds out her parka. The coat trembles as she slips into it, jamming the still-warm gun into the pocket. They gape at the moon bleaching the ground, lighting the window shards. "I'm sorry," Josh says, breathlessly. "I'm glad you know."

Outside, while Wayman warms the car, Vayda and Josh stomp the glass to smithereens. "You. Are. The shit!" Josh yells, over the crunch. "And I thought I was badass." He opens the car door. "But don't do that again. Never aim at anyone. Ever."

He waits for her to slide in beside Wayman. She drops her head back, sucks in the cold air. She reaches up and rubs her brother's bristly skull until her palms chafe. "I can't wait until you grow this out."

"Hell, yeah!" He yanks a spike of her hair before she climbs in. "Move over." He clambers in beside her.

By the time Josh and Wayman drop her off, the gun's freezing in her pocket. The tree's fitful flashes light her way upstairs. Vayda gropes along the hall. Red and blue strobe the stairwell. She stops beside her mother's half-open bedroom door.

"Vayda?" her mother whispers.

Vayda waits. Her mother steps into the hall, shutting the bedroom door. She takes Vayda's hands. "Like ice," her mother says.

"You didn't talk to me," Vayda says. "I figured his death made everybody's life go dark." She sits on the floor. Her mother sits beside her, warming Vayda's hands.

"You were only thirteen," her mother whispers. "Thirteen."

Vayda shakes her head. "The lie felt worse than the truth. Dad wasn't a liar." Her mother's face is blue, then red. She has her mother in her sights now, just like Josh. The lights flash red once more before Vayda turns and her mother pulls her close.

Tuesday Night at the Shop and Shoot

Joann Smith

DAMIAN CHECKS HIMSELF out in the locker-room mirror at 9:30 Tuesday night. White jacket. White tie. White shirt and pants. "Welcome to the Shop and Shoot," he says. "Damn, I look good."

Mort kind of rolls his eyes, the way he always does with Damian. But I nod and say, "You do," because Damian does. He takes his appearance seriously and I respect that.

Damian turns and gives me a fake punch—kind of a hard fake punch—and says, "Someday, my man. Someday you'll wear the jacket, too."

"You know it," I say, and nod again. I'm still a Buddy and Buddies don't get to wear white jackets. When I get promoted to Master Buddy, I'll wear one. "I'm with you tonight in orientation," I tell Damian.

"Good. Watch and learn. Watch and learn."

Damian always says this, and Mort rolls his eyes again. Damian just shakes his head like there's nothing to be said or done about Mort and heads upstairs for a vanilla milkshake. He always has a shake before his shift. We're allowed two free snacks a night. Of course, the Master Buddies' list of approved snacks is more extensive than the Buddies' list. We're allowed shakes, too, but smaller ones.

"He's such an asshole," Mort says.

"Yeah, but he's good at his job," I remind Mort. I like Mort. He's funny and he's a good Buddy, but I don't think he'll ever make Master Buddy. He hasn't got the drive. I look in the mirror. I think I look good, too, but I don't say it because I don't want Mort thinking I'm an asshole, too. "Welcome to the Shop and Shoot," I say into the mirror.

"You going to practice the Guidelines again?" Mort asks. "Want me to listen?" The Guidelines are the instructions for the Shop and Shoot. Master Buddies get to take the customers into the orientation room and tell them the Guidelines. The MBs have to memorize the script and be really enthusiastic and dynamic. Damian is a genius at that.

"Nah," I decide, looking at the clock. I like being on the floor early. Upstairs, Mort and I split off—he pulled the Shop tonight and I've got the Shoot.

The Greeters have already registered the new customers, charged them for membership and taken ID photos. I direct them to one of the orientation rooms and seat them. We keep things intimate at the Shop and Shoot—thirty people to a room, max. Tonight we have twenty-three. I go back for their ID cards, which I'll hand out after they get the Guidelines.

Damian blows onto the platform like a rock star, wired and ready. "Welcome to the Shop and Shoot," he calls out, applauding. The people applaud back. It's Tuesday, the crowd's quieter than on week-ends, but Damian still gets them going. "I want to release you good people into the aisles and onto the range as soon as possible, so if you'll just listen up, I'll go over some guidelines to make your time here great. Now, the most important: everyone must carry a gun."

He claps again a couple of times. "That's right. At the Shop and Shoot, everyone three and older carries a gun. Even you folks plan-ning to head for the Shop section—" MBs never say "you women heading for the Shop section" because Mr. Watsom, our boss and the owner, thinks that might make the women feel stereotyped as shoppers.

"You may think you don't require a gun," Damian continues, "but just when you're bending down to get that Dorito thirty-pack from the bottom shelf, 'someone' pushes right into your face, blocking your way. Or maybe when you're on line, 'someone' jumps ahead.

Wouldn't you like to . . . well, *shoot* that someone?" Damian smiles and nods and claps some more. "Come on, admit it," Damian says. "I want to shoot people all the time. That's why we have the Shop and Shoot."

I nod and clap to encourage folks, and they look at each other and nod, too. It's clear they're getting excited. Except this one guy, who looks unsure and won't meet anyone's eye. Sometimes people come, then think they don't really want to be here. But deep down, the guy knows why he came, just like most people know. That's the genius of this place. It gives people permission to admit what they really want.

"Now, me, personally," Damian continues, "I think the Shop's sometimes more challenging than the Shoot. Your targets are unexpected there, and you have to be alert."

Here a woman nudges her husband or boyfriend and says, "See?"

"But you shoppers, you do what you want—you can shoot all the targets that pop up or you can ignore them all and just shop. Plenty to shop for—we have it all, from cars to tomato paste. Check out Aisles 1–72. You'll find restrooms and snack bars all along the way, and plenty of Buddies to help with whatever you need. We believe in service here. And we don't just say that; we mean it."

That's another thing I admire about Mr. Watsom. He knows people are sick and tired of snotty cashiers and serve-yourself-everything-stores. He knows people want service, and he gives it to them.

"Okay," Damian continues. "So you'll all get a directory and a map. If you want to, you can stay after this part for the 3-D virtual tour. Okay? Now, here's how the Shoot works." People lean forward.

"When you go onto the range, they'll direct you to a booth. In there's a list of targets. Each kind of target has its name printed, along with a picture to help those of you who might not be sure what the picture means." The pictures are really for those whose English isn't so good, but we don't want to make anyone feel bad about that. We don't discriminate here at the Shop and Shoot.

"You'll also notice that the targets are color coded. The first group is pink. Pink targets won't get you many points, but they'll give you practice. Yes, we do track points here at the Shop and Shoot. That's for your benefit, because racking up more points earns you free targets.

"The pink targets are first, and they're inanimate things, okay? Nonliving. Paper targets, cans on stumps, the side of a barn, etc. You move on to blue targets, you raise your points a bit. Here you have your raccoons, birds, rats, mice—all those annoying little critters who won't stay out of your yard or who crap on your car."

Laughs and nods.

"In the brown group, you'll find dogs and cats. Now, *I* know you all love your pets, but *you* know there's been times when 'someone's' dog tore up your yard, or barked all night, and you just wish you could—" Damian pauses here and puts out his hand, inviting the audience.

They shout back, "Shoot it!"

"Well, now's your chance. And what about your boss? Let's talk about these green targets. Haven't we all wanted to kill our bosses?"

The truth is, I'd never want to kill Mr. Watsom. I respect him too much. I give him credit, though, for knowing that people often do hate their bosses, and I admire him for not being afraid to make himself a target, so to speak.

"And now the teens, the bright orange targets. Forgive me, you teens out there, but hasn't there been a time when everyone has wanted to kill a teenager? The loud music, the bad attitudes. I know there were a few times my mother wanted to kill me."

Some of the teens boo, but they're smiling.

"On the other hand, you guys, come on—I know, believe me, I know, I was a teenager up until a year ago—haven't you wanted to kill your mother? Or your father? Go ahead, admit it! And aim for those gray targets."

Now the teens hoot and pump their fists.

"And let's hear it for husbands and boyfriends. Yeah, I know we're impossible. And—sorry, ladies—but you guys out there, don't you just want to kill them sometimes?"

Someone yells out, "Oh, yeah."

"Yeah," Damian says. "So go for the red."

Now they're all stirred up, smiling, laughing, pointing at each other, saying, "I'm going to kill you tonight!" Everyone except the quiet guy.

"Okay," Damian says. "You can choose the beige Generic Male or Generic Female, or you can get really specific and move on to the purple targets, where you choose by race or religion: Chinese, Jewish, African, Catholic, Dominican, Indian, Irish, whatever. We put Homosexual in that category, too, because, well, where else would you put it? So go for it. Express yourself!

"That about does it, except for Scenarios and Taboos. The silver and the gold. Scenarios cost a little more. Well, actually, a lot more, but believe me, they're worth it. You pick the place: park, movie theater, train, school. We have a whole list. Your place, we load it up with people. And then—" Damian pauses for effect. "You come in and shoot to your heart's content.

"As far as the Taboos, well, I don't want to give too much away, but you folks are smart. You know what a taboo is, right?" Here, Damian shows why he's a Master Buddy. For those who don't know, but don't want to look stupid by asking, he says, "You know, something you're really not supposed to do. For example, some people say it's taboo to kill an infant. Others think it's taboo to shoot at a crucifix. See?

"Anyway, you push the big gold button under the word 'Taboos' and see what comes up. You have to be a little daring, I admit, because you don't know what you'll have to shoot.

"All right. Let's get out there." Damian used to ask if people had questions, but some woman almost always asked too many, which made the rest impatient. Now he skips questions and reminds people that the Shop and Shoot has Buddies and Master Buddies on the floor to answer their questions.

I hand out the IDs and tell people they have to wear them the whole time. "We like to know that everyone at the Shop and Shoot belongs here," I add. They like that. It makes them feel part of a special group, which they are, and it makes them feel safe.

Damian shoots me a look, then nods toward the quiet guy. He's noticed him, too. Masterful! That's my signal to follow. Damian gives me the ones who look like they're not sure; he takes the ones who look like they'll spend big. I understand; the MB who signs up the most targets per month gets a bonus.

I get next to my guy. He's easy to track because he kind of looks like me when I'm out of uniform, but older. Jeans, blue T-shirt. Short brown hair, brown eyes. My height. "Hey, I'm Zed," I say. That's not my real name, of course; we all have floor names.

"Luke," he replies.

"What kind of targets are you after, Luke?"

"I don't know. Generic Male, I guess," he says.

"Ever been here before?"

He shakes his head. "Nah."

"You're gonna love it." Luke doesn't answer. That's okay. I can do the talking for both of us. I walk him to his booth, push the beige Generic Male button for him. He picks up the gun, stretches out his arms, cups the heel of his left hand in his right palm—he's a leftie, like me—and settles into his aim.

He pulls the trigger and drops his arms slowly. He stares at the target a moment. He puts down the gun and pulls the cord, bringing the target close so he can see where he hit. Over the left eye.

"Great shot." I like it when my customers hit their targets. It makes them happy. "Hey, I'm a southpaw, too."

"Yeah?"

"Yeah. Hey, do you want to go for another target?" I ask. "Some extra points? What about an animal?"

He shakes his head. "I don't want to shoot an animal."

"Sure. Okay. What about your boss? Or girlfriend?" I raise my eyebrows to encourage him; I learned that from Damian.

"Nah." He pauses. "There's no girlfriend." His eyes move around like he's embarrassed and doesn't want to look at me. And doesn't want me to look at him. So I just push the GM button again. Another target pops up, and Luke gets ready to shoot. He hits four more targets and that's it. He's done.

"Thanks," he says before he leaves.

I nod. "No problem." I think I handled him pretty well.

Luke comes in every Tuesday for the next few weeks, and he always looks for me. He never says much, but that's fine. I think he likes me because I don't ask him a lot of questions. I just let him be, and let him know he has a place here at the Shop and Shoot.

Most people tell you who they're shooting. We're not supposed to ask, it might make them self-conscious or guilty. But people like to tell. Last Friday, I got a girl in here, maybe sixteen. Right after I greeted her, she said, "I'm going to blow my boyfriend away. He's Puerto Rican and Irish. You got a target like that?" We don't, but I showed her the Puerto Rican Male and the Irish Male, and she said the Puerto Rican looked more like him than the Irish, except that he had blue eyes. She shot twenty-five PRMs.

Not Luke. He doesn't come in angry, and he doesn't say who his GM is, and he doesn't want any other target. I find something pure in the way he sticks to that one target. Another thing I like about Luke is that he's what we Buddies call a Lone Shooter. We're of two minds about them at the Shop and Shoot. Some of us like the weekend crowds, and others prefer the weekday customers. Mort and I diverge; he's a week-end man. His crowd always comes here primed, knowing what they want. And they want it all. They come in groups and on dates.

Almost no one comes alone unless they're meeting someone. Last Saturday we had a group like that, guys who shot at their targets and kept yelling to each other, "This is you, dude!" They were also Bitch Killers, as we call them. You know, "Hasta la vista, bitch." We always get a bunch of those on weekends.

I prefer weekdays. People coming in then are more particular and thoughtful about their choices. Plus you get your regulars, and your Lone Shooters like Luke, so it just seems more civilized to me.

Tonight, I'm all set at his regular time—10 p.m.—and there he is.

"Hey, Luke."

"Hey."

"How's things?"

"Great."

But he doesn't sound like they're great. I think he's lonely; I just get that impression because he never comes with a friend. He's also pretty thin, so maybe he jogs. He's about thirty-five or forty, but I'm not a good judge of age. Tonight he looks even older. Dark circles under his eyes. Probably not sleeping. Maybe sad about something. I want to cheer him up.

"How about a Scenario tonight?" I feel like I have to try to persuade him even though I don't expect him to give in. "You could do a Generic Male Scenario. We could arrange that. Shake up the routine a little bit." I'm starting to think a change might do him good.

"No, thanks," he says. "But thanks."

He's always polite. I walk him to his booth and set up a GM for him. He hits just one target and puts down the gun.

"That's it?" I ask, surprised. He usually shoots at least five Generic Males.

"That's it," he says. "Bye. Thanks." He shakes my hand. He's never done that before. He's done something else unusual, too. I've never seen anyone shoot just one target. Never. Luke stays on my mind.

After my shift, I'm allowed five targets on the range, categories pink through red—no Scenarios or Taboos until I make Master Buddy. Tonight I pull Generic Male. I want to do just the one target, like Luke, to see how it feels. After one, though, I'm just not satisfied. I hit the Generic Male button again and wonder why Luke didn't choose race or religion.

Who does he shoot that has no race or religion? Is Luke gay, and shooting a lover who left? Still, he doesn't strike me as gay, and he never chose an HM target. I take another shot. Is it his father? Why not the Father target, then?

I set up my third target, seeing Luke the way he would set it up. Determined. Eyes narrow. Face set. Thin face. Pale. I wonder what nationality Luke is. White, yeah. Irish? Maybe. Polish? Possibly. Nothing distinguishable. Just white. I take my shot. Then it hits me. Generic Male. Luke is Generic Male.

He's shooting himself. Every week, he comes in and shoots himself.

Wow. Now I can't wait for him to come back. But I can't say anything to him. It's against all the rules to comment on a customer's choice of target, even if the target is himself. I can't risk making him feel self-conscious, making him feel like he can't come back here. Because if he can't shoot himself here, where can he shoot himself? No, I just have to be here for him.

All week, I can hardly think of anything but Luke. Tuesday finally comes, and I keep checking the time. 9. 9:30. 10. Finally. But no Luke. 11. Midnight. No Luke. All night. No Luke.

Maybe he moved, I tell myself. Or got himself a girlfriend. But in my gut, I have this feeling: Luke shot himself.

It isn't my fault, but I feel kind of guilty. Like I should have done something. Like maybe he was telling me and I should have figured it out sooner. Then I think that maybe he should never have come to the Shop and Shoot in the first place, that if there was no Shop and Shoot, maybe he would never have gotten the idea to shoot himself. I don't like thinking this way.

I tell Mort about it. He sets me straight. "First off," he says, "you don't know that he's dead. He could have just moved. He could have gotten a girlfriend. Maybe he's busy getting laid."

"Maybe."

"Don't torture yourself. A guy's got to take responsibility for his own actions. You know that. You know the rules. Don't force anyone into a target they don't want. Did you force this guy?"

"No."

"Right. We suggest, but we don't force. As Mr. Watsom says, we're not doing them any favors if in the end they don't take responsibility for their own targets. Right?" I feel less guilty.

"He came in here knowing what he wanted. And he gave himself what he wanted. That's the whole point of the Shop and Shoot, right? Just keep doing your job. Hey, and keep practicing your Guidelines. Right?" Maybe Mort understands the Shop and Shoot better than I do.

Luke stays on my mind, though, when I practice that night. I know this because I do something I've never done before. Right after I say, "The most important guideline is that everyone must carry a gun," I make my hand into a gun and point it at the mirror. At my reflection. At me. That's when the idea hits me.

My meeting with Mr. Watsom goes well. He likes the idea of a suicide target. "We might even create a High Taboo category for it," he says.

"We could use the ID photos," I say. "Blow them up and apply them to the body of any target—GM, Latin Female, whatever. Then, if a person went into the High Taboo category, up would come a target of him or her. What a rush that would be! To see your own face come up on a target. It would be the ultimate Shop and Shoot experience!"

"Great idea!" he says.

My mind works fast. "We could even have self-targets pop up in the Shop section, maybe in dressing rooms when the things people try on don't fit."

Mr. Watsom laughs. "Brilliant!" he says. "I love a Buddy who's always thinking. And clearly, *you* are thinking. Brush up on your Guidelines, Zed, because this idea of yours could bring us many more customers. So many we might need more Master Buddies. Be ready," he says, shaking my hand.

Mr. Watsom was right. "Welcome to the Shop and Shoot."

Mercy

Pinckney Benedict

THE LIVESTOCK HAULER'S ramp banged onto the ground, and out of the darkness they came, the miniature horses, fine-boned and fragile as china. They trit-trotted down the incline like the vanguard of a circus parade, tails up, manes fluttering. They were mostly a bunch of tiny pintos, the biggest not even three feet tall at the withers. I was ten years old, and their little bodies made me feel like a giant. The horses kept coming out of the trailer, more and more of them every moment. The teamsters that were unloading them just stood back and smiled.

My old man and I were leaning on the top wire of the southern fence-line of our place, watching the neighbor farm become home to these exotics. Ponies, he kept saying, ponies ponies ponies, like if he said it enough times, he might be able to make them go away. Or make himself believe they were real, one or the other.

I think they're miniature horses, I told him. Not ponies. I kept my voice low, not sure I wanted him to hear me.

One faultless dog-sized sorrel mare looked right at me, tossed its head, and sauntered out into the thick clover of the field, nostrils flaring. I decided I liked that one the best. To myself, I named it Cinnamon. If I were to try and ride it, I thought, my heels would drag the ground.

Horses, ponies, my old man said. He had heard. He swept out a dismissive hand. Can't work them, can't ride them, can't eat them. Useless.

Useless was the worst insult in his vocabulary.

We were angus farmers. Magnificent deep-fleshed black angus. In the field behind us, a dozen of our market steers roamed past my old man and me in a lopsided wedge, cropping the sweet grass. They ate constantly, putting on a pound, two pounds a day. All together like that, they made a sound like a steam locomotive at rest in the station, a deep resonant sighing. Their rough hides gleamed obsidian in the afternoon sun, and their hooves might have been fashioned out of pig iron.

The biggest of them, the point of the wedge, raised his head, working to suss out this new smell, the source of this nickering and whinnying, that had invaded his neighborhood. His name was Rug, because his hide was perfect, and my old man planned to have it tanned after we sent him off to the lockers in the fall. None of the other steers had names, just the numbers in the yellow tags that dangled from their ears. Rug peered near-sightedly through the woven-wire fence that marked the border between his field and the miniature horses', and his face was impassive, as it always was.

The teamsters slammed the trailer's ramp back into place and climbed into the rig's cab, cranked up the big diesel engine, oily smoke pluming from the dual stacks. The offloaded horses began to play together, nipping at one another with their long yellow teeth, dashing around the periphery of the field, finding the limits of the place. Cinnamon trailed after the others, less playful than the rest. Rug lowered his head and moved on, and the wedge of heavy-shouldered angus moved with him.

Another livestock van pulled into the field, the drivers of the two trucks exchanging casual nods as they passed each other. I was happy enough to see more of them come, funny little beggars, but I had a moment of wondering to myself how many horses, even miniature ones, the pasture could sustain.

More of the midgets, my old man said. What in hell's next? he asked. He wasn't speaking to me exactly. He very seldom addressed a question directly to me. It seemed like he might be asking God Himself. What? Giraffes? Crocodiles?

This valley was a beef valley from long before I was born. A broad river valley with good grass, set like a diamond in the center of a wide plateau at twenty-four hundred feet of altitude. For generations it was Herefords all around our place, mostly, and Charolais, but our angus were the sovereigns over them all. My grandfather was president of the cattlemen's association, and he raised some trouble when the Beefmasters and Swiss Simmentals came in, because the breeds were unfamiliar to him; and my old man did the same when the place to our east went with the weird-looking hump-backed lop-eared Brahmas. But they got used to the new breeds. They were, after all, beefers, and beef fed the nation; and we were still royalty.

Then the bottom fell out of beef prices. We hung on. Around us, the Charolais and Simmentals went first, the herds dispersed and the land sold over the course of a few years, and then the rest of them all in a rush, and we were alone. Worse than alone. Now it was swine to the east, and the smell of them when the wind was wrong was enough to gag a strong-stomached man. The smell of angus manure is thick and honest and bland, like the angus himself; but pig manure is acid and briny and bitter and brings a tear to the eye. And the shrieking of the pigs clustered in their long barns at night, as it drifted across the fields into our windows, was like the cries of the damned.

Pigs to the east, with a big poultry operation beyond that, and sheep to the north (with llamas to protect them from packs of feral dogs), and even rumors of a man up in Pocahontas County who wanted to start an ostrich ranch, because ostrich meat was said to be low in fat and cholesterol, and ostrich plumes made wonderful feather dusters that never wore out.

The place to our west wasn't even a farm anymore. A rich surgeon named Slaughter from the county seat had bought the acreage when Warren Kennebaker, the Charolais breeder, went bust. Slaughter had designed it like a fortress, and it looked down on our frame house from a hill where the dignified long-bodied Charolais had grazed: a great gabled many-chimneyed mansion that went up in a matter of months; acres of slate roof, and a decorative entrance flanked by stone pillars and spear-pointed pickets that ran for three or four rods out to each side of the driveway and ended there; and gates with rampant lions picked out in gold. That entrance with its partial fence made my old man angrier than anything else. What good's a fence that doesn't go all the way around? he asked me. Keeps nothing out, keeps nothing in.

Useless, I said.

As tits on a bull, he said. Then: Doctor Slaughter, Doctor Slaughter! he shouted up at the blank windows of the house. He thought her name was the funniest thing he had ever heard. Why don't you just get together and form a practice with Doctor Payne and Doctor Butcher?

There was no Doctor Payne or Doctor Butcher; that was just his joke.

Payne, Slaughter, and Butcher! he shouted. That would be rich.

The horses started testing the fence almost from the first. They were smart, I could tell that from watching them, from the way they played tag together, darting off to the far parts of the pasture to hide, flirting, concealing their compact bodies in folds of the earth and leaping up to race off again when they were discovered, their hooves drumming against the hard-packed ground. They galloped until they reached one end of the long field, then swung around in a broad curve and came hell-for-leather back the way they had gone, their coats shaggy with the approach of winter and slick with sweat. I watched them whenever I had a few moments free from ferrying feed for the steers.

I would walk down to the south fence and climb up on the sagging wire and sit and take them in as they leaped and nipped and pawed at one another with their sharp, narrow hooves. I felt like they wanted to put on a show for me when I was there, wanted to entertain me. During the first snow, which was early that year, at the end of October, they stood stock still, the whole crew of them, and gaped around at the gently falling flakes. They twitched their hides and shook their manes and shoulders as though flies were lighting all over them. They snorted and bared their teeth and sneezed. After a while, they grew bored with the snow and went back to their games.

After a few weeks, though, when the weather got colder and the grass was thin and trampled down, the horses became less like kids and more like the convicts in some prison picture: heads down, shoulders hunched, they sidled along the fence line, casting furtive glances at me and at the comparatively lush pasturage on our side of the barrier.

The fence was a shame and an eyesore. It had been a dry summer when it went in, five years before when the last of the dwindling Herefords had occupied the field, and the dirt that season was dry as desert sand, and the posts weren't sunk as deep as they should have been.

They were loose like bad teeth, and a few of them were nearly rotted through. I was the only one who knew what bad shape it was getting to be in. My old man seldom came down to this boundary after the day the horses arrived, and nobody from the miniature horse farm walked their border the way we walked ours. We didn't know any of them, people from outside the county, hardly ever glimpsed them at all.

It wasn't our problem to solve. By long tradition, that stretch was the responsibility of the landowner to the south, and I figured my old man would die before he would take up labor and expense that properly belonged with the owners of the miniature horses.

Cinnamon, the sorrel, came over to me one afternoon when I was taking a break, pushed her soft nose through the fence toward me, and I promised myself that the next time I came I would bring the stump of a carrot or a lump of sugar with me. I petted her velvet nose and she nibbled gently at my fingers and the open palm of my hand. Her whiskers tickled and her breath was warm and damp against my skin.

Then she took her nose from me and clamped her front teeth on the thin steel wire of the fence and pulled it toward her, pushed it back. I laughed. Get away from there, I told her, and smacked her gently on the muzzle. She looked at me reproachfully and tugged at the wire again. Her mouth made grating sounds against the metal that set my own teeth on edge. She had braced her front legs and was really pulling, and the fence flexed and twanged like a bow string. A staple popped loose from the nearest post.

You've got to stop it, I said. You don't want to come over here, even if the grass looks good. My old man will shoot you if you do.

He surprised me watching the horses. I was in my usual place on the fence, the top wire biting into my rear end, and he must have caught sight of me as he was setting out one of the great round hay bales for the angus to feed from. Generally I was better at keeping track of him, at knowing where he was, but that day I had brought treats with me and was engrossed, and I didn't hear the approaching rumble of his tractor as it brought the fodder over the hill. When he shut down the engine, I knew that I was caught.

What are you doing? he called. The angus that were following the tractor and the hay, eager to be fed, ranged themselves in a stolid rank behind him. I kicked at Cinnamon to get her away from me, struggled to get the slightly crushed cubes of sugar back into my pocket. Crystals of it clung to my fingers. He strode down to me, and I swung my legs back over to our side of the fence and hopped down. It was a cold day and his breath rolled white from his mouth.

You've got plenty of leisure, I guess, he said. His gaze flicked over my shoulder. A number of the miniature horses, Cinnamon at their head, had peeled off from the main herd and were dashing across the open space. What makes them run like that? he asked. I hesitated a moment, not sure whether he wanted to know or if it was one of those questions that didn't require an answer.

They're just playing, I told him. They spend a lot of time playing.

Playing. Is that right, he said. You'd like to have one, I bet. Wouldn't you, boy? he asked me.

I pictured myself with my legs draped around the barrel of Cinnamon's ribs, my fingers wrapped in the coarse hair of her mane. Even as I pictured it, I knew a person couldn't ride a miniature horse. I recalled what it felt like when she had thrust her muzzle against my hand, her breath as she went after the sugar I had begun bringing her. Her teeth against the wire. I pictured myself holding out a fresh carrot for her to lip into her mouth. I pictured her on our side of the fence, her small form threading its way among the stern gigantic bodies of the angus steers. I knew I would be a fool to tell him I wanted a miniature horse.

Yes sir, I said.

He swept his eyes along the fence. Wire's in pretty bad shape, he said. Bastards aren't doing their job. Looks like we'll have to do it for them.

He shucked off the pair of heavy leather White Mule work gloves he was wearing and tossed them to me. I caught one in the air, and the other fell to the cold ground. You keep the fence in shape then, he said. The staples and wire and stretcher and all were in the machine shed, I knew.

Remember, my old man said as he went back to his tractor. First one that comes on my property, I kill.

On the next Saturday, before dawn, I sat in the cab of our beef hauler while he loaded steers. There were not many of them; it would only take us one trip. I couldn't get in among them because I didn't yet own a pair of steel-toed boots, and the angus got skittish when they were headed to the stockyard. I would have helped, I wanted to help, but he was afraid I would get stepped on by the anxious beeves and lose a toe. He was missing toes on both feet. So he was back there by himself at the tailgate of the truck, running the angus up into it, shouting at them.

Rug was the first, and my old man called the name into his twitching ear—Ho, Rug! Ho!—and took his cap off, slapped him on the rump with it. Get up there! he shouted. I watched him in the rearview mirror, and it was hard to make out what was happening, exactly, because the mirror was cracked down its length, the left half crazed into a patchwork of glass slivers. The other angus were growing restive, I could tell that much, while Rug balked.

My old man never would use an electric prod. He twisted Rug's tail up into a tight, painful coil, shoving with his shoulder, and the big steer gave in and waddled reluctantly into the van. The truck shifted with his weight, which was better than a ton. The rest followed, the hauler sinking lower and lower over the rear axle as they clambered inside. My old man silently mouthed their numbers, every one, as they trundled on board, and he never looked at their ear tags once. He knew them.

When they were all embarked, when for the moment his work was done, his face fell slack and dull, and his shoulders slumped. And for a brief instant he stood still, motionless as I had never seen him. It was as though a breaker somewhere inside him had popped, and he had been shut off.

I made my daily round of the southern fence, patching up the holes the horses had made, shoveling loose dirt into the cavities they carved into the earth, as though they would tunnel under the fence if I wouldn't let them break through it. They were relentless and I had become relentless too, braiding the ends of the bitten wire back together, hammering bent staples back into the rotting posts. The sharp end of a loose wire snaked its way through the cowhide palm of the glove on my right hand and bit deep into me. I cursed and balled the hand briefly into a fist to stanch the blood, and then I went back to work again.

The field the horses occupied was completely skinned now, dotted with mounds of horse dung. Because the trees were bare of leaves, I could see through the windbreak to the principal barn of the place, surrounded by dead machinery. I couldn't tell if anyone was caring for them at all. I don't believe a single animal had been sold. Their coats were long and matted, their hooves long untrimmed, curling and ugly. A man—I suppose it was a man, because at this distance I couldn't tell, just saw a dark figure in a long coat—emerged from the open double doors of the barn, apparently intent on some errand.

Hey! I shouted to him. My voice was loud in the cold and silence. The figure paused and glanced around. I stood up and waved my arms over my head to get his attention. This is your fence!

He lifted a hand, pale so that I could only imagine that it was ungloved, and waved uncertainly back at me.

This is your fence to fix! I called. I pounded my hand against the loose top wire. These here are your horses!

The hand dropped, and the figure without making any further acknowledgment of me or what I had said turned its back and strolled at a casual pace back into the dark maw of the barn.

Most days I hated them. I cursed them as they leaned their slight weight against the fence, their ribs showing. I poked them with a sharp stick to get them to move so that I could fix the fence. They would shift their bodies momentarily, then press them even harder into the wire. The posts groaned and popped. I twisted wire and sucked at the cuts on my fingers to take the sting away. I filched old bald tires from the machine shed and rolled them through the field and laid them against the holes in the fence. The tires smelled of dust and spider webs. This was not the way we mended fence on our place—our posts were always true, our wire stretched taut and uncorroded, our staples solidly planted—but it was all I could think of to keep them out. The horses rolled their eyes at me.

And I tossed them old dry corn cobs that I retrieved from the crib, the one that we hadn't used in years. The horses fell on the dry husks, shoving each other away with their heads, lashing out with their hooves, biting each other now not in play but hard enough to draw blood. I pitched over shriveled windfallen apples from the stunted trees in the old orchard behind the house. I tried to get the apples near the sorrel, near Cinnamon; but as often as not the pintos shunted her aside before she could snatch a mouthful.

You know why we can't feed them, don't you? my old man asked me. We were breaking up more of the great round bales, which were warm and moist at their center, like fresh-baked rolls. The angus, led not by Rug now but by another, shifted their muscular shoulders and waited patiently to be fed. I could sense the miniature horses lining the fence, but I didn't look at them.

They'd eat us out of house and home, he said. Like locusts.

Behind me, the hooves of the horses clacked against the frozen ground.

One morning, the fence didn't need mending. It had begun to snow in earnest the night before, and it was still snowing when I went out to repair the wire. The television was promising snow for days to come. Most of the horses were at the fence, pressing hard against it but not otherwise moving. Some were lying down in the field beyond. I looked for the sorrel, to see if she was among the standing ones. All of them were covered in thick blankets of snow, and it was impossible to tell one diminutive shape from the next. Each fence post was topped with a sparkling white dome.

I walked the fence, making sure there was no new damage. I took up the stick I had used to poke them and ran its end along the fence wire, hoping its clattering sound would stir them. It didn't. Most of them had clustered at a single point, to exchange body heat, I suppose. I rapped my stick against the post where they were gathered, and its cap of snow fell to the ground with a soft thump. Nothing. The wire was stretched tight with the weight of them.

I knelt down, and the snow soaked immediately through the knees of my coveralls. I put my hand in my pocket, even though I knew there was nothing there for them. The dry cobs were all gone, the apples had been eaten. The eyes of the horse nearest me were closed, and there was snow caught in its long delicate lashes. The eyes of all the horses were closed. This one, I thought, was the sorrel, was Cinnamon. Must be. I put my hand to its muzzle but could feel nothing. I stripped off the White Mule glove, and the cold bit immediately into my fingers, into the half-healed cuts there from the weeks of mending fence. I reached out again.

And the horse groaned. I believed it was the horse. I brushed snow from its forehead, and its eyes blinked open, and the groaning continued, a weird guttural creaking and crying, and I thought that such a sound couldn't be coming from just the one horse, all of the horses must be making it together somehow, they were crying out with a single voice. Then I thought as the sound grew louder that it must be the hogs to the east, they were slaughtering the hogs and that was the source of it, but it was not time for slaughtering, so that couldn't be right either. I thought these things in a moment, as the sound rang out over the frozen fields and echoed off the surrounding hills.

At last I understood that it was the fencepost, the wood of the fencepost and the raveling wire and the straining staples, right at the point where the horses were gathered. And I leaped backward just as the post gave way. It heeled over hard and snapped off at ground level, and the horses tumbled with it, coming alive as they fell, the snow flying from their coats in a wild spray as they scrambled to get out from under one another.

The woven-wire fence, so many times mended, parted like tissue paper under their combined weight. With a report like a gunshot, the next post went over as well, and the post beyond that. Two or three rods of fence just lay down flat on the ground, and the horses rolled right over it, they came pouring onto our place. The horses out in the field roused themselves at the sound, shivered off their mantles of snow, and came bounding like great dogs through the gap in the fence as well. And I huddled against the ground, my hands up to ward off their flying hooves as they went past me, over me. I knew that there was nothing I could do to stop them. Their hooves would brain me, they would lay my scalp open to the bone.

I was not touched.

The last of the horses bolted by me, and they set to on the remains of the broken round bale, giving little cries of pleasure as they buried their muzzles in the hay's roughness. The few angus that stood nearby looked on bemused at the arrivals. I knew that I had to go tell my father, I had to go get him right away. The fence—the fence that I had maintained day after day, the fence I had hated and that had blistered and slashed my hands—was down. But because it was snowing and all around was quiet, the scene had the feel of a holiday, and I let them eat.

When they had satisfied themselves, for the moment at least, the horses began to play. I searched among them until finally I found the sorrel. She was racing across our field, her hooves kicking up light clouds of ice crystals. She was moving more quickly than I had ever seen her go, but she wasn't chasing another horse, and she wasn't being chased. She was teasing the impassive angus steers, roaring up to them, stopping just short of their great bulk; turning on a dime and dashing away again. They stood in a semicircle, hind ends together, lowered heads outermost, and they towered over her like the walls of a medieval city. She yearned to charm them. She was almost dancing in the snow.

As I watched her, she passed my old man without paying him the least attention. He wore his long cold-weather coat. The hood was up, and it eclipsed his face. He must have been standing there quite a while. Snow had collected on the ridge of his shoulders, and a rime of frost clung to the edges of his hood. In his hand he held a hunting rifle, his Remington .30-06. The lines of his face seemed odd and unfamiliar beneath the coat's cowl, and his shoulders were trembling in a peculiar way as he observed the interlopers on his land. I blinked. I knew what was coming. The thin sunlight, refracted as it was by the snow, dazzled my eyes, and the shadows that hid him from me were deep.

At last, the sorrel took notice of him, and she turned away from the imperturbable angus and trotted over to him. He watched her come. She lowered her delicate head and nipped at him, caught the hem of his coat between her teeth and began to tug. His feet slipped in the snow. Encouraged by her success, she dragged him forward. I waited for him to kill her. She continued to drag him, a foot, a yard, and at last he fell down. He fell right on his ass in the snow, my old man, the Remington held high above his head. The sorrel stood over him, the other horses clustered around her, and she seemed to gloat.

The Remington dropped to the ground, the bolt open, the breech empty. Half a dozen bright brass cartridges left my old man's hand to skip and scatter across the snow. The hood of his coat fell away from his face, and I saw that my old man was laughing.

Acknowledgments

We thank, above all, our contributors. Their enthusiasm for the idea behind this book, their brilliant imaginations, and their willingness and patience with the process helped make *Lock & Load* real.

We thank the Virginia Center for the Creative Arts, which provided a collaborative residency at a crucial moment in the manuscript's organization and development.

We thank Kevin McIlvoy and David Mullins, the book's preliminary reviewers, for their time and comments.

We thank our families, too, for their patience as we undertook additions, corrections, negotiations, details, and sticky wickets, and for essential assistance, editorial and otherwise.

Contributors

Mari Alschuler has published a poetry chapbook, *The Nightmare of Falling Teeth*. Her work has also appeared in *Shenandoah*, *American Poetry Review*, *Backbone*, *Berkeley Poets Co-op*, *No Apologies*, and *Pudding Magazine*. She received an MFA in creative writing from Columbia. An assistant professor of social work at Youngstown State University, in Youngstown, Ohio, Alschuler is a poetry therapist in private practice. She leads workshops on poetry and journal therapy, clinical supervision, and suicide prevention.

Pinckney Benedict has published a novel, *Dogs of God*, and three story collections, *Miracle Boy and Other Stories*, *The Wrecking Yard*, and *Town Smokes*. His stories have appeared in *Esquire*, *Zoetrope*, *StoryQuarterly*, and *Ontario Review*, and in the O. Henry Award and Pushcart Prize series. A professor in the English Department at Southern Illinois University in Carbondale, Benedict has also received a Michener Fellowship from the Iowa Writers Workshop, an NEA fellowship, a Literary Fellowship from the West Virginia Commission on the Arts, the Nelson Algren Award, an Individual Artist grant from the Illinois Arts Council, and Great Britain's Steinbeck Award.

Bonnie Jo Campbell has published two novels, *Once Upon a River*, which grew out of "Family Reunion," and *Q Road*. Her most recent book, *Mothers, Tell Your Daughters*, is her third story collection. Her first, *Women and Other Animals*, won the Grace Paley Prize for Short Fiction and a Pushcart Prize. Her second, *American Salvage*, was a finalist for the National Book Award. Her work has appeared in

Ontario Review, Story, the *Kenyon Review, Witness*, the *Michigan Quarterly Review*, and the *Southern Review*, which awarded her its Eudora Welty Prize. Campbell received her MFA from Western Michigan University. She teaches writing in the low-residency program at Pacific University.

Daniel Cox's short fiction has appeared in the *Mochilla Review, 3:AM Magazine*, and *Agave Magazine* and was shortlisted in the Disquiet International Literary Contest. Cox is working on his first novel and seeking publication for his story collection, *Better Times Than These*. After receiving an MFA in creative writing from the University of Tampa, Cox developed, funded, and teaches a creative-writing curriculum for inmates in Richmond, Virginia's county, regional, and city jails.

Rick DeMarinis has written ten novels, most recently *El Paso Twilight*, and seven story collections, as well as *The Art and Craft of the Short Story*. DeMarinis's stories have appeared in *Esquire*, the *Atlantic, Harper's, GQ*, the *Paris Review, Grand Street*, the *Iowa Review*, the *Antioch Review*, and elsewhere. He received two NEA fellowships and the Drue Heinz Prize, as well as the American Academy's Literature Award, the Jesse H. Jones Award for fiction from the Texas Institute of Letters, and the Independent Publishers Award. He taught fiction writing at several universities, retiring from the University of Texas at El Paso in 1999.

Mary D. Edwards has published short stories in the *Paterson Literary Review* and produced her one-act plays in the Samuel French Off-Off Broadway Short Play Festival. She also publishes articles on art and architecture and is coeditor of two books: *Gravity in Art: Essays on Weight and Weightlessness in Painting, Sculpture and Photography*, and *Wind Chant and Night Chant Sand Paintings*. Edwards is a professor at Pratt Institute, where she teaches courses on Native American culture.

Elaine LaMattina's work has been published in magazines, newspapers, and journals, including the *Buffalo News, Baseball Bard*,

Artifacts, Manhattan Poetry Review, and *Poet Lore.* She received a fellowship from the Chautauqua County Arts Council and was associate editor of *Manhattan Poetry Review.* LaMattina serves as managing director of White Pine Press, an independent literary publisher, and freelances for the Korean Literature Translation Institute. She divides her time between Buffalo, New York, and Big Sur, California.

John P. Loonam's fiction has appeared in the *Madison Review, Across the Margins, Fiction Attic,* the *Santa Fe Writers Project, Storyglossia, Slow Trains,* and elsewhere. A teacher in New York's public schools for thirty years, Loonam received an MFA in creative writing from City College, CUNY, and a doctorate in American literature from the Graduate Center, CUNY. He has lived in Brooklyn since before it was cool, with his wife Maria and his sons JJ and Joe, who were always cool.

Deirdra McAfee's fiction has appeared in *Shenandoah, Confrontation,* the *Georgia Review, Willow Springs,* the *Diagram,* and elsewhere. Her work has received the Writers Exchange Award, AWP's WC&C Scholarship, the H. E. Francis Short Story Prize, the *Seattle Review*'s Al Young Prize, and the *NMW* Flash Fiction Prize. McAfee, also an editor and book critic, earned an MFA in fiction from the New School, where she served as prose editor of *LIT.* She teaches creative writing in a community arts center.

BettyJoyce Nash's fiction has appeared in *North Dakota Quarterly, C-ville Weekly,* and the *Broad River Review*; her journalism has appeared in newspapers and magazines. She earned a master's in journalism from Northwestern University and an MFA in fiction from Queens University. The winner of the 2015 F. Scott Fitzgerald Short Story Prize, she has received fiction fellowships from the MacDowell Colony, the Ragdale Foundation, the Virginia Center for the Creative Arts, and the Tyrone Guthrie Centre. She lives in Virginia, where she has taught writing at the University of Richmond, WriterHouse (Charlottesville), and the Albemarle-Charlottesville Regional Jail.

Annie Proulx's fifth and most recent novel is *Barkskins.* She has published four story collections, as well as *Bird Cloud: A Memoir*. Her first novel, *Postcards*, won the PEN/Faulkner award. Her second, *The Shipping News*, won the National Book Award, the Pulitzer Prize, and the *Irish Times* International Fiction Prize. Proulx's stories have appeared in annual volumes of *O. Henry Awards Prize Stories* and *Best American Short Stories*, and in *Best American Short Stories of the Century*. Three collections set in Wyoming, *Close Range*, *Bad Dirt*, and *Fine Just the Way It Is*, examine the lives of early settlers as well as those of today's ranchers and oilmen.

Nicole Louise Reid has published a novel, *In the Breeze of Passing Things*, and a story collection, *So There!* Her work has appeared in the *Southern Review*, *Other Voices*, *Quarterly West*, *Black Warrior Review*, and *Meridian*. A recipient of the Willamette Award in Fiction, Reid lives in Newburgh, Indiana, with her two best boys.

Sara Kay Rupnik was named a finalist for Georgia Author of the Year for her most recent book, the story collection *Women Longing to Fly*. Her work, shortlisted for the Sean O'Faolain Prize and nominated for a Pushcart Prize, has appeared in *Chautauqua*, *Antietam Review*, the *American Literary Review*, and elsewhere. Rupnik, who received an MFA in writing from Vermont College, cofounded the Around the Block Writers Collaborative. She teaches creative writing for the Jekyll Island Arts Association.

Patricia Schultheis's story collection, *St. Bart's Way*, won the Washington Writers' Publishing House Fiction Prize and was a finalist for the Flannery O'Connor Prize. Her fiction has appeared in the *Sycamore Review*, the *Alaska Quarterly Review*, *Passages North*, and the *Dalhousie Review*. She is also the author of *Baltimore's Lexington Market*. A member of the Authors Guild and the National Book Critics Circle, Schultheis has served on the editorial boards of the *Baltimore Review* and *Narrative*.

Joann Smith's stories have appeared widely in print and online, in *Clockhouse Journal*, *Literal Latte*, the *Roanoke Review*, the *Best of*

Writers at Work, the *Greensboro Review*, the *Chagrin River Review*, *Image*, and elsewhere; *Best American Short Stories* chose her work as one of its 100 Distinguished Stories. Smith has also written a historical novel, *When I Was Boudicca*. She received an MFA in fiction from Sarah Lawrence College. The assistant director of marketing and communication at Iona College, she also edits manuscripts and tutors high school students.

Jim Tomlinson has published two story collections, most recently *Nothing Like An Ocean*. His debut collection, *Things Kept, Things Left Behind*, won the Iowa Short Fiction Award. His work has appeared in *Five Points*, the *Potomac Review*, *Shenandoah*, the *Bellevue Literary Review*, the *Pinch*, and elsewhere. Tomlinson has received fellowships from the NEA and from the Kentucky Arts Council.

Gale Walden has published a poetry collection, *Same Blue Chevy*. Her second book of poetry, *Where the Time Goes*, is forthcoming, and she is working on a memoir. Her fiction, including a story that won the *Boston Review* Short Story Contest, and her nonfiction have appeared widely in national magazines, including *Prairie Schooner*, *Mid-American Review*, and *Arts & Letters*. Walden has taught creative writing in the low-residency program at the University of New Orleans and at the University of Illinois.

John Edgar Wideman's books include *Philadelphia Fire*, *Brothers and Keepers*, *Fatheralong*, *Hoop Roots*, *Sent for You Yesterday*, and *Writing to Save a Life*, among others. A MacArthur Fellow and a member of the American Academy of Arts and Letters, Wideman has won the PEN/Faulkner Award twice, and has been a finalist for the National Book Critics Circle Award and the National Book Award. He divides his time between New York and France.

E. G. Willy writes principally in English, occasionally in Spanish. Stories in English have appeared in *Conjunctions*, *J Journal*, *Zyzzyva*, *Sand*, the *Berkeley Review*, *Oyez Review*, and the *Redwood Coast*

Review; those in Spanish have appeared in *Azahares* and *Acentos*. Willy's work has been anthologized in *Stories from Where We Live* and elsewhere. His fiction won the Laine Cunningham Novel Award and the *Trajectory Journal* WildBilly Short Story Contest.